TWO BLACKBERRY LANE

*For Jack, Ed, Emily and Frances
with all my love*

Acknowledgements

I'd like to thank my writing buddies, Frances Liardet, Nikki Lloyd, Crysse Morrison and Rosie Jackson for their endless support and encouragement.

Two Blackberry Lane

a novel

ALISON CLINK

HOBNOB PRESS

First published in the United Kingdom
by The Hobnob Press,
8 Lock Warehouse, Severn Road, Gloucester GL1 2GA
www.hobnobpress.co.uk

British Library Cataloguing in Publication Data
A catalogue record for this book is available from the British Library

ISBN 978-1-914407-24-6

Typeset in Adobe Garamond Pro 11/13 pt
Typesetting and origination by John Chandler
Cover by Mark Lloyd, On Fire Design and Art Direction

MAUDIE STRINGER

November 1943

MAUDIE STRINGER lay on the iron bed. She had never felt so uncomfortably hot. Not that it was hot, the fire in the bedroom hadn't yet been lit and the dull grey landscape outside was peppered with fog like grey cotton wool. Maudie gripped the edge of a towel with such ferocity she feared it might tear. It seemed hours since she'd sent Christian off on his bike to fetch the midwife.

The clock on the mantlepiece ticked on and with each contraction she felt the urge to push. She remembered this sensation from her previous two pregnancies, both of which had been stage-managed by both doctor and midwife. With Maudie's other babies the midwife had been by her side throughout her labour.

And yet here she was this time, alone in the marital bed, Tobias downstairs boiling water. How long did it take a man to boil a pan of water? she wondered. And where was Christian?

She felt more tired than ever before in her work-laden life. Her eyes were playing tricks on her and she felt sick. The room swayed and the photograph of her and Tobias on their wedding day no longer sat beside her hairbrush on the dressing table but swung in front of the black-out curtains. From where she lay she could hear the rain lash against the window. She closed her eyes enjoying the lull between contractions. Juniper was on the landing growling at the storm and Michael cried out in his sleep. Normally she would have gone to calm him, but nothing seemed to matter anymore except for the ache in her back and the anticipation of more pain to come. She heard the measured clunk of her husband's boots as he clumped up the stairs and tried to call him, 'Tobias!' but the word melted into nothing.

Maudie felt herself melting too and the baby, the baby was sliding – sliding into a world its mother was about to depart.

Whilst Tobias climbed the creaking stairs Maudie felt herself swiftly swimming through a shimmering hole and then along a tunnel of darkness. She experienced no fear, only relief to be free from pain as she glided into a void as calming as spring sunlight across a canvas of wintry sky.

She hovered around the places she'd lived, close to the people she'd loved and inside the farmhouse in Blackberry Lane that had been her home for the past fifteen years. She slipped away from the living, dwindling with a lingering glow, like a sinking sunset below the Mendips.

By the time Tobias opened the bedroom door and crossed the room it was too late. He abandoned his bowl of boiled water beside his dead wife's slippers and tenderly removed the tiny form of his third son from the blood-soaked bed.

PEGGY

April 1946

'WE'RE ALONG here on the right, pal,' Arthur told the cabbie. 'The new house just after the farm there.'

The cabbie slowed down. 'Bit off the beaten track. You moving in?' he asked, shielding his eyes as he squinted to the right.

'Aye,' Arthur said. He leant back again, and Peggy took the opportunity, although restricted by both their hats, to rest her head against his shoulder.

'Very nice too. You in the forces?'

'Regulars. Just home from France,' Arthur said.

'And now he's in Civvie Street,' Peggy chipped in dreamily. She couldn't fathom how Arthur could be so matter-of-fact, chattering on about the forces and France without mentioning that this was their wedding day. 'And we're just married,' she added, holding up her left hand and splaying out her fingers so the man could see her ring in his mirror.

'Newlyweds, eh? Very nice too.'

'My *husband*,' Peggy thought she might explode with happiness as she spoke the word. 'My husband is starting as a farmhand for Mr Stringer.'

'Working for Mr Stringer are you, mate?'

Peggy sighed. The man seemed determined to speak only to Arthur. 'That's right,' Arthur said. 'You know him?'

'Everyone knows everyone round here. His wife died a while back. In childbirth, so I believe. Stringer's a fair enough chap although a lot of folks around these parts think he made a bad mistake.'

'What sort of mistake?' Peggy asked.

The cabbie glanced in his mirror at Peggy. 'Got a big pay out from his wife's life insurance, apparently. But instead of using it to employ a nanny or some such to look after the sons, he used the money to build this house. The one just down here on the right opposite the farm. The one I'm taking you to now. Well, two houses it is really. Big mistake if you ask me. The man spends all the wife's life insurance on building a house and he's left with no money, and he's still got three sons to bring up. All on his own, with no housekeeper or nothing. Now that's a job I wouldn't fancy in a million years. Not a great one for kids, me.'

'Me neither,' Arthur said with a chummy laugh.

Peggy felt a little frown pinch her forehead, a small line above the bridge of her nose that sometimes appeared when she was tired or confused. Her mother had warned her not to frown as it spoiled her looks. Peggy tried to catch Arthur's eye, but the taxi had stopped, and he was rooting around for change in his trouser pocket.

'That'll be seven and six, sir.'

While Arthur was helping the driver haul their cases from the boot Peggy took the opportunity to apply a fresh bow of Rose Red Blush lipstick. She fastened the clip on her handbag and climbed out of the car, smoothing down the creases in her skirt.

'Arthur, there's someone here,' she said as the taxi drove away with a toot of his horn. A man was standing on the path swinging a key from a chain.

'That's Mr Stringer,' Arthur whispered.

The man was stocky with sandy hair that was mostly covered by a flat cap. His handlebar moustache joined forces with a pair of unruly sideburns on the lower half of his cheeks. Maroon, gravy-stained braces held up his corduroy trousers and the buttons on his shirt strained across his chest, showing a crop of wiry hairs. He looked to Peggy like a man with no wife.

Arthur carried their luggage down the path and shook hands with Mr Stringer while Peggy gazed at the house. It wasn't big and she soon realised it was divided into two, with two identical gates, leading to two identical paths and front doors. Behind her on the other side of the road was a field, and to the left of the farmhouse, a cow was standing by the fence, rubbing its chin against a bush. Peggy walked the few steps down the path to join the men as Mr

Stringer turned the key in the lock and went into the house. Peggy looked up at Arthur and fought the urge to giggle. She'd giggled at her Great Aunt Winifred's funeral the previous winter just as the coffin was being lowered into the ground. After that she'd dreaded any future deaths in the family. As Peggy took a deep breath, trying to control herself, Arthur managed to overtake her and had already removed his hat and was standing in the hallway.

Once inside Peggy was greeted by the smell of fresh paint and new linoleum.

'This here's the hall,' Mr Stringer said.

'The *hall*,' Peggy repeated, as if she were adding a new word to her vocabulary. 'Golly, we're like sardines squashed into a tin!'

'It is a bit on the small side, I'll grant you, but as you can see the house is divided in two. Makes more sense than having one big one. Drew up the plans myself. Built this house brick by brick.' Mr Stringer spoke as a father might speak of a favourite child. 'Could've offered it to the late wife's sister, but it's not always a good idea to have your relatives on your doorstep.'

'You can say that again,' Arthur said.

Peggy looked at Arthur, and for the second time in less than half an hour she wondered what he meant. She couldn't imagine anything more wonderful than having a relative living close by – not that her mother, who was basically her only relative, would ever contemplate leaving Watchet.

The three of them jostled in a circle in the hallway. Straight ahead was a staircase that led to the upper floor, and behind Peggy was a door that Mr Stringer was opening.

'This 'ere's the front room,' he said, leading the way into a longish room with a bay window which was decorated with plain net curtains and faced onto the garden path. A door at the other end of the room led to the kitchen.

'So, you built this house on your own?' Peggy asked as they stood in the middle of the room. The only furniture was a three-piece suite covered with dark brown material which didn't look very special. Certainly nothing like the floral chintz suite in Peggy's mother's front room.

'I did,' Tobias Stringer affirmed.

'Goodness me, that is clever. Isn't that clever, Arthur?' Peggy said, as Arthur didn't seem to have spoken for a while.

'Not *completely* on my own,' Mr Stringer conceded. 'My eldest boy did a lot of the lifting. Christian. You'll meet him tomorrow, Mr Blake. He'll be helping you on the land. Showing you the ropes.'

'What time will you be wanting me in the morning, sir?' Arthur asked.

'Six o'clock start. Saturday afternoons and Sundays off. Just as we agreed.'

Mr Stringer looked as if he was about to leave, even though he hadn't shown them the upstairs or told them who their neighbours would be.

'Who'll be living in the other half of the house?' Peggy asked him.

'Other half's not finished yet. Plastering's not done. The boy might have it later on.'

'So, we're Number One?' she said.

'No, this here's Number Two. Other side'll be Number One – when it's finished.'

'*Number Two Blackberry Lane!* That'll be our address,' she said to Arthur as soon as Mr Stringer was gone. 'I'll write out some cards tomorrow. Just think, Arthur. Number Two Blackberry Lane, Lyde, near Shapton, Somerset. That sounds fancy, doesn't it?'

'Aye,' Arthur replied. 'It does that, Peggy love."

Peggy lifted up one of the nets. Mr Stringer was closing their gate behind him before crossing the lane to the farmhouse. The cow mooed loudly.

'Arthur, see that cow in the field with the black heart on her face? I've decided to call her Sweetheart.'

She turned round but Arthur was loosening his tie, not seeming at all interested in the cow or what his new wife was going to call her.

'I thought he'd never go,' he sighed. 'Come on, lass. Let's inspect the bedroom.'

'Arthur!' Peggy said. 'Don't you know it's bad luck if a groom doesn't carry his bride over the threshold?'

'Whatever you say, Mrs Blake.' Arthur took her hand and led

her back outside onto the path. She squealed as he lifted her and squealed again as her arm caught the pin of the red carnation on his lapel. The flower slipped from his buttonhole onto the path.

'Arthur, your buttonhole!' They watched it blow away over the road, a speck of red against the grey.

'Never mind, Pegs. I won't be needing that again in a hurry.'

'You won't *ever* be needing it again, I hope, Arthur Blake.'

They managed to link hands as they climbed the dark, narrow staircase. At the top was a small landing with three doors, each leading to a bedroom. A large room at the front with the same bow windows as downstairs, a smaller room in the middle, and a box room at the back. In the front bedroom was an old bed that looked as if it had come from the rag and bone man.

'Come on, Peggy love.' Arthur pulled her down onto the frayed counterpane.

Peggy felt her heart move inside her chest. 'But Arthur, I'm still dressed.'

'That can soon be remedied,' Arthur said, tugging at the zip of her skirt. He managed to get it half undone when Peggy sat up on the clunky old bed.

'Arthur, I feel silly.'

'What do you mean?' Arthur said, although even he must have been able to see that his legs looked comical in his suit trousers with his best brogues still on.

'I mean, it doesn't seem right. I thought our wedding night would be well, at *night*. You know. In the dark. Look outside, it's still daylight. Anyone could see in.'

'There's no one out there except your cow with the black heart on its face and Mr Stringer, and they'd both need binoculars to see in here. I don't think I've ever come across a cow with a pair of binoculars.'

'Couldn't we just have a cup of tea? I expect there's a teapot in the kitchen... and we haven't looked at the garden yet.'

After they'd inspected the kitchen, made some tea, walked around the garden – twice – looked in the outside toilet (and used it) as well as unpacking their clothes and some of the presents, the sun was beginning to go down. This time when Arthur waited for Peggy in bed, he'd removed his shoes and his suit and wore only a vest and blue-and-white striped pyjama trousers. Peggy slipped into the nylon negligée her mother had bought for her bottom drawer. The nightdress bristled against her bare skin giving her an electric shock on her arm. She sat down on the side of the bed and brushed her hair – twenty strokes, just as Mother had shown her when she was little – and tried to steel herself for what lay ahead.

But Peggy's wedding night was not as her mother had predicted. Arthur was a gentle, attentive lover. That first night, as they lay together, Peggy knew she'd married the most wonderful man. The most handsome soldier in the British Regular Army. It didn't matter what Mother thought of him. As Arthur sat up, propped against the pillow, his dark hair almost a blue sheen against the white of the Egyptian cotton that was part of a set Mrs Craigie from next door had given them, and a freshly lit cigarette in his hand, Peggy was conscious for the first time in her life that she was an adult. A married woman whose new grown-up life was about to begin.

In the dusky half-light of that spring evening, she watched Arthur as he drifted off to sleep. How many hundreds of times in the future would they be together like this? How many thousands? She studied his face. His forehead was slightly furrowed in sleep, his moustache neatly trimmed beneath his perfectly formed nose. His dark Brylcreamed hair.

Peggy closed her eyes. She was more tired than she could ever remember being, yet sleep wouldn't come. She thought about her wedding day that was now behind her. The simple ceremony in the church in Watchet, Arthur in his navy pinstriped suit, her best friend, Sheila Arbuthnott squeezed into her lemon yellow organza bridesmaid's dress, the small gathering in their front room, the train and then the journey in the taxi that had brought them to their new home in Blackberry Lane.

But she also thought about what Arthur had said when they were in the taxi – '*not a great one for kids.*' Was he humouring the cabbie, not wanting to appear soft? Surely Arthur wanted children. Most people had children. In the six months since they began courting Peggy couldn't remember whether she'd mentioned how much she loved children. But hadn't there been something in the wedding service about 'being fruitful' and 'procreation'? She was sure that was to do with children. Eventually Peggy drifted off to sleep with a mass of confusing thoughts jiggling for space in her mind.

Peggy was scrubbing the frying pan when there was a knock at the front door. Arthur had been at work for over an hour, and she still hadn't had time to change into a day dress or style her hair. There was so much to do, what with cooking breakfast and making Arthur's sandwiches for lunch. Shopping, more cooking, cleaning. In order to wash she had to stand at the kitchen sink and still hadn't brought the tin bath indoors that leant against the back of the house.

This was her fourth morning of getting up at half-past-six and she was exhausted. She wiped her hands on her pinny and peered out of the front window. A woman was standing by the gate with a basket over her arm. A Romany family lived close to their bungalow in Watchet, and her mother always bought a sprig of heather when they called. She often invited them in to read her tea leaves. Peggy opened the window and called out 'hello.'

'Lucky heather,' the woman said holding up a sprig of flowers.

'I don't think I've got any change,' Peggy said.

'Only a penny,' the woman said. 'Lucky for you, Lady.'

'I'll get my purse. Wait a minute.'

Peggy found a penny and opened the door. The woman wore a black gathered skirt and had the most crumpled face Peggy had ever seen. Her skin looked like a screwed up brown paper bag and her temples were furrowed with deep, dark lines. Peggy recoiled, wondering for a moment how she could have been so preoccupied with her one single frown line on her forehead, when this woman's skin looked like dried earth that had cracked in the sun. Her lips were thin as two blades of grass and she stared out at Peggy under wisps of wiry hair.

Peggy handed her the penny, and the woman gave her a sprig of heather. 'Thank you, my dear,' she said. 'This will bring you luck. You should have some lavender too.' The woman held four lavender stems tied with string in her gnarled fingers. 'You can have this for free. Rub the flowers onto your clothing, Lady. They'll protect you against the cruel hands of a man.' Peggy could see when she spoke that the woman had only two brown teeth – but her eyes were pure violet.

'I won't need that,' Peggy said. 'My husband is the kindest man alive.'

'You needs luck,' the woman said. 'Everyone needs luck. You want a chavvy?'

Peggy frowned. 'A chavvy? What's that?'

'A chavvy. A baby, Lady.'

'I'm not in need of luck,' Peggy assured her, as she instinctively breathed in the smell of the lavender. It reminded her of home, of the orderliness of her mother's bungalow and the sense of safety and being looked after.

'Everyone needs luck,' the woman said again, though her voice was so low and croaky it was hard to make out what she was saying. The woman picked up her basket and left.

Peggy couldn't seem to concentrate on anything that morning. *You want a chavvy?* Why had that woman asked her if she wanted a baby? What did it have to do with her what Peggy wanted?

That night after they'd made love Peggy snuggled into the crook of Arthur's arm, as she did every night. They lay like twins in a womb, yet she had no idea what Arthur was thinking. He didn't talk much in bed, probably because he was tired after working all day.

'Arthur,' she whispered. Arthur's response was a muffled snore. She longed to talk to him about so many things. They were beginning married life together but had known each other for such a short time. She wanted to tell him about the gypsy woman and what she'd said about 'chavvies'. *Not a great one for kids.* Those words wouldn't seem to leave her. Surely that couldn't be true. And the other women in his life. Had there been any? If so, who were they? Where were they, and shouldn't Peggy know about them?

Peggy was buttering some bread for sandwiches while Arthur was in the front room unpacking the rest of the wedding presents. It was Sunday, Arthur's day off, so she'd asked him to hang a picture in the living room. The picture was a present from Sheila Arbuthnott, although Peggy couldn't imagine what had possessed her friend to give them such a thing. It had a dark mahogany frame and was a crayon drawing of a man and a woman standing together with a dog crouching by the woman's feet. The man was holding a black umbrella over them and the sky behind them was a mixture of shell pink and blue, which made Peggy wonder why they needed the umbrella in the first place. The woman wore a floral dress and a cardigan, and the man had on a suit and tie.

'A right pair of toffs,' Arthur said as he polished the glass with his sleeve. Peggy came out of the kitchen. 'I'll tell you what, though, Pegs,' he said taking a closer look at the picture, 'this fellow here reminds me of someone. It's them eyes. He's got the same dark brown bulldog eyes as Tommy Moran.' Arthur blinked and ran his hand up his forehead. 'Are you sure you want this up? It looks that much like Moran, I'm not keen on having that blighter staring down at me while I'm relaxing after a day's work.'

'I admit I only saw Tommy Moran once at that dance where we met,' she said. 'But you're being silly. How could this be a picture of Tommy Moran? Sheila Arbuthnott gave it to us – although I swear I've seen it in her mother's parlour. We'll have to put it up, though, in case she comes to visit.'

'Sheila *who*?'

'Sheila Arbuthnott. She was my bridesmaid. Surely you haven't forgotten already. After all, our wedding was all of three weeks ago.'

'Aye, I do remember. She was the one who ate four slices of wedding cake. Couldn't we just quickly hang it up if she visits? And hide all the food while we're at it.'

'No, Arthur. We could not!' Peggy said, flicking his arm with a tea towel. 'And I'll thank you not to be rude about my friends.'

Arthur hung the picture and straightened it, easing the string this way and that before standing back to admire his handiwork.

'She made *you* look prettier than ever, did your friend Sheila Whatsername. And I still say the chap in this picture looks like

Tommy. Except I can't imagine my old mate ever being togged up like that, standing under an umbrella with a sour-faced lass. No, Tommy Moran wouldn't have been seen dead in…' Arthur stopped mid flow, cleared his throat and turned the picture round so the glass was facing the wall.

'Arthur Blake!' Peggy giggled. 'Don't you know one side of a picture from another?'

'Come here,' he said taking her by the waist and spinning her round. 'Take off your apron.'

She took it off and Arthur slipped the apron over the picture as if it were a curtain. He held up his hands like an invisible trumpet and made a toot-toot sound, whipping the apron away as he swivelled the picture the right way round.

'There!' he said as he tucked one of her kiss curls behind her ear and nibbled her neck.

'I've got margarine on my fingers,' Peggy protested.

'I like a bit of marge,' Arthur said, taking her hand to suck her little finger. He kissed her on the mouth and Peggy felt her insides melt. Suddenly she wasn't bothered about margarine or silly pictures or Sheila Arbuthnott. Arthur's kisses fluttered around her neck and down to her chest.

As they lay on top of the bed that afternoon, Peggy took a deep breath. She'd been building up to this conversation and now seemed the right time to quiz Arthur about his opinion on babies. She might also get the chance to enquire about his past love life, although she realised this might be a sensitive subject.

'Arthur?' she said, stroking the side of his face, enjoying the feeling of the stubble on his cheek.

'Yes, Peggy love?'

'I've been thinking. I mean I just wondered…what you… whether you… preferred spam or corned beef with your salad?' The last few words of her sentence trailed off and after some consideration, Arthur told her that he enjoyed a bit of spam but wasn't averse to corned beef either, as long as the edges weren't dried up and curly.

In Watchet Peggy had slept with rags and kirby grips in her hair. The grips were especially uncomfortable, but she was willing to suffer for her curls. However, she had no idea what Arthur's reaction would be if he woke up next to a wife sporting a head full of metal and rags. Sheila Arbuthnott used pipe cleaners to curl her hair, which was probably the more comfortable option, although one which Arthur would surely think even more odd. But without those kiss curls that adorned her forehead would Arthur not lose interest in her? The obvious solution was to curl her hair during the day while he was at work.

As soon as Arthur disappeared over the road, Peggy combed her hair and curled her fringe with eight kirby grips using two crossed over each other for each curl. She tied rags around the rest of her hair before going downstairs to start the washing up. An hour later she was upstairs airing their bed when she heard a noise downstairs. Arthur never came home at this time. Peggy froze. She saw her face turn white in the wardrobe mirror. She heard Arthur calling her and she desperately yanked at the grips and pieces of rag. She threw them wildly into a drawer and called down the stairs, 'I'll be with you in a minute,' trying to sound as casual as she could with her heart beating like mad beneath her pinny.

'You alright?' Arthur asked as she descended the stairs demurely, fluffing up her hair as she went.

'Yes, of course. I was just making the bed.'

'You look flustered.'

'It's hard work making the bed. What are you doing home at this time?'

'I was thinking about you, and I thought *I'll just pop home to see my bonny little wife.* You sure you haven't got someone up there?' Arthur seemed amused at the thought.

'No, I have *not* got anyone upstairs. Who on earth would I have upstairs?'

'So why are you blushing? Come here. I like it when you blush. It suits you. And your hair like that. You look prettier than ever with your hair a bit wild.'

Peggy patted her hair and let Arthur embrace her.

He kissed the tip of her nose. 'I'd better get going. I feel better now I've held you but I don't want to get into trouble with our Mr Stringer.'

He kissed her once more before leaving.

Peggy had a brainwave. She had a pink checked cotton headscarf upstairs in her drawer. The next time she curled her hair she'd tie the scarf around her head in a fashionable knot and cover up the kirby grips and rags, so she'd be prepared for any unexpected visitors.

That night when she lay down next to Arthur Peggy turned to one side, then the other, then over onto her stomach. Eventually she let out a long sigh.

'What's the matter?' Arthur asked. 'Can't you sleep?'

'I don't know. It's just that I keep thinking…'

'Thinking? You don't want to do too much of that, Peggy love!'

'No, I was just thinking that … I wanted to ask you something and…'

'And what?'

'I was just wondering whether you'd had anyone special – you know, a young lady, that you were courting perhaps before you met me. I mean I walked out with Gordon Murphy a few times. I just thought we should know a bit more about each other's pasts…'

Arthur turned on the light. His hand found Peggy's hand and as he looked her in the eyes Peggy felt her heartbeat quicken.

'Have I been talking in my sleep?' he said. 'Is that it? The other chaps used to rib me about talking in my sleep. I've not told you what happened, have I? With Tommy Moran.'

Peggy twiddled her wedding ring whilst Arthur fumbled on the floor under the bed for his Woodbines. He lit one with a shaky match.

'Not told me what happened?' she replied, dismayed at the unexpected turn of the conversation. 'But you did tell me. You told me that time on the train when you'd just come back from France. He was killed…'

'Yes, but did I tell you *how*?' Arthur's voice wavered as he inhaled on his cigarette.

'Well, no. You didn't tell me how Tommy Moran was killed. But I wasn't talking about Tommy Moran. I thought you could tell me more about your past. For instance, whether you were courting or anything before you …'

'It were a German soldier,' Arthur interrupted Peggy. He was staring in the direction of the wardrobe but seeming to look straight through it. 'Tommy was lying there. Dead. Slumped in the grass, he was, by the time I got to him. I'll remember that morning till the day I die. The time was just after dawn. The grass was wet. Fresh and dewy. I stepped over Tommy's body and came face to face with the German who'd shot him. Shot my best friend, Peggy. Can you imagine how it would feel to step over the body of your best friend?'

Peggy hadn't heard Arthur talk at such length or with such animation before. And she certainly couldn't imagine stepping over Sheila Arbuthnott's body.

'That must have been a terrible thing to happen.'

'It was that, Peggy.' Arthur took a breath, cleared his throat and stubbed out his cigarette in the saucer he kept under the bed.

'I won't forget the expression on that Kraut's face if I live to be a hundred,' he said. 'The lad couldn't have been more than nineteen, but his eyes were cold and empty. Old eyes, that lad had. Cold, grey marbles, fringed with white lashes. There was something passed between us – a look – a moment of recognition that said we were both the same. Both human beings, but that was all we had in common. Then I shot him. Shot him point blank, in the head.'

'Arthur, no! You never shot a young lad in cold blood.'

'Aye. It was either him or me. I watched as the bullet blew the left side of his skull away. His right eye stayed open as he fell. Every night since, Pegs, *every night*, I've woken with a picture of those grey, empty, marble eyes staring at me over Tommy's dead body.'

Peggy wriggled further down the bed. She was beginning to wish she'd gone straight to sleep. Not that she didn't feel sad for Tommy, the way she would for any soldier who'd been killed. But everyone knew people who'd been lost in the war. She couldn't see any reason to dwell on the bad things that had happened in the past seven years. What was the point in getting in a stew about things that couldn't be changed? She tried to make all the right noises, to sound sympathetic whilst Arthur spoke about Tommy, but when he'd first told her on that train rattling its way towards the West Country, she had to admit that in a tiny, secret place inside her heart, she was relieved. Hearing what had happened to his best mate somehow meant there would be more of Arthur for her. He'd be spread less thinly, so to speak. Like a knifeful of butter with a smaller piece of bread to cover.

On the one occasion she'd been introduced to Tommy, at the dance in Watchet where she and Arthur had first met, she hadn't taken to him. He seemed the kind of fellow who might not appreciate the difference between a married man and a bachelor. The kind who'd still have expected Arthur to go out drinking, carrying on with his carefree ways even if Arthur had married.

She might not miss Tommy Moran, but in some respects, although she'd never have admitted it to anyone, Peggy did miss the war. Of course, she was as relieved as the next person when it was all over. D Day came and life seemed like the beginning of a long, wonderful party. People in the streets smiled at each other. She'd spoken to people she hadn't even met before. She'd never dreamed she could feel so happy. Yet somehow, peacetime failed to live up to expectations. There was still rationing. Recently there'd been a bread shortage and it wasn't always easy to get meat. Somehow her life seemed drabber than ever, like a row of empty fields going nowhere.

She missed the munitions factory too, the silk parachutes she'd folded that would save the lives of airmen she would never know. She'd picture the pilot – always a handsome young man with a curling moustache – floating through the air and then being dragged along the ground, with the cloth she'd folded flowing behind him. She could still feel the softness of the silk and remembered the way they were folded. She'd practised on the serviettes they had for the wedding, just to keep her hand in. Some people believed there'd be another war before long. Arthur said it would be a nuclear war and everyone would be dissolved in a cloud of chemicals. Their skin would peel off and lie in strips on the floor. What good would a silk parachute be then?

'But the thing was, Pegs, his right eye stayed open as he fell.' Arthur was still reminiscing about the German who'd killed Tommy

Moran. Peggy slunk even further down the bed. She thought about sucking her thumb but managed to resist. She suddenly felt that urge to giggle, that same urge that had overtaken her at Great Aunt Winifred's funeral. She'd waited so long for Arthur to open up but now she wondered if he was ever going to stop. She tried to disguise a muffled snort of laughter that slipped out, attempting to make it sound like a cough. She'd never been so relieved as when Arthur finally switched off the light.

'I know,' she pronounced into the darkness. 'We'll name our first baby Tommy. After your friend.'

'Our *first* baby? Who said owt about babies?'

Peggy clung to the hem of the sheet. 'I've always wanted children,' she said firmly. 'A girl and a boy. I was lonely when I was little, so I think we should have at least two.' Arthur remained silent. 'Most married couples have babies,' she said. 'It's not something you can always stop happening... '

'What if we had a baby and it turned out to be a lass? She'd look a bit funny with a name like Tommy.'

'We'd think of another name. Or we could go on having more babies – until we got a little boy, then we could call him Tommy,' Peggy said.

'I'm not sure I like the sound of that. I could end up living in a houseful of women.' At that point Arthur yawned, kissed her on the cheek and turned over, leaving Peggy to dream about German soldiers with one eye, and girl babies called Tommy.

A letter arrived from Peggy's mother. Mrs Driver had written in block capitals with just her signature at the end, *Mother*, in joined up writing. Peggy kept the letter in her apron pocket for a week after it arrived. The content was mainly to reassure her that her mother was happy and managing on her own, but to Peggy it didn't really sound like her mother speaking. The tone was formal. She hoped Peggy was happy and sent her regards to Arthur. At the end she devoted seven lines to news about the coalman who'd left her out on his last delivery and how she'd often wondered about him mainly because his hair was so ginger it was almost gold, and his eyes were too close together...

Peggy read the letter over and over, but it wasn't the same as having a conversation. There was a phone box at the end of the lane by the war memorial but that was no help as her mother wasn't on the phone. She wanted to write back, but she'd never been good at letters, or writing of any sort. She wasn't confident about her spelling. Her mother had mentioned Mrs Craigie was getting a telephone. Peggy decided she'd write back to ask for Mrs Craigie's phone number so they could communicate that way.

In the mornings after Arthur had gone over the road to the farm, Peggy sometimes had imaginary conversations with her mother. As she dusted the picture Sheila Arbuthnott had given them, she told her mother about the day Arthur hung it on the wall. Except for the bit *after* he'd hung it on the wall when they'd gone upstairs together. As she dusted their wedding photograph, she went over that day in her mind too, just as they might have reminisced together. The photograph made her think of another photograph her mother kept in the front room in Watchet. The one of Peggy when she'd been Carnival Queen.

Peggy sat down on the settee, the duster still in her hand. She leaned back on the cushion, tucking her stockinged feet under her legs. She wished they had a radio. Her mother always listened to Housewives' Choice in the mornings. Peggy yawned and closed her eyes and fell fast asleep.

As a rule, Arthur would be in bed first and would lie, propped on a pillow smoking, watching Peggy as she untied her pinny, stepped out of her dress, slipped her petticoat over her head and undid her bra. But that night he was already snoring by the time she came upstairs. She removed her clothes in silence. Arthur looked so peaceful lying on his side of the bed with his left arm hanging over the edge of the mattress.

Because Arthur was asleep, she considered putting all her pin curls in instead of just the kiss curls at the front. After all, Arthur was a deep sleeper. But then she worried that she might not be up before him in the morning, so she left it.

At two in the morning she was glad she had. She was peacefully sleeping, dreaming about a blue satin dress her mother had made her when she was twelve, when suddenly Arthur shouted out, jerking up in the bed, bringing the bedclothes with him.

'No. I couldn't help it. I didn't have any choice. You were too fucking heavy...'

'Whatever is the matter?' Peggy was as shocked by the swear word Arthur used as she was at being woken in the night. Arthur had a wild expression in his eyes which made him look like a savage, and he was shaking. Peggy squeezed his arm. His pyjamas were hot and clammy. The look on his face frightened her. He was staring ahead with a glazed look in his eyes that reminded her of a medium who'd taken part in a séance when she and her mother tried to make contact with Great Aunt Winifred.

Peggy was shaking too. 'Heavens above. There's not a burglar, is there?'

This had been one of the many reasons Peggy had married Arthur. Arthur *was* fearless – apart from a brief lapse when he'd needed an alcoholic drink before meeting her mother. He was strong, unlike the Gordon Murphys of this world, who were scared of their own shadows and no better than schoolboys in grown-ups' clothes. She'd often fantasized about a burglar breaking into their home. Arthur would grab something, she imagined, usually a crowbar, despite the fact that Peggy wasn't entirely sure what a crowbar was, or whether they had such a thing. Then he'd go downstairs with no sense of fear, he'd wrestle the intruder to the ground, grab him by the ear and throw him out, before rushing up the stairs to comfort her.

'No, Peggy love,' Arthur said between breaths. 'It's only a dream. You get to sleep.' Arthur seemed to be settling so Peggy rearranged the bedclothes before sliding down beside him. But it was hard to get back to sleep. She sensed Arthur was awake too.

'You're not still dreaming about that German soldier? The one you... shot,' she began.

'No,' Arthur stared above him as if the ceiling might offer some comfort. 'This one's "the Tommy dream". Nowt to do with the Kraut. Tommy's there, lying in the grass, dead, but still talking. It's always the same. Him accusing me of not picking him up, of deserting him in France when I could've carried him home.'

'But you couldn't have carried Tommy Moran. He was dead. How could you carry a big man like that? Especially when he's dead. People weigh a lot more when they're dead. I know it's only a dream, but I think Tommy Moran's being unreasonable.'

'Aye, lass. But you try telling that to Tommy Moran.'

On their wedding anniversary Arthur arrived home at four in the afternoon.

'I've got a surprise for you, Pegs,' he said as he washed his hands and wiped them on the tea towel in the kitchen. 'Come and have a look.'

Peggy put down her potato peeler and rushed to the front room bay window. A shiny black car stood by the front gate.

'What's that?' she said.

'It's a Humber,' Arthur replied, jiggling a set of keys in his hand.

'A Humber? But where did it come from? It's not yours, surely.'

'No, not mine, Peggy love – *ours*.'

Peggy laughed as she undid her apron strings. 'But where did you get the money for a car?'

'Been saving in the Co-Op,' Arthur said with a grin.

'You never told me you were saving.'

'And you never asked. Come on. I got the car cheap. Now, get yourself dolled up. We're going into town. There's a John Wayne at the Astoria. A good Western and a poke of chips in the car. What more could a girl ask for on her wedding anniversary?'

'You make us sound like a couple of love birds, not an old married couple,' Peggy said.

Arthur looked in the mirror above the fireplace and smoothed his hair with his hand. 'I don't know about you, Peggy love. I may be married but I'm not ready for my pension yet.' Peggy reached up and ruffled his hair then ran giggling up the stairs with Arthur close behind.

'Hey, I'll have you for that, Mrs Blake,' Arthur said, following her up, two stairs at a time.

By the time Arthur had bought the tickets from the woman behind the glass window, they'd missed the B Film and the Pathé News was about to begin. An usherette flashed her torch at a couple of vacant seats.

They had to climb over four people before they could sit down. 'Excuse me, sorry, sorry,' Arthur whispered as they clambered over four pairs of legs. Hearing Arthur apologising so many times in the dark made Peggy want to start giggling again, he sounded so comical. Eventually they unfolded the red prickly seats and sat down. Arthur took off his hat and Peggy looped her arm into his. He produced a quarter of humbugs in a white paper bag from his jacket pocket and popped one in her mouth. The News began. That music always gave her a tug of excitement inside her tummy.

The first item was about Princess Elizabeth and her fiancé who was a Greek prince. They were walking in a garden, holding hands. Princess Elizabeth looked lovely, but Peggy thought the man she was going to marry wasn't a patch on her Arthur. Peggy had a peek at Arthur's profile and snuggled contentedly into his shoulder. Her prince was definitely more handsome than Princess Elizabeth's.

The next story was about some Boy Scouts on Hayling Island and after that there was something about the battle of Monte Cassino with lots of gunfire, planes and bombs. Peggy felt Arthur's arm move then suddenly, inexplicably, he was standing, his seat snapping backwards behind him. The paper bag fell to the floor and sweets rolled like marbles towards the row in front. His trilby in his hand, Arthur clambered towards the aisle like a blind man in an obstacle race. He didn't even apologise as he fought his way back past the blockade of legs. Tuts of indignation followed him as he disappeared in the darkness.

Arthur was gone for the whole of the rest of The News. She supposed he must have been caught short and hurried to the Gents, but why hadn't he told her? Anyway, there was no sign of him near the toilets. Peggy couldn't concentrate on The News any longer, but she was afraid to go and look for Arthur in case he came back and she couldn't remember where they'd been sitting.

The interval came and she looked around in the gloomy yellow light of the cinema. When she stood up to get a better view, her seat flipped up behind her, making her jump. There were hundreds of heads in hundreds of rows of seats. Some people were filing towards the exit signs, others flocking towards the usherettes selling ice creams. She kept seeing men she thought were Arthur but when they turned around, they had goofy teeth or spectacles which made her feel horrified that she could have mistaken them for her husband. She didn't have any money, so she couldn't join the ice cream queue and in any case she wasn't hungry. To make matters worse she felt as if everyone was looking at her. Hundreds of strangers all noticing that Peggy Blake had been deserted by her husband in the middle of the picture show.

Peggy sat down and pretended to search for something in her handbag. Even when she'd been Carnival Queen, she'd felt awkward on that float high above the pavements crammed with people all waving flags and staring. The further they'd gone along the road, what with the float being pulled by a tractor spewing diesel oil, the more she'd started to feel sick and wished she could jump off and disappear.

Peggy wanted to disappear now. Other people were returning to their seats with tubs of ice cream but still there was no sign of Arthur. The next film was about to start. It was a Mickey Mouse. Normally Peggy loved a Mickey Mouse, but not sitting alone in a packed cinema. A woman to her left who was licking an ice cream wedged between two wafers gave her a pitying look. The lights were beginning to fade when Peggy grabbed her handbag and squeezed past the other people in the row, walking as fast as she could towards the Exit sign. She thought perhaps Arthur had gone back to the car for some reason.

The green and pink painted foyer was brightly lit, but empty. A cashier was counting piles of coins. Peggy's heart turned over when she saw Arthur through the glass door. He was outside, leaning against a billboard, inhaling on a cigarette.

'Arthur?'

Arthur frowned. 'I'm sorry,' he said. 'I needed some fresh air. You go back in – I'll be with you in a jiff.'

Peggy felt she'd rather scale Ben Nevis than have to negotiate her way through all those legs again.

'You left me sitting all on my own with everyone looking at me! What's wrong? Don't you want to see the John Wayne?'

'I *said* I needed some air. Leave it at that, will you. It's not such a strange thing, is it?'

Arthur didn't sound like her Arthur at all. His voice was harsh and impatient and although she tried to hold in her tears, Peggy knew she was about to cry.

'You've ruined the evening. I want to go home,' she babbled through tears. She could feel the corners of her mouth forming into an ugly shape. She felt like a baby, shuddering and crying. But once she'd started it was as if she'd turned on a tap that was stuck. The tears came from somewhere deep inside. At first they'd been the result of Arthur's desertion of her, her humiliation coupled with the strange way Arthur was behaving, but they soon changed into a general sadness about everything from the absence of her mother, the fact that her lipstick had nearly run out, to her inability to cook a shepherd's pie that wasn't soggy on the top.

She told herself to remember she was still the same Peggy who'd been Carnival Queen in 1932, still the same Peggy who'd worked in the munitions factory and folded the parachutes that had saved airmen's lives. But nothing could stop the tears. Even though she was a married woman, she felt like a useless baby. A nothing. Nobody. Arthur wasn't looking at her as he dragged deeply on the last inch of his cigarette and blew the smoke out long and slow as if that were the only way he'd be able to keep his temper. All Peggy wanted was for him to change back to the real Arthur who would take her in his arms and call her Peggy love, whilst wiping her tears with his handkerchief. But he stayed as he was, leaning against the side of the wall, smoking.

Finally he spoke. 'You wait here. I'll fetch the motor.'

'I'm not staying here while you disappear again.'

It was as if she'd done something wrong, but she had no idea what. Her sobs made her cough and two boys who were running past the cinema turned round to gawp at her. But she didn't care who saw. She couldn't make sense of anything. Why the evening had turned out so wrong, or why Arthur had suddenly changed into someone else. She grabbed hold of his elbow, clattering along beside him in her wedding shoes. Apart from the sound of her sobs, they drove home in silence and although she wanted to ask what was wrong, she felt there was no point. Arthur didn't want to tell her. That night they lay as far apart as they could, and Peggy, drained from crying, fell straight to sleep.

Stringer's farmhouse was cold and dark inside and smelled of cabbages. The floors were hard, made of flagstones with not a rug in sight. Downstairs the windows were small, each with six panes of grubby glass and framed with thin flowered curtains that were never pulled. A pair of rusty horseshoes hung above the stone sink. The kitchen also contained a pine table, six chairs and a fireplace which would have been big enough to accommodate a cow, if she stood sideways on.

Peggy went over to the farmhouse occasionally to help with the laundry. Tobias had again fallen out with Ada, his late wife's sister who had helped occasionally with the children. Gradually Peggy had ended up doing Tobias's washing on a Thursday and on Fridays she'd iron the family's clothes and bedding. This meant she had a shilling each week for herself. The first morning she went over, Tobias Stringer showed her where everything was.

'My Maudie kept everything clean as a new pin,' he told her. 'We've let things go, Mrs Blake. The place needs a woman's touch.'

Peggy also helped with Edmund who was only four and had blond curls that Peggy thought needed cutting, and no mother. She knew Mrs Stringer had died in childbirth and she pitied this poor little scrap of a boy, who followed her around like an affectionate dog.

'D'you know where my mummy is?' Edmund asked Peggy one afternoon. He shadowed her as she cleared the table and stacked the lunch plates and cutlery beside the sink.

'My mummy's in heaven with the angels,' he said, answering his own question. Peggy paused from her work to look down at him. She'd run a duster over Mr and Mrs Stringer's wedding photograph on the dressing table in Mr Stringer's bedroom many times. Mrs Stringer had had dark hair cut in a bob and looked severe, her face squarish and flat. Her dark eyes reminded Peggy of Christian's. Neither of the 'happy couple' were smiling 'Where's *your* mummy?' Edmund went on. 'Is *your* mummy in heaven with the angels?'

Peggy placed her hand on the little boy's curls. 'No, my mummy's not with the angels, Edmund. She's in Watchet in a bungalow by the sea.' She felt her voice falter. Her mother might as well have been in heaven the number of times she'd seen her since the wedding. Suddenly the bungalow in Watchet did seem a bit like heaven.

'What's the sea like?' Edmund asked.

'Haven't you ever been to the seaside? Heavens above,' Peggy said. 'We'll have to take you in Mr Blake's new car. Now let me get on with these dishes. Then we can wash that pile of sheets that I stripped from the beds this morning.'

As usual, Edmund dragged one of the kitchen chairs to the sink and climbed on it, dipping his hands into the suds, pretending to wash a pillowcase.

'We'll get this lot through the mangle and hang it out to dry,' Peggy said as she rubbed the last sheet.

They carried the bedding out to the yard. The air was rich with the smell of cow dung.

'Poo. Smelly cows,' Edmund said.

Peggy smiled. Edmund was right, there was a bit of a farmyard smell. She looked across the field for Arthur and Christian who'd been muck-spreading, but there was no sign of anyone. She folded a wet sheet over the rope and glanced across the road towards her house. The Humber, normally parked by their gate, was gone. Edmund hung a row of pillowcases onto a string she'd hooked up for him between a chair and the handle of the mangle. They went inside to boil some eggs.

After tea she helped Edmund into his pyjamas. They sat down with Michael at the table with some crayons and paper, drawing stick men under a yellow sun. Time was going on and Peggy still had to make Arthur's tea. She poured the boys some lemonade.

'Don't forget to bring the laundry in,' she said to Michael as she rushed out of the house, almost colliding with Mr Stringer. She was about to ask him if he knew where Arthur was but hesitated just in time. Supposing he thought Arthur and Christian were in the field. What would happen if Arthur was meant to be working but had gone somewhere else? Supposing he got the sack! They'd lose everything.

'Good night, Mrs Blake,' Mr Stringer said. He looked tired and headed straight to the sink to wash his hands.

'Bye, Mr Stringer.' Peggy scurried over the road, through the empty space where the Humber should have been. Of course, someone might have stolen it, but hardly a soul came down Blackberry Lane, so that wasn't likely.

Inside the house was dark and eerily silent. A knot was forming inside Peggy's stomach as she went into the front room. She hadn't had time to light the fire that morning. She looked up above the fireplace at the picture of the couple sheltering under their umbrella that had been their wedding present from Sheila Arbuthnutt. She'd started to find comfort in the simplicity of that picture, even though she knew Arthur disliked it. She knelt next to the hearth to brush the ash from the previous night's fire into a newspaper. She laid fresh newspaper, kindling and some coal, struck a match, then blew underneath the grate. As the flames flared up, she felt better, although her feet were still chilly. She knelt for a while looking at the fire. She enjoyed watching the flames gaining strength. She could get lost in thought just staring at a fire. As the flames grew and danced, they seemed to be laughing, so much so, that Peggy felt herself smiling at them.

But she stopped smiling when she realised it was a quarter to seven and Arthur still wasn't home.

Peggy had prepared a rabbit stew the night before. She went into the kitchen to stir more water into it. It was getting dark, so she returned to the front room to close the curtains, but not before taking another peek outside. The Humber was still absent.

She began one of her imaginary conversations with her mother. 'When Arthur did *eventually* come home,' she said in her head, 'well, ha! I felt so silly – all that worrying for nothing. You'll never guess where he'd been. He'd been to...' That was the point where she got stuck, so she started the conversation again.

At eight she switched the lights on, turned on the wireless Arthur had bought second hand for her birthday, and sat down by the fire. The Light Programme was playing some music. *Can't get away to marry you today – my wife won't let me...* If Arthur had been at home, they could've stood up together and had a twirl.

At half-past ten Peggy heard a car pull up outside. She'd been dozing in the chair with the radio fizzing in the background. She shivered. The fire had gone out. She got up and peeked around the curtain. She recognised the tall stooped boyish figure of Christian Stringer in the car headlights as he crossed over the road. Christian tripped against a stone. Peggy was about to run outside to check he was alright when she heard him shout, 'Fucking – ouch.' That was what he said! 'Fucking – ouch.'

Peggy could hardly believe what she'd heard, but those words made her decide against helping him. She hadn't been brought up with that kind of language. Arthur occasionally swore, but that was when he was half asleep, having one of his nightmares. Peggy opened the front door. Arthur was still in the driver's seat of the Humber. The headlights went off and he got out. Arthur swayed towards her down the path.

'What's going on, Arthur? Is Christian alright?'

'You've no need to fret, lass. He'll be fine. It's yer man you should be looking out for.' Arthur was smiling oddly. He'd reached the front door but seemed to take a lot more steps to get there than usual, and when he did arrive, he smelled like the inside of a pub.

'Peggy, love,' he slurred as he locked an arm around her shoulder. Not only was the weight of his arm dragging her downwards, but he seemed to be growling like a bear. Peggy had never seen him like this before. He seemed funny, but somehow, at the same time, not funny.

They moved together into the front room like competitors in a three-legged race. Arthur slumped down into the armchair.

'Arthur Blake,' Peggy began, a hand on either hip. 'I've been sitting here worried sick. Where've you've been all these hours?'

'Where've I've been? I've been t't pub. T't *ale* house. I had to take the lad int't town. A lad his age needs a bit of fun. All work and no play makes…some'ut. He's only got me to help him out, hasn't he? Now, my lovely lass, I want you to forget about *him* and concentrate on the man you married.'

Arthur hiccoughed and signalled for Peggy to join him on his lap. Peggy ignored the invitation. 'Look,' she said. 'I've got a nice fire going for you, or at least I had until it went out, and the stew's been bubbling for hours. You've had me so worried. I thought you might have had an accident or something."

'Ashident. Who's had an ashident? People ought to be more careful.'

'I can tell you're drunk and I'd thank you not to come home in this state in future.'

Arthur belched. 'Drunk. I'm not drunk. I am not drunk.'

'At least you're home in one piece. I suppose that counts for something. You'd better eat your stew. It's rabbit.'

'Rabbit? It's you I want, you gorgeous creature, not a plate of slop. Now come over here so I can feel you...' Arthur lurched forwards to grab her hip.

'Stop that at once. You haven't even had your tea. It's fresh rabbit with apple dumplings for afters. You can have it on a tray, and I'd thank you not to refer to my cooking as slop.'

By the time she'd arranged the tray with a cloth and a drink of water, Arthur was snoring with his chin bobbing against his chest. Peggy went upstairs to bed, leaving the tray on the floor next to Arthur. It would serve him right if he stood up and stepped straight into it. Although, if he did, he might break the plate, which would mean they'd only have three left. And it would be a waste of good food. After she'd got undressed Peggy went downstairs to return the plate safely to the kitchen.

At four in the morning, she was awoken as Arthur slid in bed beside her. His arm felt cold against hers.

'I hope you're not still drunk.' Her words should have sounded disapproving, but her voice emerged sleepy and small. Arthur tucked his arm around her stomach and kissed the lobe of her ear. He still smelled of stale beer and tobacco but having him next to her made her feel contented and forgiving. As if a part of her that had been missing was now restored. Sleeping alone didn't feel right.

'Promise you won't ever do that again?' she said.

'Do what, lass?'

'Come home like... that...'

'I promise,' Arthur said, which made her feel even more content and forgiving.

As the sun began its ascent above the dark green bank of trees at the north side of Stringer's field, Peggy lay with her head on her Arthur's chest. The relief of having things back to normal was delicious. It was almost worth the pain of the night before to feel as wonderful as she did that morning as they drifted into harmonious sleep.

They were both late going over the road the following morning. Arthur left his breakfast because he felt sick. Peggy was so tired she went back to bed at seven. Tobias Stringer gave her a queer look when she crept into the kitchen at ten o'clock.

'You ill, Mrs Blake?' he said. 'Must be something going around. Our Christian's been ill all night.'

Peggy could hear coughing and retching from upstairs. She started on the washing up, then cleared her throat. 'I was wondering, Mr Stringer, if perhaps me and Arthur might take Edmund to the seaside one day. This Saturday coming perhaps? If that's alright with you. Arthur can drive us in the Humber.'

'That's very kind of you. I'll send our Michael over with him on Saturday morning.'

Standing at the sink washing the dishes, Peggy smiled to herself. She could imagine Arthur driving the Humber, her sitting next to him her hair blowing behind her in the wind like a film star, little Edmund sitting behind them. They'd be like a real family on a real family outing.

The berries in the hedgerows were beginning to turn from green to red when Fred Pittle cycled up Blackberry Lane, wobbling with the weight of two parcels and a sack of letters in the basket on the front of his bike. The sun was warming up as Peggy hung her washing out on the line. A rabbit bounded out of the hedgerow causing Fred to swerve.

'*Run, rabbit, run rabbit run, run, run. Here comes the farmer with his gun, gun...*' She could hear Fred singing from the garden. He arrived at the gate and leant his bike against the wall.

'Mrs Blake? Oh, good, you're here. I'd never have got this through your letter box,' Fred panted. 'What with your curtains still being closed I was going to leave this parcel at the side of the house, but then I'm not supposed to leave the King's mail outside a house for any Tom, Dick or Harry to walk off with. It's against the law, see. That's why I'm glad you're up and about after all, Mrs Blake.'

'Thank you, Fred,' Peggy said.

'I mean, I could of left it in the garden, but then I'd have been worried that you or Mr B might get up, come outside and trip right over the parcel. Might've broken one of your necks. Never walked again. Confined to a wheelchair for the rest of your naturals. Then I'd get the blame, see? Probably get the sack. Then how would I find another job with a criminal record? And who'd want to marry me? A man with no job and no prospects. A bachelor for ever more. My whole life ruined just because of a parcel.'

Peggy reached for the parcel but Fred seemed reluctant to let it go. 'Strictly speaking,' he went on, 'I should be delivering this to *Mr* Blake. The label's clearly got his name on it.'

'I'm sure you won't get into trouble, Fred,' she said as Arthur appeared still in his pyjama trousers and string vest.

'Who's getting into trouble?' Arthur enquired.

'Parcel for Mr Arthur Blake, sir.' Fred saluted with his spare hand. Then he handed Arthur the parcel, jumped on his bike and disappeared up the lane.

Arthur examined the parcel. It was a large bulky square tied with string stuck down with a red button of sealing wax. Peggy followed him into the kitchen.

'You'll need a bread knife to cut that string,' she said.

Arthur cut through the string and unwrapped the paper. Inside was a silver cigarette case. He opened it and smelled the inside. A few grains of dried golden tobacco fell out.

'Here, there's a letter,' Peggy said, handing Arthur an envelope that had slipped onto the floor. Arthur began reading. *"I know Tommy would have wanted you to have a keepsake and so I'm sending his cigarette case as a memento. Etc. etc... Vera."*

'Who's Vera? And why is she sending you parcels? Look – there's some initials engraved on the top. TLM. Why would someone send you a cigarette case with somebody else's initials on it?'

'Vera, aye. You don't know her,' Arthur said reluctantly as if he'd rather not share even this small amount of information.

'But if you know her, why can't you tell me who she is?'

'She's no one,' Arthur said. Peggy frowned. 'Alright,' Arthur conceded. 'She's Tommy Moran's sister. A memento! Huh. As if I need something to remember him by. What *I* need is something to make me forget.' Arthur slipped the cigarette case into the pocket of his jacket that hung in the hall. Peggy was about to go back inside when she saw two little figures walking towards her.

'I've brought our Edmund for the seaside outing, Mrs Blake,' Michael said with one hand holding Edmund's and the other gripping a metal bucket. Edmund wiped his feet on the mat, shuffled into the hall, and took off his cap.

Arthur ruffled Edmund's hair. 'Hey that's a grand bucket you've got there. We'll have that full of sand in no time.'

The three of them sat, resting against the wall by the groin, eating meat paste sandwiches that crunched where the sand had got in. The turn-ups on Arthur's trousers flapped in the wind and Peggy only managed to keep herself decent by tucking her skirt between her knees. Edmund knelt in the sand digging furiously against the tide.

'So, how well did you know this Vera?' Peggy pushed one of her curls out of her eyes.

'Vera? She was alright, was Tommy's sister,' Arthur said wistfully.

'So you were quite… close with her?'

'She were just a mate's sister. Why do you ask?'

'No reason. I just wondered, what with her sending you the cigarette case. She must have gone to some trouble to find you.'

Arthur shrugged. 'Must have got my address through my mam. We'll go back to the car soon, Pegs. It's not really seaside weather.' Arthur stood up to chase the pages of his *Daily Herald* as they blew along the beach.

'It's only a bit of wind, Art. Let's not go yet,' Peggy said. 'I want this afternoon to last for ever. Just you, and me, and little Edmund. It's so special – the three of us here… like a real family.' She began wrapping up the rest of the sandwiches. 'Just think,' she said, packing the picnic things away, 'this is how it will be when we have our own little one.'

The beach was deserted except for some squawking seagulls circling overhead hoping for a stray crust of bread. A roll of grey waves tugged endlessly at the shingle further down the beach. Rolling in and pulling away. Peggy could have watched it all day. But she had half an eye on Edmund and half on Arthur. In fact, she often felt like this when they went out together. It was because of that night at the John Wayne. She had to make sure Arthur was all right, that he wasn't going to turn strange again. Arthur returned with his paper and shuffled the pages together. The sea rolled, Arthur tapped the ash from the end of a cigarette he'd just lit, and Edmund burrowed deeper into the sand.

Arthur seemed so deep in thought Peggy wondered whether her words had been swallowed up in the wind. 'It is grand having Edmund with us for the day, isn't it?' she tried again. Arthur sucked on his Woodbine. 'I mean,' she went on, 'when I sit here looking at little Edmund beavering away in the sand, it makes me wonder what *ours* would be like.'

Arthur exhaled a cloud of smoke. 'Our what, Pegs?'

'Our... *baby,* of course. I wonder what our own child would be like.'

'Like us I expect,' Arthur said, poking his newspaper into his jacket pocket.

Peggy sighed as loud as she could. She'd been waiting all day for a chance to have a serious word with him, but sometimes having a conversation with Arthur was like collecting water in a sieve. A rivulet of tide swirled under the bridge Edmund had just built, causing the bridge to collapse in the middle and Edmund to cry. She thought about helping him build another one further from the water. Her father had played with her on the sand for hours when she was Edmund's age. Once he'd buried her legs and built a pretend car around her body with sand. She could still remember the sensation of the cold, damp sand on her skin.

'Art?'

'What is it?'

'You know our ... *little Tommy,* well I think...'   A r t h u r stood up and flicked the end of his cigarette into the sand. 'Arthur? What's wrong?'

'Nothing. Look, there's a hotel up there at the top of the cliff. I noticed it on the way down. It says *Open to Non-Residents*. I'll be up there in the lounge. I've had enough of this wind. I'll see you there when the bairn's finished playing.' Before Peggy had a chance to protest, Arthur began to disappear along the beach. He still had his shoes on and his heels sank into the sand making him look comical as he walked. Peggy wrapped herself in the blanket they'd been sitting on, feeling strangely relieved at being alone. She sank back into the sand and an outbreak of goose pimples pricked the tops of her arms. Edmund had stopped crying and was reconstructing his bridge, banging the wet sand with the palm of his hand.

Two hours later Peggy trundled up the coastal path with Edmund trailing behind her. She was carrying his bucket with the paper flags they'd bought from the beach kiosk, her own bag, and the rolled-up rug.

'Are we there yet, Mrs Blake?' Edmund's hair was blown into a mess by the wind and his nose was running.

'Not far, love. You can see the hotel there at the top of the cliff.' Peggy stopped, licked salt from her lips, bent down to wipe Edmund's nose before letting him climb onto her back. He was heavier than she'd expected which made her wonder if it was such a good idea. At the top of the path, she kneeled down to let him off and they stood together on a patch of brown grass, outside the front bay window of the hotel next to the sign Arthur had mentioned. *Lounge Bar. Open to Non-Residents*.

Peggy pressed her face against the glass whilst Edmund peeled some flaking green paint from the windowsill. She could see Arthur inside, sitting on a stool talking to a barman. Arthur was holding something in his hand and a half finished pint sat beside him on the bar. She tapped on the glass but neither Arthur or the barman heard.

'You look after the things, Edmund, while I go inside to get Mr Blake,' she said.

'Can I come with you?'

'No. You're too young. You're not allowed. That's what's called *licensed premises*. You have to be a grown up to go in. I won't be a minute. You wait here like a good boy.'

Edmund stuck out his bottom lip. 'But a big wave might come and wash me away. I want to go home.'

'There's no waves up here. Look how far away from the sea we are. Now, be good. I won't be a minute. If you stand on tiptoes you'll be able to see me when I'm inside.'

It took a few moments for Peggy's eyes to adjust to the gloom in the hallway of the hotel. The walls were decorated with different sized mirrors, some with writing on, adverts for cigarettes and ale, some plain and tarnished around the edges. A single bulb hung from the middle of the ceiling. The overriding smell was of furniture polish and stale cigarette smoke.

She could hear Arthur's voice. 'See this?' he was saying. 'Arrived this morning in the post. Cigarette case – sterling silver. Worth a bob or two, this.'

The barman mumbled something. 'See the initials, TLM. D'ya know what they stand for?' Arthur was slurring his words. 'Thomas Lester Moran. Best pal a man could have.'

'Nice,' the barman said.

'Yes, his Vera sent it me. Voluptuous Vera, that's what we called her. And I can testify to that, if you catch my drift. A man could get a decent handful with Vera.' Arthur laughed.

'And I'll bet you did.' The barman laughed as well.

'D'ya know something else?' Arthur lowered his voice and Peggy couldn't make out what he was saying. But then he banged his fist on a towel that was on the bar and spoke louder. 'I have nightmares about that man. Thomas Lester Moran. The man's like an albatross tied around my neck.'

The barman mumbled something again, which Peggy couldn't make out.

'Sometimes,' Arthur went on, 'sometimes when I hear youngsters talking about World War Three, I feel like smashing something.' He thumped his fist onto the bar again. The barman looked up from the glass he was wiping. 'Kids nowadays talk about war as if it's a game. Like the lad I work with. Always asking me what it was like being a soldier in the war and I tell him it was a job that needed doing, not some game. Do you know what he said to me?'

The barman scratched his neck and looked bored, but Arthur carried on. 'He said " I bet you can't wait for World War Three so you can get back into uniform and blast those Commies to smithereens." I mean, I've told the lad. War's an evil thing. Not a game. And anyway, I didn't travel the world. I never went beyond France. Huh! France. I wish I'd never heard of the place.'

The barman leaned his elbows on the bar and yawned. 'Really? He said. 'Why's that then?'

Arthur went on. 'Because that's where Tommy Moran died. You'd think that bastard would leave me alone. But he's at me every night and it's always the same dream. We're standing at a bar – bit like this one. Tommy's ordering the drinks, but as he turns round to pass me my pint – that's the point where I wake up, shaking and sweating. Because it's not Tommy's right face. It's Tommy with his dead face. But he still speaks and laughs, d'you understand? He drags on his ciggie, except the smoke's like a grey line coming from the bullet hole in his head. And the bastard keeps asking why I didn't stay. Why I didn't hang around long enough to pick up his fucking body…'

At that moment Arthur noticed Peggy and tried to get up from the stool but his foot became entangled in the bottom rung and he only just managed to stop himself falling onto the greasy carpet. 'Hello, Peggy love.' Arthur smiled a lopsided smile and slipped the cigarette case into his pocket. 'I'd like you to meet…'

'Arthur, you should wash your mouth out with soap! Nobody wants to hear about Tommy Moran again and again. I think it's time we went home.'

'I'll just have one more pint,' he said, sliding the empty glass towards the barman.

'The little boy's waiting outside,' Peggy reminded him. The smell of polish was making her nauseous.

'Boyz? What boyz?'

'Edmund, of course. What's wrong with you?' she snapped, but all Arthur did was to stare at the ceiling, while the barman refilled his glass.

'Oh, aye,' Arthur suddenly seemed to return to the real world. 'Little Edmund. One of the other lads from the farm over the road,' he said by way of explanation to the barman who looked about as interested as Peggy felt. 'Three lads, half orphaned. Mother died in childchurch. Wife here likes helping them out. What is it about women that they're always wanting to mother anything half-orphaned?'

The barman laughed again. His laughter reminded Peggy of the cabbie who'd brought them to Blackberry Lane when they'd first moved in. 'I'll wait for you outside. With Edmund,' she said as if to make a point.

As they walked to the car Peggy held Edmund's hand while Arthur shuffled ahead of them, zig-zagging from one side of the path to the other.

'Take deep breaths,' Peggy told him. 'Are you sure you'll be able to drive properly?'

'Drive properly?' Arthur turned around and lurched towards Edmund. 'Hey – did you hear what your Aunty Peggy said? Me drive properly? I'll tell you something, a few pints goes a long way when it comes to driving. Sharpens the brain. You ask your daddy if I'm not right.'

Edmund examined his bucket. The rain started just as they reached the Humber. Great big drops plopping on the windscreen. A strip of rubber on the windscreen wiper that had become unhinged waved manically at them as it flipped and flopped backwards and forwards. Peggy sat in silence with her handbag on her knees at the far end of the front seat and Edmund slept in the back slumped against the bolster in the middle. Every so often she glanced behind to make sure he was alright. His little chest was moving up and down. She could see the pin on the speedometer touching fifty miles-per-hour and Peggy started to feel sick.

'Arthur!' she said, opening her handbag to find her handkerchief. 'Can you slow down? I think I'm going to be sick.'

Arthur pulled in at a lay-by. 'What's the matter with Mrs Blake?' Edmund's sleepy voice came from behind them.

The accident happened soon after she'd been sick on the side of the road, got back into the car and told Arthur what she thought was wrong with her.

'I'm over a week late,' she said. 'I think I might be expecting.'

'Expecting? Not a bairn?'

'No, a bus. What do you think I'd be expecting? Of course a *bairn.*'

Moments after that exchange they seemed to be on the wrong side of the road with a motorbike coming towards them. Luckily only the motorcyclist was slightly injured but the police were called. If Arthur hadn't started shouting at that copper, things might not have turned so bad.

***

PEGGY STRETCHED out on the sofa in the front room watching the sun go down behind the nets that hadn't seen soap and water in weeks. She'd given up believing Arthur would come home from work at five and had stopped preparing his tea for ten past. The Ring O' Bells was in the centre of the village between the post office and the village hall. Arthur could walk there from Stringer's Farm – which was just as well for him, because he'd lost his driving licence and had sold the car after the court case.

Since she'd been expecting, Peggy didn't feel much like eating normal meals at normal mealtimes. Instead she stuffed herself with large quantities of any food she had in the larder, which seemed to calm her sickness. The big sick hole inside her stomach was mainly filled by thick slices of doughy white bread plastered with the blackberry jelly she'd made the previous autumn. It was too much like hard work cooking tea just for Arthur and too upsetting looking at a meal on a plate with nobody there to eat it.

The front room was bathed in the last orange of the setting sun before sinking into a shadowy semi-darkness. She couldn't be fagged to get up to turn on the light. Instead she closed her eyes and lay like a lazy cat rubbing her balloon belly.

Recently she'd spent many afternoons lying on the sofa, just thinking. Somehow, despite the fact that she'd always wanted to be married, if she was honest, life had seemed better when she still lived in Watchet with her mother. When they'd had long chats into the evenings and trips to the shops at the weekends.

Peggy opened her eyes. The baby had kicked the inside of her stomach. That was a kick that could only come from a boy, she thought. She could see the outline of a tiny leg undulating beneath the material of her maternity smock. If only Arthur had been there to see it too.

Then something wonderful happened. Peggy heard the key in the door, the lights went on and suddenly Arthur was there beside her, still in his working clothes, smelling of earth and fresh air, kneeling on the rug next to the sofa, unwrapping a fish supper.

'I went into the village with the lad and stopped for some fish and chips. I knew you'd be hungry,' he said on his way into the kitchen for some vinegar.

They ate cod and chips out of the newspaper, with vinegar dribbling down their chins. Arthur had even bought her a pickled onion which she popped into her mouth, crunched up and swallowed in one go. She didn't care if it gave her indigestion. After they'd eaten, Arthur got out the playing cards and they had a couple of games of Gin Rummy. Peggy won the first game and Arthur won the second. Before they tidied up the cards, Peggy placed Arthur's hand on her stomach.

'Here,' she said. 'Can you feel the baby? It's been moving a lot today.'

'I'll be blowed,' Arthur said. 'I did feel something, Pegs. I think our bairn's going to enjoy a fish supper.'

At that moment Peggy knew precisely why she'd married Arthur. She loved him more than anything. More than anyone. She felt as if the world was him. In that room, in that house, with him. With Arthur. She didn't need anybody else. Except for their baby and she longed for it to be born so they could be a proper family. They'd be parents. She'd hardly dared think that far ahead. They'd have a real live child. Maybe there'd be another baby – and another. With a house full of children Arthur surely would have to come home straight from work every night. As she lay on the sofa watching Arthur clearing away the playing cards, the newspaper and left over chips, Peggy felt convinced that her future was going to be the happiest any woman could dream of.

The night she fell down the stairs was one of Arthur's pub nights. He'd invited Christian in for a nightcap after they'd staggered home, even though it was an empty invitation. There was no alcohol in the house, except for an inch of Harvey's Bristol Cream left from Christmas.

Peggy was in bed when the sound of voices downstairs woke her. She opened her eyes and froze. Her heart was thumping. Maybe a burglar had broken in. But surely, she reasoned to herself, it could only be Arthur. The voice sounded like his. But how could she be sure it wasn't a burglar whose voice was similar to Arthur's. Or two burglars. There was obviously more than one person downstairs. She lay still as a corpse. If they were being burgled, why did it have to happen when Arthur wasn't there to protect her? She turned gingerly onto her side, eased herself out of bed and bravely stepped onto the landing.

She sighed with relief when she realised for certain that the voice downstairs was Arthur's. She could see the top of his cap as he stood in the hallway, grappling with his key.

'What's up with this friggin' key?' he muttered. 'It's stuck in the friggin' lock.'

'I'll do it for you. See, it's easy enough when you know how,' Christian said. Both men began laughing.

'Peggy!' Arthur called up the stairs. 'The lad's come in for a nightcap. Peggy? Where are you?'

Peggy stood at the far end of the landing in the shadow.

'Come on, lad,' Arthur went on. 'Come upstairs – we need to find Mrs Blake. She'll make you a cup of cocoa.'

'I'd best be getting along. Mrs Blake won't want to see me. She'll be asleep.'

'Nah. She won't – she gets all that indigestion. You should 'ear her burp. Never heard nothing like it. Puts any farm animal to shame, she does. Come on. She won't bite.' Peggy heard a clatter as they both tripped on the first stair.

'Let go of me, Mr Blake. I've never laughed so much. I think I'm going to piss myself.'

Peggy took a few steps forwards and stood at the top of the stairs looking down on them. Their faces looked ridiculous. Christian was grinning, his expression a mixture of confusion and hilarity and Arthur somehow managing to distort his good looks with an idiotic twisting of his lips. Christian, recently grown taller than Arthur, with his brown greasy hair combed away from glazed eyes, and Arthur holding onto him by the arm, dragging him upwards towards her.

'Peggylove, I'd like you to meet…whatsh 'is name. What is your name, again? Oh yes. Peggy, I'd like you to meet Chrishtan. A fine name for a fine…He lives acrosh the road there.' Arthur waved in the direction of the farm.

'Arthur, don't be so ridiculous. Of course I know Christian. But will you please send him home. Do you have any idea how late it is?'

'Why're you shouting? Hey, Chrishtan, lad, what's she got to shout about?' Arthur swayed on the fourth stair from the top with his arm still linked to Christian's. 'It's like being in the army with her around. She's always shouting. T's like being married to a sergeant major, and just look at her. She's as big as a tank. I married a lass who's more like a fucking Chaffee.'

Peggy had one hand pressed into her hip and the other tensed into a fist. She tried with difficulty to control her breathing.

'Err… I think I'll get home now, if it's all the same to you. Mrs Blake,' Christian slipped his neck from Arthur's grasp but Arthur was carrying on up the stairs.

'Come here, my little tank.' He lurched towards her.

'Don't touch me. I don't want you anywhere near me when you're like this. In fact, you can sleep in the baby's room.'

'Ooh! The *baby's* room is it? The *baby's* room.' Arthur climbed the last couple of stairs and poked her arm with his finger.

As Arthur poked her she lost her footing on the curve of the top step and felt herself bump-bump down the top couple of stairs. She caught hold of the banister but still bumped down another step until she landed on her bottom in the middle of the staircase.

'Oh, Peggy, love. Phew. I've got you. What a weight you are, though!' Arthur seemed sober within an instant and with his hands under her armpits managed to haul her back to the landing. 'I never meant…you tripped. You should be more careful. Peggy, are you alright? How on earth did that happen?'

He helped her into the bedroom. She was too shaken to cry. She sat down at the dressing table trembling as she pulled her brush through her hair. She stopped after fifteen strokes. All she wanted was to sleep, but before she'd had a chance to take off her dressing gown, Arthur had collapsed across the bed so she couldn't get in. She pushed his arm and even shouted at him but she knew from experience that it was no good trying to wake or move him. Peggy spent the night on the camp bed in the middle bedroom.

The midwife arrived at four in the afternoon, and the doctor came soon after. Arthur said he'd wait downstairs and listen to the radio.

'Try not to scream, Mrs Blake,' Dr Connor said, as the contractions intensified. 'You'll worry Mr Blake.'

'I don't care about Mr Blake,' Peggy moaned. 'He's never coming near me again.'

'Now, you don't mean that,' the doctor tried to calm her. 'All you young mothers have a funny five minutes before the birth. It's nearly time to push. Just hold on for a few more breaths...'

'I never knew it'd be like this ...I never knew it'd be... aghhh...'

At two in the morning the midwife called down the stairs and Peggy heard Arthur rush up. The midwife let him into the room. The doctor was standing at the end of the bed, a short rotund man with sparse grey hair. His head only came up to Arthur's shoulder. He placed his bag on the floor and offered Arthur his hand.

'Congratulations, Mr Blake. You're the father of a baby boy. Mother and baby both doing well.'

Arthur shook the doctor's hand. The doctor took a handkerchief from his top pocket and wiped his forehead.

'Can I get you a drink, Doctor?' Arthur asked.

'It's been a long night, though thanks for the offer. I'll be getting home. Now you see to that wife of yours – and your son. Take care of them, mind.'

Dr Connor wrote out his bill and both he and the midwife left. Arthur stood beside the bed. 'It's a little lad,' he said, peering towards the baby.

'Yes, it is – a boy. Come and look at your son. He's got all his fingers and toes. Everything in the right place.' Peggy was holding the baby wrapped in a towel and beckoned to Arthur to sit down on the bed.

Arthur craned his neck to see inside the bundle. 'I'm not sure I feel like a father, Pegs. It's hard to get used to.'

'But you *will* get used to it. I think he's here to stay. At least for the next twenty-odd years.'

'If you put it like that, I reckon I will.' He hesitated. 'I hope we get on,' he said. 'I never got on with my old man.'

'I'm sure you will. Here, have a look at him properly.'

'I've never taken much notice of babies before.'

'Do you want to hold him?'

Arthur took a pack of Woodbines from his shirt pocket, shook one out, tapped the end against the bedstead and dug into his trouser pocket for his matches. 'I might drop him, love,' he said. 'I think it's best if you take care of him, at least to begin with.' He lit the cigarette and blew a ring of blue smoke into the air. Peggy was propped up on the two pillows, Arthur's and her own, stacked up behind her. Her damp hair stuck to her forehead. 'I must look a mess,' she said after a long silence.

Arthur stroked her wrist. 'I've never seen you look so bonny,' he whispered and kissed her forehead. They sat in silence for a few more minutes before Arthur began to fidget.

'Would you like a brew?' he asked.

'Not until you've said hello properly to our son.'

'I've not had a wash.'

'That doesn't matter. Come on.'

Arthur stood up, crossed the room and opened the window a fraction to stub his cigarette out on the sill. The night was calm with only a slight rustle in the horse chestnut over the road. Apart from the dreamy hoot of an owl it felt to Peggy as if the rest of the world was asleep. She shivered and Arthur closed the window quickly, smiling a tight, apologetic smile for the cold air he'd let in. Arthur took his place beside her again. Gently Peggy lifted the top of the towel to reveal a tiny head with a crust of dark blood on matted black hair.

Arthur squinted at the baby. 'Oh! He looks… what's that on his head?'

'Dried blood. The midwife said I should pat it with a damp flannel in the morning.'

'Oh. I expect he'll look better tomorrow then. He's a little belter, Pegs,' he said uncertainly. 'I can tell he's going to be a little belter. Now, can I get you anything?'

'That tea would be nice and then perhaps you could lay him in the crib.'

'I'll put kettle on. I'd be afraid to lift him. He looks so frail. You lay him down, Peggy love. I won't be long.'

Arthur tiptoed out of the room and disappeared downstairs.

Days passed and the blood on the baby's head had turned a dark brown colour and dried so hard Peggy was reluctant to scrub his delicate skin. She hadn't washed herself either and had been wearing the same nightdress, never getting dressed from morning to night. If she wasn't asleep, she was propped up in bed trying to suckle the baby. Her nipples were swollen and red and although she didn't want to give up trying to coax him to feed, she'd started to dread those hard little gums clamping onto her flesh. There was none of the softness she'd imagined from a baby. And she'd never experienced real tiredness before. What people called being "dog-tired" or "exhausted" was nothing compared to the feeling of being completely washed out by lack of sleep. She could have fallen asleep standing up – the way horses do. Then every time she did nod off, within moments, or so it seemed, she'd be woken by that awful rasping sound of her baby's hungry cry. She could almost believe he was intentionally trying to upset her. It wasn't even proper crying with tears. Sometimes she wanted to shout at him. Squeeze his throat. Anything to stop that unending whine that cut through everything. She didn't squeeze him, of course. What sort of mother would harm a baby? She took a deep breath and lifted him into her bed, where sometimes he calmed himself or else carried on with that shivering whimpering until he surrendered to fretful sleep.

The more Peggy gazed at his tiny features, his dull blue eyes, the peck of a nose and the flappy ears, the more she began to think her baby looked odd. The shape of his head reminded her of something Arthur or Christian might dig up in one of the fields. A potato or a turnip. Dr Connor had used forceps, so maybe that was why. Perhaps her baby's head would return to a normal shape eventually. But as the days wore on, the more she studied this little scrap, the more she felt guilt. Guilt that she'd gone out onto the landing that night when Arthur had come home drunk, instead of turning over and going back to sleep. Guilt that she'd shouted at Arthur and riled him. Guilt that she'd stumbled on the stairs.

Guilt that she'd produced a baby with a head the shape of a potato.

She decided to go into the village as soon as she was on her feet again to see if there were any other babies around that she could compare hers with. She wished her mother were there and wrote a letter inviting her to visit. She knew she'd want to see her grandson, and Peggy had never felt more in need of seeing her.

Two weeks after the birth Arthur said he'd walk into the village at lunchtime to see if he could get the midwife to visit.

'Someone who might be able to give us something to stop the bairn crying,' were his exact words.

The baby was asleep when Peggy came downstairs to make some tea. She took the stairs one at a time sideways on, gingerly making her decent. As she hobbled through the hall she heard a knock at the door. She knew it couldn't be Arthur. She was still in her nightdress so she only opened the door a fraction. Immediately she recognised the wrinkled brown face of the woman who'd come to the house selling lavender soon after they'd moved in.

'Lucky heather,' the woman pressed some flowers towards her face.

'No, no thank you,' Peggy said, closing the door. But the woman, who wore dirty, oversized brown lace-up shoes, had her foot on the step. She produced something else from her basket. 'Hazelnuts' she said proffering a handful of nuts. 'For good fortune. And milk thistle for your man. Look, lady, here's some tarragon for the health of your little one.'

'My baby's perfectly healthy, thank you,' Peggy said.

'A mother shouldn't take risks.'

'I don't know what you're talking about.' Peggy felt a folding in her insides as she heard the baby whimpering upstairs. 'I need to go, my baby's crying.'

'Take this,' the woman persevered, pushing some leaves into Peggy's hand. 'You're a bonny one. Don't let any man hurt you.'

The following day Peggy heard someone open the gate. She went to the window and pulled back the net curtain. Thank goodness she'd dressed for the first time since the baby was born, although she was only wearing an old maternity dress her mother had posted to her months ago, but it was clean and had a starched, white collar. A young lady in a green uniform and hat stood on the path.

'I'm Miss Cray,' the woman said. 'Midwife. I found your husband's note last night when I got home,' she explained as Peggy showed her into the front room. 'I'd been meaning to visit you. You had one of my colleagues, I understand, for the birth. Where's Baby?'

Miss Cray wore a bottle green dress with a watch pinned above her ample bosom. Her hat had a badge on the front and hid most of her tidy brown hair that was rolled into a coil at the nape of her neck. She was tall and upright, and when she spoke, she tilted her head to one side. Her smile produced a pinprick of a dimple in each cheek.

Peggy led her upstairs where the baby was snivelling in his cot. Mary lifted him firmly and with a confidence that both impressed and deflated Peggy. 'He's a bit damp down below, that's all. When did you last change him?'

Peggy picked her way through her tired brains. It was like trudging through muddy fields in heavy boots. 'This morning after his feed, I think.'

'I'll change him for you. Let's take him down to the kitchen and give him a wash first. You've to keep Baby clean and dry, then Baby will be happy. I know it's hard,' she said as she carried the baby downstairs. 'You've still your husband to look after. Dinners and so on to make. Having a baby is always a lot more work than we imagine. You'd never dream such a little mite could create so much work. But you'll manage. The first one's always the hardest.'

Miss Cray boiled a kettle while Peggy sat down at the kitchen table with her head between her arms. 'That's right. You make the most of any opportunity to rest,' Mary said as she placed the baby on top of a towel she'd laid on the table. 'Do you have any relations nearby who could help? A mother or sister?'

'My mother's in Watchet. She sent a card after the baby was born but I heard from her the other day. She's got shingles and isn't keen to travel.'

'Oh, and has Baby got a name?' she asked as she wiped his face with a flannel.

'We haven't decided, but probably Thomas.'

'Ah! Tam, as they say in Scotland. Sorry, my love, but I did my training in Glasgow. A few years ago now, but I can tell you I met some men up there who'd put a woman off marriage for life.' Miss Cray laughed as she wiped the baby's bottom with the same flannel. 'You wouldn't believe some of the sights I saw. Men rolling home drunk minutes after their wives had given birth and climbing into the bed with them, bold as brass and with me still at the other end, trying to cut the cord.'

'My Arthur's not like that...' Peggy began.

'Oh, goodness me, no. I didn't mean... I was just saying... some of the sights you see in other parts of the country. D'you know I even helped a woman give birth once in a double bed with a couple of kiddies asleep at the other end while the father was away on a bender. I'll tell you in confidence, Mrs Blake, that I vowed I'd *never* marry after some of the things I saw. I decided there and then, I'd die as I was born. Miss Mary Cray. Spinster of this parish.' Mary Cray laughed to herself again as she pinned the neatly folded nappy around the baby and passed him back to Peggy like a new parcel. 'You'll need to get him registered sooner or later, so you'll have to decide for definite on his name. What have you been calling him?'

'Nothing really...' Peggy was interrupted by the sound of footsteps. Arthur came in wearing a white collarless shirt and braces. His hair looked blacker than ever against the whiteness of his shirt. He smiled when he saw Mary Cray, and Peggy noticed how bright his eyes were and how perfect his teeth. Arthur had been sleeping on the camp bed in the middle bedroom, which meant he was the only one in their little family who'd been sleeping at night. Seeing him smile like that Peggy realised she'd hardly noticed him for weeks. She thought how wonderfully handsome he still was. A handsome stranger. Although he did need a shave. He washed his hands in the stone sink and dried them on a tea towel.

'I'm right glad to see you,' he said, shaking Mary Cray's hand. 'Sorry I'm talking quiet. We've got used to whispering what with the little'un being such a light sleeper.'

'Ah, Mr Blake. I can tell you're a northerner by your accent.'

'Aye,' Arthur said. 'Barnsley born and bred.'

Mary Cray smiled. 'I thought as much. There's no need to whisper, though. He's awake at the moment, bright as a button. I've just given him a lovely wash, haven't I, little man?' she said running the back of her finger along the baby's cheek.

'He looks calm,' Arthur said. 'You must have the magic touch.'

'I'm not sure about that. It's a lot easier to deal with Baby when you haven't been deprived of sleep. Anyway, I'll be off now.'

'I'll see you out,' Arthur said.

Peggy could hear Arthur thanking her for coming. 'You got my note then?' he said.

'Yes, and everything seems fine. I've weighed Baby. He's lost a few ounces but that's to be expected in the first couple of weeks. He'll catch up soon enough. Your wife's very tired, but I've left her a tonic and some gripe water to settle the baby.'

'Thanks for coming, Nurse.'

'It's been nice meeting you all. I'll pop in again in a couple of weeks.'

Peggy picked the baby up and stood by the door so she could carry on listening as they moved down the hall.

'Is that normal?' she heard Arthur say.

'Is what normal?' Mary Cray said.

'I mean, is it normal to keep popping in, like?'

'It depends what you mean by normal ... and how busy I am. With some mothers it's fine to leave them to get on with it. Others need a bit more help.'

'So, how soon before we'd know if there was ... anything *wrong* with the bairn?' Arthur went on. Peggy held her breath, straining to hear Mary Cray's reply.

'How do you mean *wrong*?'

'It's just that he seems to cry a lot and he looks...' Arthur lowered his voice so Peggy was unable to catch the end of his sentence.

'All babies cry, Mr Blake. It's what babies do,' Mary Cray said dismissively. 'And he looks ... completely fine to me.'

Peggy sighed, and still carrying the baby, who stared up at her with vacant eyes, went out into the hall and stood beside Arthur. They watched Mary Cray cycle away down the lane, her thick ankles pumping at the peddles until she disappeared behind the hedge at the crossroads by the war memorial.

-2-

THE DAY before his fifth birthday Peggy sat Thomas down at the kitchen table.

'Tomorrow you will be going to school,' Peggy said. 'Isn't that exciting? You can wear the new jumper I've been knitting for you. You know where the school is. We've walked past the field at the side of the playground lots of times, so I won't be far away.'

'Where will you be? I want you to come to school with me.'

Peggy frowned. 'I'm not allowed to come to school with you. All children have to go to school when they're five and their mummies collect them in the afternoon.'

'But I want to stay with you.' Thomas's dangling feet kicked the chair leg.

'I like having you here, but every little boy and girl has to go to school. That's how you learn about the world. Reading and writing and sums.'

Thomas began to cry and Peggy knelt down and hugged him close. She loved his little smell and the way his fingers clung to her.

'You'll enjoy school,' she said. 'School is where you make

friends. I met my friend Sheila Arbuthnott at school. And you still spend Saturdays and Sundays at home with Mummy and Daddy.'

The next day they walked along Blackberry Lane, turned right at the war memorial, over the style and past the corn fields. They'd taken that path hundreds of times when they'd collected conkers or the wild oxeye daisies that grew in the long grass. Eventually they were greeted by the black iron gates of the playground.

Miss Arnold was standing in the playground with a whistle hanging on a ribbon round her neck. Boys, who all looked a great deal older than Thomas, were playing tag and kicking balls, and four girls were skipping, whilst others sat in huddles on the low walls by the toilets.

Peggy tightened her grip. 'Mummy you're hurting my hand,' Thomas said. 'When can we go home? I don't like it here.'

Miss Arnold swung a bell with a wooden handle. The noise made Peggy jump, but every child stopped what they were doing, and the air became still. Miss Arnold told them all to get into line and the two lines of children filed inside the building. Boys on one side, girls on the other.

Miss Arnold strode across the playground towards Peggy. She had a deep, manly voice and wore a grey skirt, which was plain and straight. She took Thomas by the hand and led him towards the building, leaving Peggy to follow behind, until she had to hurry her step just to keep up with them. Thomas looked round a couple of times with frightened eyes and Peggy knew he was about to cry. Once she caught up with them inside the corridor that led to Miss Arnold's office, she took him in her arms.

Miss Arnold had an angry look on her face that reminded Peggy of Arthur when he came home late at night in one of his moods. She felt shaky inside. She'd never liked school and the smell of this one reminded her of the unhappiness, all those years ago, when she couldn't recite her nine times table.

'I want to go home,' Thomas said, tugging the hem of her dress once she'd put him down.

Miss Arnold took Thomas's hand again and led him into her office. Whatever fresh air smelled of Miss Arnold's office was the opposite. 'I think perhaps it would be better if you waited outside whilst I interview Thomas,' she said. Peggy bit her lip and Thomas cried some more.

'Deary me. We have got a cry-baby here. It looks like we'll have to carry out the interview with you here after all, Mrs Blake.'

Peggy and Thomas sat opposite Miss Arnold's desk. She produced a pile of cards from her desk drawer, each with a different sum written in large black numbers.

'Now Thomas, can you tell me the answer to this sum? One plus one?'

Peggy cleared her throat. 'Come on, Thomas.' Peggy felt hot. Thomas looked down at his fingernails. Peggy looked down at her own hands, her face fixed with an anxious smile. She pulled the cuff of her cardigan over a yellowing bruise on her wrist.

'I'm sorry. It's not Thomas's fault. I never realised I was meant to do things like this with him. Teach him sums and such like.'

'Not to worry,' Miss Arnold said returning the card to the drawer with a sigh. 'Does he know how to spell his name?'

'I'm not sure. I don't suppose he does.' Peggy tidied Thomas's fringe, even though she'd combed it through a dozen times that morning.

Miss Arnold sighed again and looked up to the ceiling. 'Does he at least *recognise* his name?'

Thomas sucked his thumb. 'No, I don't suppose he does,' Peggy said, feeling her voice fade.

'Can he read any words?' Miss Arnold sounded as if she might drop off to sleep if this went on much longer.

Peggy coughed to give herself time to think of an answer. 'I'd never really thought about teaching him how to read. I thought he'd learn that sort of thing at school.'

Miss Arnold stood up, so Peggy stood too. Miss Arnold towered above her. She must have been a good six inches taller even than Arthur.

'Bring him in tomorrow at a quarter to nine. We'll see how he gets on. He'll have a bit of catching up to do, but he should be fine. We'll see you tomorrow, Thomas,' Miss Arnold added making the words sound like a threat.

Peggy arrived outside the school at half past three so as to be in good time for the bell at four. Edith Pittle and Myrtle Dobbs were standing there waiting, although both turned away when they saw Peggy.

'She must *know*,' she heard Mrs Pittle say under her breath.

'But why stay with the man when he's been up another woman's skirts?' Peggy was aware of the two women sniggering.

'That's a very good question, Mrs Pittle. Maybe she's nowhere else to go.'

'With a nurse too! I thought nurses were supposed to look after people.'

'Maybe that's what she is doing!' Both women sniggered.

Peggy stood on the other side of the gate. She peered into the playground, willing Thomas to appear so they could hurry off home where she had some biscuits baking in the oven. She wished she had a friend to stand with. For his first couple of days Miss Arnold brought Thomas out through the playground and handed him over to Peggy, but this week she had to wait with the other mothers as Thomas was no longer 'new' and was to come out with all the other children. Suddenly she heard a loud bell, the big green wooden door, marked 'Boys' was flung open releasing a group of boys into the playground. One of them was Edmund Stringer, who was acting the fool, play-fighting with his satchel, pretending to wallop one of the bigger boys. Peggy peered beyond Edmund and his pals, but there was no sign of Thomas.

As the boys approached her, Peggy called out. 'Edmund! Have you seen our Thomas?'

Edmund stopped running. 'He's just coming, Mrs Blake,' he said before putting on a spurt to catch up with his friends. Peggy heard them all laugh as one of the one of the biggest boy chanted, 'Nitwit Blake, nitwit Blake, couldn't even eat a piece of cake!'

Peggy looked behind her to see who'd spoken but the boys had disappeared.

Gradually more children came out. Some girls and a few younger boys, all of whom eventually hooked up with the gaggle of mothers who'd been waiting at the gate. Peggy watched as Myrtle

Dobbs and Edith Pittle walked away, swinging their handbags and holding the hands of their offspring and wondered who they'd been talking about, and even wondered if it was her. Eventually the playground was empty, except for one little dot that gradually turned into Thomas as he dawdled across the tarmac, his newly-knitted, over-sized jumper drowning his shorts. He was crying again. Peggy knelt down and hugged him as soon as he got to the gate.

'Miss made me stand at the front, and those other boys all call me stupid,' Thomas mumbled between sobs.

'Stupid! You're not stupid. Why would they say that? They're the ones who's stupid. And you can tell them I said so!'

As the weeks passed Peggy had taken to standing as far away from Myrtle Dobbs and Edith Pittle as possible when waiting at the school gates. She didn't care about their sniggering. She remembered what her mother had said to her when a group of girls made fun of her when she was at school. 'They're only jealous, Peggy. Because of your looks. Because you look like a film star and the best they could ever look would be like an extra playing the part of a plane Jane.' The problem was that she did care because they made her feel lonely, but she cared a lot more about Thomas and her reward for standing there day after day was the sensation of his little hand in hers as they turned together away from the school to begin their walk home.

On the fourth week Miss Arnold came out of the school building just as they were about to walk home.

'Mrs Blake?' she said. 'If you've got a moment perhaps we could go inside for a word.'

Miss Arnold marched, straight-backed ahead of Peggy across the playground, her long legs taking strides that Peggy again found impossible to keep up with. In the classroom Miss Arnold pulled out one of the children's chairs. 'Do take a seat,' she ordered.

Peggy squeezed into a miniature chair that had been designed for a five-year-old. Thomas stood beside her staring at his shoes. Miss Arnold wrote a large letter A in white chalk on the blackboard.

'Now, what's that letter, Thomas?'

Thomas looked up. 'Don't know, Miss.'

Miss Arnold sighed and drew a large cartoon of a cat on the board. 'Now, can you tell me what that is?'

'Don't know, Miss,' Thomas mumbled.

'Come on, Thomas. You know what that is,' Peggy coaxed him.

'Come here,' Miss Arnold said beckoning him nearer to the board. 'Now tell me what letter that is.'

'Letter A, Miss,' Thomas whispered.

'What is *that*?' she said, pointing once more to the cat.

'Pussy cat,' he said in a tiny voice.

Peggy sighed with relief. She knew Thomas wouldn't let her down. He had learned something since he'd been at school – even if it was just the first letter of the alphabet.

'Myopic!' Miss Arnold declared.

'I beg your pardon.'

'Glasses. The child needs glasses. He can't see the board. Thomas has enough trouble keeping up without the added handicap of myopia. You'll need to take him to the optician's in town. The child clearly needs spectacles.'

Peggy didn't know what myopia was but promised to take Thomas to the optician's.

They took the bus into Shapton the following Saturday. Peggy and Thomas sat together and Arthur perched on the edge of the seat behind them.

'Where are we going, Mummy?' Thomas asked as Peggy produced a paper bag containing six sherbet lemons.

'To the optician, lad,' Arthur said over his shoulder.

'What does the 'optishern' mean?'

'It's a place where they look at your eyes and if you need glasses, they will give you a lovely pair of glasses. Then won't you look grand?'

'What if the lad doesn't need glasses?' Arthur said, leaning both elbows on the back of Peggy's seat. 'That Mrs Arnold's a know-all if you ask me. She should've been a man and now she's taking it out on the rest of us. Why would the lad need glasses? Neither of us wears glasses. Look, lad, tell me what you can see out of the window?' The bus was travelling through the hub of the village, past the post office and the butcher's. 'You see the picture of the little pig in the butcher's window?'

Thomas didn't reply. 'He's eating a sweet,' Peggy said.

The optician, who wore a mustard-coloured jumper and thick spectacles, spent a long time testing, measuring, and shining lights into Thomas's eyes. A fortnight later they went into town again to collect his glasses.

'Just think how exciting it will be to have glasses,' Peggy said as they alighted from the bus at the marketplace and rushed to escape a burst of squally grey rain that made them shiver as they covered the short distance to the optician's.

'You'll be the first one in our family to have glasses.' Once inside the shop Peggy shook rainwater from her rain hat. 'They'll be brand new ones, made especially for you by that nice man we met last week.' Peggy was aware that her voice had become loud and rather squeaky. Thomas gazed down at his shoes and frowned. 'I don't like that man,' he mumbled.

The optician sat Thomas down opposite him and opened a small brown case. Inside were the glasses that he was to wear every day except when he went to bed, had a bath or went swimming. Peggy wanted to tell the man that Thomas had never been swimming, not even to the sea, but he was busy leaning over Thomas, coiling the ends of the glasses around his ears.

'Ow, that hurts,' Thomas said, trying to turn round. The optician leant over to adjust the bridge on his nose. The man twisted the glasses to the left and to the right but whichever way he moved them they still seemed lopsided. Arthur was sitting next to Peggy, gazing out of the window, when suddenly he stood up.

'I'll meet up with you later. By the bus stop,' he said, making his way towards the door. 'I need some air.'

'Arthur…' Peggy began. Thomas turned round again, his little face now half covered in the two circles of wire magnifying his confused blue eyes. Peggy felt her own eyes mist over, although she wasn't sure whether the tears were to do with Thomas looking so odd or because of Arthur's need for some fresh air. She wiped her eyes with the sleeve of her raincoat and diverted her attention away from the plight of her son to watch her husband who was walking towards the main road, but not heading in the direction of the Wagon and Horses as she'd expected. She craned her head around the window stretching as far as she could without toppling over on the chair. Arthur had stopped to talk to someone. A woman Peggy recognised. A woman wearing a dark green raincoat who was holding a black umbrella. She watched as Arthur ducked underneath the umbrella, as he took it from her to hold it himself, so it provided space for his extra height above the woman. As the woman reached her hand to Peggy's husband's cheek and laid the palm there with such tenderness as if she were wiping away a spot of rain. Peggy thought about the picture that still hung in their front room. The one with the couple sheltering under the big black umbrella. She stood up and moved towards the door. She put one foot outside onto the pavement.

'Mummy,' she heard Thomas call her. 'Where are you going?'

Peggy paused on the threshold. 'I won't be a moment,' she called behind her to the optician as she ran towards the main road where Arthur was standing with Mary Cray.

'Arthur,' she cried. She felt herself stomp her foot. 'What are you doing? What are you doing with … that woman?'

Mary's expression remained as calm as the morning she'd held Thomas in her arms and lulled him off to sleep. 'Good afternoon. Mrs Blake, isn't it?'

Peggy placed a hand on each of her hips. 'Mrs Blake isn't it?' she mimicked. 'Why, I don't know how you've got the nerve.'

'Pegs!' Arthur took hold of her arm. 'I just bumped into the midwife here when I was on my way to get some tobacco. Why are you behaving like this? Where's the lad? You haven't left him in the optician's on his own?'

'Oh, your son's in the optician's? Is there something wrong with his eyesight?'

Peggy clenched her fist. 'You know he's in the optician's,' she accused Mary. 'I bet you know everything there is to know about him, about me, and not to mention *my* husband.'

Arthur tightened his grip on Peggy's arm. 'I don't know what's come over you, love,' he said. 'I must apologise for my wife, Nurse.'

Mary looked at the pavement. 'I have to get on now, I'm afraid. I do hope your wife recovers.' She gave Arthur a sideways glance, just the shadow of a smile flitting across her plain features.

Arthur was sheltering in a shop doorway, smoking when Peggy and Thomas eventually emerged from the optician's.

'Your new specs are getting wet, lad,' he said through an exhalation of smoke. Peggy was still shaking with anger as she bent down to remove the glasses that were splashed with drops of rain.

'That's better,' Arthur said. 'You look much better without those things.'

Peggy glared at her husband as she wiped the lenses on her handkerchief. 'I don't agree, Arthur. These are the nicest glasses I've ever seen. I think our Thomas looks very clever in them.' She placed the glasses back on Thomas.

Arthur stubbed out his cigarette with the heel of his boot. 'Right you are, Peggy love.' He ruffled the boy's hair. Peggy smoothed it flat again.

'Arthur?' They were standing in the queue for the bus so she spoke softly. 'Why do you like her? What has she got that makes her more attractive than me?' Tears burnt her eyes.

'Sorry, love. I don't know what you mean. I was low on cigs. I didn't want us to miss the bus.'

The bus came and they got on. As Thomas's glasses slipped down his nose he pushed them up with his thumb.

'Are you sure that optician knows what he's doing? The specs don't seem to fit the bairn.'

For once, Peggy wasn't concentrating on her son. All she could think about was the woman in the green raincoat. 'I knew there was something going on,' she said. 'Now I know for certain what it is. Ha! The midwife who came after our Thomas was born. With her plain face and her fat ankles.' The midwife, who'd made her feel so reassured. So cared for.

Arthur looked bemused and even glanced around the bus at the other passengers, as if demonstrating that he had no idea what his crazy wife was on about. The bus turned a corner and they all slid along the seat. The conductor came up to them and Arthur took some change from his coat pocket and seemed preoccupied with counting out the correct coins before handing them over.

Peggy tried to recall whether any other children she'd seen coming out of school wore glasses but couldn't think of any.

'Just see how smart you'll be now you've got your posh new specs,' she said when she dropped Thomas at the school gate on the Monday. 'You look very handsome in them.'

But when she picked him up at the end of the day it seemed having glasses was making school more difficult. She heard the chant before she'd even caught sight of Thomas emerging from the big green door.

'Hey Specky – what's two plus two? Four! Specky four-eyes, Specky four-eyes!' Tommy dawdled across the playground and stumbled into her arms. His shoelaces were undone. Peggy bent down to take the glasses off so she could wipe his eyes.

'I'll have a word with Miss Arnold tomorrow about those nasty boys,' she said, tying his laces, although what she really wanted to do was to grab each one by the collar and shake them.

Peggy walked to the school the following day at lunchtime to confront Miss Arnold. She arrived at the gates and stopped for a few minutes and looked through the railings. All the boys she saw were playing tag or kicking a ball around, except Michael Stringer and another of the bigger boys called Bernard Dobbs who Peggy had met when he'd come for tea at the farmhouse, who were tearing around the playground pretending to be jet fighters. Four little girls with ribbons in their hair were skipping with a long rope that looked like a washing line. The only child on his own was Thomas who stood in a corner by the drains. Peggy turned and decided to leave before he saw her. Tears blurred her eyes as she hurried home.

She found some washing that needed doing, some of Arthur's trousers and a blouse she'd made for herself that had a gravy stain on the sleeve. She looked at the pile of ironing in the kitchen corner by the sink, and some socks with holes in, but she wasn't in the mood for any of her normal jobs. Her mother had sent her an old copy of *Woman's Realm*, and a knitting pattern for a child's cardigan. She sat down in the front room and flicked through the magazine and read about other people's lives.

Arthur was helping a friend in the village to do up his house. He'd go there straight after work sometimes, and if they were late finishing, Arthur would stay over. He'd never been one for doing things around the house in Blackberry Lane, but Peggy didn't mind that he'd suddenly become interested in home improvements. She didn't bother to ask who the friend was. Eventually it was every night and Arthur collected the bulk of his clothes one afternoon while Peggy was out picking Thomas up from school.

Life seemed easier now Arthur had a friend. Thomas stopped biting his nails and he didn't ask where his daddy was. The days passed, months went by. A year. From the bedroom Peggy could see Arthur arrive for work in the mornings if she was awake. Sometimes she'd watch him leave from the front room window in the afternoons. Often she'd sit with Thomas in the kitchen playing Happy Families or Snap. She let him win at Snap and when they played Happy Families she helped him collect the families. She held her head high as she walked past Edith Pittle and Myrtle Dobbs and the other women at the school gates.

Peggy was on her way with nine-year-old Thomas down the long hospital corridor when she realised the man walking towards her was her husband.

'Arthur! Goodness me. What are you doing here?' She held tighter onto Thomas's hand. They'd passed each other, but each of them turned awkwardly in order to speak.

'They've done some x-rays,' Arthur said. 'Just routine, but they say there's a shadow on my lung.' He coughed, a deep rattling cough in his chest. Peggy noticed his hands were shaking. 'There's not a lot they can do – so they claim.' Arthur went on, reaching in his shirt pocket for his Woodbines.

'Not a lot they can do? What do you mean by that? That's a queer thing to say.'

'It's only a shadow. Nothing serious. They don't do anything with a shadow, apparently. I've to come back in a fortnight. Anyway, enough about me. What brings you here, Peggy?'

'It's our Thomas. He's had a hearing test – the school referred him. There's always *something* – I'm beginning to think you were right when you said Miss Arnold picks on Thomas on purpose.' Peggy spoke in a whisper to shield the little boy from what she was saying, although she was beginning to wonder if this was necessary. He hid his face in her skirt as Arthur tried to ruffle his hair.

'I expect it's nowt to worry about. That's schools for you. Better be getting along,' Arthur said. 'Don't know how much longer I'll be working, though. This cough's a blighter. You might have to start looking for another place – you know, if I'm not working like – for Stringer any more…'

'We'll manage,' she replied, as if she didn't care either way. 'We can always go to Mother's. In fact, I telephoned her last week and she's started decorating my old room. Just in case.'

Two nurses with starched white caps passed them in the corridor, both turned around and looked at Arthur. Peggy found Thomas's gloves and hat in her handbag.

'I'll let you get on,' Arthur said. He paused to draw on his cigarette. 'Are you alright? You know. I was just wondering. I know Christian would tell me if there was owt wrong. You've got enough – financially, like?'

'We're fine, thank you. Now we'd better be getting along. The bus leaves in twenty minutes.' Arthur looked as if he'd lost weight. If he was ill there was no point in starting an argument about the fact that he'd left them to fend for themselves with just a few shillings every week. That he'd let her down. That he'd forgotten his wedding vows. Forsaking all others…

'Hold on a minute. You know, Pegs,' he said. 'I'm not that good with words, but, the truth is … she makes me feel safe. She always made me feel safe. From that first day that she came to the house when our Thomas was born. The dreams – you know – they went away … as soon as I …I can sleep at night now…'

Peggy felt a pulse begin to ring inside her head. This was the conversation they'd never had. Like so many other things in their marriage, the subject of Mary Cray had been buried beneath the minutiae of everyday life. When they'd first married she'd worried about the women Arthur might have known before her but had never found out who they were or whether they even existed. The strands that had held them together had unravelled like wool in a loosely knitted scarf. Peggy knelt down on one knee to put Tommy's hat and gloves on for him and straighten his glasses.

'Safe. Yes.' Peggy did understand. She felt a pang of envy, more for her husband than for Mary Cray. What must it be like to have someone who afforded that cushion of safety? A mother-like figure who provided a sense of contentment and protection. She knew for certain at that moment that she would return to Watchet.

Arthur coughed into a handkerchief and Peggy noticed some red against the white of the cotton. He touched Thomas on the shoulder. 'I've to collect some pills from the pharmacy. Cheerio, lad.' He pinched the side of Thomas's ear. The boy flinched. Arthur held the top of Peggy's arm squeezing it a bit too hard. She knew the squeeze was meant to be affectionate, yet it reminded her of something else.

They watched Arthur as he walked across the path past a low wooden building painted in the same green as the corridor. For all the times he'd made her suffer, and even though he looked too thin, he was still a good-looking man and for just a fraction of a moment Peggy longed to walk down the street with her arm linked through his – just once more. To dance a waltz together with his arms around her, take the bus into town, share a poke of chips and a pickled onion. Deal the cards out for a game of Rummy. Just once more to show off her handsome soldier to the world. Maybe she should have fought for him. He was her husband and after all, what *did* Mary Cray have that Peggy Mabel Blake didn't? Her mother said she should have put up a fight – but the strangest thing was, that for quite a few reasons, on balance, life seemed infinitely easier without him.

The seventeenth of November 1954. Arthur Blake's funeral service was marred by a fall of snow the night before. Eleven people shivered in the front pews inside Lyde Village Church. Tobias

Stringer, his sons, Christian, Michael and Edmund, Peggy and Thomas Blake, the landlady and four of the regulars from the Ring O' Bells. Peggy stood perfectly still, her gloved hand locked into that of her son, her black hat pinned neatly amongst the gold of her curls. A delicate veil of netting concealing the top half of her face. Thomas was dressed in his warm coat, gloves, scarf and a woollen balaclava which he kept pulling at to itch his head. After they'd sung *Breathe On Me Breath of God* and *The Lord's My Shepherd* and listened to a prayer and eulogy by the vicar, the mourners moved outside to re-group beside the grave.

Freshly dug clods of earth sprinkled with snow, like a row of Christmas puddings topped with cream, marked the spot where Arthur was to rest. Peggy watched Christian Stringer as he walked away from the other mourners, along the path, past the grave of his mother, towards the church gate, his working boots scuffing the gravel. Her heart felt heavier at the sight of his distress than with the weight of her own.

A woman stood by the gate and spoke to Christian as he passed. Mary Cray – still in her green uniform. They stood together for a while, Mary with her arm around Christian's shoulder.

After the coffin had been lowered into the ground, and the last prayers mumbled, Peggy looked up again. Christian was still by the gate kicking the toe of his boot into the path and Mary was cycling away, her fulsome ankles clad in thick brown stockings, her left hand holding on to her hat. Peggy looked down at her own trim ankles in her best nylons and took hold of her son's hand ready to walk home.

JOHN McDONALD

April 1955

JOHN McDONALD always kept a spare shilling in his trouser pocket in case of emergencies. Not that this was an emergency, but he produced the coin and flipped it into the air.

'Heads you have the big room, tails it's mine. Oh dear,' he said as the shilling rolled towards the top of the stairs.

'Here, let me.' David had a half-crown which he also flipped and caught expertly on the back of his hand, revealing the bearded profile of King George V. 'Heads it is,' David said. 'Best of three?'

'No, you've won. I'll be fine in here.' John opened the door to the middle bedroom. 'It'll be warmer. Besides, I always had the big room at home.'

'But this house belongs to you, John. You should have the best bedroom. After all, you're the oldest, and if you hadn't been so lucky on the pools, we wouldn't be here.'

'Ah, but you won the toss, so you have the best room. That's what we agreed. All's fair in love and war, as they say.'

John carried a box of books upstairs with David following behind. David shivered as he opened the door to the big front bedroom. 'You're right about this room not being as warm.'

'We could swap. It's not too late, if you're not happy,' John said.

'No. I'll be fine,' David assured his brother. 'Here, let me help you with those boxes.'

The boxes were packed with John's management training manuals. At home they'd resided beneath his bed, but now they'd have their own room.

'Besides,' John added, 'I've got the small box room for my books, so that makes it completely fair.'

The following week John walked up the path to the gate and out into the lane. The warm spring sunlight flickered through the leaves of the horse chestnut trees. He breathed in the fresh air mixed with just a hint of the smoky sweetness blowing over from the fields. In the distance he could see the paperboy cycling towards him.

'Two Blackberry Lane. *Times* and *Goal*!' the boy shouted as he skidded to a halt and handed John his copy of *The Times* and David's football magazine.

'That yours, mister?' the boy said, scrutinising the front page of the magazine. 'Billy Wright. He's the greatest. Wish I could have a magazine like that.'

'Perhaps you could use some of the money you make from your paper round to buy one.'

'Fat chance. I gotta give all my wages to me mum.'

John smiled to himself. Financial independence was one of the rewards of being in his twenties – and of winning a small sum on the football pools. The boy cycled off towards the other end of Blackberry Lane and John went inside. He left David's magazine on the kitchen table, rolled up his copy of *The Times* and secured an elastic band around it. He still had ten minutes to walk as far as the war memorial to catch the eight-fifteen bus that would take him to Reckitt's Paper Mill on the outskirts of town.

On the bus journey to work John always sat in the front near the driver. For the first five minutes he'd drink in the view of fields and trees, then as they passed through the village, he enjoyed looking at the shops and at the other end of the village, the recreation ground, and more fields. After the bus had picked up a couple of people who always got on at the post office, he'd unroll his paper and devour the day's news.

The headlines that day concerned a woman called Ruth Ellis who'd been charged with murdering her lover. The picture on the front page showed her in a low-cut dress, holding a Martini glass. Her hair was bleached blonde, her sharp nails painted with dark varnish, and, although she was smiling in the photo, her expression was so hard it extinguished any sense of joy.

Her smile seemed false, and the more John looked at the picture, the more he could imagine this woman killing someone. The article said she'd shot her lover in the head. John looked at the photograph again. She was the sort of woman some men would find attractive. David might admire a woman like that at first, but probably wouldn't bother with her for long. Her eyes were empty, as if she had no soul.

As the bus chugged along John felt a bit sick, so he folded his paper up and closed his eyes. He couldn't help thinking about that woman in the paper, though. Violence of any kind was anathema to him. Yet he was loath to pre-judge a person. If Ruth Ellis was convicted of murder, she would hang. John had recently put his signature to a petition calling for the abolition of capital punishment. Whatever this woman had done, no man had the right to end her life.

As the nausea wore off, he opened his eyes and looked at the photograph again, focusing on the spot on her neck where they would tighten the noose. You could tell how soft the skin on her neck was, where it wasn't hidden by the glass she was holding. John turned the page with a sigh. The next article he read was about some new gimmick they'd come up with to encourage people to go to the cinema. A photograph showed rows of cinema-goers wearing cardboard glasses with red and green lenses which apparently made films appear in 3-D.

Whatever would they come up with next?

He was in his office, sitting at his desk, by nine. There was a knock at his door. Two of the canteen girls stood outside.

'Mr McDonald, can we have a word?' The woman who spoke was called Gillian and was in charge of cleaning. The other girl, whose name John couldn't immediately recall, sniffed into a handkerchief.

John showed them to the two chairs that sat facing his desk.

'Mr McDonald,' Gillian said. 'Valerie here has got a problem.' Gillian nudged Valerie's arm. 'Go on, Val, tell him.'

'It's like this, sir. Some of the men on the factory floor have been making … you know…saying things about us.'

'"Us"? What sort of things, Valerie?' John asked, although he had an uneasy premonition of what was to come.

'Saying I've been going out at lunchtimes – which I have, sir, because I been visiting my nan who's had a fall and I been helping her with her lunch and things…'

'Go on, Val,' Gillian encouraged her friend.

'It's because you, Mr McDonald, because you been going out at lunch too. They are saying that we are … you know…'

'Doing it, sir,' Gillian kindly interjected.

'Doing what? …Oh, I see…' John said, looking up at the clock and wishing this interview would soon be over.

'Go on,' Gillian said, 'tell Mr McDonald the rest.'

Valerie examined her fingernails. They were painted in dark varnish, like Ruth Ellis's in the photograph in *The Times*.

'They said I been doing it with…' at this point her voice became a whisper. 'With… you, sir, of a lunchtime. Jack Drew says I done it with you so that's why you don't eat in the canteen no more. They're making things up to spite me.'

John wished he understood how women's minds worked. 'Why would anyone want to spite you, Valerie?' he asked. Sometimes, although it was just a small factory, he also wished he wasn't the manager responsible for personnel. 'I shouldn't take any notice. I'll have a word with Jack.'

'Tell him to keep his nasty rumours to himself, sir,' Gillian said. 'I mean, I know why Valerie goes out at lunchtime. I expect you got a good reason too. A lot of people talk about things and if they don't know the facts, they make 'em up. They all says you've got a young lady, sir. Because that's what their minds are like. They ain't got nothing better to think about.'

John adjusted the knot on his tie and Valerie plumped up the dyed blonde bun that was balanced on top of her head. 'I'll have a word with Jack,' he reassured her. 'Now run along. I'm sure you've got lots of work to do.'

'Thank you, Mr McDonald.'

John turned around from his desk and gazed out of the window that overlooked the factory floor. Sheaves of paper flowed from the machines in immense waves of white. Pure and perfectly straight sheets of parchment filling the air with a fresh woody smell, like the smell of a new book. Presently he saw Gillian and Valerie tottering along towards the corridor where the kitchen was situated. John made a note of the conversation in his diary with a reminder to talk to Jack Drew. Not that he was about to explain why he left the building every lunchtime. That was none of their business.

At twelve-thirty Jack Drew was sitting opposite John. The chair looked too small for him as he lounged backwards, his long legs splayed on either side as if he were astride a horse. He wore drainpipe trousers and winkle-pickers with his hair teased into a quiff.

'I won't keep you long,' John began.

Jack sniffed.

'I'll get straight to the point. One of the girls from cleaning has expressed concerns about rumours that are circulating...'

Jack sniffed again.

'She... actually, you might as well know...Valerie. Although I'm not a hundred percent sure I should have told you who it was. But on second thoughts you may already know. Anyway, *Valerie* was somewhat upset this morning. To be perfectly honest ... I can't have this kind of thing going on...'

'What kind of thing?' Jack straightened himself on the chair in a pose that John found rather intimidating.

'It's only gossip, Jack, but Valerie seems to think you've been spreading unkind rumours about her...'

'What rumours?'

John adjusted the knot in his tie. 'Rumours concerning the way she spends her lunch hour...' Even as he spoke the words, John was aware of how silly they sounded.

Jack made a snort implying derision. 'I don't know what you mean.'

John felt hot. 'I think you probably do. I realise it's only her word against yours – although to be fair she did have another girl with her, so it wasn't just Valerie's point of view. Maybe we'll just leave it at that, if you don't mind.'

'Hold on, sir. You're right, it is her word against mine. You can't accuse me of something I never done. I'm in the union, you know.'

John took a handkerchief from his pocket and wiped his forehead. 'Look, I'm sorry if I've upset you. Perhaps as a compromise you could just be more careful about what you say in future, especially in relation to female members of staff.'

How had John ended up being the one to apologise?

John took his briefcase and umbrella and left the building. He walked along the high street, past the bank and the butcher's and crossed the road by the ironmonger's. The spring sunshine had enticed a few shop girls to eat their lunch by the lake, but John preferred to sit alone in the bus shelter to eat his sandwiches. He propped up his umbrella by the bench and took his lunch from his briefcase. As he ate, he read the various messages people had chalked or painted onto the walls. 'LV loves MC,' and 'JT loves?' Some of the other things people had written were so vulgar John avoided reading them. However, on the inside wall by the bus timetable someone had written a poem that he always made a point of reading. It was printed in red paint on the wood of the shelter. The perpetrator had clearly been determined that their handiwork didn't get washed away by the rain. As he chewed his way through his cheese sandwich, John read it again.

I strove for none, for none was worth my strife. Nature I loved and next to Nature, Art. I warm both hands before the fire of life. It sinks and I am ready to depart.

John intended to memorise this verse and discover whether it was a proper poem and, if so, who the poet was. The words seemed specifically written for him. Not that he was 'ready to depart' – far from it, but he still took comfort in the words, despite the fact that in the last twenty-four hours some vandal had inserted a 't' after the first 's' of the word 'sinks'. John tutted. He felt a mixture of betrayal and embarrassment.

He opened his library book. He was coming to the end of *Martin Chuzzlewit* but, with forty pages still to read, knew he wouldn't have time to finish it that lunchtime. But it was due for renewal. If he was quick, he'd make the library before his lunch hour was over.

After he'd eaten his sandwich and the apple he had for afters, he hurried towards the library, cutting through the alley by the fish shop, past the tobacconist's. The sun had become lost in a cover of dark cloud and drizzle turned into large drops of rain that trickled down his neck. He opened his umbrella and was almost running by the time he reached the library.

He shook his umbrella, went into the building, past the desk where the librarians sat, and savoured the warmth and hushed stillness of the library. The central heating, mixed with the smell of books and furniture polish seemed even more comforting than usual.

The orderliness of the shelves of books gave John a glowing feeling inside. Books were like a reassurance that all was well in his world. A reassurance that some things would live forever. If some *things* were eternal, then why not life itself? *I warmed both hands before the fire of life. It sinks and I am ready to depart.* There, he'd remembered some of the poem. Words defied death, illness and loss. Everything that was written about Ruth Ellis, for example, would survive her, and ultimately all those who wrote about her. The library was wall to wall words. Knowledge that had been passed down the centuries, packed inside thousands of book covers.

On his first visit to the library, John hadn't known where to begin. His parents kept no books at home and both he and David had left school at fifteen. John had used textbooks for the business course he'd done at night school. In the library he saw classics he'd heard of, but knew nothing of what lay within their covers. He'd started in the fiction section with the authors whose surnames began with the letter A, then B and so on. Jane Austen had been a bit of a struggle and he gave up half way through *Northanger Abbey*. He skipped most of the Brontes, although there was something about *Jane Eyre* that made him persevere. He enjoyed Joseph Conrad, though, *and* A.J. Cronin and now he was on Charles Dickens.

John couldn't specify exactly when he first noticed the young librarian with the soft blonde hair that was tied at the nape of her neck with a blue velvet ribbon. A grey-haired woman had stamped his books when he'd first visited the library. His awareness of her fair-haired colleague had been gradual. He'd half noticed her without giving her any thought, then registered her presence, eventually allotting her a fraction of space in his subconscious.

He proceeded to the counter where he placed *Martin Chuzzlewit* on the desk. The grey-haired librarian was not there, but the young one with blonde hair was.

'I'd like to renew this, please,' he told her. After she'd stamped the book, she smiled as if he were a special friend. 'That's due back on May the twentieth.' She handed him the book. Unlike the older woman, who snapped the books shut, she'd closed the book carefully as if it were a precious keepsake.

'Thank you,' he said and carried on into the library to find the E – F section in preparation for when he'd finished *Martin Chuzzlewit*.

When John returned the next day, the blonde librarian was again on the front desk, stamping a book for an elderly gentleman who leant heavily on a walking stick. She looked at the old man with a smile.

'Thank you,' she said as she gave the book to him. John accidentally caught her eye and looked away. He hid for the next five minutes in the History section in an agitated state, picked up a book at random and flicked through the pages pretending to be interested in the life of King Charles the Second. But all the time John was thinking about something else. Something completely absurd. Why had the blonde librarian given that old gentleman the same friendly smile she'd given him the previous day? That smile had seemed especially reserved for him, yet there she was giving the same smile to just any old man who happened to be borrowing books. It was unbearable. He slotted the book about King Charles the Second back on the shelf and left.

John spent the next week at home, lying in bed, reading. He'd contracted a head cold and didn't want to spread his germs at work. On the Wednesday he wondered if the blonde librarian had missed him coming into the library, although he knew this was a ridiculous notion. A girl as wonderful as she would surely never notice someone as ordinary as John.

As he lay in bed shivering and sweating, sneezing and coughing, he couldn't help imagining what it would be like to have a girlfriend to visit him. Maybe after she'd finished work, she might bring some ginger biscuits, make him some tea, refill his hot water bottle. Gradually the vague image of a 'girlfriend' turned into the blonde librarian. She'd cook meals for him, serve them on a tray, wash his pyjamas and handkerchiefs, ask if he was feeling better. Maybe even sit on the side of the bed, although not too close because of the germs.

As it was, John struggled downstairs to make his cheese sandwich for lunch and rinse his hankies in the sink.

On his first day back at work John took all four of his books to the library during his lunch hour. As soon as he entered the building, he was dismayed to see the grey-haired woman at the desk. The sight of her made him feel depressed. The aftermath of the 'flu most probably. He needed cheering up. He stood in the fiction section wondering what sort of story would lift his spirits. He'd heard P.G. Wodehouse was amusing, but that would mean skipping ahead to U – W, which would be cheating.

He picked up a book by someone called Kingsley Amis which looked entertaining, but would mean back-peddling to A. As he passed the returns trolley, he noticed the name Wodehouse on the spine of one of the books. He hesitated before picking it up but decided that if the book was on the returns trolley it wouldn't be cheating if he read it. As he reached towards the trolley, he nudged it with his knee. The trolley was on wheels and, as it moved away from him, he heard a loud 'Ouch!' and was horrified to see the blonde librarian stumbling on the floor.

'I'm most terribly sorry,' John whispered. He moved towards her in order to help her to her feet. She was wearing a pink blouse with long sleeves. As he took her by the arm, he felt her elbow through the fabric. John hadn't been this close to her before. She was smiling as she thanked him. Her white teeth were perfectly even. She wore no makeup, but her lips were coral pink.

'It's alright. I'm perfectly alright,' she kept saying. John was about to apologise again when he felt a sneeze building up inside his nose, a straggler from his cold unreasonably making its exit at this most inconvenient of moments. He fumbled for his handkerchief, managing to pull it out of his pocket just in time.

'Bless you,' the librarian whispered, and she smiled again with that smile that made John feel happy from the tips of his ears to the soles of his size eight feet.

John left the library as swiftly as possible. He didn't want anything to spoil the moment. He floated along the pavements back to the factory on a cloud of joy.

The following morning the hours ticked slowly by till lunchtime, but when John got to the library the blonde-haired librarian wasn't behind the desk. Mondays, Wednesdays and Fridays. That was it! The young woman with the smile that made him feel wonderful all the way down to his socks, only worked there three days a week. John felt like kicking himself. Why had it taken him so long to fathom that out?

John had a plan. He would engage her in conversation. He'd ask her a question, she would answer, he'd ask another question, and again listen to her reply. It would be easy. But the problem was choosing the right question. He didn't want to appear nosy by asking anything too personal. The most obvious topic would be books. She must be interested in books, which meant they already had something in common.

He went to the library on the Wednesday, put the Wodehouse down on the counter and cleared his throat.

'That was a thoroughly enjoyable book,' he said.

She smiled as she slipped the ticket into the little pouch.

'I don't suppose *you've* read any Wodehouse?' John ventured.

'No, I can't say I have.'

'I'd really recommend it. It's very funny. If you like humorous books, of course. It's about a gentleman and his butler…'

John heard his voice trail off into nothingness as she turned to a woman in the queue behind him in order to stamp her book. He'd written out the poem from the bus shelter and had the piece of paper in his pocket ready to ask her if she knew of its origin. But he realised at that moment that he'd never have the courage to show her the poem. He could tell from the expression on her face that to her he meant nothing.

There was only one solution. He would stop visiting the library. He'd read newspapers, buy second-hand books, anything to put an end to this absurd infatuation.

John kept his resolve for the next three weeks. He ate in the canteen at lunchtimes, only stepping outside briefly for some fresh air. He sat on a table by himself, aware of the whispering between Jack Drew and some of his cronies. He noticed Valerie there too. Apparently, her nan had been taken into hospital.

But a fellow couldn't stop going to a library when that was what he enjoyed most in the world. Besides, he still had four books, one of which was overdue. The obvious solution was to visit on Tuesdays or Thursdays when the blonde librarian was elsewhere. John couldn't help wondering exactly where 'elsewhere' might be.

Despite his new plan, the following week John wasn't in the mood for the library on the Tuesday, so he popped in on the Wednesday after all. After he'd paid his fine, as he made his way towards the fiction section his legs became weak when he realised that the object of his infatuation was in fact standing on a small stepladder by a bookcase marked Cookery. She wore flat shoes and was on tiptoe, replacing a book on a high shelf.

John tried not to stare as he passed her. He'd never wanted anything more than to stop at the Cookery section and casually strike up a conversation, but he feared he might appear ridiculous if he suddenly affected an interest in cookery when previously, apart from his brief dalliance with King Charles the Second, he'd always been a fiction reader.

Casually he flicked through the pages of *The Portrait of a Lady*. The book was about an American lady and partly set in Italy. He preferred books with settings he could relate to. Still, he'd try to broaden his mind and would give Henry James a go. He looked up surreptitiously. A small portion of the librarian's legs showed beneath her skirt. Her ankles and the lower part of her calves reminded him of a woman's legs he'd seen in an advertisement in the newspaper for *Pretty Polly* nylons. John couldn't help imagining what happened to the shape of her legs as they travelled up above the hem of her skirt.

He waited until she was back on the desk again.

'We've missed you,' she said as she stamped the inside of *The Portrait of a Lady*. 'Thought you might have moved away.'

'Er...no,' John said. 'I'm still in the same house...'

'By the way.' She gave him his ticket. 'I read the P.G Wodehouse. You were right. It was funny.' As she spoke her smile incorporated a little chuckle at the end of the sentence, as if she were remembering an amusing passage in the book. John played that little chuckle over and over inside his mind for days.

John scraped three burnt sausages onto David's plate and two onto his own. David poured gravy over his sausages and covered his mash in brown sauce. After he'd rinsed the pan, John sat down to eat with his brother.

When he'd finished eating, John cleared his throat. 'I wonder if I could pick your brains, David,' he said.

'Fire away!' David was soaking up his gravy with a slice of bread. He wiped his mouth with the back of his hand. John stood up to fill the kettle.

'It's to do with a woman. A girl, I mean.'

'You've met a girl? That's great news. Is she pretty?'

'Yes, very pretty, as it happens. She's more than pretty, though. I'd go as far as to say she's *enchanting*. She works in the library in Shapton. Although I have *met* her, I can't claim to *know* her. I mean, she's stamped my books and we've exchanged a few words. But I'd like to get to know her. To tell the truth, I can't seem to think about anything else...'

'Sounds like love to me.'

'Love! Goodness me, no. You could hardly call it *love*. As I say, I don't *know* her. But I mean, I do know her...oh, I don't know. It's all so complicated and confusing.'

David laughed. 'Women tend to be complicated and confusing. Half the women I've been out with have been complicated and the other half confusing.'

'But at least you've been *out* with women. I mean, I know it seems a silly question and hardly one I should be asking my younger brother, but how do you get to go out with a woman?'

'Going out with them is the easy bit.'

'Yes, you say that, but you've got the knack of making things seem easy.'

'You must have been out with girls in the past. Didn't you go out with Patricia Moore when we were in Minehead?'

'Yes, but if you recall, it was Patricia Moore who asked *me* out and although she was a nice girl, she sounded like a hyena when she laughed.'

David smiled. 'Oh yes. I remember that squawk. You'd need ear plugs to spend any amount of time with her.'

'Exactly. So how do you do it? I mean how do you go out with the girls you like? Ones who don't sound like hyenas. You've never had any trouble asking girls out and you always seem to land the prettiest.'

John poured David's tea and sat down.

'Alright,' David said. 'I'll give you a few tips.'

'Please do. There's nothing I'd like better.'

'Right.' David spooned sugar into his tea. 'The first question you have to ask yourself – *is she married*?'

'Married? Of course she's not married.' John paused. 'She works in the library so she can't be. Although, I suppose she could be. How would I know?'

'You could ask her.'

John's eyes widened. 'Be realistic. I can hardly say "Can I have this book out, and that book out and renew this one and, oh, by the way are you married?"'

'I don't see why not. Have a look at her ring finger then. She might be engaged. There's no point in wasting your time daydreaming about a girl who's already spoken for.'

John stood up, bumped his knee against the table and caused his tea to spill into the saucer. 'David, you're a genius. None of this would have occurred to me. And I *can* recall her hands. They're small with white unblemished skin and perfectly rounded nails. I don't think she wears a ring... but now I come to think of it, she might have one. I can't remember. I don't think she has, but I'm not sure...'

'So, next time you see her, have a butchers. If she's wearing a ring you leave well alone. No ring and you ask her to go out with you. I'm surprised you didn't think of that. It's simple.'

'It's easy for you to say that.'

'Nothing ventured, nothing gained. If you don't ask her, you'll never know whether she'd have said yes. The longer you leave it, the more chance there is that some other fellow will get in there before you.'

The following lunchtime when John visited the library the blonde librarian was at the desk with both hands firmly stuck inside the pockets on either side of her skirt. John didn't have a book to exchange, as he'd only just started the Henry James. He hovered in the K-M fiction section, ostensibly deciding which book he might borrow next, whilst at the same time keeping an eye on the blonde librarian in case she took her hands out of her pockets. She did, of course, as soon as the next person went up to the desk to have their book stamped. Then he saw it. Her left hand – as unadorned as the day she'd been born. With a silent prayer of thanks, John secretly celebrated the fact that, not only did she have no ring on her finger, but also no rings were hanging on a chain round her neck. He'd come up with that possibility himself.

So the blonde-haired librarian with the perfect smile and the exquisite ankles who worked in the library on Mondays Wednesdays and Fridays (and sometimes Tuesdays) was free, unmarried, and unengaged.

Of course, that was not to say she wasn't courting. Surely she wouldn't be without admirers. John's spirits dipped as he strode briskly back to work in the rain.

Jack Drew arrived outside John's office just as he was about to take his lunch break. He knocked and John opened the door, letting in the burr of factory sounds; the whirr and clunking of the paper machine, the hum of conversation mingled with the sweet powdery aroma of shaven wood.

Jack leant against the door frame. 'It's about Valerie Grimwood,' he muttered out of the corner of his mouth.

'I thought we'd discussed this, Jack,' John answered.

'That was then. Things are different now. Either she goes or I do. And you know you'll never get a better machine operator than yours truly.'

'What on earth has happened? I'm sorry but you can't give me that sort of ultimatum. Surely there's a simpler solution.'

'No, sir.' Jack raised his voice and John looked at the clock. 'That...*slut* has only been spreading gossip about me. We *was* courting. Now she's telling everyone she's in the family way.'

John felt his brain tangling itself in knots. 'Please, Jack, don't use words like that in my office. If you don't mind me asking, why *were* you going out with her – if you were – if you didn't have... strong feelings for her? Although I realise that's nothing to do with me, but how could she possibly be *in the family way* as you put it, when surely there hasn't been enough time since I last spoke to you for things to have advanced to ... or at least I don't think there has...I mean when did all this happen?'

'I never said I had strong feelings for her.' Jack leaned back on the chair, so the front two legs left the floor. 'I never done nothing with her like that to put her in the family way in the first place. And anyways, that was months ago, so if she had been going to get in the family way, it wasn't with me.'

'This does seem rather complex. Leave it with me. I'll have a word with Valerie this afternoon,' John assured him.

People like Jack and Valerie could be from another planet, John thought as he walked towards the library. The way they took things for granted. Easy come, easy go. John was sure that if Jack knew how long John had agonised over just asking a woman out, he'd probably roar with laughter and yet he felt momentarily empowered by the other man's audacity. But suddenly his old fear returned. The fear of rejection. The girl in the library was as different from Valerie as she was from that Ruth Ellis woman.

But less than twenty minutes later, as John handed her his book to stamp, he suddenly heard himself asking the question he'd rehearsed and pondered over for weeks. He simply placed the book on the desk.

'Thank you,' the blonde librarian said, as usual.

'Thank you,' John said. 'Er…I don't suppose you'd like to come out with me?'

He could hardly believe what he'd said. What he was still saying. 'I was thinking of going to the fair this Saturday and I wondered if you'd like to join me?' John's breathing quickened as he awaited her reply. She was staring at him. Her eyes were blue, the whites so totally pure they had a tinge of grey.

'Yes,' she said. Just the one word. *Yes.* John wanted to run down the road, crying, laughing. He wanted to skip along the pavement like Gene Kelly in *Singing In The Rain*. But he couldn't leave it at that. He had to say more.

'That's marvellous. I'll meet you at eight…' He almost ran towards the door.

'Hold on,' she called after him. John turned around, acutely grateful that there were no other customers at the desk. 'You didn't say where to meet.'

He returned to the counter. 'I'm sorry, I don't even know your name,' he said once he'd clarified the arrangements to meet outside the ironmongers, all the while thinking that it would just be too wonderful to know her name as well.

'Susan,' she said.

'Hello, Susan,' John said.

'Hello, John,' she replied.

John got off the bus at the ironmongers on the corner of the high street at a quarter to eight. The sounds of the fair floated over the roof tops of the row of shops on the other side of the road. Carousel music, clashing with rock and roll, mixed with faint screams, bells clanging and the cracks of gunfire borne along on the lull of the May evening breeze.

His anxiety increased with every second that Susan was not there. The bus journey had made him nauseous, and he prayed he wouldn't be sick. He'd hardly eaten. All he'd had was a boiled egg at lunchtime, although he'd left the toast on the side of his plate. He didn't know which way to look as he had no idea which direction Susan would be coming from. He'd avoided the library for the past few days just in case she might change her mind about their outing.

John hadn't been to a fair in years. Fairs were places he'd visited with his parents when David and he were children. Now he wondered whether he'd made the right choice of activity. The fair was loud and brash. The opposite of Susan. She might not like the noise and bustle. Perhaps he should have suggested the pictures or a coffee bar.

Perhaps she wouldn't turn up.

But she'd said 'yes' when she could easily have said 'no'. Pretended she was busy, or washing her hair. Wasn't that what girls said when they didn't want to go out? John looked at his reflection in the window of the ironmonger's. Luckily, as it happened, since a clump of his hair was sticking up just above his left ear. He smoothed the offending strands down. Apart from that, he didn't look too bad. He wore his best weekend jacket, a plain navy blazer, teamed up with a new shirt and a blue tie he'd borrowed from David. In his head he heard his mother's voice, 'you'll do', a phrase that offered neither encouragement nor criticism. Of course, David had always been the good looking one, with his darker hair and better dress sense. The fact that he was a few inches taller than John made him feel he'd drawn the short straw where looks were concerned. But 'he'd do'. He'd have to 'do' because Susan would be there soon. Wouldn't she?

John looked at his watch. It was almost five to eight. He glanced down the road to the left of the ironmonger's and down the other end towards the bus stop. He didn't even know how she'd be getting there. Presuming she *was* planning to get there. For all he knew she had no intention of turning up. Maybe she'd agreed out of embarrassment. Or, even worse, pity.

At four minutes past eight John was shocked to see Susan crossing the road towards him. Despite everything, he felt mentally unprepared. He fumbled with the knot in his tie. He put his hands in his pockets, then remembered his mother had told him this was a sign of bad manners, so swiftly removed them. He wanted to grab

Susan by her waist and twirl her around in the air. Instead, he stood there like a sack of bricks.

'Sorry I'm late,' she said. She looked smaller away from the library desk. Daintier. 'The bus was *so* slow. We were stuck behind a tractor for a good ten minutes.' Susan was laughing as she spoke, her voice clear as music.

'I see you're wearing a raincoat,' John said. 'That's very sensible considering the weather we've been having recently.' John heard his voice saying these words, yet had no idea why he was talking about her choice of apparel in relation to the weather, when really he wanted to tell her how beautiful she looked, how her eyes shone with the exertion of running across the road, how much more lovely she was than even he had recalled – how *honoured* he was that she was there with him now.

How perfect she was in every way.

They walked through the field towards the fair, their feet sinking into the grass. Susan wore white shoes and laughed as one of her heels got stuck in the ground. John held her bag while she pulled it out. What would David have done? Taken her by the hand to help her balance? Pulled the shoe out for her and placed it on her foot like Prince Charming in Cinderella. As it was, John stood like a human hat stand, clutching her bag until she'd regained her balance. Although delirious to be in possession of something so intimate, he returned the handbag to her at the first opportunity. As they carried on walking, she swung it back and forth. Her hair was still tied in the same bow she wore at work, except a strand at the front had come loose and fell against her cheek. John longed to lift that strand of hair and secure it behind her ear – but it felt presumptuous – much too soon. He longed to hold her hand too, but her handbag created a barrier between them.

The sun was a perfect ball of pink fire sinking towards the horizon. The air smelled of candyfloss and burnt sausages. As they neared the entrance to the fair, lights flashed white, red, blue and green. Music mish-mashed, loud and enticing. Crowds of people bustled and queued for rides.

'Oh, look! Dodgems! Shall we go on the dodgems? Or the big wheel? Look! A carousel!' Susan's voice rose above the clang of noise.

John paid and they clambered into a dodgem car.

'I can't drive!' John shouted, as he took the wheel and skirted the outside of the track, managing to avoid any major collisions. Susan screamed at each near miss. Afterwards she climbed onto a horse painted red and blue with swags of gold and a black braided mane and bridle. John mounted the horse behind and watched the back of her head as they swirled around, up and down, Susan always a yard in front of him.

'John, look! A waltzer. Let's go on the waltzer!' They bundled into the carriage. A Teddy Boy wearing black drainpipes swung from car to car as he climbed across the metal pole that fixed the cars to the block in the centre. He held out an impatient palm whilst John fumbled in his pocket for a sixpence. The cars began to roll forward before the Teddy Boy had got off. John watched him, anxious that he might not make it in time, but he vaulted effortlessly to the safety of the booth in the middle like a monkey moving from branch to branch.

The carriages rumbled over the wooden slats, slowly at first, then gathering speed. As theirs began to twirl they clung tightly to the bar that locked them in. The sides of their bodies were forced together by the momentum. When Susan's shoulder pressed against John's she squealed. A hundred light bulbs overhead flashed, blurring into one swish of electricity. Music clattered and scraped relentlessly at the inside of John's head. Susan slid away from him on the slippery seat and squealed again. Their thighs crushed together once more, until gradually the machine slowed and ground to a clunking halt. John trembled as he helped her out of the carriage.

'I think I might have to sit down for a moment. I feel a bit dizzy,' he said, but Susan was already off in the direction of the shooting range.

'Come on!' she called behind her, holding out her hand. He ran forward, but by the time he caught her up she was sorting through her purse for some money. A gang of teenage boys crowded around the guns. Each had a cigarette clamped between his lips as they fired the rifles before slinking off in search of something more profitable. A row of yellow plastic ducks floated on a stream of water at the back of the range. John was the first to pull the trigger. The ducks bobbed on unperturbed.

Susan tried her luck. 'Four shots for the lady.' The man who spoke had black scowling eyes and strutted up and down behind the stall. He stared at Susan as she positioned herself behind the gun and screwed up one eye.

'You look very professional,' John said. The man stood close to them with his arms folded across his chest. He didn't turn to look at the ducks, even when Susan's final shot sent one of them flying backwards into the water.

'Hurrah!' John said. The man showed no emotion as he reached for Susan's prize. His dark, expressionless eyes remained fixed on her face as he rewarded her with a goldfish in a plastic bag. Susan held up the bag bulging with water so that John could see her fish.

Beside the shooting range was a painted caravan with a sign outside. 'Fortune Teller'.

'I've never had my fortune told,' Susan said.

'Here you are,' he said. 'Sixpence. It's customary to cross a gypsy's palm with silver, I believe.'

'You'll have to hold the fish while I go in.'

'Alright.'

'Or you could come in with me. Why don't we go in together? I'd be nervous on my own.'

'I'd rather not,' John said. 'I don't believe in that sort of thing.'

'Neither do I, but it's just a bit of fun. Come on,' she said reaching for his hand.

They climbed the few steps to the caravan doorway which was covered by a heavy cloth. Inside were two women, an elderly crone who sat in the corner smoking a clay pipe and a younger woman with a shawl over her head and a crystal ball in front of her. Brightly coloured scarves were pinned around the windows. The air smelled of paraffin mixed with the smoke from the woman's pipe. John was unable to supress a cough.

'Lady first.' The woman beckoned at Susan to sit down and took her sixpence. She peered into her crystal ball. 'This looks interesting,' she said. 'I can see something…something … a book.'

'Ah!' Susan said. 'That's because I work in a library…'

'Oh, yes, Lady. I see lots of books... true love too. A husband too.'

John looked down at the goldfish.

'You'll get what you want from this life,' the woman went on. 'Eventually – but on the other side of the earth.'

'The other side of the earth? What does that mean?'

'The crystal's fuzzy. You'll need more money.'

Susan took another sixpence from her purse.

'I see babies – but they're ... they're conceived with love. Your life's long and filled with love.' The woman pulled her shawl around her shoulders. 'What about the gentleman?' she said. The old lady in the corner coughed on her pipe.

'Me?' John said. 'No, I don't think so.'

Susan was smiling as they walked away from the caravan. 'Lots of children. Sounds like I'm going to be busy.'

'Surely you don't believe all that tosh,' John said, even though he thought the tosh sounded rather appealing.

Susan laughed. She seemed to laugh a lot when she was away from the library. Her laughter was unexpected, and it made John ache for her.

Their next outing was to the park the following Sunday. They walked around the paths for an hour before stopping at the café on the south side by the swings.

'So you live at home with your parents?' John asked as he placed the teacups on the table and sat down on a rickety iron chair.

'Yes. My parents have lived all their married life in the same house. My dad works in the bottling factory, you know, the one on Hazeldown. He's due to retire the summer after next, but we don't know if he will...'

'I work in a factory. In the office though...'

"Yes, you told me. But no one can imagine Dad as a pensioner. He's worked every day in that factory since he was nineteen. He's never changed jobs and he's never moved since they got married.'

"My parents bought a bungalow in Weston-super-Mare. So my brother and I were forced to find somewhere else to live, and it so happened that I won a bit on the football pools..."

'Yes. I remember you saying…I bet your mum's proud of you in your office job. Mine's so proud, it's embarrassing. She's always telling people I'm a librarian. Anyone would think I'd written all the books the way she goes on, when the only thing I've written in my life is my boring little diary. But no, you'd think I was the most famous person in the world!'

'I'm sure you could be anything you wanted to be.'

Susan smiled. 'I doubt that's true, but it's very nice of you to say.'

'All the same, I hope you don't stop being a librarian,' John added.

'I love my job, but I might leave. If I married and had children.'

What was the right response to this? He'd just said he hoped she didn't stop being a librarian, so how could he now suggest she should get married and have a family instead?

'I'm sure whatever you do with your life you will be successful,' John said as he bit into a Bakewell tart.

The following week they went to the park again. The leaves on the oak trees outside the tennis courts threw shade over the children's playground. In the café a woman sat at the next table with a baby on her lap and a toddler in a sun hat.

'Aren't they sweet!' Susan said. 'I'd love to have children one day. Five at least! Remember what that fortune teller said?'

'I wouldn't read too much into *that*. But five? Goodness, that is a lot.' John imagined himself and Susan in the kitchen at Blackberry Lane with five children (all miniature versions of Susan) standing in a semi-circle around them. Susan, his wife. Susan McDonald. He let the name play around in his mind.

'Wouldn't you like children?' she asked.

'I've never really thought about it. It sounds like a big responsibility. But, yes, I suppose. One day, if I was married. Can I get you another biscuit?' As he stood up, he caught his shoe on the leg of his chair.

John had made a pot of tea and had just sat down to eat some toast and read the paper when David came downstairs clutching his football kit.

'There's a brew on the go,' John said. David sneezed, poured milk into a cup, balanced the tea strainer on the rim and removed the tea cosy from the pot.

'See they've got that Philby chap. A bunch of Commies if you ask me,' David said reading from the back page of John's paper.

'He'll get away with it. Sure as eggs is eggs. They're all Cambridge graduates from rich families. People like that always do.' John replaced the tea cosy on the pot.

"Don't suppose you'd like to come along to the match this afternoon?' David asked between swigs of his tea. 'We'll be going for a couple of jars afterwards, if you fancy it.'

'I would like to. Very much. But I've invited Susan round this afternoon.'

'Susan?'

'Yes, she's the girl I've been out with a few times recently. You know – to the fair. A couple of times to the park. She works in the library.'

'Oh, yep. Cor, this tea's stewed,' David spat the dregs into the sink. 'I'd best get going. It's one o'clock kick-off.'

'Make sure you thrash them.'

'I will.'

John cleared away the breakfast things, polished around the picture rails and the skirting boards and tidied up the hall where David had recently taken to leaving muddy football boots.

He had bread and cheese ready to make sandwiches – hopefully Susan wouldn't be expecting anything as elaborate as cake even though he'd invited her for afternoon tea. After he'd lit the fire John flitted the Eubank round the carpet, the plan being that he and Susan would sit together in the front room talking, although he knew in his heart that they should have progressed beyond the talking stage by now. It was a month since they'd been to the fair, but he hadn't touched Susan since she'd taken his hand outside the fortune teller's caravan. There was an aura of purity around her, like a halo of silver light. A barrier that seemed impossible to cross. Not that he wanted Susan to think the only reason he liked her was because he wanted to touch her. But at the same time, he didn't want her to think he wasn't interested in a physical relationship. Sometimes it seemed as if he thought of nothing else.

As he straightened the cushions on the settee, John pictured the afternoon ahead. If they both sat on the settee (although it was a three-seater) they might somehow drift closer together as the afternoon progressed, until they were really very close, and eventually something might happen.

Something might happen. John was angry with himself. Such vagueness. 'Define the word *something*,' he said to himself. 'What you really mean is that you want to kiss her.'

Yes, of course I do, you numbskull. You know I want to kiss her.

'Go on. Do it, man. What are you waiting for? Christmas?'

You know yourself, it's not as simple as that!

'Okay, make a deadline. Tell yourself that if you don't kiss her this afternoon, you'll take her all the way home and make sure you jolly well kiss her outside her garden gate.'

Good thinking. Willco.

John often had conversations with himself. After all, apart from David, he was the only person he could rely on to listen to his problems and offer sensible advice. It was only that awkward *first* kiss that was the obstacle to his happiness with Susan. Once that particular mountain had been scaled, more kisses would inevitably follow with far less planning. Then as more kisses were achieved, he'd gradually be able to forget about the enormity of what he was doing and begin to enjoy himself.

The clock on the mantelpiece said five past two. John looked out of the window. The morning's rain was beginning to break through again. He opened the front door and walked down the path. Susan was hurrying towards Stringer's Farm, looking lost, wet and bedraggled with the collar of her raincoat pulled up.

John could have kicked himself. He should have met her at the war memorial or offered to accompany her from her house, rather than expecting her to find Blackberry Lane with just the aid of a piece of paper scribbled with directions. That way she wouldn't have arrived looking drenched and forlorn. He could've taken an umbrella and held it over her all the way from the bus stop. Two people beneath an umbrella would by necessity be physically close. She might have linked her arm through his. He might even have kissed her on the path before they went inside.

He still *could* kiss her. He could kiss the tip of her nose where a drop of rain was about to run onto her lips. Or he could go straight for her lips which would undoubtedly taste of fresh rain and her. They could stand together in the rain, embracing, not caring about the weather.

As it was, John stood at the gate waving. Susan waved back, running the last few yards to the house.

'John,' she said laughing. 'You should have told me. I had no idea you lived so far from the village.'

'I'm sorry. You're absolutely right. I should have warned you. We are a bit out in the sticks. But you found it in the end. I do hope the journey wasn't too arduous.'

'No, not at all. I met someone further up the lane. A man with a young boy. Said he knew you.'

'Oh, Mr Stringer. He lives over the road. I'm so glad he was able to point you in the right direction.'

Once inside the house Susan patted her hair and gave John her raincoat. He shook it outside, and, after showing her into the front room, hung it on the nail in the hall.

'I've got the fire going. Come in and take the weight off your feet.'

'This looks cosy. Lovely and warm.' Susan rubbed her hands together and he pulled up the armchair nearer to the fireplace so that she'd benefit from the full heat of the fire.

Immediately John realised his mistake. His plan had been that they should both sit on the settee. Susan might as well have been miles away on the other side of the county.

'Let me know if you're too hot over there.' John spoke louder than normal.

'No. It's lovely. Very comfortable, thank you,' Susan said.

By the time John heard the sound of David's motorbike outside, Susan was on her second cup of tea and third sandwich.

John was just telling Susan that the bike she could hear was his brother arriving back from his football match when David barged into the living room. 'Oh! Sorry,' he said making an about turn. 'Sorry, John. I'd forgotten you had company. I'll go upstairs… could do with a lie down. Throat's killing me.'

'David, hold on. I'd like you to meet someone,' John said. It seemed rude not to introduce Susan to David. She'd been eating sandwiches for what seemed like hours and the conversation was beginning to flag. If David joined them, things might liven up.

'David, I'd like you to meet Susan. Susan, this is David, my brother.'

'Nice to meet you.' David came into the room and flopped onto the settee. He was shivering, his dark hair damp from the rain.

'I won't get too close,' he said. 'I think I'm coming down with the flu. My bones feel like sticks of ivory.'

Susan put her head on one side and smiled a sympathetic smile.

'So, tell us about the match, David. Did you win? David's the footballer of the family,' John said.

Susan smiled again, tilting her head to the other side.

'Slaughtered 'em. Five nil.'

'What position do you play?' Susan asked.

'Centre forward.'

'My brother Christopher plays football. He's a goalkeeper,' Susan said.

'Goalie, eh? Important job. The most important, if you think about it,' David said.

'I'll tell him you said so.' Susan laughed and looked down at the teacup on her lap.

'Susan, your tea must be stone cold. Let me get you some more,' John said, standing up and taking her cup. 'I expect you'd like one too, David."

'Could murder one. Thanks, John.'

From the kitchen John could hear the murmur of David's deep voice followed by Susan's softer one, until the whistle of the kettle blanked them out. He was relieved that they seemed to be finding plenty to talk about. He remembered the poem from the bus shelter. Now would be the perfect time to ask whether she knew its origin. The afternoon looked as if it might be a success after all.

He'd bought a packet of biscuits, the same kind Susan had chosen when they were in the park café. Custard creams. John emptied six onto a plate and carried the tea tray into the front room. As he walked into the room Susan was asking David what he did for a living.

'I'm an airline pilot.'

'Goodness, are you really?' Susan looked wide-eyed.

'No, not really.' David laughed. 'I'm a plumber. Just coming to the end of my apprenticeship. But I'd rather be an airline pilot.'

Susan laughed again and took her tea from the tray John had set down on the floor near the fire.

'What do you do?' David asked.

'I'm a librarian.'

David gave John a look that told him he'd just put two and two together and realised this was the girl John had asked his advice about. John raised his eyebrows and held up his left hand just a fraction to secretly show David that he'd checked her ring finger. The room was quiet for a few moments before David spoke again.

'So, you're a librarian?' he said. 'You don't look like my idea of a librarian.'

'What's your idea of a librarian?'

'Oh, some old biddy. Stern, with thick glasses, a grey suit, and woolly stockings.'

Susan giggled. 'We're not all battleaxes.'

'Thank goodness for that,' David said. 'It sounds an interesting job. Did you have to go to college?'

'I go to the Tech twice a week, but mostly we train on the job. It's perfectly easy, once you get used to it.'

'A bit like plumbing, then.'

They both laughed.

As John passed the biscuits to Susan, he noticed something tender in David's voice and a kind, gentle, concerned expression that softened his eyes. Maybe it was the cold or flu he had. That sort of thing could knock the stuffing out of a chap. But as John watched David dunk his biscuit into his tea, he recognised the feeling that was taking hold of *him*. It was the same feeling he'd had when he'd invited Robert Cole home for tea when they were at primary school. David had taken Robert outside into the street to kick a ball while John stayed in his bedroom flicking through his Scout Annual on his own.

But John decided not to dwell on the past and instead to bring up the subject of the poem from the bus shelter. *I strove for none, for none was worth the strife...*

'Susan, I was wondering if you could answer a question that's been niggling me for some time. It's to do with a poem. It goes something like this...' John recited as much of the poem as he could from memory until he felt himself faltering in a turmoil of embarrassment. Susan was listening to him, but her smile seemed slightly patronising, as if the poetry recital was making her feel uncomfortable.

'It does sound vaguely familiar,' she said with a frown. 'But I couldn't honestly say who wrote it. Was there any particular reason you wanted to know?'

John shrugged the poem off, but he couldn't help thinking about the plans he'd made for that afternoon – about his intention to kiss Susan. To touch her properly as more than a friend and show her his true feelings. But somehow the more she and David chatted away, the more John felt his plans crumble, and the certainty of that kiss begin to fade.

Outside the rain had stopped and the summer evening sky was lit with dunes of tangerine. The sound of the cows lowing, and the bleating of sheep folded across the air from the farm over the road. As the three of them sat together drinking tea in the front room of Two Blackberry Lane, with the sun slowly slithering lower and lower behind the net curtains, casting a block of dull orange across the carpet, John began to wish he hadn't invited Susan to the house. It was rushing things, especially as he was still uncertain of her feelings for him.

'Librarianship is nothing at all like plumbing,' John suddenly heard himself saying. 'I mean, as far as I can imagine, training to be a librarian is nothing at all like training to become a plumber.'

His words came out from somewhere deep inside of him, almost unbidden. Beyond his control. He spoke more loudly than he'd intended and David and Susan both turned to look at him. It was as if they'd both forgotten that he existed.

SUSAN McDONALD

Sunday 25 August 1957

THIS MORNING I went to church feeling *so happy.* As usual it was damp and cold inside and Reverend Olive spat on the people in the front row, *and* went on and on about the *Parable of the Sower,* but after the sermon we emerged into bright summer sunshine and the world seemed a wonderful place. I have truly been blessed by God.

'Thank you for a most uplifting sermon,' I said, as I shook hands with the Reverend.

'Good to see you again, Mrs McDonald.' I detected an underlying tone in his words that implied disapproval, perhaps because this was only the second time I've been to church since our wedding. Or maybe he thought David should be there with me.

Mr and Mrs Pittle were standing behind me with their son, Bertie, the boy who delivers the papers. Mrs Pittle offered a black-gloved hand and the Reverend moved onto them, greeting them with fervour. Anyway, thank goodness he hadn't tried to engage me in a long conversation or attempted to discuss the *Parable of the Sower* in any more depth.

How different this visit to my last, eight weeks ago, when I'd prayed with every fibre of my being. When I'd squeezed my eyes together so tightly that tears ran down my cheeks. When I'd begged God for something *very special.* That morning I'd taken in every sentiment of the lesson, sung my heart out during the hymns and repeated the prayers as if my life depended upon every word. Since my prayer has now been answered, my visit today was my way of saying 'thank you'.

I opened the church gate and turned right, beginning my walk towards the crossroads. The other thirty or so people who'd made up the congregation were leaving in dribs and drabs, filing back towards the main hub of the village. Myrtle Crabtree was amongst them. I'd turned down her offer to join the Women's Institute, when she arrived at the house with a Simnel cake soon after I'd moved in. I realise I'm a married woman now, but things like joining the Women's Institute make me feel really old. The Jessops were there, and the couple from the post office, Mr and Mrs Coleman, I think they're called. She's always friendly, although I left my umbrella in there once and when I went to collect it the whole shop went quiet. I've heard people say you need to live in a village for at least twenty years before you're accepted by the locals. Still, I don't care. I've got David, and soon I will have our own, precious baby.

The men from the congregation were heading for the pub, the women rushing home to prepare the Sunday lunch, as I was. I was thankful to be away from all that chit chat and out of the chilly church. It was warmer outside than in. The summer sun beat hard against my shoulders as I strode along the lane. I took my coat off and undid the top button of my blouse.

The walk from the crossroads along Blackberry Lane to the house reminded me of the first time I'd done it – almost two years ago. That day it had been raining and I was relying on the scribbled notes David's brother had given me to direct me to the house. I know the date of that first visit. I drew hearts around it in my diary. July 9th 1955. The most important date in my life.
The day I met David.

I won't need this diary any more to keep records of my time of the month. Eight weeks now with no show. No one could be more aware of what that means than I. 'Thank you, thank you, God,' I repeated all the way from the church to the war memorial.

My legs felt tired and heavy as I turned right into Blackberry Lane. The horse chestnuts at the side of the fields cast mottled shadows on the road. I began counting them to keep my mind off my aching calves. There were nine trees. Three on the right and six on the left. Ticking them off in my head seemed to make my journey go faster.

As I approached Stringer's Farm I heard the crack of gunfire, followed by the squall of pheasants fluttering away. I watched as the birds scrambled to lift off the ground.

'Go on, boys. Quick, before he gets you!' I called out softly. There's something comical about pheasants. I love the way they scuttle along the ground, only taking flight when they absolutely have to. Christian Stringer was in the field with his dog Queenie, and his rifle. He must have spent half his life out in that field either working or shooting, while Evie spent hers indoors washing nappies. A row of dripping nappies always hung from the washing line in the garden of Number One. Soon my washing line would be the same, although I'd make sure mine were gleaming white and not the dull rabbit-grey of Evie's.

Just before I crossed the road Christian appeared on the other side of the hedge.

'Not playing football this morning, Christian?' I asked.

He stood with feet apart, his gun slung over his shoulder glaring at me with that gloomy scowl. 'Injured hamstring,' he explained.

I tried to look sympathetic but I was finding it hard not to laugh out loud and spill my joy into the world, although Christian Stringer was the last person I'd choose to share my good news. As I walked away from him I felt his eyes bore into me. At least that would be one of the advantages of being pregnant. Once the baby was showing Christian Stringer would hopefully stop watching me with that penetrating stare as if he could see right through my clothes.

I opened the gate and walked down the path. The house is hardly recognisable as the place I visited when David's brother lived here. The rose bushes I planted around the door now hang heavy with pink blossoms. Where I've sewn aubrietia seeds along the tops of the walls, seas of purple petals pour from every crevice in the stone. On either side of the path a row of purple dahlias saluted my arrival. Inside the house I could smell the lamb roasting. As I dropped my bag on the floor, for some reason I started thinking about the wallpaper David put up in the hall, the living room, all the way up the stairs. Now I needed to tell him about the box room. It hasn't been touched since John took his books out. The perfect room for a nursery.

I hurried to the kitchen to check the lamb which was sizzling nicely in the pan with the sprig of rosemary only slightly singed, and unlocked the back door. If John had turned up now, he would have been amazed at the sight of the garden. What with the three sapling apple trees David planted, not to mention the vegetable patch where he'd dug ridges of fresh earth for the potatoes and carrots. Last summer fresh green runner beans scampered up the canes, showing off their vermilion buds. The tomatoes and onions we planted took as well. David says he never realised he had green fingers until he met me.

I put an apron on and changed my shoes. I just had time to go outside and do a bit of weeding and plant out some of the new potato crop before David got back from football.

I crouched down and began to dig.

I stopped digging.

The sun still beat hot on my shoulders, but my skin had turned cold. I stayed as I was, frozen in a crouching position. The cramp was like a metal belt tightening around the lower half of my abdomen. I allowed the blood to leak out. Not that I had any choice. It came in a steady flow down both my legs and dripped onto the soil. I was shaking and my first instinct was to get the clothes off that were soaked in blood. Still in the vegetable patch, I rolled my underwear into a bloodied ball. My skirt, which, a few moments before had been a mixture of yellow sunflowers on a white background, was hideously blotched with crimson. As I stood, slowly, carefully, aware that I might faint – as I had done last time – I steadied myself against one of the apple trees, and just caught sight of the shadow of someone at the upstairs window of Number One. I grabbed my clothes and hobbled quickly inside, but I couldn't avoid the sight of that horrible row of nappies that always hung like a line of victory flags on next-door's washing line.

Sunday 8 September 1957

David's converting the middle bedroom into a bathroom. He's run pipes through the house to take the waste outside to the cesspit and he's replaced the stone kitchen sink with an aluminium one.

I don't know how he does all these things. Of course he should be able to do them – it's his job, but – he's so clever! After he's finished with the bathroom, the only job left will be to decorate the box room. Dare I even say it? For our *baby*. I know I've had all the miscarriages, and I know I'm not pregnant again *yet*, but no matter what happens, that room will always be kept for our baby.

Wednesday 25 September 1957

This morning I went into town on the bus to look at wallpaper samples in Keele's. The problem is choosing a colour. Pink would be a disaster if it was a boy. I can imagine what David would say if I came home with rolls of pink wallpaper.

But a little girl wouldn't look right in a blue nursery. Although I suppose that's not as bad as putting a boy in a pink one. Of course there's always the possibility that we might have twins. This is how the conversation went at tea time:

'I've been looking at wallpaper in Keele's today. You know, for the nursery…'

'Susan, you're not telling me that you're…'

'No,' I said. 'But I might be – soon. I wanted to choose the wallpaper so that you could get on with the room. Only, the problem is whether to get blue or pink.'

'Darling, can't we just wait. I'm sure I've heard it's bad luck to buy things for the baby before it's born, never mind conceived…'

'Or, we might end up with twins! One of each, then what would we do?'

'Or triplets!' David laughed, joining in at last, although I think we both knew in our hearts that none of this mattered. Boy, girl, pink, green, sky blue yellow.

All we want is our own precious little baby.

Tuesday 15 October 1957

I've decided that our house should have a name. Number Two is so impersonal. So dull. When I was little I had a story book about elves and fairies. In the book they all lived together in a house made out of the trunk of a gnarled old oak tree with a sign over the door saying '*Cosy Nook Cottage*'. I vowed I'd have this name for my own house one day. David made a wooden plaque and painted the name in black and hammered it onto the gate with two nails. Sometimes I think there's nothing he wouldn't do for me.

I thought I was so happy. But tonight this month's curse came and I cried myself to sleep in David's arms.

Sunday 27 October 1957
Went to church today, although I couldn't persuade David to come. I suppose there *are* limits to what he'll do for me, after all. And football *is* his second love.

I've started to think of the church as an insurance policy. It is a comfort, although I suppose I should get all the comfort I need from David, but it's to do with needing to understand how God works. If God exists, that is. What on earth would all those people in the village say if they could hear me? The Pittles and Myrtle Crabtree, not to mention the Reverand Olive. All those people who believe in God and live their lives around that belief. But since we started trying for a family I'm not sure what to believe. During the service I mimed instead of singing the hymns out loud, and hoped He didn't notice. (If there is a He, of course!) I'm always afraid I'll be heard above everyone else with my wobbly out-of-tune notes. But I did listen intently to the sermon, which was about Paul and Silas. I remember this story from Bible studies at Sunday School. It stuck in my mind because Saul changed his name to Paul, which I thought was a shame because Saul is such a beautiful name.

Reverend Olive spoke about Paul and Silas being falsely accused, beaten and thrown into jail. The point of the lesson was, that despite the way they'd been treated, Paul and Silas still sang praises to God. At the end of the service the Reverend asked us all to think about the story of Paul and Silas. Where do we turn when we experience something really difficult in our lives? He maintained that we automatically turn to God in the same way Paul and Silas did. 'In God's presence only is there the fullness of joy.'

I'd heard it all before at school. I don't know what made me imagine church sermons and the Bible would be any different now that I was an adult. They were still the same, although maybe the message behind them was easier to unravel.

During the prayers, I lowered myself to the floor and knelt on the embroidered cushion. The cushion was sewn with a background of blue thread and a grey image of a cross superimposed over the picture of the church. Mrs Pittle told me the cushions were embroidered by members of the Women's Institute. Funnily enough, despite my lack of faith, I felt at that moment, as I settled myself on the floor, closed my eyes and put my hands together, that God actually did know I was there, and that He'd intended for me to have the most beautiful cushion to kneel on. On the side of the cushion the words 'suffer the little children' were embroidered in purple thread.

Is it possible that God *does* know the pain I've suffered? Could He feel the emptiness in my heart, and could He understand the disappointment each month when that first spot of blood brings with it the realisation that, yet again, I'm not to be a mother?

If so, how could He let this go on happening?

As I knelt on that cushion, in that church, I prayed silently. I asked God what I had done to deserve this? I've led a blameless life. I've never hurt anyone, stolen anything, been unkind to anyone or anything. I think I can honestly say I've never even had a bad thought.

Despite all this I promised God I'd be a better person. Maybe I was deluding myself. Maybe I hadn't been as good as I thought. Of course, there was David's brother.

I'd sensed John's hurt when David and I had fallen in love. But John was just a friend. It wasn't as if he was my boyfriend. John hadn't shown any interest in me in that way. He'd never even tried to kiss me. He did move out of the house, which was sad. But David bought the house from him, so it wasn't as if he'd lost any money, and his job had been relocated to Newcastle, so he'd have had to leave anyway.

Maybe God was less convinced of my kindness than I. Perhaps if He could see how much I was trying to improve, He'd let me get pregnant again, carry a baby to term. I vowed I'd try to be a better wife, a more attentive daughter, a more caring sister, and, please God – given the chance – a mother. I held my hands together in prayer and screwed up my eyes until they stung, pleading with a man I'd never met, a man I would never know or see, who I'd imagined somewhere up above the clouds driving a chariot pulled by horses with steam billowing from their nostrils. I'd taken this image from one of the classical art books at the library and somehow this man had become my God and, despite my lack of religious belief, was, irrationally, the image I'd endowed with the responsibility for my future happiness.

Monday 18 November 1957
Please. A baby. Such a small request. Lots of people have them. Every other woman seems to be pushing a pram. Babies are everywhere. Next door, Evie's nappies continue to flap in the wind. On the bus, in town, in prams, pushchairs, in pictures, in the street, in the parks, everywhere – babies. Surely there is space for one more child on this earth.

Wednesday 27 November 1957
Took the morning bus into Shapton. Chose some material for a new skirt. In Keeles I had a flick through the *Style* book. Some pretty patterns for dresses – and a maternity dress with smocking at the yoke.

I accidentally landed on a page of romper suits. The babies modelling the clothes were drawings but they looked adorable – the boys in blue with little straps, and pink frills for the girls. I spent at least half an hour choosing my favourites – just so I'd know where to look when the time comes.

I didn't have a pen on me, so I memorised the page numbers by repeating them over and over in my head on the bus home – 1176 to 1179.

Wednesday 11 December 1957
Braved the fog and took the bus into Shapton. Was in Keele's all afternoon but decided to wait a while before I choose a pattern for my skirt. After all, I might need maternity clothes soon.

Went to the cafeteria for a cup of tea before I caught the bus home. Had to go through Home Furnishings to get to the lift – in the bed department they had four cots on display. One was painted white with six red and blue balls suspended on metal rods at either end. I hope no one else buys it before we have the chance to put down a deposit.

Wednesday 15 January 1958
God has answered my prayers. My time of the month has come and gone – twice. I could cry with joy. My nipples are hot and tender. I'm exhausted by five in the afternoon. My life is now, finally, complete. Our marriage fulfilled. I am pregnant!!

Monday 20 January 1958
Appointment with Dr Connor. Feeling horribly sick but I wasn't going to miss seeing him. In the parlour that he uses as his surgery Dr Connor looked at me over his glasses and asked me the date of my last period. I told him it was November the fifteenth. Dr Connor scribbled some calculations on a pad of paper. 'Mrs McDonald, your baby is due on August 22nd,' he declared. A summer baby. What could be more perfect? I couldn't wait to get home and write the date in my diary.

When I got home David was lying on the kitchen floor adjusting the pipes under the sink.

'David,' I said, 'I've been to the doctor and guess what? I'm expecting! I'm certain this time everything is going to be alright.'

David banged his head on a pipe as he twisted around onto his knees.

'Ouch! Sit down, Susan,' he said clambering to his feet. 'I'll make you a cup of tea. You must be careful. Did you walk from the bus stop all by yourself?'

This made me laugh. 'Of course I did, but I will be careful. Don't worry. I know this baby will be fit and strong. I can feel it, and Dr Connor said everything is fine, so there's no need to worry.'

David *made* me put my feet up for the rest of the day.

Friday 7 February 1958
I have never felt so sick in my life, to the point where I wanted to die. David was upset when I said this – because of what happened in Munich yesterday. Manchester United is his favourite team, so

he's devastated. I had a little weep for the players who died, and for their mothers. Every one of those men was some mother's son.

Friday 28 February 1958
Never again. I feel so terribly ill. Dr Connor gave me some new pills for the sickness but I don't know what I did with them so I haven't taken any. This baby will definitely be an only child. I could never go through this again.

Monday 7 April 1958
Today I haven't felt sick once. Hurray. My body's changing. My face is fatter. I've never had rosy cheeks before – David says they suit me. So now I know he's good at lying, the way he's good at everything else! Mr Coleman in the post office said I was 'blooming' which is exactly how I feel – now that horrible sickness has gone. This time I feel so different from the other times. I *know* this time is different. I can't wait to hold my baby. I can't wait to find out if it's a boy or a girl. I can't wait to meet our child.

David will be a wonderful father. I hope I don't feel jealous of her relationship with David, if our baby turns out to be a girl!!

Wednesday 7 May 1958
Caught bus to Shapton. Wanted to go to Keeles to visit the cot with the coloured balls on the ends! I'll ask David if we can put a deposit on it. I've been saving halfpennies in a jar. In the wool department I bought a pattern for some matinee jackets. I chose yellow and white 2 ply and some green ribbon to thread around the cuffs. They had buttons in the shape of teddy bears, which I couldn't resist.

Wednesday 14 May 1958.
The cow parsley is spectacular this year with its white frills decorating the side of the lane like fronds of filigree lace. I decided to pick some on my way back from the bus stop after I'd been to Shapton. David gave me two shillings for the romper suit patterns. I chose soft winceyette decorated with yellow chicks and a cream poplin.

At home I emptied one of the drawers in the bedroom and lined it with some left-over wallpaper so I'd have somewhere special to keep our baby's clothes. I'll get started on the romper suits tomorrow. I've got some tissue paper to wrap them in when they're finished.

Thursday 15 May 1958
There was a knock at the door this morning about eleven. I admit I felt excited. How often does anyone visit us here? Even Evie would shout over the fence if she wanted anything.

A woman I'd not seen before stood outside holding a basket. At least it wasn't that awful busybody from the WI – Mrs Pittle. Although on second thoughts, I did recognise this woman. I'd seen her outside the butcher's selling lavender bags. She had some in her basket, as well as sprigs of heather in bunches. I realised she was the woman we met at Shapton fair when I went with John. She was telling fortunes then, now her violet eyes bored into me.

'Lavender, Lady, lucky heather,' she said pushing the basket towards me. She held up one of the lavender bags so it was practically touching my nose. She moved nearer until her foot was on the threshold. Up close her skin was like the husk of a walnut. Each of her fingernails curled over the tips of her fingers. They reminded me of a book we had in the library with pencil illustrations of witches.

'Lavender, good for all sorts,' she said. Actually, I had thought of getting a lavender bag to put in the drawer with the baby's clothes.

'Make tea with the leaves. That will halt the sickness.' She nodded at my stomach.

'I'm past the sickness stage,' I said, feeling proud she'd noticed the baby. 'But I might take some lavender to freshen my layette.'

'Put lavender under your pillow for a good night's sleep.'

'Sleep!' I exclaimed. 'I seem to do little else!'

'Here, take this,' she said, handing me something that looked like a whole nutmeg. 'This will bring good luck to your little girl.'

'My little girl?' I said. 'I don't have a little girl.'

The woman smiled, revealing brown teeth. ''Tis the way she's low slung. Take care of y'self, Lady,' she whispered. 'There's no one else will. Tuppence for the lavender, and the nutmeg is a penny. Will bring you luck, Lady.'

I went into the kitchen to get some money and when I came back, she was inside the hall. She took the pennies, slipping them greedily into her apron pocket. 'Here, take some camomile,' she went on. 'Only a penny. Will calm the temper of the angriest of men.'

I recoiled from her, wishing David were here and that she'd get out of the house. 'I won't be needing that,' I told her. 'My husband doesn't have a temper. But he will be home soon and he might be angry if he finds someone here selling things. He's not keen on people selling door to door...'

'You mean he might be cross with you, Lady? Put some camomile in his tea. Look, only one penny for you. I can see you need it.'

'I doubt that very much, but here you are.' I gave her another penny. 'If you don't mind, I have a hundred things to do, and no doubt you're busy too.' I walked towards the woman, forcing her to back out of the door.

'You do take care of y'self. Make the lavender into tea. Good for baby.'

As I closed the door behind her I dropped the nutmeg and it rolled under the hallstand. I got down on my knees to retrieve it but felt a twinge in my side like a stitch. What was I doing crawling about the floor in search of a nutmeg? I hauled myself up, went upstairs and put the heather in the drawer under the baby clothes. As I went, I tried to recall our meeting at the fair that time with John. She'd definitely said something about lots of babies. What rubbish. I'm sure I won't have lots of babies. All I want is this precious one. I boiled the kettle and infused some of the lavender I'd taken from the bag, but when I drank the tea it made me retch.

Thursday 19 June 1958
I've finished the third romper suit and placed it in the drawer wrapped in tissue, but not before holding it up and imagining our baby in it. The smell from the lavender bag was making me feel sick so I threw everything the gypsy woman had given me into the dustbin.

Saturday 21 June 1958

I can feel our baby getting bigger each day, filling my belly. How I long to hold it, dress it, and bestow on it all the love I've held in my heart for so long.

Ps. I think our baby is a girl, even though I don't believe that gypsy woman could possibly tell. I feel in my heart it's a girl.

Monday 23 June 1958

At the doctor's this morning there were five other people waiting– people who looked ill. A man who wore a trilby, even indoors, kept sneezing, and an elderly woman next to him perched on the edge of her chair looked like a collection of bones held together by the thin fabric of her coat.

But I felt wonderful. *I* wasn't seeing the doctor because of illness. Quite the reverse. A woman smiled at me in the street before I arrived at the surgery. Being in the family way is like belonging to a secret club. Last week a shop assistant in Keele's asked me if this was my first baby. I hesitated before saying 'yes', because it's true, this is my first baby. Those five aching clots of blood were nothing but lost dreams.

Dr Connor took my blood pressure and said he would write a letter to the cottage hospital booking my confinement for the middle of August, as well as a letter to Miss Cray, the midwife.

Wednesday 25 June 1958

David's still with that building contractor on the new Greenside Estate. I watched him leave for work this morning on his motorbike. The BSA Bantam – as he keeps reminding me – not just an ordinary motorbike. He's had it for a year now and although I used to love riding pillion, I haven't been on it for months. I'm not taking any risks.

I can't help thinking that if he sold the bike, we'd have enough to put towards a car on the H.P. Life would be so much easier once the baby is born if we had a car. I'll ask him tomorrow.

Thursday 26ʰ June 1958

David's not keen on my idea to sell his bike. 'We could get a sidecar,' he said. He'd do anything rather than give up that bike. I must admit the thought of me and the baby bumping along together in a sidecar made me giggle so much I had to rush to the bathroom.

Friday 27 June 1958

At five this morning the midsummer sun darted through the gap in the curtains, warming the bedroom and casting an orange glow against the wallpaper. I get heartburn at this time of day and once it wakes you up it won't let go. I decided to pick up some Milk of Magnesia later on when I walked into the village. I just couldn't seem to sleep properly anymore. David was up at half-seven looking for clean socks.

'Do you want anything before I go, darling?' he asked. He was sitting on the end of the bed pulling socks on that definitely weren't a pair. A green one that his mother had knitted, and a black one from a pair I'd bought him for Christmas.

'Are there any pickled onions left?' I asked.

David shook his head with an indulgent smile. 'No, I emptied the jar for your sandwich last night. I'll call into the chippy on the way home.'

He stood up and fastened his belt. I turned over and *burped*, which I know is so undignified, especially in front of my husband. As usual David squatted down beside the bed. He's used to me being windy. We kissed again and again.

'Do you still love me, even though I'm fat and can't help burping?' I asked him between kisses.

'Of course I do,' he said fluttering more kisses all the way down my neck, finishing with the most gentle on my stomach. 'I might be a bit late tonight,' he said. 'If there's any overtime on offer, I'll carry on for an hour or so.'

'Try not to be too long.'

'I'll try.'

'Love you.'

'Love you – and you,' he said stroking my belly.

I sighed as David closed the door behind him and, for some reason, started thinking about the library. I hadn't given a thought to my old job since I'd been married. For the first time I appreciated the fact that I could turn over and go back to sleep. I don't know why it came into my head at that moment. But I started thinking about John, because I'd met him at work, so if I hadn't worked in the library, I'd never have met David. And I started wondering if we're all destined to meet the one we love. In other words, I'd have bumped into David somewhere eventually. For example, his football team might have played against our Christopher's. Not that I ever went to see Christopher play.

I heard David go downstairs, the front door close and the engine revving up. I turned gingerly onto my other side, stretched out across the bed and drifted off to sleep.

When I woke it felt late. I could tell by the way the shadows of the trees outside fell across the bed and I recognised the afternoon sunlight that stretched languorously across the field. I reached for the clock but as I twisted my body I caught my breath. A pain, so intense I thought I'd die if it didn't stop, stabbed my insides. I daren't move.

When the pain lifted, I reached for the clock again though without twisting my body this time. One thirty-five. How could I have slept for so long? I had to make a decision. Although it was late, I couldn't stay in bed waiting for David to come home. Gradually I levered myself up and sat for a while on the side of the bed.

As I stood, warm water poured down my legs onto the linoleum. I was only seven and a half months gone and my waters were breaking. Not only was it too soon, but I'd never imagined it like this. I'd expected a trickle rather than the flood that was drenching the lino. I shouted for David, even though I knew the house was empty. The sound of my voice echoed round the room.

I wondered if Christian Stringer was outside or whether Evie would hear me if I banged on the wall. After all, we could hear *them* shouting at each other most nights. But Evie wasn't likely to be upstairs in the bedroom at this time of day if she was home.

Using what strength I had, I hobbled to the bathroom, where I found a towel to hold between my legs. If I walked carefully down the stairs, I'd be able to phone the hospital. But as I went out onto the landing the pain got worse. I bent over as much as was possible with the size of my belly and, before I had time to realise what I was doing, found myself at the top of the landing on all fours, like an animal. I must have sounded like an animal too, the noises I was making, gasping for breath and moaning with pain. I remember being relieved David didn't have to witness his wife behaving like a wild beast. Eventually bad turned to unbearable, and with it came an uncontrollable urge to use the toilet. I crawled towards the bathroom, grasped the side of the bath, the cold, hard linoleum chaffing my knees. The toilet is next to the bath, but I didn't manage to crawl that far. I felt myself pushing. There was nothing else to do but push.

The head slid out first. I could see it under my nightdress. I'd grabbed a flannel from the side of the bath and screwed it into a ball, forcing it inside my mouth. I bit hard on the flannel and pushed again. The pain was agonising but suddenly vanished as I felt the whole precious thing slithering out of my body, a tiny limp purple being, still attached to its thick blue cord.

The pain had gone but a new agony was beginning. Surely this was not the beloved baby that had been growing inside me for the past seven and a half months. I thought this thing must have come from somewhere else. I put my hand across my stomach. The real baby must surely be still inside. But the skin on my stomach which had been so firm was now flat and floppy. I reached for another towel from the side of the bath, covered up the purple thing and fainted.

I awoke in a bed with bright flowery curtains pulled back in bunches. Sunlight streamed through huge windows that took up the whole of one wall. The bed had paper-white sheets tucked tightly into either side of my arms. I looked around me. There were five other beds, one with its curtains pulled around it, shielding it from view.

I was just about to call out for someone to help me when the door swung open and a nurse carrying a baby swaddled in a white blanket strode towards me. Suddenly everything became clear. The pain, the purple baby on the bathroom floor. I'd had our baby early. I hoisted myself up ready to receive the little bundle into my arms.

But the nurse kept walking.

She walked past my bed and placed the baby into the arms of a smiling black-haired woman who was propped up on a pile of pillows in the bed next to mine. The nurse slashed the curtains around her bed and hurried back towards the door.

I called her. 'Nurse? Excuse me, could you tell me where my baby is?'

'Your baby? Wait a moment, dear, and I'll find out for you.'

'Oh, and before you go, could you tell me what day this is?'

'Thursday, dear,' she said.

'No. I mean the date. What date is it?'

'Oh. The twenty-ninth, no, tell a lie, it's the twenty-eighth of June. I should know – it would have been my mother's birthday.' The woman smiled sadly before turning to go.

I lay my head back on the pillow. If it was only the twenty-eighth of June the pain and the tiny purple baby on the floor must have been a dream. I touched my stomach. It was concave, the skin flabby and soft. Wads of cloth padded my pants. A woman in the bed on my other side was reading a magazine.

'Do you know where my baby is?' I asked her.

The woman sounded sleepy. 'It'll be in the nursery with all the others.'

'Where's the nursery?'

'Out of the main door, turn left. It's just along the corridor. But they'll bring your baby to you if you ask. Are you breast or bottle?'

'I don't know.'

The woman gave me a strange look. I hauled myself out of the bed and hobbled out of the ward. Shuffling along, I clung to a banister on the side of the corridor wall. I passed several doors before reaching a long glass window. Through the window I could see rows of cots. I opened the door. Each cot contained a baby with its surname written in pen on the side. I searched for McDonald.

A nurse came in wearing a dark blue dress and a different, more elaborate hat than the nurse on the ward, like a folded serviette balanced on her head.

'Mrs McDonald!' the woman spoke in a sharp whisper that cut through the snuffling sounds of the nursery. 'What are you doing in the nursery?'

She gripped my arm and led me back to the ward. Once I was in bed again, she swished the curtains roughly around the bed, where they swung for a few seconds, unconnected.

She stood over me, next to my bedside cabinet, which, unlike all the others, was bare, apart from a jug of water.

'Now listen to me, Mrs McDonald,' she hissed. 'You'll need to be strong. I'm sorry but your baby died. I think you already know that...'

'No, that can't be true.'

'The little mite was dead when the ambulance arrived at your house yesterday. You've had a stillbirth. It's very unfortunate, but it happens. You're to stay here for observation. Now make the most of the rest. You'll be discharged within the next forty-eight hours, all being well.'

I focused on a single flower on the curtain. It was a pink tea rose, like the ones that grew around our front door. Tears burned my eyes and the rose shimmied and blurred into the flowers around it.

'Where's David? I want my husband!'

'Calm down, Mrs McDonald. You'll upset the other mothers. If you carry on like this, I'll have to administer a sedative. Your husband went home last night. We don't allow fathers to hang around the wards indefinitely. No doubt he'll collect you soon.'

'I want my husband!'

'Mrs McDonald. Please! Try to have some self-control. You're causing a disturbance. Concentrate on building your strength. I suggest you aim for a bowel movement within the next twenty-four hours. I'll send Staff Nurse over with some cod liver oil and a bedpan.'

Wednesday 2 July 1958
David drove the bike down the side of the house and switched off

the engine. He unlocked the back door before helping me off the pillion and into the kitchen. I had to squeeze past the pram we'd bought on the drip which was still parked in the hall.

'Damn thing,' David said. 'I should have got rid of it. I'll make some tea, love.' I felt like an invalid as he helped me into the armchair. 'I'm sorry. I should have thought. I should have asked someone for a lift rather than bringing you home on the bike. Christian would have helped us. But I haven't even told anyone. When I came home on Friday night and found you upstairs, I thought I'd lost you both. The ambulance man had to comfort me almost as much as he cared for you during the rush to the hospital.'

'So what happened to our baby?' I whispered.

'In the midst of the panic I can't remember much about the baby. The ambulance man took it away. I know this has been awful for you, darling, but for the past week the house has been like a morgue. I've just been going through the motions of waking, eating, working and sleeping. I'm so relieved to have you home.'

'I'm glad to be home.' My voice sounded flat, like a robot.

David gave me a funny look. 'You go upstairs to rest,' he told me as soon as I'd finished my tea.

'But we will try again,' I said, prising myself from the chair. 'Promise me you won't get rid of the pram?'

David frowned. 'Don't you mind it sitting there in the hall? Surely it will remind you every time you walk past it.'

'But we're not going to give up. I couldn't bear it if we gave up.'

'We'll see. You need time to get over this. And so do I.'

At night as I lay in bed I could hear Christian and Evie Stringer yelling at high volume. I strained to listen. David and I had never raised our voices at each other, and I wondered what they found to fight about so often. I couldn't hear exactly what they were saying, except that the tone was belligerent. First he'd shout, then it would be her. Him again, then her and so it went on. Then there'd be the sound of the baby crying and the shouting would stop briefly before resuming with even more aggression.

Their latest baby, Martin, who's about five months old, must still have been sleeping with his parents because I could hear him crying. Something wet and cold was seeping through my nightdress. My breasts, already solid as boulders, hardened more, swollen with the milk which should have nourished our baby. The liquid dripped like a broken tap.

Tuesday 8 July 1958
It. David referred to our baby as *it*. I can't help wondering whether our baby was a girl or a boy. Since I've been home we've hardly mentioned the baby except for the time he called the baby 'it'. But I need to know if the baby was a girl or a boy. Then at least if we speak about the baby we can say 'he' or 'she'. I don't want a baby called 'it'.

Saturday 26 July 1958
David's team beat the Young Farmers and he scored so I knew he'd be in a good mood. I stood up to clear away the plates after tea.

'David,' I said, 'you remember that evening …' I turned away from him to fill the sink with water. 'You know – when you came home and… I've wanted to ask you for a long time now…' I looked around at David, drying my hands on my pinny. He was standing up and pushing his chair under the table. 'Don't go,' I pleaded. 'I just want to know. Was our baby a girl or a boy?'

David sat down again, the expression on his face said he didn't have any choice, as if he'd resigned himself to my irritating questions. I turned the tap off and joined him.

'I don't know,' he said, fiddling with the lid of a bottle of HP sauce. 'I didn't look. I realise now that I should have looked, but I didn't. I don't know and I never will know, so let's leave it at that. We don't need to know about something we haven't got.'

I fought my tears. *Something we haven't got.* First 'it', now 'something'. That's what David is calling our baby.

I went to bed early with a headache but couldn't sleep. When David came up, he got into bed and turned the light out.

'Are you awake?' he asked in the darkness.

'Yes,' I said.

'That evening. You know, the evening …I've been trying not to think about it, but I can't seem to get it out of my head. When

I got home and found the house in darkness, and when I called and you didn't answer. I went upstairs. You were in the bathroom and I could see the baby was dead. It might seem strange, but I wasn't thinking about the baby. All I was thinking about was you. I thought I'd lost you – and all for a baby that was dead anyway. I didn't want to look at it, let alone work out its sex.'

David stopped. It seemed he was crying. I'd never seen him cry. I lay there without moving, wishing he'd just *made up* an answer. Not that I'd ever want David to lie to me, but a white lie – he could have just said 'darling, she was a girl,' or 'darling, our baby was a little boy.'

Monday 25 August 1958

A woman came to the house this morning while I was upstairs, resting. I feel so tired all the time, but I dragged myself from the bed.

'Good morning,' she said as I opened the door, squinting in the sunlight. 'Mrs McDonald?'

She was wearing a green dress with a matching hat.

'I'm the midwife. Come to weigh Baby. Is it alright if I leave my bike by the gate?'

Christian Stringer was in the field staring over at the house. 'I was a bit concerned,' she went on. 'You haven't brought Baby to the clinic for weighing...'

I suppose I should have sent her packing, but in a strange way I was glad to see her.

'Didn't anyone tell you?' I asked.

The nurse looked at me as if she was boring deep into my soul. 'There's something wrong, isn't there, my love?' she said.

'I had a stillbirth. Nothing to weigh.'

'Oh, my dear, I'm so sorry. I've been given completely the wrong information. Please, don't let me keep you,' she said turning to leave. 'I'm sure you don't want the likes of me bothering you.'

Actually, she was wrong. I felt comforted by her presence. 'No, no. Not at all. Do you have time for a cup of tea, nurse?'

'I'm Mary. Mary Cray. Yes, I'd love a cup of tea. But only if it's no trouble.'

I led her into the front room and she sat by the window.

'I see you've changed the wallpaper,' she said.

'Yes, my husband redecorated the house when I moved in. How do you know about our wallpaper?'

'I was here, a long time ago.' The midwife gazed wistfully around the room. 'A family called Blake lived here. I visited them just after they had a baby. A little boy. No doubt you've heard the gossip...'

I looked at Mary Cray. 'No,' I said. 'What gossip? I haven't lived here long so I don't know any gossip.'

'That's probably not a bad thing. Anyway I'm not here to talk about myself. I'm so sorry you lost your baby. How is your husband? Men can change when a wife has a baby. I hope you're looking after him. Two cooked meals a day with everything in its place when he gets home from work.'

'Of course,' I said. What sort of wife did she think I was? 'Are *you* married?' I asked her.

She laughed. 'No, my dear. There was someone – once. But he was already married, so the situation was difficult.' She gazed around the room again as if she was looking for something. She was beginning to unsettle me. 'He died, though,' she added as an afterthought.

'So you don't have any children of your own?'

Mary looked down at her lap. 'No, I don't. I've brought plenty into this world but none of them my own. Not that I regret it. Men change when there's a baby around. I've seen it too many times. Arthur was enough for me. I didn't need anyone else.'

'I'll make some tea,' I said and went into the kitchen. As the kettle boiled on the hob I felt hot tears sting my eyes. Suddenly I was crying. I wiped my eyes and carried the tray into the front room.

'I suppose David, my husband, should be enough for me,' I said once I'd poured the tea. 'But I still long for a baby. Maybe there's something wrong with me. David doesn't seem to have the same need, but I'm tortured by the thought that I may never hold my own child.'

'But it's your duty to respect your husband's needs,' Mary said as she sipped the tea. 'Try your best to be a good wife, and if he doesn't want children perhaps you should find the strength to honour his decision. After all, you don't want to lose him.'

'It's not that he doesn't want a child. It's more that he's worried about me.'

'You mean he doesn't think you can cope?'

'No. Maybe. I don't know.'

'You seem upset, which is understandable. But if you let your husband see you smiling, I'm sure that will help. Maybe, before you know it, another baby will be on the way. I'll alter your notes as soon as I can.' Mary Cray drank her tea swiftly in large gulps.

'Just one thing,' I said as she stood up to leave. 'Before you go. I would like to know whether the baby I had was a boy or a girl. Could you find out for me, please?'

'I'm sorry, but it would probably help you if you didn't think of it as a baby. The corpse would have been incinerated at the hospital. I'm so sorry, but they can't keep bodies indefinitely.'

After she left, I slept for the rest of the day.

Wednesday 17th December 1958

In Keele's they've hung tinsel around the counters and rows of paper chains from the ceiling. The assistants all wore coloured paper hats like the ones from Christmas crackers. I had two pounds David gave me. 'Treat yourself to something nice to wear for Christmas,' he said this morning as he left for work.

I've looked around the ladies' fashion department on the ground floor so many times, imagining what I'd buy if I could afford something new, so why did I suddenly find myself walking downstairs to the basement where the toys were?

The toy department reminded me of when I was little – all those rubber dolls with blonde curly hair or dark straight hair. There were dolls' clothes, even a dolls' wardrobe. The boys' toys were equally enticing. Guns, cowboy outfits, a submarine in kit form.

I wandered around in a daze when an assistant came up to me and asked me if I needed help.

'I'm just looking,' I said, and the woman returned to her till. I should have gone back upstairs to the fashion department, but I couldn't help thinking *what might I have been buying for my baby this Christmas?* There was no harm in thinking about what might have been. If the baby had been a girl, I'd definitely have chosen the doll with blonde curls. It was displayed in a box covered in cellophane. I longed to unwrap it, to feel the texture of the curls, to feel the softness of the doll's body. Or what if our baby had been a boy? A wind-up monkey dressed in a red waistcoat, or a teddy with soft golden fur that seemed to be smiling at me? I lifted the teddy, enjoying its softness and new smell. Now, he *was* irresistible. Before I knew it, I was standing at the till with all three. I carried them home in a big bag with the word Keele's on the outside.

Thursday 18 December 1958
This morning David started quizzing me about the dress. 'Did you get a new dress? Come on let's see you in it!'

'I didn't get a dress. There was nothing that suited me, but I've chosen some material. I'll get it next week.'

There. I'd lied to David.

'Good,' David said as he kissed the top of my hair, a kiss that implied our baby was far behind us now, and no longer a problem.

Monday 22 December 1958
I've decided to call the baby 'Pip'. David and I usually make important decisions together, but I chose the name on my own. Once I'd thought of it, I knew it was the right name. A pip is a seed, and Pip could be a boy's name or a girl's. There was a boy called Pip in *Great Expectations* and there had been a girl called Pip in my class at school. Pip is an androgynous name which is perfect for our baby. I went into the library to look up the name. It means 'something wonderful'.

Pip would have been wonderful.

Tuesday 6 January 1959
This evening David announced he's leaving his job on the Greenside Estate. 'I've applied for a job in Charlesdon. It's only five miles west of Shapton. I'll be working on the new municipal swimming pool.

I feel as if I need a fresh start. Going into work every day seems to remind me of that day...'

'Which day?' I asked.

'The day of the...stillbirth.'

I know he's trying to spare my feelings but the 'stillbirth'!? Why does he have to call our precious baby by such a horrible, clinical name?

'The job starts in two weeks. I'll have to leave the house fifteen minutes earlier.'

'That means an extra half hour on my own each day,' I said.

'You could join a group,' David suggested. 'What about that woman from the WI who came round? You said she was trying to get you to join something. Maybe that would help.'

'Help what?'

'It's something different. It might help to take your mind off things...'

Thankfully, David didn't say the word again. The Stillbirth. Instead his sentence just petered out as he went upstairs for a wash. I said it for him though. In a whisper I said the word 'Pip'.

Monday 19 January 1959
David seemed happy when he got home today, mainly because he's made a friend called George at his new job.

'He reminds me a bit of John,' he said. 'Very organised. Brings a lunchbox to work every day. But he's unsettled. George says he's determined not to be a plumber all his life helping make swimming pools for other people to enjoy and profits to go into other men's pockets. And do you know, darling? I think he's got a point. I mean, I've never thought about it before but that's the way things are. I work long hours, yet we struggle to make ends meet. When do we get a chance to have fun in a swimming pool?'

Monday 2 February 1959
David says George has bought himself a one-way ticket to Australia.

'The ticket cost ten pounds. Ten pounds! Less than a week's wages. He's leaving next month.'

I thought it a shame that David was losing his new friend, but I had been getting a bit fed up with hearing about George non-stop. George this, George that…

'All George talks about now is how he'll be sunbathing on the beach by this time next year and I'll still be here, fixing pipes and wiping down spanners.'

'But he'll have to work, even in Australia,' I pointed out.

'True. But according to George, after work he'll be straight down to the beach for his tea. That's how they do things out there. Work and play. Surf and sand. Christmas dinner on the beach. It's the good life out there, according to George.'

Thursday 19 February 1959
After David left for work, when I'd cleared away the breakfast things, I opened the drawer where I keep Pip's clothes. I laid the romper suits out on the bed with the cardigans and considered which outfit Pip might wear today. I knew in my heart that Pip would probably have outgrown them all by now, but somehow that didn't seem to matter. I held each one up to my cheek just to feel the softness of the fabric. I breathed in the smell, and flattened them with my hand, so I could refold them and place them in the tissue paper in a neat pile in the drawer.

(I've hidden the toys in a cupboard in the box room, still in the Keele's bag. I'm sure David never goes in there.)

Friday 13 March 1959
As soon as I smelled the fresh morning air and saw the daffodils swaying with heavy heads along the bank by Stringer's farm, I decided it would be the ideal day to take Pip out. The first blue sky for weeks was like a magnet drawing me away from the house. The pram's been sitting there for so long it's about time it got some use. I put a pillow embroidered with yellow flowers inside the pram, and the cot blanket. I hooked the rain cover on either side of the hood so that if I met anyone, they wouldn't be able to see in. I've never pushed the pram before. It was much lighter than I'd imagined, more bouncy.

I'd noticed Evie taking her brood across the road to the farm earlier, which meant she'd be over there all day. I needed some stamps for a competition in a magazine I wanted to enter. The first prize was a car. If I won the car there would be no need for David to sell his bike. We could have both. I was sure I had a good chance of winning. The competition was to compose a rhyme about one of the new Bubblecars. Mine is: *Drive a Bubble without any trouble.* I know it's not perfect, but it's worth a go. If I won, there'd be a spanking new Bubblecar parked outside Two Blackberry Lane.

Apart from the stamps, I needed bread and some mince from the butcher. Sometimes carrying the shopping home makes my arms ache. With Pip's pram I could put it in the rack at the bottom.

As I wheeled the pram around to the front path, I kept an eye out for anyone who might be around. Or rather, I kept an eye out for Christian Stringer, since he's the only one likely to be around. But it was market day when most villagers go into Shapton.

It took me a quarter of an hour to walk to the post office, and as I neared the shop, I noticed another pram parked outside. There was no mistaking that pram. After all, hadn't I seen it day after day in next door's garden? So Evie must have decided to come into the village after all.

The hot spring sunshine streamed down onto the baby's face. I knew this to be Martin, the latest addition to Christian and Evie's family. His cheeks were red and shiny, his eyes swollen from crying, his breathing punctuated with silent sobs. The pram should have been turned the other way to keep the sun out of his eyes. Evie Stringer might have three children, but the woman didn't have a clue. I could hear her inside the post office talking to Mrs Coleman. *Yak, yak, yak.* I stood for a while listening. Evie was telling her about her brother-in-law, Michael, who's studying to be an architect in London. She was chattering on about how well he was doing.

I put the brake on Pip's pram, but I didn't want to talk to Evie, especially as I might have had to explain why I was pushing a pram when I didn't have a baby to put in it. I decided to carry on up to the baker's and get my stamps later. But before I did, I just had to shift Martin's pram so his little face wasn't in the sun. He looked so uncomfortable, poor love.

If children could choose their parents, then Evie and Christian Stringer would be at the bottom of the list, that's for sure. How could a child develop into a stable adult with parents who argued non-stop? I looked at Martin – he was so tiny, and I thought, at his age, he still had a chance. If, for example, he was brought up by a loving, caring couple who respected each other and could provide a stable, happy home, he probably wouldn't even remember the first few months of his life.

Suddenly I realised I had a duty as a churchgoer and a responsible adult to help this child. After I'd turned Martin's pram round, I looked up and down the high street. Old Mrs Gladwin was just disappearing into the baker's so I waited, pretending to be looking for something in my bag. When I looked up again, she'd come out of the baker's with a loaf under her arm, and was heading in the opposite direction towards the bus shelter. There was no one else around.

I lifted Martin out of his pram. Evie hadn't even secured him properly with the reins that hung uselessly on either side of his pillow. He was so light. No heavier than a couple of bags of flour. His bottom was damp, and he smelled of wee. His nose had a snail's trickle of snot that melted into his top lip. I slipped him under the blanket in Pip's pram.

Pip's pram, Martin's pram. Martin's pram, Pip's pram.

Martin coughed and his eyes twitched.

'There you are, my baby,' I said. 'It's about time I got you home.'

I tried not to run. *Keep calm,* I said to myself, *keep calm, everything's going to be all right. Walk at a steady pace. Don't draw attention to yourself.*

Blast, I'd forgotten my competition entry. I didn't want to miss the closing date but I daren't go back to the post office. I repeated the verse I'd made up for the competition in my head. *Drive a Bubble without any trouble, drive a bubble without any trouble, drive a bubble, drive a...* Lord above – as I turned into Blackberry Lane, I thought I might faint. Christian Stringer was walking towards me.

He called Queenie to heel.

'Hello, Christian. I think it's coming on rain,' I gabbled, as I quickened my pace. 'Just look at those black clouds.'

As Christian looked up at the sky, I made my getaway over the road and arrived at the gate before he'd had a chance to answer. I pushed the pram round the side of the house and stood there for a moment. I was so hot and out of breath I had to compose myself before going inside. I manoeuvred the pram up the step and left it in its usual spot in the hall. As I took my coat off, I heard the baby stir and begin to grizzle. I undid the hood, lifted him out, held him close, and stroked his hair. He smelled of the sweetness of sweat. He looked up at me and began to cry.

'Hush, hush, my darling. There's no need to cry.'

His bottom was soaked – even wetter than when I'd first picked him up. I carried him upstairs and filled the sink with warm water. I laid a clean towel on the bathroom floor, patting its softness before gently placing him on it.

Martin wore a home-knitted cardigan which might once have been yellow but was now a dirty beige colour; a grey vest, stained with brown at the neckline; some shorts, and a sodden towelling nappy. How often had I averted my gaze from these nappies on Evie's line? Now I was unfastening one myself. Unclipping the giant safety pin and sensibly re-closing it to avoid any accidents.

I threw his dirty clothes into the bath. Martin was chubby with little pink fold lines around his knees and elbows. His skin was soft, like silk. I'd never imagined skin could be this fine. The floor space in the bathroom is limited but there was just enough room for us both. I ended up on my knees beside him. He looked up at me with his blue wondering eyes, and I kissed the top of his head. He was lying on the exact spot where Pip had been born.

I lowered him carefully into the sink. He looked uncertain, but as I swilled the warm water around his toes, his smooth, chubby legs and his sore bottom, he gurgled.

'Is that nice, my love? You like this, don't you?'

Martin gurgled some more and after his bath I wrapped him in the towel, hugged him and kissed him again. I took him into the bedroom, laid him on the bed and sprinkled talcum powder over his bottom. His skin was red raw where the nappy had been. I didn't have any nappies, but I had a small towel which I wrapped around him in the shape of a nappy and fastened with the pin I'd removed from his dirty one.

Inside the drawer all the clothes I'd made for Pip were still neatly packed away.

'Now, my little Pip, what are we going to wear today?'

He giggled, a deep throaty chuckle that made me want to laugh too. But there was no time to enjoy him now. I had days ahead of me when I could laugh and giggle and do all the things a real mother does. I took out one of the matinee jackets I'd knitted. The yellow one with the duck buttons. The wool was soft and virginal. Unworn. I could see straight away that the jacket didn't fit Pip now. He'd grown so. None of his clothes were the right size. So I decided to wrap him in a blanket. I took the other clothes out of the drawer and placed Pip inside, stroking his head until he slept. I washed his clothes and hung them over the bath to dry, then lay down on the bed next to the drawer.

The sound of David's voice woke me. 'Hello!' he called up the stairs. I came down and found him in the kitchen holding his sandwich tin.

'I've got something to show you,' he said, producing a dog-eared brochure from inside the empty tin. Sleepily I deciphered the words on the front. *Welcome to Australia – The Land of Opportunity.*

'George let me borrow it. I've been thinking about this a lot, what George is doing, and do you know? I think we should consider emigrating. Of course, we'd have to sell up, which would be a shame after all the work we've put in here. It would mean I might never go to another decent match again.' David laughed. 'We might never see our relations again. But John might as well be in Australia himself the amount we see him, and Mum and Dad weren't too bothered about us when they shoved off to Weston. And we hardly hear a peep out of your lot. You can telephone Australia now. It might cost a lot, but you can keep in touch with everyone at home. It's not as if we wouldn't know anyone out there. We'd know George. Or at least I'd know George, and you'd soon get to know him. I'm sure you'd like him, and, maybe if we lived somewhere hot, a more carefree lifestyle, you'd be able to have a baby. We could try again. In a warmer climate everything could be different.'

I yawned and rubbed my eyes. 'What time is it?'

'Just after six. What's for tea?' David folded the brochure and put it in his pocket. 'We could talk about this later. Are you expecting anyone? I think there's someone outside.'

I followed David into the front room. 'Good Lord, it's the police. Probably looking for Stringer. It wouldn't surprise me if he was in trouble with the law. He's that type, and I doubt it's the first time either. Drunk and disorderly probably, or wife beating.'

There was a loud knock at our front door. 'You'd think they'd know which house he lives in by now.'

I heard a man's voice. 'Good evening. Constable Dobbs, Shapton Constabulary. Are you Mr David McDonald, sir? Might I enquire whether Mrs McDonald is at home?'

As I went into the hallway, I caught sight of myself in the mirror. My hair was limp and untidy, my cheeks sleepy pink. A policeman as tall as the doorway stood on the step, the top half of his helmet hidden by the lintel.

'I'm Mrs McDonald,' I said.

The policeman removed his helmet and placed his gloves on the rim, holding it upside down like a bowl.

'Would it be possible to have a word, Mrs McDonald?'

'Not really. I'm rather busy at the moment.'

David looked at me as if he'd never seen me before in his life. 'Darling?' he said. 'What seems to be the problem, Constable?'

'It's something of a delicate nature, sir. Perhaps we could discuss it inside, in private, so to speak.'

'You're welcome to come in,' David said opening the door wider.

'No!' I whispered.

David looked at me with the same incredulous expression.

'If you don't wish me to come inside the house we can discuss the matter out here, or I can get a warrant.'

'You'd better come in,' David said.

'I'd like to ask you both a few questions,' the constable began. 'You do both know Mr and Mrs Christian Stringer of Number One Blackberry Lane which I understand to be the dwelling attached to the dwelling we are at present…within?'

'So this *is* to do with Stringer. I thought as much.' David spoke with obvious relief.

'You are aware that they have a young baby?' the constable carried on, ignoring David and glancing down at his notebook. 'Goes by the name of …er …Martin?'

'Yes, of course,' David said. 'We know them. They live next door. I play football with Mr Stringer sometimes.'

'I see. Could you tell me when you last saw the baby – Martin Stringer?'

'Last saw Martin? Goodness me, I've no idea. I've seen him outside in his pram I suppose. And I've seen Evie in the mornings taking the children over the road to her father-in-law's.'

'What about you, Mrs McDonald? When did you last see Mr and Mrs Stringer's baby?'

I smoothed a strand of hair away from my face and held my hands neatly together in the prayer position in my lap. 'I've never seen him,' I said.

'Never seen him? But they live in the house adjoining this one, don't they, Mrs McDonald?'

'What my wife means,' David said with uncertainty, 'is that they live next-door but Evie and my wife aren't close friends. You can go for days without seeing anyone down here. It's a very quiet place to live.'

'I see, sir. So, Mrs McDonald,' the constable said turning the page of his notebook, 'although the Stringer family live so close, you have *never* seen their youngest child?'

'No.'

'Susan?' I could feel David staring at me, but I wouldn't meet his eye.

'Perhaps if you could tell us what this is all about, Constable, maybe my wife or I could be of more help.'

'This is a serious state of affairs, sir. A baby has been kidnapped. Master Stringer was abducted this afternoon sometime around fifteen hundred hours from his pram outside the Lyde village post office.'

At that moment the rasping sound of Pip crying came from

upstairs. I could feel David trying desperately to get my attention, but I remained motionless on the edge of my seat.

'Do you have children, Mrs McDonald?' Constable Dobbs went on tilting his head to one side as if to hear better what was going on upstairs. I wondered if there was any point at which this man would give up with his ridiculous questions. For some reason we both answered simultaneously.

'No.'

'Yes.'

The constable looked at me and then at David, then at me again. 'I see,' he said in his imbecilic, monotonous voice. 'So you, Mr McDonald, don't have children – and you, Mrs McDonald, do.'

Again we answered in unison.

'No.'

'Yes.'

'I see. So the baby I can hear upstairs belongs to you, Mrs McDonald, but is not the child of Mr McDonald?'

I stood up. 'I'd better go and see to him. He'll be hungry.'

David was about to follow me. 'Don't,' I told him. 'I can manage on my own.' All the same, I was aware of him behind me as I went into the hall. He caught up with me at the bottom of the stairs and held my arm. 'David,' I said, 'you're hurting my arm.' The baby was still crying, and I didn't want to neglect him.

'Susan, darling, there's a baby upstairs. Whose baby is upstairs? What's going on?'

'Nothing is *going on.*'

'But why did you tell that policeman you had a child? Susan, you don't have a child, you know that, darling.'

'Let go of my arm, David. You're hurting me. I have to go. Pip's crying.'

'Who in God's name is *Pip*?'

'David you must know who Pip is. Pip is our baby.'

'But Susan, our baby…our baby…'

'Why are you being like this? He's crying. I never leave him when he's crying. Not like Evie does, for hours on end.'

I climbed the stairs. Somehow they seemed steeper, higher and longer than usual. I knew David was following me but when I looked down from the top step, I saw the constable standing at the bottom, his arms folded across his chest, like a guard.

Pip was snuggled inside the drawer whimpering. 'There's a cot in Keeles…' I began. David stood by the drawer and seemed to be having difficulty speaking. 'It's white with red and blue balls at either end…'

'Susan. Susan,' he touched my shoulder. 'This is Martin Stringer, isn't it?'

I lifted Pip out of the drawer, holding him close to calm him. 'The cot. We should get it. Pip would be so much more comfortable in a proper cot…'

'Here,' David said, taking him from me. He held Pip and stroked his head. He was a good father. 'There, there,' he said. 'Time for you to go home, little man.'

I touched Pip's foot, running my fingers along the silky skin of his calf. David turned towards the stairs and we went down.

Constable Dobbs was still positioned at the bottom of the stairs blocking our way. As David approached him, he unfolded his arms.

'Is this your baby, sir?' he asked.

'Of course not. I've already told you – I don't have a damn baby.'

'Alright, sir, there's no need to raise your voice. Am I correct in presuming that this is Martin Stringer?'

'*I don't know.*' David took a deep breath as if he was trying to hold in his anger. 'I imagine so. Most babies look the same to me, but yes, I suppose this must be Martin Stringer.'

'If you'd be so kind as to pass him to me, sir, I will proceed next door with the infant.'

We followed him down the path and out of the gate. It was dark outside, and a film of drizzle dampened my face. The air smelled of rain and smoke. Pip began to cry.

'If I were you, I'd go home. I don't think it wise to confront the parents at this juncture. I'll talk to you both again once the child is formally identified and reunited with his parents. And I might warn you both not to go anywhere until we've spoken again.'

Neither of us took any notice and the constable had his hands full so there was nothing he could do to stop us following him. David opened the Stringer's gate to let him through. Their curtains were closed but the light through the gaps lit the pathway and the front door opened a split second before the policeman had a chance to knock. Christian Stringer stood there, his eyes wild and red rimmed. He wore a grey shirt with the top button undone and a thick belt held up his trousers. At least he wasn't staring at me now.

'Mr Stringer, I have reason to believe your baby has been recovered. Would you be kind enough to identify the child?'

Christian was standing in the hallway of his house, which was a mirror image of ours, crying. He fell onto the baby.

Inside the house was full of people, like a party but with the main lights on and no noise except for the sound of Evie sobbing. Nicholas sat on the floor at her feet, Tobias, Edmund, and a few other people I didn't recognise were huddled round the dining table. As soon as Evie saw the baby she screamed.

'Praise the Lord,' an elderly lady said, crossing herself.

'Where was the babby found, Constable?' Tobias asked.

'He's here now, safe and sound. That's all that matters,' David said. Everyone turned to stare at us

'I suggest you return home now, sir.' Constable Dobbs' suggestion sounded more like a warning.

One of the women looked at David with rheumy eyes. 'Why is he here with the constable? Is he the one who found the babby? The least we can do is offer him a glass of sherry.'

Evie was cradling Martin, her face streaked with tears. 'Where exactly *was* our Martin found?' Her expression changed as cold realisation dawned. 'Wait a moment. It was *her*, wasn't it? *You*,' she said turning on me. 'Christian was right when he told the constable he'd seen you acting strange, wandering about pushing that pram when you don't have no baby to put in it. What sort of a woman goes about pushing an empty pram?'

I felt the room buzz as if a swarm of hornets had just been let loose. Suddenly I was aware of an uncomfortable movement and Christian Stringer had his hands around David's neck.

'You bastard. How dare you come into my house acting the hero.' At this point several gasps came from the group sitting round the table. 'Your wife's a loony. None of our kids is safe with her around. She wants locking up.'

The constable pulled Christian away. Nicholas was crying and Evie clutched Martin tightly to her chest.

David rubbed his neck as he shook himself free from Christian's grasp. 'Christian, let's talk about this man to man. Okay, maybe Susan did take your baby. But look at it from her point of view. She still hasn't got over the little one we lost. Think about it, man. She didn't mean any harm. Susan wouldn't hurt a fly. You only have to look at her to know that. And it could have been worse. The baby could have been taken by a complete stranger. Maybe in future your wife will keep a better eye on her children.'

Christian's face grew redder. He balled his right hand into a fist. His father stood up to restrain him.

David carried on talking. 'Susan took care of Martin for the short time she had him. Didn't you, darling?'

'Yes! I … he needed changing. I changed his nappy. It was very wet…'

'There. You've heard her. She was trying to help. Now, don't let's be rash here. I'm begging you, mate. Don't press charges. I'll do anything. Imagine if the tables were turned and your Evie was in trouble. Anyway, we're moving. That's right. We're going to Australia. Soon. Look, I've got the brochure here in my pocket.' David grabbed the crumpled brochure that George had given him from his trouser pocket. 'That proves it. See? We'll be gone in a matter of weeks. You'll never see us again. For God's sakes, man, have pity. She didn't mean any harm. I'm begging you. Let all this business drop and we'll be gone before the end of the month. I swear on the life of my dead baby. We're leaving. You can tell the bobby now. Tell him you want to drop the whole thing. Have some compassion. If not for Susan's sake, then for mine. We've always got on, haven't we?'

I slumped by the wall, shivering as David made this speech. When he'd finished he put his arm around my shoulder. Meanwhile Christian was breathing heavily. He opened a bottle of beer that was on a sideboard, poured it into a cup, drank and belched.

'Alright, McDonald. But I'll not say it was Evie's mistake if this goes to court. Evie could get done for neglect, or even wasting police time. Dobbs, you can make a note of this. We don't want to press charges. But you'd better be gone by the summer, or I swear I'll drag you both out of that house and put you on that boat myself.'

"Fine,' David said, and we left.

Friday 5th June 1959

We're standing on the quayside with our hand luggage by our feet, surrounded by a circle of people, like the farmer and his wife in the game we used to play when I was little. *The farmer wants a wife, the wife wants a child, the child wants a dog, the dog wants a bone.*

I stare at the boat. I never imagined it would be so big. Such a monster casting its shadow over the quay. A huge rusty chain rests on the ground, like a chain for a giant convict about to sail to Australia. The gangplank is alive with people going up and down. Crew and passengers – other people like us who are leaving England to try something new. Sunshine in winter, a carefree life, Christmas dinner on the beach…

But do I really want something new? Why would anyone want to eat Christmas dinner on a beach? I imagine sand in the mashed potato, pebbles in the gravy.

Our bags have already been carried aboard. The romper suits are in there, at the bottom wrapped in the tissue paper. They will make the journey with us to the other side of the world. What will it be like? Australia is a hot place but the baby – if we ever have one – might need a woollen jumper in the winter. They do have winters, I believe.

I take one last look behind me, hold tightly onto David's hand, and step onto the gangplank.

CHARLIE MULLETT

January 1960

CHARLIE MULLET struggled from the van with his cocktail cabinet between his arms. He managed to tango towards the gate, only to jam the damn thing between the fence and his stomach. Getting a firm grip on the underside was proving difficult without Maureen there to help.

Charlie looked around for some sign of life, but all he could see was a pair of cows watching him above a blackberry bush on the opposite side of the road. The curtains were drawn in the adjoining house and the farmhouse over the road also appeared to be asleep.

'Curses!' Charlie muttered the word under his breath, even though in the circumstances it was an effort to speak. Not only was nobody around to lend a hand with his cocktail cabinet, but there was nobody to even notice that Charles Mullet Esquire, Master Butcher, and newly appointed owner-occupier of Number Two Blackberry Lane, possessed such a thing.

The rest of their belongings were due to arrive at lunchtime. Charlie had a friend whose brother owned a removal company, who'd be along soon with all his worldly goods. Except for his cocktail cabinet. He wanted to be sure that particular chattel arrived in one piece. Even a second-hand cocktail cabinet didn't come cheap, and this one had two whisky bottles and a bottle of *Cinzano Bianco* attached to their optics. You never knew what a gang of removal men might do with two bottles of whisky and five inches of *Cinzano Bianco*. Drink it probably and leave Charlie with just the bottles topped up with *Tizer* and cheap lemonade. The exact same thing had happened to one of his friends' cousins who'd lost a whole crate of ale in the process of moving house. Charlie knew a lot of people with unfortunate removal stories. A man had to be on the ball when it came to moving house.

Charlie and his cocktail cabinet came crashing into the front room. He needed to sit down, his heart was galloping like a frightened horse. He looked around him. There wasn't even a chair to sit on. Thank heavens Maureen wouldn't be back from Felixstowe for a while.

He regarded the fire surround. It was old fashioned – just crying out for someone with a bit of flair to modernise it. He'd already ordered a box of tiles from a man he knew who was in tiling. They were cut price, due to the fact that the odd one might be chipped. But they could easily be patched up, his friend had assured him. The sooner he covered the old stone fireplace and installed the imitation log gas fire Maureen had set her heart on in Keele's, the better. This house might be bigger than his old flat over the shop, but it needed bringing up to date. And who better to steer the place into the sixties.

Even at the age of fifty-three Charlie embraced the modern styles. His taste was impeccable. It had to be – Maureen would never have married a man without impeccable taste. Both her previous husbands had had impeccable taste.

Charlie had a lot to live up to.

Maureen had booked a seat on the two-thirty train from Paddington on the first Friday in February, which gave Charlie a week and a half to get the place up to scratch. It was a fair amount of time, but he felt pressurised. And when he felt pressurised Charlie's heart fidgeted inside his chest. There was so much to do, plus he still had to work all day, not to mention eat, sleep, wash – that sort of thing. A butcher of Charlie's calibre couldn't be seen slicing best fillet of beef with lumps of grouting under his fingernails.

The box of tiles for the fireplace arrived but there was only enough to cover a fraction of the fire surround. He realised half-way through that maybe he should have started from the middle top section and worked his way outwards on either side. That way, if he did run out of tiles, at least the overall effect would be balanced, and he could have finished the job off with a different colour. After all, beige went with anything.

The telephone rang. Charlie answered it still holding the trowel.

'Is that you, Charlie?'

'Hello, Pumpkin.'

'Hello, Mump.' Charlie had forgotten how shrill Maureen's voice was.

'When are you coming home, Pumpkin?'

'That's what I was ringing about. Elsie's asked me if I'd stay another week, so I said I would.'

A blob of grouting slid from Charlie's trowel onto the floor.

'But, Maureen, you've already been gone for three weeks...'

'I know, I know.' Maureen lowered her voice. 'It's Elsie's Eric. You remember I told you he's got the conversational skills of a mute? Well, Elsie's enjoying having me here to chat to. It's just for a little while. Say you don't mind. You don't mind, do you, Charlie?'

If he was honest, Charlie did mind. He hadn't foreseen enforced celibacy as an integral part of marriage. *I promise to love, honour and leave you on your tod whenever I happen across a friend who needs a bit of conversation.* That hadn't been one of the wedding vows. It had been almost a month now. But when he thought about the half-tiled fireplace, the leg on the cocktail cabinet he'd snapped, not to mention the sliding doors he'd promised Maureen to separate the kitchen from the front room which were still in the shop, he gave Maureen a truthful reply.

"Of course not, my Pumpkin. As long as we make up for it when you get home. If you know what I mean.'

"I do know what you mean," Maureen said down the phone, two hundred miles away, in Felixstowe.

Eight days later Charlie drove to the station.

'Help me with these bags, will you? I've already snagged my nail on one of the handles,' Maureen pleaded. Charlie staggered towards the boot with Maureen's suitcases while she sat on the front seat of his Cortina with her vanity case balanced on her knees.

'You should see Elsie's new twin tub, Charlie,' she said as he squeezed into the driver's seat. 'Eric bought it her last week. He treats her like royalty, her Eric does.'

As Charlie regained his composure after carrying Maureen's

luggage down four flights of stairs, he reflected on Eric's supposed shortcomings in the conversational department, which had necessitated Maureen's prolonged stay on the east coast.

'I thought you said her Eric was a waste of space.'

'No. You don't listen. I said he doesn't *talk* a lot, but that's not to say he doesn't have a good job. He bought her a hostess trolley for their wedding anniversary.'

'They must do a fair bit of entertaining if they need one of those. The chap must speak sometimes.'

'We could do more entertaining now that we've got the house, Charlie.'

'I dare say we could.'

'A hostess trolley would look lovely in our lounge.'

'Yes, I dare say it would.'

Charlie dropped Maureen's cases on the front step and fiddled in his pocket for his key. His heart was doing that fluttering dance again as if a swarm of butterflies had been let loose in his ribcage. Where had he put that key? Maureen shivered theatrically.

'Hurry up, Charlie, it's freezing out here.'

He'd had it a minute ago. Must have had it to drive the bloomin' car. Maureen looked behind her.

'There it is, you mump head. Look – by that bush thing.'

Charlie felt a stabbing pain in his chest as he bent down to pick up the key which had fallen beneath a rose bush. He knew he should get his ticker checked out at the quacks, but Charlie disliked doctors. They always told him to lose weight. Most of them were jealous. A scrawny, undernourished profession who didn't have time to eat properly if you asked him.

Maureen handed her vanity case to Charlie and scuttled around the house, opening doors. She'd only been to Two Blackberry Lane once before when Charlie had made the initial offer. He'd bought the house from a couple who were emigrating to Australia. Mr and Mrs McDonald had seemed in a hurry to sell up, which was why Charlie had got the place cheap.

'We'll have to do something about this décor,' Maureen complained as she followed Charlie upstairs. 'It's so plain and ordinary. Like that woman who lived here before. She looked plain and ordinary. In fact I was only describing her to Elsie the other day. "She's the type who wouldn't know what to do with a pair of false eyelashes if they flew onto her eye lids," I told her. Wouldn't last five minutes in Felixstowe.'

Charlie puffed as he dropped Maureen's bags by the wardrobe.

'The husband seemed nice, though. Quite good-looking, in fact,' Maureen carried on as she opened her bag and hung up the first of her pencil skirts. 'Kind eyes and an athletic physique. Hmm … wasted on her, if you ask me.' Maureen folded a salmon pink corset and placed it in a drawer.

When she'd finished unpacking, Charlie led the way down to the kitchen.

'Mump, how long do we have to put up with this wallpaper?' Maureen sat down and began shaping her thumbnail with a nail file. 'I'd prefer something like Elsie's kitchen wallpaper. She's got an orange brickwork pattern running along the walls with pictures of fruit and some flower things curling all over the place. It's very classy. I'll have to start looking for something nice as soon as I can get to the shops.'

'But you do like the place, my Pumpkin?' Charlie asked, as he slipped a chubby arm around her waist.

'I *quite* like it,' she said, leaning her head on his chest. 'But I'm telling you now, I won't be able to live with this wallpaper, although I'll admit it's a darn sight better than being cooped up in that flat with carcasses of dead animals hanging in the basement and pigs' heads dripping blood in the larder.'

'I never knew you felt like that about meat,' Charlie said.

'Poo,' Maureen pinched her nose. 'That place was a step up from living in an abattoir. *Any* house is a move in the right direction. Not that I haven't lived in a house before. Both my other husbands owned houses, as you know. Neville even had a detached bungalow – although of course he had to move into that bedsit after the divorce.'

'Divorces can be costly affairs,' Charlie mused to himself. Not that he'd been divorced or even married before. But he was beginning to realise that marriages were rather costly too. Especially if you were married to Maureen.

Maureen opened the sliding doors which had kept Charlie up half the night.

'Are these the ones I chose, Charlie?'

'The exact same, my Pumpkin.'

She pushed them shut. 'Hmm. They don't exactly meet in the middle.'

Charlie yanked the handles together. 'There,' he said. 'They almost meet.'

'Move out of the way, you mump head! They should meet flush on and lock together, surely. Otherwise they could cause a draught through to the kitchen.'

Charlie caught his breath. 'Draught?' Charlie abhorred draughts and recently draughts had been on his mind. In fact he'd given a lot of consideration to draughts over the past week or so. For a start the house had no porch, and a house with no porch would by definition be draughty. As soon as the penny dropped that he'd bought a house with no porch, Charlie had been on the blower to a builder he knew. Charlie had specified exactly what he wanted. All breeze blocks and lots of glass. The gaffer told him he'd have to wait for the job to be done. They were booked up until the other side of Easter, he said. But that was before Charlie brought up the subject of his best silverside. Suddenly one of their jobs had been re-scheduled and they were able to fit Charlie in straight away.

On their first night together in their new home Maureen snuggled up to Charlie in bed.

'What's up, Mump?' Maureen asked. 'You seem a bit quiet.'

'There's nothing up, except … maybe there is. I thought you'd be more enthusiastic about the house. Are you sure you like it?'

'Don't be soft. Of course I like it! Although, there's obviously a lot to do. It'll take a while to get up to the standard of Elsie's place – and it is a bit remote.'

'How do you mean remote?'

'I mean it's not near anything. Surely you're familiar with the word remote. For a start, how am I meant to get to the hairdressers'?'

'There's a bus twice a week into town or you could walk to the village. It's not far.'

'Walk? With my feet?'

Charlie had forgotten about Maureen's feet.

'You could always get a lift into town with me in the morning, if you've some shopping to do.'

'But what if I wanted to go later in the day? Why would I want to go into town at eight o'clock in the morning? I'd be hanging about for hours.'

'I could collect you at lunchtime.'

'But that would be too late. I'd want to be *there* at lunchtime if I was having lunch with Linda or something.'

Charlie scratched his head. It was difficult arguing without his teeth in.

'How about if I learned to drive?' Maureen thought aloud. 'I could do with a car, stuck out here.'

'I'll think about it, my Pumpkin.'

'Wasn't there someone you used to know with a second-hand car lot in Furnival Street?'

Charlie perked up. 'Bill Brennan. In fact if my memory serves me right he had his own driving school.'

'Kill two birds with one stone.'

'Exactly, my Pumpkin.' Charlie wriggled his fat butchery fingers under Maureen's negligee. 'We'll see how things go,' he lisped.

Charlie was about to shut the shop for lunch when Archie Jones came in for two pounds of sausages. Charlie lifted the sausages like treasured pets from their tray beneath the counter and lowered them onto the scales.

'Two pounds, spot on Archie.' He reached down for a couple more. 'And another few for luck, eh?'

Archie looked suitably grateful as he handed Charlie half a crown. Charlie lingered over the change.

'Was that your cousin who owned a driving school in Furnival Street, Archie?'

'Driving school? – no, that was our Iris's neighbour's son-in-law. Went bust months ago.'

Charlie's mistake was like a stab in the side. Tarnation. It was too late to ask for those extra sausages back.

'Not thinking of learning to drive, Charlie, old mate? Thought you had a car.'

'No, no. I was thinking about my Maureen. Wants a little runabout now we're out in the sticks.'

'Can't blame her for that, Charlie, my old mate. Women get restless stuck at home all day. Say, why don't you teach her? Save yourself a bob or two. Thanks for the bangers. See you soon, mate.'

Maureen sat in the driver's seat of Charlie's Cortina wearing a pout worthy of a fashion model. Charlie felt uncomfortable and odd, squashed into the passenger seat, out of reach of the controls. It was a bit like being on the wrong side in bed.

Maureen leaned forward to peer out of the windscreen before slumping backwards with a dramatic sigh. 'When I suggested driving lessons, Charlie, I imagined a proper driving instructor turning up outside the house in a Vauxhall Viva, like Elsie's. Surely I shouldn't be expected to drive this thing. It's like a bus.'

Maureen checked her lipstick in the mirror and practiced moving the steering wheel.

'Be gentle, Pumpkin. Gentle. You'll break the bloomin' steering wheel doing that. You're only meant to turn it when the car's in motion. Now, put her into gear, pull out the choke, press down on the accelerator with your right foot, ease your left foot up from the clutch, take your other foot off the brake until you feel the bite.'

Maureen glared at Charlie. 'That's all very well for you, droning on about clutches and bites. *You* know what all these things mean. You know how to drive, besides, I'd need three feet to do all those things at once. Nobody normal could do all those things at once.'

'Three feet? What are you talking about? This isn't getting us anywhere.' Charlie wound down the window and breathed in the fresh air. 'Come on,' he said. 'Move over to the passenger side. I'll drive. You observe.'

Charlie got out while Maureen slid across the front seat. Once he was on the driver's side he turned the key. He drove down Blackberry Lane and turned left at the war memorial.

'Where are we going?'

'I don't know where we're going. Does it matter? So long as you learn to drive.'

'But don't people learning to drive usually sit in the driver's seat?' Maureen said with an even bigger pout.

'Don't complain. And don't be sarcastic. I'm learning you, aren't I? What more do you want?'

'Stop the car!'

'What?'

'Stop the car and turn round. I knew this was a daft idea. I want to go home.'

The next morning Charlie wolfed down his usual breakfast of egg, bacon, sausage, black pudding and beans. He consulted his watch. 'I'd better get going or they'll be queuing on the pavement.'

Maureen lit a Consulate. 'There's not enough to do here, Charlie,' she sighed through an exhalation of smoke. 'I've been thinking…'

'Make it snappy, Maureen,' Charlie said, struggling with his jacket sleeves. 'I haven't got all day. There's a pile of pigs' trotters waiting for me at the shop.'

'I've been thinking…about fitted carpets.'

'Fitted carpets?'

'Yes. Fitted carpets are quite *normal*, Charlie. You make them sound like something from outer space. Most people have fitted carpets nowadays. I mean, just look at that green linoleum with just a square of carpet in the middle. It's so cold and horrible bits of fluff collect in the corners. I don't want to spend the rest of my life sweeping up horrible bits of fluff from corners of linoleum.'

Charlie was making for the door clutching at his chest.

'I mean, Eric bought Elsie proper carpets years ago. Carpets that cover the *whole* floor.'

'We'll talk about it tonight,' he said stepping into the new porch.

'I've seen some in Keele's with a swirly space pattern on them.' Maureen was following him. 'It's supposed to be something to do with that Jury Gregarin. You know, a memento of that foreign spaceman chappie.'

Charlie thought about fitted carpets while he chopped a side of brisket for Mrs Pittle. He might have to work through his lunch hours for a few weeks. But, yes, fitted carpets would reduce the draughts and anyway he knew a man who owned a warehouse where they sold end of rolls. He went home at lunch time to make a few phone calls so someone could come to the house to measure up. They'd have to shuffle things about to make the remnant fit. There'd be a few joins here and there, but what were a few joins if it meant saving a few quid, and keeping Maureen happy?

But even surrounded by fitted carpets Maureen complained of boredom.

'You could visit our neighbours. That woman with all those nippers is around during the day,' Charlie suggested as he sawed through the lamb cutlet Maureen had grilled for his tea.

'Yes,' Maureen studied the pompom on her slipper. 'I was going to invite her round to look at the new kitchen wallpaper, but she's got all those *children*. Imagine the mess they'd make with drinks and biscuits all over the new carpet. Anyway, I don't know her well enough.'

'*Evie*, I've heard the husband calling her. Why don't we invite them round one evening for a cocktail. You said you wanted to entertain more. Just for an hour or so. They can't do much damage in an hour.'

'I suppose so. But I still haven't got a hostess trolley. I don't feel ready for entertaining without a hostess trolley.'

'I doubt anyone around here would expect you to have a hostess trolley and anyway, we've got the cocktail cabinet. I bet she hasn't seen many of those in her lifetime!'

'Sometimes I'm afraid to take my eyes off of our Martin. After what happened to him,' Evie said, as Charlie handed her a Bloody Mary.

'What can I get you to drink, Christian?' Charlie asked returning to the other side of his cocktail cabinet with a white dishcloth slung over his arm.

'Beer'll do me.'

'Are you sure I can't get you something else? A Cinzano, or an eggnog perhaps?'

'No. Ale's fine.'

'Why? What happened to your Martin?' Maureen asked Evie, failing to suppress a yawn.

'Didn't you hear about the people who lived here before you? Everyone in the village knows about them.'

Maureen looked at Evie out of the corner of her eye. 'Heard what?'

'That Mrs McDonald what lived here before you, only stole our Martin from outside the post office in broad daylight. Took him home and tried to pass him off as her own.'

Maureen sat up straight on her chair. 'She never did.'

'I swear on the lives of my boys that's what she did. She was a right mental case,' Christian said, sitting down with his beer.

'I only met her once, but I thought she looked a bit strange. A baby snatcher! Who'd of thought.'

'Yes. She should be in prison by all rights now for what she done. They immigrated to Australia, you know,' Evie said.

'Best place for her,' Maureen added.

'That's what I said. Further away the better.'

'Did she hurt the baby?'

'I don't know – he weren't old enough to say.'

'Suppose not. The husband looked alright,' Maureen observed wistfully.

'David. Yes, he was alright. Couldn't give her a baby, though.'

'Firing blanks, eh?' Charlie laughed.

'You ever been to Canada, Mrs Mullett?' Christian asked when Charlie had turned round to adjust the optics on his cocktail cabinet. Evie had gone upstairs to the bathroom and Christian was sitting on the sofa beside Maureen with his sleeves rolled up, still in his working boots. His eyes were directed at a spot in the distance beyond Maureen's new gold striped curtains.

'No I haven't. But my Linda's often spoke about moving out there.'

'That's where I'm planning to head for. Canada, or the Falkland Islands. Somewhere like that."

'The Falkland Islands? But they're in Scotland aren't they?'

Christian laughed. 'No, off the coast of Africa. As soon as our Edmund finishes college, you won't see me for dust.'

'But what about Evie and the children?'

Christian scowled and gave her a sideways look. 'They'd come with me, of course.'

Charlie turned around. Maureen looked as if she'd been in on a promise but had lost out at the last minute.

They stood by the sink, Charlie washing whilst Maureen dried.

'That wasn't so bad, was it? Seem like a nice enough couple. He can fair put the drink away, though. I'd 'ave had to make a trip to the offy if they'd stayed any longer.'

'At least they didn't bring all their brats,' Maureen said, handing Charlie a cocktail glass to dry. "But did you hear what she said about that McDonald woman. I knew there was something dodgy about her. We're living in a house previously owned by a mental case. A baby-snatcher. I don't like it, Charlie. I mean I don't like it one little bit.'

'But she's not here now. She's gone. Australia. Couldn't get much further away if she tried.'

'I knew there was something up the minute I clapped eyes on her. This kitchen still has the feel of her. Even now with the new wallpaper her presence is still in this house. In this room. Now I come to think about it, I've felt it since day one.'

'Don't be silly.'

'I'm not being silly. I've been thinking. About one of those fitted kitchens. I think we should rip this lot out. The sink where she washed her pots, the cupboard where she kept her cabbages or whatever she ate. Get rid of this old table and chairs where she sat when she was planning her kidnapping. Everyone in Felixstowe has fitted units. A stainless steel sink. Matching cupboards with red handles and a Formica table. I'll tell you something for nothing, Charlie. We'd be social outcasts in Felixstowe with a kitchen like this.'

'But we're not in Felixstowe…'

Maureen emptied the water from the sink. 'In fact, I was talking to Elsie the other day on the telephone…'

'Not for too long I hope, Pump. You know how the bills mount up, my petal.'

'You and your bills. What do you expect me to do all day if I'm not on the phone? Sit crocheting doilies? No – and you'll never guess what Elsie's got. A dishwasher! Her Eric had it shipped over from America. "I've thrown my Marigolds in the dustbin," Elsie said. And Audrey Mickelthwaite – you know the one I told you about. Elsie's friend – plucked eyebrows and bandy legs – well, Audrey was so miffed, she sent her Stanley off straight away to order one for her. And look at me. I haven't even got a twin tub. I must be the only woman this side of London who still has to scrub everything in the sink. Imagine the difference a twin tub would make to my feet…'

The more Maureen spoke, the more Charlie felt his spirits drain and the hope that he might be able to shut the shop for a couple of weeks during the summer fizzled into an unattainable dream. 'I don't think we can afford any more gadgets at the moment,' Charlie said.

'Gadgets? Dishwashers and twin tubs are essentials to people like Elsie and Audrey. So why shouldn't they be to us? I don't refer to your knives and meat hook thingies as *gadgets*. I'm going up,' she said, hanging up the dishcloth. 'I've got a headache.'

'Evie's learning to drive,' Maureen told Charlie over dinner. 'Christian's teaching her. I saw them go off together in that awful Morris Minor this morning.'

Charlie aimed more tomato sauce at his sprouts. 'Maybe she'll offer you a lift into town once in a while.'

'She might. But that's not the same as having my own car. If you remember, you did promise me a Vauxhall Viva, like Elsie's.'

'When did I promise you a Vauxhall Viva like Elsie's? I've never even seen Elsie's Vauxhall Viva.'

'You promised, Charlie! Just like you promised you'd teach me to drive. Do you know what? I think I'll ask Elsie to teach me, even if I do have to go all the way to Felixstowe for a month.'

'No, no. There's no need for that. I'll ask Stringer if he'll learn you. A Morris Minor is every bit as good as those new Vivas.'

Christian Stringer parked his sheep truck outside Number Two and honked the horn.

Maureen had just finished gluing her second eyelash into place. She looked out of the window and blinked in disbelief. 'If that thing's meant to be in the same league as a Vauxhall Viva then you're Gregory Peck,' she told Charlie.

'At least there's no sheep in there, Pump. Could be worse. You'd better get a shift on. He's waiting.'

'Ugh – but there's a dog on the seat. You know I can't bear animals.'

'Hurry. You can't keep him waiting – he is doing us a favour, you know.'

Maureen arrived home an hour later.

'How did it go?' Charlie asked.

'Mr Stringer drove to the other side of the village. He said the roads round here are too narrow for a learner. We stopped by the football pitch and swapped places so I was in the driving seat. I put both hands on the steering wheel at ten-to-two, which is like this,' Maureen demonstrated the ten-to-two position. 'Then he told me what to do. He said I had to... look in the mirror, turn the key to do something to the engine, put my right foot on one pedal and my other foot on the clutch thing and wait till I felt the bite. If that dog hadn't been there whining on the seat beside me every time the engine stalled, it would've been easy as pie.'

'That's pretty much what I told you to do. But it went alright? I mean I've already paid him several times over in faggots plus the promise of a goose this coming Christmas.'

'Yes. It did go alright. Christian kept saying "Never mind, Mrs Mullett. You're doing fine." He was a lot calmer than you, Charlie, a lot more encouraging. He's picking me up the same time next week. I'm looking forward to it already.'

After her third lesson when Maureen came home Charlie opened the door for her but she pushed past him and ran straight upstairs. Charlie noticed one of her eyelashes was hanging like a dead spider on her cheek.

'Are you alright, Maureen?' he asked.

'Fine,' she called down from the landing. 'Just tripped getting out of that infernal truck. Is there any hot water? I'm going to have a bath.'

When she came downstairs, she was in her dressing gown and her wet hair made a damp patch on the material between her shoulder blades.

'How about a spot of tongue for tea?' Charlie said as he reached for the dinner plates. 'How did the lesson go?'

'Fine. I'm not hungry, though. I'm cold,' she said, pulling her dressing gown belt tighter round her waist. 'I think I might be coming down with something. I'm going to have an early night.'

Charlie sat alone at the kitchen table masticating his way through his tongue and pease pudding, reading the paper as he ate. Eventually after he'd watched a bit of *This Is Your Life* and the news, and had a drop of brandy, he stomped up the stairs, went into the bathroom and took out his teeth.

In bed, Charlie's heart was racing. Maybe he should drop that medicinal nightcap. The house was silent except for the sound of his heart beating and Maureen's breathing. She hadn't closed the curtains properly so he could see the black sky through the window with a perfectly full moon. A barn owl hooted. Some of the country sounds could be eerie. Unsettling. He thought about Christian and Evie Stringer in bed on the other side of the wall. He and Maureen listened to them sometimes. Occasionally they'd hear raised voices, more often than not, children crying. Tonight, though, all was still and within moments Charlie was snoring. He was dreaming. In his dream a sheep was standing outside his shop holding a shopping bag and a shopping list in its mouth. Suddenly it was speaking – in Maureen's voice.

'Charlie?' Maureen slipped her arm half-way over his stomach.

'What?' he said. 'You gave me a fright. I thought you were a sheep, I mean asleep.'

'Do you love me, Charlie?'

'Huh?'

'Charlie, I'm cold.'

'You're not on about central heating again, are you?' Charlie mumbled. 'How many times do I have to tell you? We aren't on the gas mains and if we had electric, it would cost...'

'I'm not thinking about heating. It's the driving lessons. I'm not going to have any more.'

'Alright.'

'I don't get on with Christian Stringer.'

'Really? Why not? He seems a decent enough chap.'

'We've got nothing in common... I do love you, Charlie.'

'What?'

'Nothing. I just said I love you.'

'And I love you. But I still don't want to be giving away good meat to pay for driving lessons that nobody's going to have...'

'I wish that Stringer family were a million miles away. I wish they'd go to Canada or the whatsit Islands, or wherever they were going.'

'What have they done to deserve that?' Charlie yawned and resumed his rattling snores before Maureen had a chance to answer which meant he didn't see the patch of wet Maureen's tears made on her pillowcase.

Charlie had considered borrowing money to invest in a second shop, but whenever he thought about anything to do with his finances those little butterflies banging against his ribs made him stop. The last time he'd exercised his rights as a husband, he'd thought his chest might explode. He felt so tired these days, he couldn't even be bothered with his usual bit of bedtime reading before he turned off the light. Charlie's December copy of *Meat Marketing Monthly* lay unopened on the floor by his bed. It was time to admit defeat. Charlie made an appointment with the doctor for lunchtime the following Thursday.

Dr Webber conducted his surgery in his house. His lounge had been converted into a waiting room, and he saw his patients in what had once been the parlour. The waiting room walls were flanked with chairs. Several matching dining chairs with hard hide seats, some kitchen chairs and stools, and a pair of armchairs. Posters covered the green distemper on the walls. *Coughs and Sneezes Spread Diseases*. Free Orange Juice for children under Five.

Drinka Pinta Milka Day. Charlie sat on one of the kitchen chairs and flicked through an old copy of *Punch*. Most of the jokes were to do with men playing golf, others showed couples looking out of panoramic windows in fancy houses. Charlie had never played golf and although he was sure Maureen would have loved one of those modern houses, he couldn't see what was funny. None of the jokes made him laugh.

The doctor called Charlie's name. He went into the surgery, puffed and sat down. He was breathless but Charlie put that down to the anxiety of abandoning his body to the mercy of a member of the medical profession. There was something about doctors. As far as doctors were concerned it didn't matter who you knew or who you knew who knew someone else in the know. Having contacts counted for nothing in the world of medicine.

'Take your shirt off, Mr Mullett.' As Dr Webber spoke, the phone on his desk rang.

'Yes, yes. Put her through, please,' the doctor said. 'Ah, yes – the results of your test. Now ...' He flicked through some pieces of paper on his desk. 'It's good news! Your test was positive!' Dr Webber put the phone down and scratched his head.

'Now that's a strange coincidence...' he began, but then gave Charlie an uncertain look as if he were about to say something but changed his mind.

Charlie wished the quack would get on with it. He sat on the other side of the desk in his vest and trousers with his braces dangling, gazing out of the window as Dr Webber took his blood pressure. A jackdaw had landed on a bird table in the middle of the lawn and was nicking away at a bag of nuts. Charlie always marvelled at the paucity of flesh on birds.

'Now, Mr Mullet. If you'd like to get dressed...' The doctor took a fountain pen from his top pocket and wrote with a flourish on a prescription pad. 'You're most likely suffering from angina. Take these,' he said, presenting him with the prescription, 'and come back in six months.'

Charlie strode out of the surgery as if his life had been saved. Like a man who'd been condemned to death, only to have his sentence revoked a moment before the noose was due to be tightened around his neck. Angina. That didn't sound too bad. It didn't have the words 'heart' or 'attack' in it. Angina was a calm, friendly word. Charlie didn't mind having Angina. He felt so relieved, he could have skipped off to the chemist to get the prescription made up – if he'd been younger…and thinner …and didn't have angina.

That night he poured himself a double whisky from the cocktail cabinet and a *Cinzano Bianco* for Maureen. Maureen hardly touched her drink, but Charlie was too preoccupied with his pork chops and tinned peas to mention the fact. After tea, while they sat in the front room watching *Take Your Pick*, Maureen took a deep breath and closed her eyes.

'Charlie?' she said. 'I've been meaning to tell you about a friend of Elsie's.'

'Oh, yes…' Charlie said, without taking his eyes from the screen.

'This friend of Elsie's, she lives near Felixstowe, and she asked Elsie, and Elsie asked me… if I knew of anyone who….'

'If I knew what? Where to get the best pork chops and pigs' livers in Somerset?' Charlie chuckled. 'A bit far for a home delivery, Felixstowe.'

'No, don't be daft. What she was asking was… whether I knew anyone who… performed … abortions. I don't suppose you know of anyone, do you?'

'Hold on, I'm trying to watch this.'

'But, Charlie, I said I'd phone her tonight. I said I'd ask if you knew of anyone in that line. I don't suppose you do?'

Charlie turned his attention away from Michael Miles. 'Back street abortionists? How in the name of the devil would I know anyone like that? You can tell that friend of a friend of yours that I'm a butcher of defenceless animals not human beings. Whatever does that Elsie take me for? You can tell her from me that a woman shouldn't go getting in the family way, not nowadays when men can have the snip on the National Health. Look at me. I've had it done. Easy as pie. What your friend of a friend needs is a bottle of gin and a knitting needle.'

'But you do know a lot of people,' Maureen persisted. 'You've got contacts. You do pride yourself on your contacts. And there's contacts of contacts. I just thought you might know of someone who…' Maureen looked as if she might be about to cry. Michael Miles was offering the contestant sixty pounds for her box. 'Take the money!' Charlie shouted at the television. 'Take the money! Did you see that? The silly woman won a bag of sweets. Ha. I said she should've taken the money!' Charlie was so agitated, bouncing up and down on the settee, that the annoying pain came back. He went out to the hall to take one of the angina pills he had hidden in his coat pocket, then went upstairs and pulled the chain so Maureen would think he'd only got up in the middle of *Take Your Pick* because he needed the toilet.

Inside an old copy of *Meat Marketing Monthly*, under the bed, Charlie hid what he called his "special book", a magazine with pictures of naked women. Since his visit to the doctor Charlie felt like a new man, confident that he could once more do what he wanted with Maureen without those pains interrupting his pleasure. But now he had his ticker sorted Maureen had presented him with a fresh set of problems. In fact he'd never have married her in the first place if he'd known she was going to turn frigid on him.

Charlie could hardly bring himself to tot up the amount he'd shelled out on wallpaper, the log effect fire, the new porch and the sliding doors, fitted kitchen, fitted carpets, even the laminate encased hostess trolley. Now she had another gripe. There was an unpleasant smell coming from their garden.

'Charlie. That smell really is the last straw. It's making me feel sick. I think we should look at one of those new houses on the Greenside Estate. I've heard they're really nice.'

'I'm sure they are nice, Pumpkin. They're probably a nice price too. That smell is the cesspit. It needs emptying, that's all. Next time I see Hershaw, I'll get him round.'

Maureen hesitated and shook a last *Consulate* from a packet in her dressing gown pocket. 'I'd like to move, Charlie. I met a woman yesterday. A gypsy selling lavender in the village. She asked me if I lived in Blackberry Lane. It was frightening, Charlie. She said I should leave here immediately. She really put the wind up me.'

'What nonsense. Those gypsies will say anything to sell a clothes peg.'

'But she said we should leave if we wanted happiness. Charlie, I think she was right. Some of those gypsies have special powers, and since I packed in the driving lessons… I know I'm never going to be able to drive. I can see that now. I haven't got the coordination. I could walk into town from the Greenside Estate. And there wouldn't be that foul smell.'

Hold on a minute. Stopped driving lessons? Since when did you stop driving lessons?'

'Weeks ago. I told you…when we were in bed, remember?'

'Stopped driving lessons! That Stringer's a sly one. I've paid that blighter enough faggots to run a bloody driving school.'

'Please don't say anything, Charlie. It was my idea to stop. I did tell you. We were in bed. You must remember. Or, maybe you were half asleep at the time. But I wasn't learning nothing with Christian Stringer. I'm no good at driving – you were right. I'm more of a passenger.'

Charlie was about to resign himself to a lifetime's chastity when Maureen surprised him by snuggling up to him the following Sunday morning. She stroked his lower back in the place he liked to be stroked. Before long he was heaving his bulk on top of her, chugging up and down like a pair of bellows. In out, in out. Puff, blow. Puff, blow.

'Charlie?' Maureen said when he'd finished.

'What, my Pumpkin?'

'Was that nice?'

'It's been a long time, my Pump. I'll say that.'

'But worth waiting for?'

Charlie kissed her ear by way of an answer.

'I was wondering, Mump,' Maureen went on, '…do we have any spare money? Only I need twenty pounds… to lend my Linda.'

'Twenty pounds?' Charlie sat up in bed. 'What does your Linda need twenty pounds for? She hasn't lost her job, has she?'

'No, of course not, but she needs some cash … for a deposit on a new flat.'

'New flat? What's wrong with the old one?'

'I don't know. I just promised I'd get it for her. She's never asked me for money before. You don't understand what it's like having children, Charlie. If you had any of your own, you'd realise it's only natural to want to help them.'

'Your Linda's hardly a child. Anyway, why doesn't she ask her father? Perhaps he'd be better at understanding what it's like to have children.'

'Herbert doesn't have any money. If you lent her the money, I could ask her for interest. That way you would make a profit.'

Charlie thought it over. True, he did have some spare cash set aside. And he liked the idea of making some interest on it. And he'd just had sex for the first time in months.

'I'll have a look for my post office savings book,' he said.

A pile of boxes that neither Charlie or Maureen had got round to unpacking was stacked in the little room at the back of the house. The room was hot and musty. It had no curtains and the morning sun picked out speckles of dust in the air.

Charlie remembered which box he needed. It had *Ovaltine* written on the side and Charlie quite enjoyed a mug of Ovaltine in the winter. Inside were some of Maureen's things. An envelope containing her Pitman's typing certificate (ninety-five words a minute); her shorthand certificate (thirty); her birth certificate; all her marriage certificates, and her two decree nisis, as well as several piles of Green Shield stamp books which were held together with an elastic band.

Charlie took out one of the Green Shield stamp books. When they'd first met Maureen had showed them to him, flicking through the pages as though sharing a photograph album. Some stamps she'd stuck in individually, others had come in large sheets, some she'd simply stuck the wrong way up as if she'd been in too much of a hurry to bother. Now most of them curled at the edges from age, some pages were fused together. The books represented the story of her life – the things she'd bought and the stamps that had been her reward for spending her husbands' money. Maureen had been saving for a set of table mats with London scenes on them.

St Paul's in the snow, Piccadilly Circus in the rain, the Houses of Parliament glowing under a setting sun. Charlie had seen the catalogue, although she'd obviously never cashed the books in. He counted them. Twenty-three. Maybe she'd collected enough for one table mat and a plastic tumbler to go on it, Charlie thought, as he tucked the books back into the elastic band.

Charlie's bits and pieces were in an envelope underneath. His post office savings account and some Premium Bonds. He picked up his National Savings Account book. The last amount scribbled on the page was thirty-four pounds, seven shillings and six pence. He might be due a few shillings in interest, but thirty odd quid, twenty-three Green Shield stamp books, and a few Premium Bonds was hardly an impressive amount of savings between them.

Charlie was about to leave the room when he noticed a small door on the wall opposite the window. It was wooden, flush with the wall, with an old fashioned black circular wrought iron handle. He hadn't noticed this cupboard before. If he had, he'd certainly have thought about getting rid of that awful handle and replacing it with a red plastic one.

Charlie had to move some of the boxes to get to the cupboard. He turned the handle, still holding his post office account book, and peered inside. The damp smell was like a fug of mould. A spider scuttled away into a corner, but, although the cupboard appeared at first to be empty, he thought he could see something. Charlie stood on one of the boxes so he could reach inside. It was a bag. A large shopping bag with the word Keele's printed on the side. So, Maureen had been on secret spending sprees during her trips into town. But Christmas had already gone and Charlie's birthday wasn't until October. Still, it was their anniversary in June. But why would Maureen buy a secret present for their anniversary when in the past they'd only celebrated with a couple of fillet steaks? He tugged at the side of the bag so that it slid towards him. When Charlie looked inside, he recoiled as if he'd just been confronted with human remains. But in a way, as far as Charlie was concerned, it contained something equally sinister. The bag was stuffed with children's toys. A doll, a teddy bear and a clockwork monkey. All brand new, still with price tags on them. Charlie stepped away from the bag. Why would Maureen buy toys? She didn't know anyone who had children – except for Evie. Could she be buying toys for Evie's children? She didn't even like them. Was her Linda expecting? She'd never been with a man, as far as Charlie knew. In fact, he'd always suspected she preferred women. If Linda had been expecting, Maureen would surely have told Charlie, not gone out secretly buying toys. And what was all that nonsense about knowing someone who performed abortions? If her Linda was expecting and wanted an abortion, then why buy toys?

Charlie arranged them in a row on the floor. They all looked disconcertingly human, staring up at him with glass eyes. Presumably Maureen hadn't bought them for *herself*. She had that infernal Gonk plonked on her pillow every night. Surely she wasn't planning on increasing the number of stuffed things on their bed. Or, maybe they were substitute children. They'd agreed together on Charlie's vasectomy but perhaps she was getting broody after all. But no. Charlie understood how Maureen felt about children. She'd had her Linda when she was seventeen and would be the first to admit she'd never been a natural when it came to motherhood.

Inside the bag was a receipt. The toys had come to a total of nine shillings and sixpence. He felt like returning them to the shop. Yes, that was what he'd do. Spending his money on toys! That would teach her.

Charlie took the bag downstairs when Maureen was in the bath, put it in the boot of the Cortina and popped into Keele's during his lunch hour the next day. The store guide indicated that the toy department was in the basement and his heart sank when he saw the steep staircase leading down from the ground floor, but he carried on down and placed the bag on the counter.

'I'd like a refund on these, please.'

The shop assistant peered into the bag. 'Do you have the receipt, sir?'

'It's in there.' Charlie felt anxious to escape. He'd left his tablets at work and beads of sweat were running down his neck.

The woman asked him to fill out a form she produced from under the till, stating the reason the goods were unsuitable.

Just as he started on his address the woman interrupted him. 'Er... excuse me, sir, but when did you say you bought these?' she asked scrutinising the receipt through a pair of glasses she had hanging on a chain around her neck.

He cleared his throat. 'I didn't buy them myself. I'm returning them for a friend.'

'It appears your friend bought these in December 1958. Goods have to be returned within six months of purchase for a refund, sir, not four years!'

He was getting hotter and hotter. 'I hadn't read the receipt properly,' he snapped. 'They're not mine anyway. Just keep the damn things.'

The woman at the till flinched and Charlie returned to the steep staircase. All this for nine shillings and sixpence – that he didn't even get. He climbed the stairs slowly, pausing halfway to catch his breath and mop his neck with his hanky.

The butcher's was quiet for the rest of the afternoon. Charlie was glad of the peace and the fact that he didn't have to make conversation with customers who seemed to do nothing but complain about strikes and the price of beef. He picked up the cloth he used to wipe his carving knife. He liked the feel of the blade beneath the cloth. He dampened it, then used it again to wipe his chopper, his meat cleaver, and the wooden chopping block. He unhooked the carcass of beef hanging behind him and lifted up the chopper. Bang. The bone split in two. Charlie wiped the blood from the chopper, took one half of the carcass and cut it into chunks. Each one exactly an inch thick. Butchery was a trade of precision. He knew Maureen thought he just sold chunks of meat wrapped in paper bags to customers who chatted about their bunions, but he wasn't called a Master Butcher for nothing.

At half past four he'd just started cashing up when the bell jangled and Brian Hershaw came in for some black pudding. Charlie weighed out the black curly sausages, wrapped them in a sheet of white paper and handed them to Brian.

'Say, Brian,' he said as Brian handed him some coins, 'you still in the cleaning business? Only I'd be much obliged if you'd have a look at our cesspit– it's been a bit pongy these last few weeks.'

'When would you like it doing? Just say the word. Up by Stringers now, aren't you?'

Charlie nodded. 'Soon as possible,' he said. 'Here, take a half pound of mince – on the house.'

Brian handed back the paper parcel for the addition of the mince.

When Charlie got home the house was in darkness. He switched on the lights and fetched a whisky from his cocktail cabinet. He noticed the gin bottle was missing from its optic. That was odd, he thought. All the bottles had been there the night before, and Maureen wasn't a spirit drinker. She wasn't much of a drinker at all these days. Recently she'd hardly touched the Cinzano Bianco. Surely she wasn't turning to the hard stuff. When he went upstairs, he realised Maureen was in fact home and was in the bath again. The door was locked but the window above it was steamed up.

'I'm home,' Charlie shouted. 'Shut up early. Maureen, are you alright in there?'

There was no answer, so Charlie went into the bedroom to change his trousers. As he undid his braces he thought he could hear the sound of retching coming from the bathroom.

He went onto the landing and banged on the door. 'Maureen? Are you alright in there?'

Maureen appeared wrapped in a towel, looking sheepish. Her black hair hung limply around her face, some strands stuck to her pale cheeks.

'Maureen, whatever's the matter? You look like you've seen a ghost. And why have you got the *Gordons* up here? And you're not planning on taking up knitting…'

Charlie's breathing became laboured so he couldn't finish his sentence and Maureen began to cry.

'Rape? You're saying Stringer – *raped* – you? When he was meant to be learning you how to drive. Maureen this is… this is… I ought to go round there and strangle the bastard now.'

'No, Charlie. Don't do that. I don't think he meant any harm.'

'What're you talking about? You said he tried to *rape* you. That he *did* rape you. How could he not mean any harm? In the name of the devil, was it rape or not? If it is, it's a matter for the police.'

'It was rape. I swear it was. As good as. I would never have encouraged him... Charlie you know I wouldn't have. But I don't think we should go to the police.'

Charlie lowered himself onto the bed, the springs creaking under his weight.

'The man's a danger to the community. Why didn't you say anything before?'

'I don't know, Charlie. Keep your voice down. They might hear. I didn't want any trouble and I was afraid. I mean, they live so close. And I didn't come on to him. I don't even like him.' Maureen sat on the bed next to Charlie. She was shaking as she held her Gonk close to her chest. 'Please, Charlie. Can't we just get an abortion and put all this behind us?'

'How can we do that, Maureen? Abortion's illegal. Rape's bloody illegal.'

'Please don't shout, Charlie. Don't be angry. If you throw me out, I don't know what I'll do. I mean, you've never minded things being illegal before.'

'Throw you out? Why would I throw you out? I am angry, though. I'm angry with that bastard, Stringer. And the odd bribe with a pound of sausage meat. A cheap bit of carpet off the back of a lorry. That's hardly the same thing as a man raping my wife. In broad daylight. And an abortion. Where would you get an abortion in this country that wasn't in some back street hovel?'

'I don't know, Charlie. I don't know...'

'And the expense. This is going to cost, Maureen.'

'I think it's only twenty quid.'

'*Only* twenty quid! Which reminds me – that friend of yours who was looking for an abortion – and that twenty quid for your Linda. That was all to do with this, wasn't it? A deposit on a new flat, my foot. Why couldn't you tell me the truth?'

'I didn't want to upset you.'

'I am upset, though. You think a man's going to stand by while his neighbour interferes with his wife? I'll tell you for nothing,

Maureen, I'll swing for that bastard, Stringer, next time I see him.'

'Charlie, there's no need for that…'

Charlie stood up. 'In fact, I'm going round there now, hang the consequences. Nobody makes a fool of Charlie Mullet. Where's my coat?'

'Charlie – no. Violence won't solve anything. He'd only lie and say I made a pass at him. Anyway, I doubt he'd be in. He spends most of his evenings in the pub. So you'd only be upsetting Evie and the children.'

Charlie sat down and rubbed his chest. 'I suppose you're right. If he's not there, he's not there. And if I did go round, Evie could warn him, so he'd be ready for me. I reckon he could be violent – especially if he's had a skinful. Maybe I should wait…'

Maureen lifted her Gonk to her cheek. 'Yes, Charlie. Please don't do anything hasty.'

'And those toys? What about those toys I found in that cupboard in the box room?'

'What toys? I've never even opened the door to that cupboard.'

'Kid's toys. A bag full of them.'

'They probably belonged to that mad woman. The one who was always stealing kids.'

There had been films Charlie and Maureen had watched together where abortions were performed by dodgy characters in grimy half-lit rooms. They'd seen one where a girl handed over a wad of notes and waited while an old woman with a flannel and a bowl of steaming water in the background counted the money with greedy fingers. The scene switched from the room to the corridor outside, with the girl's screams echoing down the hallway. Charlie tried to think – there must be someone he knew in this line of work.

He turned to the classified page in the local paper… A. Animals for sale. Articles for Sale. B. Books for sale. Books wanted. He realised he was being absurd. As if illegal abortions were going to be advertised in the local rag under A for Abortions.

On Tuesday morning Charlie felt too ill to open up the shop. Instead he stayed in bed until nine. When he came downstairs Maureen was standing at the ironing board working her way through a pile of his shirts. Swish, swish, back and forward, fold and start again. She'd got behind with the laundry which meant Charlie had worn a dirty shirt to work the previous morning. In fact, she'd got behind with all the housework, despite the twin tub and the Hoover Charlie had got her on the drip. He'd practically bitten her head off when she'd mentioned an electric toaster though, and told her to stick the bread under the grill like everybody else.

Charlie's shirt was pale blue with a detachable collar. Maureen ironed down one arm, down the other and over the large expanse of the back. She sprayed starch on the collar and pressed the label. Size sixteen-and-a-half. There had been a time when Maureen had commented on the manliness of Charlie's size. Both her other husbands had only been fourteens.

Maureen hung the shirt on a hanger, and Charlie noticed she'd missed a bit on the front, but things like that no longer seemed important.

'Maureen, I think you should ask the quack for an abortion. I'm already spending more than I'm earning. And I'm not well. He knows about it. The quack already knows. Not only that, but I'm too old to be a father. And you – I mean you could be a grandmother – if your Linda had ever had any boyfriends, that is…' Charlie coughed. 'Tell him what I said. There must be some circumstances where he could arrange to get rid of it on the National Health. Plead with him, anything.'

'What do you mean you're not well? You don't mean you're going to die?'

'Die? Hells bells, no. It's just the chest,' he said patting his ribs. 'The ticker, to be precise…'

'Your heart? Charlie, you need to lose some weight.'

'No, no. It's nothing to do with weight. The quack says it's something called Angina. That's what them pills are for.'

'The vitamin pills in the brown bottle?'

'You haven't been taking them, have you?'

'No, of course not.'

'I didn't want to worry you. But Webber gave them to me for my ticker. It's a bit dodgy sometimes. Nothing to worry about, but it might be a reason for him to put you forward for an abortion.'

'But it's not *my* heart that's dodgy.'

Charlie banged his fist on the kitchen table. 'You could try, Maureen. Try phoning him now.'

Maureen jumped. She blew her nose, turned off the iron and went into the hall. She picked up the receiver only to put it straight down again. 'Evie's on the phone,' she said with a sniff. 'If she's talking to one of her friends, she could be hours.'

'Here let me do it,' Charlie said, going over to the phone. I'll tell her to shut the hell up and get off the line.'

But just before he picked up the phone, he stopped. There was a noise outside of an engine followed by a knock at the door. Brian Hershaw stood in the porch in his navy overalls.

'Here to empty the cesspit, Charlie. Morning, Mrs Mullet! Might want to make sure all the windows are closed. Smell can be a bit iffy.' Mr Hershaw laughed and Charlie noticed Maureen smile for what seemed the first time in weeks.

The windows were already shut tight. Unbattened windows meant draughts and Charlie had had all the windows sealed for the winter. It was a cold morning with a westerly wind blowing across the fields opposite.

'Least the wind's blowing in the right direction,' Mr Hershaw pointed out. 'You don't want an easterly, for example. That would mean the smell would waft towards the house,'

Maureen shuddered at the thought.

'House is north facing, if I'm right?' Hershaw went on.

Maureen looked blank. 'I'm not one for geography. Could never see the point of it at school,' she explained before turning to Charlie.

'Yes, north-facing, Brian,' Charlie confirmed.

As Brian Hershaw lugged his hose along the side of the house and out to the far corner of the garden, Maureen filled the kettle and took three cups and saucers from her best tea service. She and Charlie peered through the tiny kitchen window and watched as he levered open the stone covering to the cesspit in the corner of the garden by the smaller apple tree and sunk the hose into the hole.

'I never knew that was the cess-thingy,' Maureen said. 'So that's what that dreadful smell was.'

On his way back to the lorry, Brian Hershaw passed the kitchen window, doffed his cap and gave them both cheery grin. He jumped up into the driving seat and started up the engine. The noise invaded the house, and despite the closed windows, the smell crept in too. The purring of the engine mingled with the sound of the steam blowing from the kettle gave Charlie goosebumps on the tops of his arms and he forgot about the abortion, wanting to kill Christian Stringer, and Evie being on the party line. When he'd finished, Brian Hershaw knocked jauntily on the back door and gave Charlie the bill.

'I'm afraid I'll have to settle up with you later. Although I've got some ribeye steaks in the fridge...'

Hershaw looked disappointed, as if his favourite game had been ruined. Or maybe he was remembering that extra half pound of mince Charlie had passed his way and hoping that wasn't presumed to be in lieu of payment.

'...but my Maureen'll make you some Bovril if you'd like to come in.'

Brian looked down at his overalls. 'Wouldn't want to dirty your lovely kitchen,' he said.

'That's all right. I'll get some newspaper.' Charlie opened a copy of the *Daily Express* and made a pathway of paper from the back door to the kitchen table, while Maureen placed a page on the chair for Mr Hershaw to sit on. He laughed as he took giant steps, carefully moving from page to page as if he was in a game of hopscotch.

Maureen handed him his Bovril.

'How long you been here now?' Brian asked. 'I've only emptied you this once. You were pretty full.'

'We've been here over a year, but the people before us were a bit vacant,' Maureen explained. 'The woman was, anyway. Probably didn't even know they had a pit-thingy.'

Brian frowned with disbelief.

'Where is it you live now?' Charlie passed the biscuit tin to Brian.

'I've just bought one of them new houses on the Greenside Estate.'

'The Greenside? Where all those detached houses are?' Maureen joined in. 'I bet your wife likes it up there.'

'Wife?' Brian chuckled. 'No. I live on me jacksy.'

'You're not married then?'

'Never have been. Always looking for the perfect woman. Never found her yet.' Brian chuckled some more and Maureen offered to top up his Bovril.

'How long have you been doing this job?' she asked pointing vaguely towards the garden.

'Years. Years and years. Though it's not a job, if you don't mind me saying, Mrs Mullett. Cleansing is what you would call a career, a vocation, a *calling*. There's something very satisfying – and necessary – about the egress of dirt and human waste.'

'I can imagine.' Maureen clutched her stomach. 'I'm just popping upstairs,' she said, leaving the room.

Charlie coughed to break the silence. 'I don't suppose you would know anyone who…'

'Who what, Charlie?' Brian said, blowing on his cup of Bovril.

'Anyone who could …extract other kinds of matter …'

'Other kinds of matter? You mean silage?'

'No, no. It's just that a friend of mine is in a bit of bother. She's looking for someone to… you know,' Charlie leant over the table and whispered, "perform an abortion.'

Hershaw roared with laughter. 'I don't think I'd ever get that hose of mine up your friend!'

'No I don't suppose you would.' Charlie coughed again and rubbed his chest. He began busying himself by clearing up the cups and plates and arranging them around the washing up bowl.

'I've been thinking,' Maureen said as she sat at her dressing table back-combing her hair. 'About what that cess-thing man said about his new house on the housing estate. I mean, couldn't we have a house there? I've seen them and they're lovely new modern houses.'

'But we already live in a new house, Pumpkin.'

'Hardly,' Maureen said with a snort. 'It's over twenty years old. More like a museum. Plus it's a semi. The estate houses are all detached. Please, Charlie. I don't like it here anymore. It smells of cows and with him next door... '

'I see your point. But those houses are expensive.'

'I'm sure I'd be much happier somewhere else, and if I was happier I think you would be too. We could start all over again.'

'I'll make some enquiries next time I'm passing.'

Just as Charlie was shutting up shop the following evening Brian Hershaw arrived.

'Hello,' Charlie said. 'What brings you here? I'll get the money for you at the end of the week.'

'It's not about the money, Charlie, mate,' Brian said with a smile. 'To do with that "friend" of yours. You know the one who was looking for an ...' he silently shaped his mouth into the last word.

'You'd best come in,' Charlie said. 'Is there anything I can get you? I've got a good piece of rump fillet. Been hanging in the fridge for a fortnight. Nice and dark. Would go down a treat in a mixed grill...'

'No, Charlie, thanks all the same, but I'll get straight to the point. Didn't like the look of your Maureen yesterday. No, no... let me finish. I don't mean nothing bad by it. I mean your Maureen – she's a looker. Not that I'd ever... you know, but I always thought she had something of the Sophia Loren about her. Though obviously your Maureen's much thinner and less...you know...in the ...' Brian cupped both hands in front of his chest. 'But she wasn't looking herself yesterday, and then you came out with that stuff about abortions, so, to cut a long story short, I reckon I might be able to help you there. If the problem's what I think it is.'

Charlie wiped the end of his knife with his cloth.

'This woman I know,' Brian went on. "Used to be a nurse. Visited her years ago with my in-growing toenail. I could put you in touch with her. All hush-hush. She does it to help women who are in trouble.'

Charlie wiped another knife.

'So, where is she, this nurse?'

'Mary Cray? She lives in the village. Involved in a bit of a scandal, she was – long time ago. Had an affair with a married man – ex- soldier, died years ago, used to be a midwife, and now she's pretty much a recluse. She likes helping other women, though. Knows what she's doing. Strong-minded. Thinks all women got the right to choose whether or not they bring a new life into this world. She probably needs the bit of extra cash too,' Brian finished with a sympathetic smile.

At lunchtime Charlie drove to the new estate in Greenside. He parked outside the show house which was one of rows identical in design. Each had an open porch and a yard of grass in front of the bay window. Charlie felt uneasy. He'd got used to his closed-in porch in Blackberry Lane. Still, if he did decide to buy one of these houses, he could probably find someone to finish the porch off with a door, some double-glazing and a few more breezeblocks.

All he had to do was find some money, which meant increasing his trade. Recently things had been looking up. Fresh chickens were the latest thing. He'd struck a deal with a chicken farm near Shapton. A hundred chickens a week for only seven-and-six each. He reckoned if he sold each chicken for fourteen and three ha'pence he'd be able to put all his money worries behind him – and take out a bigger mortgage to buy a house on the Greenside.

Charlie walked up the path of the show house. Inside a woman sat at a desk reading a book.

'I'm interested in these houses,' Charlie said in his best upper-class accent. 'Perhaps you'd be kind enough to tell me who's in charge of sales?'

The woman folded the corner of the page she was reading.

'I'm very sorry,' she said removing her glasses. 'You're too late, I'm afraid. All the houses on this estate are sold. We're closing up the show house tomorrow and moving to Slough.'

Charlie twiddled his thumbs. He hadn't realised how important the new house had become to him. Suddenly it seemed as if the future of his marriage depended on it. Maureen deserved more than a poky semi in the middle of nowhere. He could see that now.

'Your only option would be to wait until someone on the estate decides to sell up. Unless, of course, you were interested in this house. Mind you, it has been a show house for the past couple of years so it's not "as new" you understand. But we could probably come to some arrangement to take into account the wear and tear.'

Charlie felt his heart pound. He was like a shark with the first faint smell of blood filtering through water.

'What exactly might that *financial arrangement* entail?'

'You'd have to speak to Mr Wood about that.'

Charlie found the aforementioned Mr Wood arranging pieces of paper in a filing cabinet. By half past one he had signed one of Mr Wood's pieces of paper pledging a two hundred pound deposit on the show house. He couldn't wait to get home to tell Maureen the good news. If this little coup didn't cheer her up, nothing would.

Charlie drove up Blackberry Lane and parked the Cortina by the gate. He'd left his tablets in his other jacket and wanted to pop in for them. Signing a cheque for two hundred pounds had brought on a mild angina attack. As Charlie got out of the car he noticed Brian Hershaw's lorry parked up the lane past Stringers Farm. This seemed odd. He hadn't expected anyone to be around, especially as Maureen had started taking the bus into town on market day.

As he opened the gate he looked up the lane again at the lorry and did a double take. Maureen was standing by Hershaw's lorry without a coat. It had been raining on and off all day. She seemed to be shivering and had the sleeves of her cardigan stretched over her hands.

He called her. 'Maureen? Didn't you get the bus?'

Maureen looked surprised. 'I missed it,' she called out. 'Mr Hershaw offered me a lift.'

'Afternoon, Charlie,' Brian called out from the cab of his lorry with a chirpy wave.

Charlie's heart missed several beats.

'I need to talk to you, Maureen. Just wait while I go inside…'
The pain which had arrived like an uninvited guest as he left the

Greenside Estate was now impossible to ignore. Charlie tried to walk as naturally as he could. He went inside and fished for the pill bottle in the inside pocket of his coat. Maureen was close behind, coming up the path. Charlie swallowed the pill without water.

'What've you come home for?'

'Does a man need a reason to visit his own house?'

'No, of course not. It's just that I was about to go out. A few minutes later, and you'd have missed me.'

'I'm glad I caught you,' Charlie said after a few deep breaths. 'I've just been up to that new estate. There's some cracking houses up there.' Charlie stopped to compose himself. 'I ... I reckon we could afford one if we sold this and tightened our belts. Would you like to have a look? I've put down a deposit on one of them.'

'I could, but I've already said I'll have a lift with Mr Hershaw.'

'So what's that got to do with the price of fish? Why's Hershaw hanging about here anyway? I've told him I'll pay him.'

'He was just passing, Charlie. I think he was emptying the Stringer's pit thingy. But he's given me the address.' Maureen held out a piece of paper. 'You know for the... He's only trying to help. But I'll tell him not to wait for me if that's what you want.'

Charlie took the paper from Maureen. 'Yes, that is what I want, Maureen.'

Mary Cray was in her late forties, tall and stocky with thick legs. Her grey hair was rolled into a bun at the nape of her neck. She ushered Charlie and Maureen briskly inside into the dark hallway of her house. They followed her past a mahogany hat stand into a room with a tiny kitchen off it and a window that looked out onto a yard and an outside toilet.

'Before we begin,' she said, 'the fee is twenty-five pounds.'

Charlie scratched his chin. 'I've only got twenty pounds, and seven shillings. But I could let you have some offal. I own the butchers in the high street. Sure I've seen you in the shop.'

'It's usually thirty,' Mary said with a smile which produced a dimple on either cheek. 'But you can give me the rest later on.' Charlie handed Mary an envelope. Mary put on her glasses, sat down and counted out the money, just like the woman in the film

Charlie and Maureen had watched together.

Mary explained to Maureen what she was going to do. It was basically an injection that involved soap and something else. Charlie could hardly bear to listen. Maureen just kept nodding. The room was cold and smelled of carbolic.

'Perhaps you wouldn't mind waiting in the hall, Mr Mullet.'

Charlie sat in the hall on the bottom stair reading the evening paper. He had a rather uncomfortable snooze and did the quick crossword. When Maureen emerged, her face was so bloodless it looked grey.

They left by the kitchen door, through the yard and round by an alleyway back to the car.

At home, Maureen lay down on the sofa.

'The pains are beginning. That's what the nurse said would happen.' Her voice was a whisper. Charlie winced. He didn't like to think of Maureen in pain.

An hour later it was all over. The baby that might have been, would now never be. If it had lived, developed, grown, would it have resembled Stringer? Possibly, but Charlie could have brought it up as his own. That's what some people did. Nobody would have been any the wiser. The little dot that had been flushed away might one day have been heir to Charlie's meat empire. For a moment Charlie felt unexpectedly bereft. They'd just destroyed the blueprint of a real person who deserved a chance the same as everyone else. They'd exerted their power as human beings to deny life. Charlie sat in his chair in the front room beside the cocktail cabinet. He rubbed his hands together and then tucked them between his knees as if in prayer. He didn't know whether to be sad or happy, and ended up feeling empty. He heard Maureen pull the chain and call him. Charlie staggered up the stairs. She was lying on the bed so he lay down beside her, slipped his arm around her shoulder and held her.

'Are you okay, Pump?'

'Not now, Charlie,' Maureen said without opening her eyes.

'No, no. Of course not, I didn't mean…' Charlie said as he fingered the strands of Maureen's hair. 'How do you feel? I mean how is it now? You're back to normal, so that must be a good thing.'

Maureen shuddered with a supressed sob. 'Normal, Charlie. I don't think I will ever feel normal.'

'What do you mean, Pumpkin?'

'You won't understand,' Maureen managed between sobs.

'I might if you told me what was wrong.'

Maureen turned so she was facing Charlie. 'It's like...like when I had our Linda. Everything feels dark, Charlie. As if nothing matters. Nothing.'

Charlie thought for a minute. 'Of course things matter. And we've got the new house, you know, on the Greenside. We've got a lot to look forward to there and ... I reckon you deserve a toaster when we move in. Or how about a record player? We've never had one of those, now have we?' We could collect records, decide what sort of music we like.'

Maureen breathed in and sighed. 'Music? I'm not that keen on music.'

'Everyone likes music. Elvis Presley. Lots of people like him.'

'But I'm not everyone. I never felt like everyone else. Even when I was little I didn't. And there was no music in our house. We didn't have a radio or a piano like most people. Nobody visited. Just as well because we didn't have anything.'

'That was then, Pump. People didn't have a lot after the war. Nobody did.'

Maureen began to sob again. 'I don't want a record player. I don't want a toaster, Charlie.'

Charlie frowned. 'No? Well, we could stick with the grill.'

'I don't want a grill. I don't want anything.'

Charlie took his arm away from Maureen's shoulder. 'Now you're being silly,' he said.

When Charlie came home from work the next day, he was surprised to find the house deserted again. He went from room to room calling Maureen. Finally he concluded she must be out. But where? She wasn't the type to leave a note. Charlie and Maureen didn't communicate via the written word. She'd never left him a note before, so there was no point looking for one now. To be frank, there hadn't been much of any kind of communication between them recently, even with all the abortion carry on, *and* the fact that Charlie had put the deposit down on one of the Greenside houses. They'd only spoken to each other out of necessity.

Now suddenly Charlie felt desperate to talk to Maureen. He wanted to discuss the exciting news about the estate house properly. He'd spent all that money on the deposit. His bank balance had taken a serious nosedive into the red – he wanted her to acknowledge the sacrifice he'd made for their new life together. Where the hell was she? Charlie took a cold chicken leg from the fridge and gnawed it to the bone. He phoned Linda to see if she'd heard from Maureen. Linda seemed surprised and said she hadn't seen her mother for weeks. Charlie sat down in front of the television and watched Double Your Money and the News. He must have fallen asleep because the sound of the phone ringing woke him up. The television screen was blank and making a whistling noise.

'Lyde four, double five, nine.'

'Charlie, is that you?'

'Maureen? Where the devil are you?'

'I'm staying the night with our Linda. She's been poorly...'

'Your Linda? But I rang her hours ago. She sounded healthy enough then.'

'Did I say Linda? I meant Elsie. Sorry. I've had a long journey.'

'A long journey? Where the hell are you?'

'In Felixstowe, of course.' Maureen's voice became fainter.

'How did you get there? What's going on?'

'Nothing's going on. Please don't shout at me. It's ... Elsie's Eric. He's got ... he's got the flu...'

'Flu! What has that got to do with us? Hells bells, Maureen. Would you care if I had flu? Would you care if I was ill?'

'You're not ill though, are you? I thought you said it was only that vagina thing and you've got those tablets for that. It's Elsie's Eric who's ill. Hold on, I think that's her calling me now. I'd better go.'

'But wait, Maureen...' Charlie felt his heart banging. 'I want to talk to you about the new estate house.'

'I'll ring you tomorrow.'

'*Maureen…*'

The line went dead.

Charlie needed some air. He went out into the porch and stood on the step. Suddenly he was aware of someone out there. In the darkness he could just make out the silhouette of Christian Stringer ambling up the road. As quickly as he could, Charlie bumbled back into the house and dislocated the Cinzano bottle from its optic. He took the bottle outside and with measured precision cracked it against the wall.

'Stringer, you bastard,' Charlie confronted Christian Stringer in the middle of the road. 'You dirty bastard, mess with my wife, would you?'

Christian seemed unsteady on his feet. 'What?' he said.

'You – you bastard. Rape – that's what I'm talking about. Rape. On that so-called *driving lesson*. Driving lesson my foot. You took advantage of my wife. An innocent woman…'

'Took advantage?' Christian sneered. 'Ha. That's funny. She was gagging for it, mate. Maybe you don't know your wife as well as you think.'

'How dare you,' Charlie swung the Cinzano bottle towards Christian.

Christian backed away. 'What are you going to do with that? It's your wife you should be having a go at. Turned up for every lesson dressed up like a dog's dinner. If I hadn't given it to her someone else would've.'

'Why you…' Charlie lunged towards Christian with the jagged remains of the bottle. But as he did so he felt the mother of all pains. Not the annoying angina pain but something far worse. He slumped heavily against the wall. Christian's voice echoed above him.

'Mr Mullet, what's wrong. Hold on there. I'll get Evie to phone for a doctor.'

Wearing a new pair of red and green checked pyjamas, Charlie rested against a stack of pillows in the Men's General Ward. It was only a mild attack. A warning, all the same. He couldn't think about his wife. Did she say she was in Felixstowe? He'd sort everything out later once he'd regained his strength. He'd thought about the estate house, though. It would be a new start for them both – if she ever came home.

Charlie asked a nurse for the phone and got Elsie's number through the operator. Eric answered and passed him on to Elsie who said they hadn't seen Maureen for months. None of this made sense, but at least the cocktail cabinet would look just right in the new house. It never fitted in properly in the old place. It would need a replacement bottle of Cinzano, though. He didn't want Maureen coming home to a cocktail cabinet with no Cinzano Bianco.

When he was discharged Charlie took a cab to the house in Blackberry Lane. Most of Maureen's clothes, shoes and jewellery were gone. There was an empty space where her vanity case had been in the wardrobe. Charlie re-opened the shop but let the house on the Greenside Estate go. He lost his deposit but moved back into the flat above the shop. Mrs Jessop, who came in every Friday for six chops hesitated before putting them into her bag.

'Was that your Maureen I saw the other day up on the Greenside Estate? I was visiting our Sandra and I could have sworn I saw her. She was with that nice Mr Hershaw – you know, the cleansing chappie…'

Charlie doubted Hershaw would be able to satisfy Maureen's demands for long. She'd come running back to him with her tail behind her legs by the end of the month if she knew which side her bread was buttered on. Meanwhile, he decided to keep the Blackberry Lane house, as a kind of insurance policy. Just in case the bottom fell out of the meat market. He'd had a little brain wave. He'd rent the house out. Should be a nice little earner. What was the name of that man? Rachman. Yes, that was him. Charlie Mullet would be the Peter Rachman of Lyde…

COLIN

April 1971

COLIN UNHOOKED his rucksack from his back and sat on it. Wow. He'd just walked past those cool rocks at Stonehenge. Man, how did those ancient dudes build shit like that? At university they'd never even touched on that kind of stuff. The sun burnt the top of his head. He could've done with one of those cowboy hats, the kind Fabian was wearing last summer.

Colin stuck out his thumb. A dark blue sports car was coming up behind him on the A303. The car overtook him, but the driver slammed on the brakes a hundred yards up the road. Colin picked up his rucksack and ran.

The woman driver leant over the passenger seat to open the door. She looked about the same age as his mum.

'I'm going as far as Exeter if that's any good to you?' She had an upper-class voice, like the Queen or that other one ... Princess Margaret. So, nothing like his mum. Colin got in. The upholstery smelled of leather, mixed with the woman's perfume. Every time she changed gear a gold bracelet rattled on her wrist.

'Where have you come from?' she asked. She'd just negotiated a couple of roundabouts so Colin hadn't said anything in case he put her off. Women drivers and all that.

'Norwich,' he said, adjusting the weight of his bag which was becoming uncomfortably heavy on his lap.

'You can put that on the floor, if you like,' the woman said. He squashed it down the side of his leg. The car wasn't exactly roomy. It had a radio, though, but it was tuned into some classical music. Not really Colin's scene.

'Goodness, that's a bit of a journey.' The woman seemed keen to chat. He'd had lifts from people like her before. Bored with driving and looking for someone to entertain them.

'You've hitchhiked all the way from Norwich?'

'Yeah.'

'Are you on your way home for Easter?'

'No.'

'Visiting friends?'

'Yeah, sort of.'

'Where would you like to be dropped off?'

Colin fished out the scrap of paper with the directions Fabian had given out that night in the pub. The name of the place was Lyde.

'Lyde, did you say?' She turned the radio down. 'I think I've seen that signposted. It's near Shapton, if my memory serves me right.'

He re-folded the paper and stuffed it into the side pocket of his rucksack.

'Was it easy? Getting lifts, I mean?'

'Yeah, not bad.'

'How long did it take?'

'About seven hours.'

'Are you from Norwich?'

'No, London.'

'Are you at the university?'

This old bird would have got a job in the Spanish Inquisition. 'Er ... yes,' he said. Well, *er...no*, actually, he thought to himself. *Not any more I'm not.*

Colin closed his eyes and pretended to be asleep, making little snoring noises from time to time to add authenticity.

'What subject are you studying?' The woman was at it again with the twenty questions routine. Feigning sleep obviously hadn't worked.

'Geography, but I've left now...'

'Geography! And you've graduated? Well done. That's marvellous.'

'Thanks,' he said. There was little point in destroying the illusion. She'd be dropping him off soon and he'd never see her again. But Colin hadn't graduated. Colin would never graduate. He'd had it up to the neck with Geography and essays and cliques of cool-looking people who all seemed to know each other and all seemed to know everything about everything. Fuck. Fuck the University of East Anglia. Fuck Geography. Fuck the lot of them.

Some people seemed to have a secret formula that made them popular. If Fabian had been at East Anglia he'd have swaggered into lectures wearing that old army coat he got from Kensington Market. He'd have shown them the true definition of cool. Colin would have a real laugh with Fabian when he told him about this rich old bird who'd given him a lift in her posh car. Talk about capitalism personified. Fabian would be in hysterics. Children of the revolution. People like this woman would be the first for the chop when capitalism was abolished. Bring back *la guillotine*.

'Your parents must be very proud…'

'Yeah.' Colin looked out of the window and pretended to read something on the side of a lorry they were overtaking. He felt his cheeks turning hot and red. He hated it when they did that. Not that he'd told a lie or anything. His mum *was* proud of him. Unfortunately. Seeing as she didn't have a clue that he'd dropped out. And his dad – no doubt he would have been proud too if he'd ever bothered to find out where Colin was. As things were, they could have passed in the street and not recognised one another.

The woman turned the radio up. Colin shut his eyes again but he couldn't sleep. The music on the radio was something classical, then a play came on that was set in ancient Scotland with lots of shouting and gunfire. He was scared to open his eyes in case she started talking to him again. Not that it would be bad to talk, but that sort of thing was heavy going and even if he'd wanted to make conversation, Colin couldn't. If his mum had been good at small talk maybe he'd have picked it up from her.

He remembered lining up in the queue for school dinners and she'd always be there standing behind a cauldron of something runny and hot, wearing a white hat and a white overalls, not looking like his mum, dishing out gravy and mashed potatoes. When Colin got to the head of the queue, she never seemed to know what to say to him. She didn't say much to any of the other kids either, although she always gave Colin an extra large helping when it was chocolate pudding and custard.

No doubt Fabian's mum spent all morning gardening and baking bread before changing into whites to play tennis on the lawn, followed by cocktails in the evening. She'd have had the small talk gene all polished up and ready to pass on to her offspring.

Colin peeked out of the window under his fringe. They were at another roundabout and took the exit for Shapton. He closed his eyes again. He remembered hearing Fabian mention Shapton in the pub in Blackheath on Christmas Eve when he'd invited everyone to his pad in Somerset. Colin had arrived at the pub late and they'd all been stoned, or drunk, or both. Fabian and his friends were ex-Dulwich College boys, but they were pretty much out of it, so Colin had mingled in easily. At one point he was actually sitting at the same table as Fabian. That was when he'd issued the invite.

'Come and stay,' Fabian had proclaimed. 'You're all welcome.' He flung his arms out wide to include everyone. Someone asked for directions and Colin memorised them and wrote them down when he got home.

The woman had dropped her speed. Having his eyes closed for so long was beginning to feel odd, like he'd gone blind or some weird shit. He felt so freaked, he had to open them.

'Oh, you're awake,' she said. 'We're in Lyde now. Whereabouts is your friend's house?'

'You can drop me at the war memorial,' Colin said. That was the thing he'd written down. Turn off at the war memorial, go down Blackberry Lane, past a farmhouse on your left and the house is on the right. Fabian had spluttered the directions between swigs of rum and Coke.

Colin sauntered down Blackberry Lane, past the row of horse chestnuts to his left and the fields where a herd of cows mingled in a peaceful group by the hedgerow. He saw the farmhouse with its five-bar gate and mud-spattered entrance. He stopped for a moment to adjust his rucksack. Instead of having it hooked over each arm like a rambler, he slung it over one shoulder, so he'd look more cool – less keen. He could tell he was getting closer to

Fabian's place when he heard strains of Jefferson Airplane drifting through the warm April air, across the road from the front garden of a red-brick, semi-detached house that stood on its own opposite the farmhouse. He crossed over to the other side of the road. It *was* a road, although a tuft of grass grew down the middle of the tarmac making it look more like a disused path.

The sounds made it easy to suss out which half of the house was Fabian's. Colin had heard him talking about Jefferson Airplane in the waiting room at Bromley South Station once and he'd saved up for *Crown of Creation* as a result.

Lather was playing. That was the one Fabian liked. *Lather*. Fabian said you could live your life by the lyrics of *Lather*. Colin had written them down and contemplated their meaning (or lack of meaning) for months.

He pushed the gate open, dumped his rucksack on the path and knocked on the porch door. The music was loud and no one seemed to hear him. He peered through the front window. The curtains were closed but there was a small gap where they didn't meet properly. A group of people were sitting in a circle on the floor. Colin screwed up his eyes to see if one of them was Fabian, but it was too dark to tell. He knocked on the window. Someone inside screamed. Colin looked round and saw Fabian standing in the porch.

'Yeah?' Fabian said, squinting in the sunlight.

'Oh, hi,' Colin said. 'Hi, er, I made it. Hope you don't mind me turning up…you know. I was in the area and just thought I'd …'

Fabian shielded his eyes and looked at him again. 'Oh … oh… shit, man. Good to see you, man. How's things?' He held out his hand for Colin to shake. Colin wiped his palm down the side of his jeans and shook hands with Fabian. Shaking hands. Fuck. This guy had so much style.

The music stopped, leaving only a crackling sound between tracks.

'Who is it, Fabe?' a girl called from inside.

'It's… er – shit, man – wow, it's really good to see you. How did you come to be in these parts? Hey man, don't just stand there.

Come inside.'

Colin picked up his bag and followed Fabian through the hall into a room that was thick with cigarette smoke and the smell of joss sticks.

Fabian wore purple loons and a tie-dye T-shirt. His long hair brushed against his shoulders. Sitting cross-legged on the floor beside a large piece of white paper with letters written around the outside edges were two girls who appeared to be in the middle of playing a game. One of them had dark, cropped hair and long dangly earrings, and other was tiny with bright blue eyes and long straight fair hair that hung almost to the floor.

They both stared at Colin.

'Hi,' the dark-haired one said.

'Hiya,' the blonde girl said.

Fabian crouched on the floor between the girls. 'Hilly,' he said, 'Angel, this is …'

'Colin.' Colin helped him out as Fabian was probably too stoned to remember his name.

'This is Hilly,' Fabian said putting his arm around the dark-haired girl's shoulders.

'And I'm Angel,' the other girl said.

Colin sat on his rucksack next to an upturned box that seemed to serve as a coffee table.

'Hey! What's the game?' He was trying to sound interested but at the same time blasé, as if he could take it or leave it.

Hilly looked at him as if she'd just noticed an unpleasant smell. 'It's not a *game*, it's a Ouija board.' The brusqueness of her remark coupled with her public schoolgirl accent caused Colin's cheeks turn the colour of an overripe peach.

He tried to hide under his fringe until his face had returned to its natural paler shade of white. He wanted to impress Fabian with his anecdote about the woman in the car with all the gold, but somehow he knew he couldn't. He'd imagined them getting stoned together – with maybe a few of his mates – eventually crashing in the early hours. But if he'd really thought about it, he'd have guessed that a guy like Fabian would have at least one chick in tow.

'Would you like some tea? I'm sorry, I didn't catch your name,' the blonde one said.

'It's Colin, and yes please, milk and three sugars.'

'Three sugars?' Hilly guffawed. 'We don't have any sugar, and it's herbal tea. Mint or chamomile. So you won't need milk either.'

Colin felt the ripe peaches reinstate themselves in his cheeks. 'Oh, yeah. Mint would be a gas,' he said, shaking his fringe to cover his face again.

Fabian looked thoughtful. 'Colin! Hey, man. Weren't you at Dulwich College in the year below me? I remember you from somewhere.'

'No. I was at the Grammar. You know. From the… the waiting room at Bromley South…?'

'The waiting room…' Fabian pulled at his beard thoughtfully. 'Yeah, I do remember you, come to think of it. Kind of. Hey, man, what brings you out this way?'

After Hilly had made the tea, she sat down again on the floor facing the Ouija board.

'Right, let's try again,' she said with an exasperated sigh. Hilly, Fabian and Angel all placed their index fingers on the upturned glass in the middle of the board. Colin wondered if he should do the same but there was no room for an extra finger, and anyway he felt embarrassed by his bitten nails.

He peered through his fringe as they moved the glass around the board. First the glass went to the letter A, then R, and then T.

'ART! Hey, wow. Far out. I'm starting Art History minor next term,' Angel said.

'Shush, Angel. Let it go on. That could just be the beginning of a word,' Hilly said.

The glass slid towards H and U. The room was so quiet Colin could hear the squeak of the rim of the glass against the paper. Suddenly Hilly jumped up and screamed causing him to slip backwards from his seat on his rucksack.

Luckily no one seemed to notice Colin as he gingerly returned to his perch.

'Cool it, Hill!' Fabian took his finger from the glass and pushed his hair behind his ears.

'Arthur! That's my dad's middle name. Shit. It's a sign. Something's happened to my dad!' Hilly shrieked.

'Cool it. You don't know that. We had a cat called Arthur that got run over when I was twelve. It might be him returning from the dead, trying to tell me where all the mice hang out.'

As Angel dissolved into a paroxysm of giggles a strand of her hair tickled Colin's wrist. Hilly sat down and replaced her finger on the glass. The glass carried on towards the R before sliding to the L, the O, the V, the E and the S.

'*Arthur loves...* wow!' Angel whispered. 'Carry on. Let's see what the spirit is trying to say.'

The glass moved towards the letter M and then the A. Hilly and Angel held their breath as it settled on the R and then the Y.

'Arthur loves Mary,' Hilly whispered very slowly. 'We must have reached the spirit of someone who lived here before. Arthur and Mary. Maybe they owned this house hundreds of years ago. I think their spirits are still here. Wow! Crazy.'

'This house wasn't here hundreds of years ago,' Fabian corrected her. 'Mr Mullet told me it was built in the forties.'

'Who's Mr Mullet?' Colin ventured.

No one seemed to hear him or be bothered to answer his question. 'Okay, thirty years ago. It might be some dude who died during the war,' Angel said.

'The war ended in forty-six,' Fabian pointed out.

'He could have survived the war and died here.' Angel's eyes sparkled at the thought.

'Whoever Arthur is, he's got strong connections with this house,' Fabian said. 'Let's see if we can talk to him again. Arthur? Is there anybody there? Knock once for 'yes', twice for 'no'.'

Colin took a last gulp of the foul-tasting tea Hilly had made for him and accidentally banged the cup down clumsily onto the box. The cup made such a clatter both girls jumped to their feet and screamed.

'For fuck's sake,' Hilly said when she realised that the noise was merely the sound of Colin's cup. 'I thought that was the spirit of *Arthur* knocking once for 'yes'.'

Colin took refuge behind his fringe again. 'Shit. Sorry, guys. It was just my cup,' he mumbled. 'Cool tea, though.'

Hilly made a macrobiotic bean salad which they ate sitting on the floor. Fabian put *Blind Faith* on the record player. While Angel was making more tea, he'd kissed Hilly full on the mouth for what seemed like hours. They rolled together on the carpet still locked in a kiss, as if Colin wasn't there. Colin took his book out of his rucksack and found the page he was up to in *On The Road* by Jack Kerouac, although he couldn't concentrate on the words. He was glad it was the girl called Hilly Fabian was rolling around with.

Angel brought a cake from the kitchen with the tea.

'It's homemade,' she said, cutting it into slices. Hilly laughed as she took a slice. Angel offered some to Colin.

'Actually,' she said 'it's dope cake. You don't have to eat it if you don't want...'

'No. I mean yes,' Colin said as she gave him the slice. 'Cool cake,' he said as he took a first mouthful. Fabian had a packet of Moroccan Red and a pot of grass on the mantelpiece. After the cake was all gone he rolled joint after joint – it was the leftovers from the cake, he said. The girls both giggled at this and each time Angel passed the joint to Colin he breathed in her musky scent.

By one in the morning Colin felt sick. His brain was swaying, his buttocks were sore from sitting on his rucksack, and he needed a piss. Fabian stretched and yawned. 'You can crash in Crazy Mike's room if you like, Col.'

'That would be far out.' Colin stood up and stretched too. 'I hope he won't mind.'

'No sweat. Crazy Mike's a head. He's away in search of mescalin and magic mushrooms at a commune in Wales.'

'Cool,' Colin managed in the midst of a yawn. He followed Fabian upstairs, leaving Angel unrolling the sleeping bag she'd pulled out from behind the sofa.

At five o'clock in the morning Colin's eyes felt like boiled sweets. His brain was buzzing like a hive of bees. Was it the grass or the fact that Crazy Mike's room had a black ceiling and no curtains? Outside the first birds of the morning began to twitter and chirp. How did this Crazy Mike dude get any sleep in living accommodation like this? Maybe that was why he was crazy. Sleep deprivation must have messed with his sanity. Dawn was breaking and a hazy cream of light lit the sky. The top branches of one of the apple trees in the garden seemed to be waving at Colin in the breeze.

He leaned over out of the bed to grab his book from his bag and noticed a smell of peppermint. Fuck. He'd been sitting on it for so long his tube of *Colgate* had burst all over Jack Kerouac. But even without the sticky mass of toothpaste smeared across the cover, he doubted he'd be able to get his head round what Kerouac was trying to get across. He was reading the same sentence over and over. Words and thoughts, concepts that had previously seemed fascinating and relevant to his life, now seemed flat and meaningless. He put the book down. On the door a poster with a picture of Ché Guevara stared at him with dark, menacing eyes. He tried counting sheep, listening to the birdsong, lying on his front, lying on his side, curling up like a baby, but whatever he did, all he could think about was that girl, the one with the long hair down to her waist. The one with the little elfin face, the turned up nose and surprised blue eyes.

The one they called Angel.

Colin pulled on his jeans and crept down the stairs. In the middle of the staircase, attached to the wall with drawing pins was an Indian shawl, and beneath the shawl someone had painted over the wallpaper with purple paint that appeared to have run out halfway through the job. He was only a few feet from the front room where Angel was. He carried on downstairs until he was in the hall. He swivelled the doorknob and opened the door to the front room a fraction. The room still smelled of stale grass and joss sticks and that musky perfume that was hers.

'Angel?' As he whispered her name, Colin felt his heart thumping under his T-shirt. He could see her outline on the sofa by the window. She was curled up in the sleeping bag, her hair hanging over the edge of the sofa, skimming the floor. The room was as they'd left it a few hours before, the armchairs on either side of the Ouija board – a pile of plates and four coffee cups were on the floor. The beige tiled mantelpiece that was home to the packet of grass was to his right as he crept across the room, carefully avoiding any of the discarded crockery. He knelt as if at a shrine on the carpet beside the sofa where Angel lay. As softly as he dared, he touched the bare flesh on her forearm.

'Hi,' she said, opening her eyes. She didn't seem shocked that he was there. Her voice was soft and a bit croaky. Even in the semi-darkness he could see that delicate blue of her eyes.

'I couldn't sleep,' Colin said.

'Me neither, it's the dope cake. It lies in your stomach like a brick.'

'Yeah.'

Colin picked up a record from a pile by the fireplace. 'Fairport Convention? Is this yours?'

'No, I don't actually live here,' Angel said. 'Fabian and Hilly let me crash sometimes. Most of the stuff here belongs to Hilly. They're third years. They've been here for ages.'

'Cool taste,' Colin said anyway, flicking through the sleeves. 'Electric Lady Land. Did you ever see Hendrix live?'

'Yes, at the Isle of Wight, just before he died.'

'Hey, I was there too! He was something else, wasn't he? I don't remember seeing you there, though.'

Angel laughed. She had a perfect row of white teeth, like milk teeth. 'I don't remember seeing you either,' she said.

'Hey, maybe we walked past each other on the beach and instead of speaking just carried on walking. It's weird when you think about it. You know, how people's paths cross. All the people we should have met, but somebody sneezed at the wrong moment, and we looked around to see who sneezed. Maybe we were meant to meet at the Isle of Wight and we missed each other.'

'Yeah. Maybe someone sneezed and we looked the other way,' Angel said.

'Maybe that's why I dropped out of East Anglia and headed down here today.'

'You dropped out of East Anglia? Why?'

'I was studying Geography.'

'Geography! Wow. Heavy.'

'Yeah – I know – bad vibe.'

Neither of them spoke for a few minutes. Colin picked at one of this fingernails.

'So… you split? That was a bit drastic. Couldn't you have switched courses or something?'

'I don't know…' Colin hesitated. Switching courses hadn't occurred to him. He'd written a letter to his tutor, telling him he was leaving. He'd pretended it was the course, but really it was the loneliness. He didn't know anyone at East Anglia and he hadn't made any friends. All the other students seemed to be in groups, hanging out together in the coffee bar and the students' union. Colin cut about on his own, pretending he thought he was better than them, imagining he'd have been fine if someone like Fabian had been there. Some days he spoke to no one and despite his high 'A' level results, lacked the self-belief to speak in his tutor group. When he handed his letter to the faculty secretary she'd opened it while he was still there and called him back. 'Mr Monk,' she said. 'Mr Monk!' He hadn't realised at first that she was talking to him. The woman had suggested counselling. Colin wasn't sure what that meant and refused the offer. But he'd never thought of switching courses. Maybe that's what the counsellor would have suggested. But changing courses wouldn't have helped him make friends.

'Anyway,' he said. 'I chucked it in. Kicked the establishment in the teeth. All that middle class shit.'

'You sound like Fabian,' Angel said.

'Yeah. Sod the lot of them. I didn't even say goodbye to the guys in my block. I said to myself *today is the first day of the rest of your life!'*

Someone had written that slogan on one of the walls in the halls of residence. From that day onwards, Colin Monk could do what he wanted. He still had some money left from his grant. He could go around the world. Fuck Geography. Fuck all the cliques of trendy students in the corridors. Fuck the lot of them.

'Wow,' Angel said.

'…Perhaps I… left because of you,' Colin suggested.

She sat up, still wrapped in her sleeping bag. 'Me? That's a bit of a heavy trip to lay on a stranger.'

'Sorry. But you don't *feel* like a stranger.'

Angel propped herself on her elbow and frowned. 'What do you mean?'

Colin felt his cheeks heating up again. 'I feel as if I've known you for a long time. Hey! Maybe we were hooked up in another life.'

'Wow! Do you really think so?'

'Anything's possible if you think about it.'

'But how would we know?'

'Do you believe in ghosts? I bet there's a few in this house.'

Angel frowned again, wrinkling her nose. 'Don't – you're freaking me. Like the Ouija board. That was really freaky, wasn't it? *Arthur loves Mary*?' Angel shivered. 'Let's talk about something else. Like … how do you know Fabian?'

'We both went to school in south London.'

'He's a great guy,' Angel said dreamily.

'Yeah. The main man.'

Angel was wearing a white nightdress with a lace collar that was torn at the edges. She cosied her sleeping bag further up around her shoulders and Colin moved closer to the sofa. Wrapped up in the sleeping bag with her hair hanging outside she looked like a mummified mermaid.

'I like your hair,' Colin said. Angel smiled. 'It's a bit cold in here.' He blew into his palms. 'You know what they say. The darkest hour is just before dawn.'

Angel sat up, put her finger on his cheek and – Colin could hardly believe what was happening – she kissed him. He felt the softness of her lips on his. He kissed her back, allowing his tongue to fill her small mouth. He tasted her teeth, her cheek, the lobe of her ear. She unzipped the sleeping bag and Colin stepped out of his jeans, leaving in a heap by his feet. He slipped in beside her. With both of them inside the sleeping bag they only just managed to balance on the sofa. Angel's legs felt hot against Colin's. She cradled his head in her arm, stroking her fingers through his hair as he nestled in the space between her breasts.

'I think you're really nice,' he said.

'Do you actually believe we were destined to meet?' she asked.

'Yeah.'

'But how would we know for sure?'

'I don't know. It's in the stars, fate, the universe, the cosmos. That sort of thing.'

'Wow,' Angel said as Colin's fingers travelled down her body, exploring the slight curve of her hip bone and the silky skin on the inside of her legs until they melted into the moisture inside of her.

Colin walked into the village for milk. Some *people*, it seemed, didn't understand the need for milk. On his way back he noticed a phone box just past the war memorial. He stopped and looked into the box through one of the grimy panes of glass. Inside was the phone with its list of instructions, the box to put the money in, the usual dog-eared pile of phone directories. One of the side windows had been smashed but, even so, the inside smelt of stale tobacco. Fabian had given him ten pence to buy a *Guardian*. There was a phone in the hall at the house, but Colin didn't want everyone listening to him. He put Fabian's change on the shelf and the bag with the paper and the milk on the floor. There was some graffiti above the shelf. The word 'Michael' and a heart were drawn in black ink. He pushed a two pence piece into the slot, lifted the receiver and dialled. 'Mum? It's me. I just wanted to tell you… I've split from the course at East Anglia.'

'Colin? Is that you, love? What do you mean? Where are you?' His mum sounded hundreds of miles away. Which she was, of course. He could imagine her at home in the lounge speaking into the phone as if it were some futuristic gadget she'd accidentally stumbled across whilst looking for the *TV Times*.

'I've dropped out. Don't freak, Mum. It's no big deal.'

'Colin. Talk properly. What do you mean? You've left the university? Surely not.'

'Yeah.'

'What about the work you did to get there? What about your grant? You can't just *leave*.'

'I'm running out of change. I'll ring you another time. Are you alright?'

'I was – until just now…' she said. She was crying. He held the phone away from his ear. When he felt strong enough to listen again she was in mid flow. 'Colin? Are you still there? Answer me, please. If you've left university why aren't you at home?'

I'm not coming home, Mum. I'm dossing down with friends in Somerset. There's no need to worry.'

'Somerset? We don't know anyone in Somerset. I don't even know where Somerset is. Colin you should carry on with your studies. Don't throw everything away… all those exams. You worked so hard and I'm so proud. I've told everyone at work. Even the supervisor hasn't got a son at university. I've never been so proud. Talk to me…'

When the pips went Colin put the phone down. He felt unsettled, but at least his mum knew he'd left East Anglia, so that was cool. She might not approve, but that was her problem. She'd had her chance at a life. Now it was his turn.

As Colin shared Angel's sleeping bag, the nights got shorter and the sun higher in the sky behind the backdrop of the endless green of Stringers Farm. In the daytime calves gathered by the hedges and small buds appeared on the blackberry bushes on the other side of the road. Colin began to enjoy his morning stroll to the village to get Fabian's paper. It was a relief to get away from Hilly watching him all the time whenever he spread some butter on a slice of bread or peeled a carrot. He missed Angel when she went into the university to a lecture or one of her tutorials and it was something to do to fill the time until she came home. As April drifted into May and June followed on, everyone was revising for exams. Except for Colin. By mid-June Fabian and Hilly announced they were packing up ready to move on. As Colin walked in with that day's copy of the *Guardian* he was greeted with the sight of Fabian struggling down the stairs carrying a full-sized skeleton.

'You got the paper, cool,' he said.

'I'll put it in the kitchen with the change,' Colin said, knowing Fabian would never notice how much change there was. Hilly came into the kitchen with an empty box. She went around the cupboards filling it with saucepans, crockery and cutlery.

'Are you ready, Hill?' Fabian was jiggling the keys to the van he'd hired.

'What's happening, guys?' Colin said. Hilly had taken the mug he'd just made tea in, rinsed it out and added it to the other things in her box.

'We're leaving this afternoon. I've only got the van for forty-eight hours. Going to hook up with Crazy Mike in Wales. Hilly's planning to start an organic farm. You two would love it. Why don't you come along?'

'Yeah, man. That sounds … a gas,' Colin said as he looked through the cupboards for another mug. 'But I think Angel likes it here…'

'Not everyone's got the same energy,' Hilly said. 'Personally, I'd suffocate and die an early death if I lived in this house for another day.'

'Alright, Hill. It's not that bad. You never know, we might have to come back if it doesn't work out in Wales,' Fabian said.

'Yeah, but surely your dad could pay for a different place. I don't think we're ever going to be that desperate. Three years here is enough for me. Enjoy the rest of your life, Colin,' Hilly said with a dismissive flick of her wrist.

Colin sat opposite the clerk in the Shapton DHSS biting his nails while she flicked through a box of cards. The rent cheque for August from Fabian's old man hadn't arrived. He'd obviously realised his son no longer lived at the house in Blackberry Lane. So that was why Colin was sitting in front of this clerk who was trying to fix him up with a job.

'I'm sure I'll be able to find you something,' the woman said, peering at him over her spectacles. She had a spot on the end of her nose that Colin couldn't quite get past. 'Now, is it office or manual you're after?'

Colin bit another nail. This ultra-keen clerk chick was freaking him out. Angel reckoned you just sign on and they give you dole money. Everyone she knew did it. All the students were on the dole during the vac. Colin scratched his head. How had he landed himself with a weird zealot whose mission was to hook everyone up who was unemployed with some kind of *work*.

'Ah. Here we are.' The woman beamed at Colin. 'The frozen pea factory in Mannering Lane in Shapton. Quality control. Thirty pence an hour. Start tomorrow night.'

When Colin got home Angel was in the kitchen sliding a cake from the oven.

'Wow,' he said. 'I thought we'd run out of dope.'

Angel placed the cake on the table. 'It's not dope cake, silly,' she said. 'I bought some sugar and a bunch of rotting bananas from the post office, and I found some organic flour in the cupboard that Hilly left behind.'

'Cool,' Colin said. Even though the cake was burnt on one side it smelled amazing and Colin was very hungry. Angel scraped black crumbs into the sink, placed the cake on a cracked plate, and dusted the top with icing sugar.

'I like the way you do that, Babe,' Colin said. He took one of the two knives that Hilly had also overlooked. 'It's really professional.' Angel smiled and flicked her ponytail over her shoulder. Colin cut a chunk of cake – about a quarter of the whole thing, in fact, and shoved it into his mouth. Crumbs fell to the floor. 'Mmmm. I'm starving,' he tried to say, although he could hardly speak with so much cake in his mouth.

Mrs Stringer from Number One lent Colin a bike. She seemed okay, not stuck up or anything, although Colin had never really spoken to her. She had three sons who worked on the farm. But the whole Stringer family looked as if the world had passed them by. Their clothes were museum exhibits from the last decade. What was it with these cats? The social revolution of the sixties hadn't even skimmed the surface of their universe. They were from another world, with their ludicrous haircuts that looked as if they'd shared a pudding basin. And they didn't even wear flares. They had a half-decent bike though, and Colin peddled off on it to the frozen pea factory at five o'clock in time for the night shift.

Colin spent the night shivering at the side of a conveyor belt. They'd made him tie his hair in a ponytail with an elastic band *and* he had to wear a hair net. Fuck. He felt like a prat. A cold prat. He'd have to remember to wear a woolly jumper the following night. Angel had a big baggy one she wore over everything else when the evenings were chilly. She'd probably let him borrow that. Colin watched the peas as they wobbled along like a thousand half-hearted competitors in a pea race. His job was to pick out the bad ones, the tiny ones, the ones that had turned black. The brown ones. The rejects. Fuck. This was the most boring job since … since fuck knows what. It was the most boring thing he'd ever done, that was for sure. He had a problem staying awake. Except it was so bitterly cold it was impossible to sleep either.

After each shift at the pea factory Colin cycled home as dawn broke over the Mendips. He looked forward to this bit of the day. The way the streaks of grey, blue, pink and gold lit up the sky just above the horizon was practically psychedelic. It was almost worth suffering the humiliating hours spent in the pea factory to watch the night sky glide into pink. If he never saw a pea again in his life, he thought he'd be a happy man, but now he'd discovered this dawn trip, Colin was hooked, like he was on some kind of drug. As the first fingers of each morning sun stroked his shoulders, he thought about Angel curled up in bed, waiting for him to snuggle in beside her. Early morning sex was the best, when the fresh smell of the wind was still in his lungs and the heat of sleepy musk was still in her hair. As he peddled along, he drank it all in. The air smelled pure and yet at the same time, intoxicating, and he had at least another ten hours before he had to stare at that poxy pea marathon again.

As Colin sped down Blackberry Lane, he saw the postman going into the farmhouse over the road. Colin always peddled extra hard down the last bit of the lane. He swerved to the right before skidding to a standstill. He propped the bike at the side of the house, put his key in the door and stepped on a letter. Colin picked up the envelope. It had Angel's name written in longhand on the front.

Except it didn't say Angel but 'Miss Angela Grey'. The envelope was white, which ruled out the DHSS with their dingy brown efforts. And they always had those see-through windows to save them the bother of writing your address out twice. Lazy bastards.

He was still holding Angel's letter when he put the kettle on for a cup of tea. He'd made a muddy footprint on the front when he'd trodden on it. While he was waiting for the water to boil, he quietly closed the kitchen door and held the envelope up to the light. It was made of thick, expensive paper so Colin couldn't see what was inside. He dabbed a spot of water onto a tea towel and wiped the muddy mark his shoe had made, but rubbing it only seemed to make the mud spread, and, not only that, he'd made a bit of the flap come loose where it had been stuck down by…by who? By whoever had written Angel's letter.

He'd soon find out who'd written it when he gave it to her. But supposing she didn't open it. She might just put it to one side to open later when he was at work. The kettle was coming to the boil, and he held the underside of the envelope near to the steam. It drooped and crinkled at the edges. Colin unglued the flap.

Inside, on headed university note paper, was a hand-written letter from Angel's tutor, and another typed piece of paper with her exam results on it. She'd failed in Art and English. The tutor's name was Professor Gabriel Posner and according to the letter, Professor Posner wanted Angel to see him to discuss her disappointing results.

It wasn't as if this was a love letter or even a personal letter from a friend. Colin knew he shouldn't have opened her mail. His mum had always told him not to open hers. She said 'the Royal Mail is the property of her majesty the Queen. You can go to prison for opening other peoples' mail.' Colin had always thought that was unlikely.

Angel was still in bed reading a book called *The Female Eunuch*.

'This came for you,' Colin said. 'I opened it by mistake. Thought it was from the Social.'

Colin gave Angel the letter. She propped herself up and pulled the letter out of the envelope roughly, tearing some of the paper.

She scanned it, frowned, and chucked it onto the blanket.

'Who's it from?' Colin asked.

'Gabriel Posner.'

'Who's Gabriel Posner?' he said, trying to make the question sound as casual as he could.

'My tutor.'

Colin pulled Angel's jumper over his head and started undoing his trousers. 'A professor?'

'Yeah. Hey – how d'*you* know he's a professor?'

'I must have heard one of the others talking about him.'

'Pretty impressive, eh?'

'I suppose. If you're into that kind of thing.'

Angel frowned. 'He's a nice guy,' she said, cocking her head to one side.

'Gabriel Posner. Pretty poncey name if you ask me.' Colin slipped into the warmth of the bed.

'He's cool,' Angel said. 'For a start he's quite young – for a professor. And he's really helpful. He got one of my marks put up in the first term. *And* he keeps a bottle of Liebfraumilch in his filing cabinet.'

Colin shivered. 'So why is Mr Nice-Guy Professor writing to *you*?'

'Something about my exams. I knew I'd fail. I'm no good at exams anymore. He wants me to go in and talk to him about next year.'

'You're not going, though?' Colin leant over to Angel's side of the bed and moved a strand of her hair that was stuck to her cheek.

'Why not?'

'Because it's a waste of time. If you've failed your exams in the first year, you're never going to make it in the second and third years. You should give up while you've still got your pride.'

'Maybe. But I could still go in. See what he's got to say.'

'And share some Liebfraumilch? Perhaps I should come with you. The guy's obviously a pervert.'

Angel rolled over onto her stomach. 'Don't be silly. Of course he's not a pervert. Come here,' she said kissing his cheek. 'You look frozen.'

'I've just spent the night in a frozen pea factory.'

'I know you have, and I'm very impressed. I think you're the best frozen pea factory employee in the world. Here, give me a hug. I've missed you. Come on, Col. What's wrong?'

'Nothing's wrong. I'm just tired,' he said, although for some reason, even though he'd been thinking about this moment for the past hour, longing for it, in fact, he suddenly felt … like … he didn't know what he felt . Like he didn't want to touch her, even though he did want to touch her. His skin tingled with the anticipation of touching her.

'What's the matter? Haven't you missed me?' Angel asked.

'Nothing's the matter.'

'Col, there is something wrong – what's happened? Is it your job? Has something happened at the factory?'

'The job's shit, but everything's cool,' he said with a yawn.

Angel laid her arm across his stomach and pinched his skin. 'Don't be cold, Col. You're beginning to turn into a frozen pea. Why are you being like this?'

Colin didn't answer her because he didn't know the answer. They lay in silence for a few minutes until he removed her arm from his stomach. 'Angel,' he said slowly. 'Promise me … you won't go and see this… this professor guy.'

'What?'

'Go on, say it. Say you promise you won't go into the university to see him.'

Angel sighed. 'Okay, I promise I won't see Professor Posner or even speak to him ever again. Girl Guides' honour.' She saluted her forehead as if she was a Girl Guide – which obviously she wasn't, and probably never had been. 'Now please can I have that cuddle?'

Colin realised he'd been holding his breath. The air shuddered from inside his lungs in a long shaky sigh as he wrapped her in his arms.

'There's a card in the post office asking for part time help in the shop.' Colin was getting ready for work, fastening the buttons on the shirt he wore over his T-shirt. 'I asked the guy about it,' Angel went on. 'His wife's expecting a baby, so they need someone in the afternoons. Twenty-three pence an hour. He said I could start tomorrow.'

Colin tucked his shirt into his jeans. 'Sounds pretty straight, but I guess we need the money. Are you sure you wanna work in a *shop*, though, Babe?'

'Are you sure you want to work in a *pea factory*? It's not like it's going to be my career for life. Anyway, I quite like the idea of meeting new people – I get bored here when you're asleep all day. It's near enough to walk, *and* I don't have to be there till one in the afternoon.'

'But what time will you be home?' Colin put Angel's jumper on over his own. One of the cuffs was beginning to unravel.

'One till half-five. I'll be home before six.'

'But I leave at six. We'll never see each other.'

'It's only temporary and we'll still see each other in the mornings.'

Colin left Angel in the kitchen and went upstairs to his look at his stick insects. He kept three jars of them in the box room. Since Martin Stringer had given them to him, he'd really started to get into them. He'd given them all names. The longest one was called 'Branchy', a baby green one was called 'Greeny' and a tiny black one was called 'Sticky'. He'd never had any pets before. His mum always said there wasn't enough room in the flat, although other families in the same block had dogs and cats. One family had four dogs, five snakes and a rabbit. But then Colin and his mum didn't count as a proper family, since there was just the two of them.

The box room still had its black ceiling and the poster of Ché Guevara on the door. Colin always thought of it as Crazy Mike's room, even though Crazy Mike had never shown up to move back in. The room reminded him of that first sleepless night when he'd spent half the time trying to sleep and the rest in Angel's sleeping bag. He'd started going up there whenever he felt upset. He'd sit watching the stick insects as they climbed to the top of the jars then toppled down again. They'd struggle up with those spindly black legs, but the minute they'd made it to the top of the jar, they'd plop right back down. Colin decided if they had any more babies, he'd call the next one Mike in honour of Crazy Mike whose room they lived in. Angel called the stick insects anorexic beetles.

Colin took the jars down from the windowsill and placed them on the floor by the bed. He preferred to watch them like this, from above, and he always made sure he left the door open so he could hear what Angel was doing downstairs. He unscrewed one of the lids to rearrange the leaves he'd put in the jar for Greeny. The phone downstairs rang. Colin stared at the jar. The ringing stopped. Angel had answered it and he could tell by what she was saying that her mother was on the line. Or at least he heard her calling the person 'Mummy'. He strained harder to make sure he'd heard right. She definitely did say 'Mummy'. Unless, of course, she was pretending to say 'Mummy' when actually she was speaking to someone else. What was that pervy professor called? Gabriel. No, the name Gabriel couldn't be confused with 'Mummy'. He heard Angel say 'How's Daddy?' Colin smiled to himself and nodded at Greeny. Everything was cool. He put the lid on the jar and went into the bathroom to wash his face before he left for work.

As winter deepened, so the mornings became darker. The ride home that November morning was cold. A wet wind carried brown and yellow leaves that splattered him in the face. When Colin got home Angel was already dressed, standing in the kitchen mixing something in a bowl.

'What are you doing up so early?' Colin kissed her ear. The kitchen had a familiar warmth that he was beginning to cherish. She had her hair tied in a pony tail with several lose strands framing her little pixie face.

'I'm making a cake.'

Colin filled the kettle. 'Isn't it a bit early to be making cakes?'

Angel laughed. 'Let me tell you what happened. It all started yesterday.' She spoke breathlessly. 'One of the old biddies that come into the post office, Mrs Cartwright I think she's called. Anyway I was standing there, yawning as usual when Mrs Cartwright comes in and asks if we're out of bread. So I looked at the bread shelf, which was empty like it always is in the afternoons, and I honestly had to bite my tongue. I mean, some of the villagers have to have everything spelled out to them. Then I thought about Marie Antoinette – you know, the one who said 'let them eat cake', and was just about to suggest she bought some *cakes* when I realised we were out of cakes too. Anyway, we started talking about bread and cakes – she's quite a nice old lady really – and she said she needed a cake for her granddaughter's christening. She asked me if I knew anyone who made cakes as she was no good at baking and a woman in Lyde who used to sell her cakes had died. So, ten minutes later I'd got an order to make a Christening cake! Isn't that fantastic?'

'Yeah, great,' Colin said, trying not to yawn. All this bakery talk so early in the day was a bit heavy. 'Aren't you coming back to bed, Babe?'

'I'm just going to finish this icing and I can't take the cake out of the oven for another twenty minutes. I don't want it to burn. This is going to be the most beautiful cake ever.'

'But have you made a Christening cake before? I mean that's one of those really elaborate things with icing and words on it. You won't be able to do all that shit.'

'I don't see why not. And if Mrs Cartwright doesn't like it, I'll be able to sell it in the post office to someone else.'

Colin took his mug of tea upstairs and got into bed on his own.

It was a late afternoon when Colin found Angel in the kitchen. 'How's it going, Babe?' She was at the sink washing up. Colin kissed the top of her head. Her hair smelled of shampoo and that musky smell, like burnt chestnuts.

'Col,' she said turning round and wiping her hands. 'You'll never believe what's happened. Mrs Cartwright *did* like the cake and so did everyone else at the Christening party, so Mr Robinson's asked me to make more cakes, you know – to sell in the shop.'

'Wow. I hope he's going to pay you.'

'Of course. Forty pence a cake.'

'I wish I could get forty pence per pea.'

Angel threw her head back and giggled. The tips of her ponytail reached down to the belt on her jeans.

'I love the way you laugh,' Colin said. He took her in his arms and stroked his hand down the length of her hair. 'I wish I didn't have to go to work,' Colin said after they'd kissed.

'Me too. But I've got loads to do.' Angel kissed him on the lips again. 'I love you,' she said before disentangling herself from his arms. 'But I must get on…' She reached into the cupboard for a packet of flour. '…and so should you, Col. You don't want to be late.'

'You look really happy, Babe. When you're baking and stuff.'

'I am. You make that sound like a bad thing.'

'I wouldn't have thought making cakes would be enough to make someone happy, that's all.'

'But I love making cakes.'

'I thought you loved me. Now all you seem to care about is flour and shit.'

'I just told you I love you, silly.'

'Angel if you really love me, don't start baking before I get home tomorrow morning. Stay in bed, please.'

As the new year kicked in, the factory seemed colder and further away. As he cycled home, a north easterly wind caught Colin's knuckles on the handlebars of the bike. He wished he had gloves. Wearily he filled the kettle when he got home. He was glad Angel had listened to him and was no longer downstairs baking in the mornings when he got home. Carrying his mug of tea, he climbed the stairs and flopped into the bed next to her. Angel stroked his cheek with her warm hand. 'You're icy,' she said.

Colin slipped his jeans down his hips. Angel put her arms around his cold shoulders and caressed his hair. After they'd made love, she went downstairs. Colin reached for the alarm clock he'd found in Crazy Mike's room which he kept on the floor under the bed. However, instead of setting it as normal for four in the afternoon he set it for two.

When the alarm went off Colin was dreaming about a pea war on the conveyor belt where giant brown peas were slaughtering baby green ones. He got up and dressed, put on his coat and his old college scarf. The air was raw, and he could see his breath like steam from a kettle as he cycled up Blackberry Lane, past the war memorial and down the village high street. He parked the bike a little way away from the post office, pulled his scarf up to his chin, ambled along the other side of the road, and stopped to look in the window of the fish and chip shop. He pulled the scarf up higher until only his eyes were showing.

He could see Angel through the post office window. She was standing behind the counter. Her hair was tied in a loose ponytail, the way she always wore it for work. He could just about make out a shadowy figure who he took to be Mr Robinson. They looked as though they were chatting. Angel had hardly mentioned Mr Robinson since she'd been working there. It hadn't occurred to Colin that they got on well. Now he wondered why she hadn't mentioned him, since they seemed to be such friends. He walked up the road away from the fish and chip shop, then down again. A man went into the post office. He was youngish – at a guess in his thirties. He wore a herringbone jacket and freshly ironed jeans. As soon as the bell jangled Angel looked up. Colin ducked round the corner of the alleyway at the side of the fish and chip shop and waited. This guy was in the post office a long time. At least ten minutes.

When the man eventually came out, all he had was a newspaper. How long does it take to buy a fucking newspaper? Colin wondered. The man crossed the road, which meant Colin got a good look at him. He hadn't seen him before in the village. He was dark-haired with sallow skin and looked a bit like that actor, Tom Conti, from *Adam Smith* on TV. Now Colin thought about it, Angel had made a point of watching every episode of *Adam Smith* on the old black and white television Fabian had left behind. Colin had suspected that Angel liked Tom Conti and he'd even turned the television off one night in the middle of the programme just to see what she'd do. She hadn't protested but simply watched the news on the other side. She seemed interested in the news item about Greenham Common. Although, now that he thought about it, she could have been pretending to be interested Greenham Common to put Colin off the scent.

Colin hid in a bush as the man walked down the road to get into his car. It was a green Citroen. A thought struck Colin.

This Tom Conti lookalike could be the Professor who dished out Liebfraumilch from his drawer. He looked that type. Angel had promised not to go to his office to discuss her grades, but that didn't mean he wouldn't visit her. Colin cycled home feeling sick.

'Did you meet anyone interesting at work today?' Colin was waiting on the sofa for Angel to come home before he left for work.

She collapsed next to him, still in her duffle coat with her chunky woollen scarf covering her hair. 'Not especially – did you meet anyone nice last night at the pea factory?'

'Hardly.'

Angel laughed. Colin had to stop himself from wrapping her in his arms. He longed to feel her next to him, to stroke her hair and wind the tips around his finger. 'I've been in a post office all afternoon. It's not exactly a discotheque.' As she spoke she pulled at the elastic band in her hair so it tumbled onto her shoulders.

'But you do meet people when you're at work,' Colin carried on, picking at one of his fingernails.

'Whereas you only meet peas. Col, most people who come into the post office are collecting their pensions. They enjoy a bit of a gossip, but I wouldn't call it *meeting* people.'

'They can't all be old.'

Angel frowned. 'No – they're not all old. Why the sudden interest in the customers at the post office?'

'No reason.'

'No reason?' Angel looked into his eyes. 'You're not *jealous* are you?'

'Of course I'm not.'

'Well then, silly. I've just got to get some butter and sugar mixed up, then I'll make some spaghetti before you go.' Colin followed her into the kitchen. She poured some sugar from a half pound bag onto the scales. 'But it would be quite cool if you were jealous,' she said as she scrutinised the dial on the scales. 'I think that's sweet. It means you really do love me lots.'

Colin sat down at the table. 'I'm not going to work tonight,' he said. Angel stopped what she was doing. 'Why not?'

'I got the push.'

'Fuck. Why?'

Colin fiddled with the buttons on his coat. 'Fell asleep on the line – they let you off twice but the third time you get the push.'

'Bummer.' Angel scraped some butter from her knife.

'Yeah. But so what. Sit down, Angel. Forget about the pea factory and the butter for a minute. I want to talk to you.'

'That sounds serious. What's up?'

'Just sit down…'

'Col. You're freaking me. You're not leaving, are you?'

Colin looked at her face. Her blue eyes shone against the pinkness of her cheeks. A strand of her hair hung across her cheek, and she had a speck of butter on the side of her nose.

'I want us … I want us to get married.'

'Married? You're not serious.' Angel laughed. 'Married! I thought you were going to tell me you were going away or something horrible…'

'No. I'm not going away. Where would I go? And anyway, I don't want to leave you. We *could* get married. Why not? Lots of people get married. Fabian and Hilly were always talking about getting married.'

'Yes, but they didn't. And they'd been together for ages. Anyway, Fabian's dad is loaded. He could do what he wanted and…'

'If you really loved me and nobody else, you'd want to marry me.'

'Of course I love you, but wow! Married.' Angel spoke the words to the weighing scales in front of her on the table. 'Married!' she said again, as if this was the craziest word in the dictionary.

'Will you? Please say "yes".'

'I suppose I could make the wedding cake,' she said. She turned and met Colin's gaze. 'Ok! Let's get married. Let's do it. It's insane, but, hey, what's to stop us?'

Colin picked up the bag of sugar and what was left of the butter and dropped them in the bin. 'Ok. Forget about cakes and come to bed.'

'Col why did you do that? I need those for my cake…'

'What's more important – your future husband or a cake?'

Angel shrugged her shoulders, shook her head so her hair swung across her back.

'My future husband!' she squealed as he grabbed her hand and they ran together towards the stairs.

For their wedding Colin wore a purple velvet suit that Fabian had left behind in the wardrobe. The trousers were too long but Angel sewed up the hems. He borrowed a tie from Mr Stringer, and Angel found a green silk dress in the Oxfam Shop. Colin's mum travelled down by coach. Colin hardly recognised her. She'd lost weight and had obviously splashed out on new gear – an orange and green frock that showed her knees. Colin wasn't used to seeing her knees. They were round and flat like two saucepan lids and made him feel embarrassed. She clutched her brown plastic handbag, the same one she'd had for years.

In the registry office Mrs Grey sat motionless beside her husband, her fingers laced around her crocodile handbag. She was wearing a pink dress with a matching collarless coat and hat like Jackie Kennedy's. The old man's threads were equally freaky. He had on a pin-striped suit with a waistcoat and a blue tie, finished off with black brogues. Italian or something, Colin guessed. Shit. Colin hadn't imagined Angel's parents would be like this. Right wing, middle class, middle of the road Conservatives. Probably belonged to the Rotary Club, whatever the fuck that was. He felt sorry for his mum having to sit next to them. Then he felt ashamed. At least the Greys were a proper married couple. There were two of them. A united front. Whereas neither Colin nor his mum had a clue where Colin's dad *was*.

After Angel and Colin had made their vows they kissed and turned around to smile at their parents. Angel's mum and dad were looking down at their respective laps. Colin's mum was dabbing her eyes with a handkerchief – one of those real cloth cotton jobbies with embroidered violets round the edges. Why couldn't she have Kleenex like everyone else?

Once the papers were signed, the five of them stood outside the registry office on the pavement with ordinary people doing their shopping or taking their lunch breaks having to walk around them. Colin bit his thumb nail as their parents shook hands stiffly and exchanged uncomfortable smiles. They drove home in Angel's dad's

Rover – Mr and Mrs Grey in the front and Colin and Angel in the back with Colin's mum. His mum said 'Couldn't you have at least got your hair cut, Colin,' but she spoke quietly so no one else heard. She'd always had that confidential way of speaking to him. Colin played with his fringe instead of answering her.

Angel was beside him, gazing out of the window so he could see her perfect profile. Her neat little nose, pale cheeks that looked like they'd burn in even the weakest sunlight. Her hair was in a plait that she'd somehow wound around the top of her head. She'd threaded a green ribbon and some daisies through it and a strand of hair that had escaped, hung like a thread of gold on her bare neck. Colin squeezed her hand and felt the unfamiliarity of the ring. He couldn't wait to get her into bed that night and wished everyone else would disappear.

Back at Blackberry Lane they ate the wedding cake Angel had made and drank elderberry wine in the front room.

'We should've brought champagne,' Mrs Grey said. 'We did suggest everyone came to our house. We've recently redecorated,' she carried on, addressing Colin's mum. 'But Angela can be a bit headstrong.'

'Elderberry wine from tea-stained cups,' her dad spoke with a bewildered shake of his balding head.

Colin looked at his mother. She was still wearing her hat, a small creation that looked like a green upside-down paper boat. She had a cup balanced on her knee, her handbag leant against her foot, and was trying to shove as much cake as she could into her mouth without dropping any crumbs. She took a sip of elderberry wine to wash it down. 'It's a nice place you've got here, Colin, love,' she said in that whisper again, as if she was afraid anyone else would hear.

Mr Grey obviously had heard though. He surveyed the room. 'If you call a semi the size of a matchbox at the end of a muddy track *nice*,' he said.

Colin wondered how it would feel to punch his new father-in-law in the face. He'd never punched anyone but he felt the urge to try now. On his first day at school a boy in the year above, Robin

Cotton, had punched him in the stomach when they were in the toilets. He'd never told anyone and felt ashamed that he hadn't retaliated. He didn't know how to fight, and his dad had never been around long enough to teach him. He took a deep breath. He could quite easily have taken the couple of steps across the room and clocked Mr Grey right in the face. He could imagine the feel of the bone in his nose against Colin's fist. Not to mention the blood. There would be a lot of blood. But what would happen afterwards? Angel would hate him. Mrs Grey would probably faint. Mr Grey might die. Colin would be a murderer. For what? To get revenge on this tosser and his snide remarks.

His mum wiped the crumbs of cake from the corner of her mouth with another hankie she had hidden up her jacket sleeve. 'It's small but they wouldn't want a big place, would you, Colin? I mean, there's only the two of you living here...' her voice trailed off as she lost the confidence to carry on. She refilled her mouth with cake.

'It *will* only be the two of you, Angela?' Mr Grey's gaze relocated to his daughter's stomach, 'I hope you're not...this isn't a shotgun wedding, is it? I mean to say, you're in the middle of your degree!'

'Daddy, it's *Angel* and, for your information, I'm *not* pregnant. I can't believe you're being so uptight.'

Colin's mum's cake seemed to have gone down the wrong way. She coughed into her hankie, at the same time shaking her head, begging everyone to ignore her plight and carry on with whatever they were doing and not mind her. Angel looked at Colin with fear in her eyes, entreating him to help his mother before she choked to death. Colin chose to ignore them both and buried his eyes behind his fringe.

'I'm extremely glad to hear that you're not pregnant,' Mr Grey carried on when Colin's mum had recovered. 'But your name was definitely Angela half an hour ago when you got married to whatsisname.'

'Daddy! Will you stop this? His name's *Colin*.'

'Now, now,' Mrs Grey interrupted. 'No arguing on your wedding day. She's not pregnant, Geoffrey, so let's leave it at that. In fact, I was actually thinking she's looking rather *thin*. Are you eating enough, Angela? You look so small. She's never been robust,' she added, looking at Colin's mum. 'We even saw a consultant when she was younger – because of her size.'

'Yes,' Mr Grey interrupted. 'You look as if you need looking after. Remember Angela, your room's still waiting for you at home if you need it.'

'Both of you, Daddy means, of course,' his wife added.   Mr Grey sucked on the end of a stubby cigar he'd produced from the top pocket of his jacket.

'Daddy – how many times do I have to tell you – I don't answer to Angela now – and more to the point, why *would* I come home? I'm married, in case you hadn't noticed.' Angel fiddled with the curtain ring she'd found in a kitchen drawer which was now on her left hand.

'I'm only saying your room's there, should you need it. And, as your mother says, Kevin can come too, after all it's big enough. Triple aspect,' he nodded towards Colin's mum.

'Daddy, can't you get anything right? It's *Colin*, – and we're happy here.'

'Can I wrap some of this cake up for the girls at work?' Colin's mum asked.

Colin was sure that if he didn't leave the room immediately, he'd be tempted to ram that cigar down Mr Grey's throat. 'Mum, would you like to come upstairs to see my stick insects?' he said.

'Oh, stick insects? I didn't know you had stick insects. What are they? Yes, love , that would be…'

Colin scaled the stairs two at a time with his mum trailing behind still carrying her handbag and a plate of cake.

She said she thought the stick insects were very interesting and asked where the toilet was. Colin stood in the middle of Crazy Mike's room, relieved at last to be alone. He could hear Angel talking to her dad downstairs, but it was impossible to work out what they were saying. He heard his mum pull the chain and came out to meet her on the landing. 'It's a bit chilly up here, Mum. We may as well go back downstairs.'

His mum retrieved her plate and handbag before following her son downstairs. By then Angel was washing up in the kitchen. 'We'll dry, won't we, Geoffrey?' Mrs Grey slid the doors closed that divided the kitchen from the living room. Colin cut his mum another piece of cake, still trying to eavesdrop through the gap in the doors.

'Angela,' he heard her dad say. 'You look like Cinderella standing there at the sink in that dress.'

'*Angel*, Daddy!'

'Think about what I said. If you're giving up your studies, and you're old enough to get married, you need to start thinking sensibly. Believe me, buying property is the way forward. Not renting. You need security, a decent place for you and ... to live. And you should be thinking about proper jobs with index linked pension schemes.'

'You mean me and *Colin*, Daddy.'

'Yes. That's the fellow. What do you say, Angela?'

'I'll have to talk to Colin about it.'

'And Angela...'

'*Angel*, Daddy. How many more times?'

'Alright. But I don't know what's wrong with your proper name. Are you happy?'

'Yes of course I'm happy, Daddy. It's my wedding day. Everyone's happy on their wedding day.'

At this point Mr Grey lowered his voice. Colin screwed up his eyes, straining to catch what he was saying. 'But this chap – this *Colin*. Seriously, what does he *do*? Where is he from? What do we know about him? He doesn't say a lot.'

'He's shy. That's all, Daddy. Once you get to know him, you'll...'

'But he's a dropout by the sound of things. What prospects does he have? Which school did he go to? He doesn't look very...surely you could have met someone more..."

The kettle started to whistle, and Angel's father came through into the front room still chomping on his unlit cigar.

That night after they'd had sex Angel sat up. She took her hairbrush from the floor beside the bed.

'You know when you were showing your mum the stick insects?' she said sliding the brush slowly through her hair. 'Well, Daddy was talking to me in the kitchen while Mummy was helping with the washing up. He said he wants to help us.'

'Help us? We don't need help.'

'That's what *I* said, but *he* said all newly-weds need help. Him and Mummy have talked it over and they've decided… they want to buy us a house for a wedding present. Isn't that just the coolest thing?'

'A *house*.' Colin made the word sound obscene.

'Yes. I know it sounds weird, but Daddy says it's the best investment anyone can make and if we had a house, we'd have security. When they got married, they didn't have anything. They lived with my grandparents for a year. I don't think we'd want to end up in that situation. So what do you think? Isn't Daddy the most incredibly generous person?'

Colin rubbed his cheek whilst he thought about what she'd said. He took a deep breath before he spoke. 'That's a bit over the top, isn't it? I mean a *house*. Especially when my mum only gave us those tea towels and the new kettle.'

'That's what I thought at first,' Angel said. 'But then I thought, well, the house would be an investment for him. But we get to live in it rent free.'

Colin reached under the bed for a record sleeve, the dope and some tobacco. He rolled a joint and blew a stream of yellow smoke across the blanket.

'My first blow as a married man,' he laughed.

Angel smiled. 'I don't know what Daddy would say if he saw you now.'

'He can't see me now. He doesn't like me anyway. You know what this house thing is really about,' he went on before she had a chance to claim otherwise, 'it's his way of holding on to you. Your old man's jealous. I sussed him straight away. He kept looking at me. It's one of those father daughter things. Oedipus complex in reverse. It's a way of keeping control. We should definitely say "no" to the house idea.' Colin's joint had gone out. He re-lit it and sucked on it in short blasts before passing it to Angel.

'*I think* he just wants me to be happy,' Angel said.

'But typically, with his middle-class values, happiness is equated with ownership.'

'Not really. His theory is that there will be a big property boom soon, so unless we buy now, we might never be able to afford our own house.'

'"Property is theft." Haven't you ever read Proudhon? All people like your old man want to do is own things, own people. Happiness doesn't come from *owning*, Angel. I don't want to move, anyway. I certainly wouldn't want to live in a house your old man had bought. What would it be? On some middle-class housing estate surrounded by accountants and shit.'

With the frozen pea factory a distant memory and his P45 tucked in his jeans' pocket, Colin took the bus into town to sign on again. Luckily, as the pea emporium had given him the push it wasn't Colin's fault he was unemployed. The mental zealot from his previous visit must have left or been on holiday because he got some spotty dude who was unable to come up with any jobs to suit Colin's requirements. At last it seemed he was eligible for benefits.

'Are you living on your own?' the clerk asked, holding his biro with a flourish in the air ready to write down Colin's answer.

Colin hesitated. He knew there were lots of rules about co-habiting, but he wasn't sure what they were. He knew even less about the implications of being married.

'Yeah,' he said. He chewed on a fingernail. 'Yeah. Just with my wife.' As he spoke the word, Colin realised that was the first time he'd referred to Angel as his wife. He had a *wife*. Wow.

'Is your wife working? Because if she is, that will make a big difference to your benefits.'

Angel came home after her last afternoon's shift in the post office. She sat in the kitchen making patterns on the table with some sugar Colin had spilt.

'I don't understand how you can feel pissed off about leaving that job,' Colin said. 'It wasn't exactly stimulating.'

'It was okay. I liked meeting people. Anyway, Mr Robinson said I could still sell my cakes in the shop. What's this?' Angel said, picking up a letter from the table.

'I don't know. I didn't bother to open it.'

Angel tore into the envelope. 'It's from Mullet. He says we're behind with the rent. He wants to evict us! Says he "needs the house for his own occupation". Great. So now we'll have to leave. No home and no job.'

'I shouldn't worry, Babe. Now you're not working the Social will pay the rent. Anyway that's the oldest trick in the book. Typical capitalist landlord preying on the vulnerability of their proletariat tenants. *Needs it for his own occupation*! That's just a lie to freak us out.'

'But can he really chuck us out?'

'I'm not sure. As a capitalist landlord he's got the state on his side, don't forget.'

'I could ask Daddy. Uncle Timothy is a solicitor."

'No. Don't. I'll check at the Social.'

A fortnight later another letter arrived – from Mr Mullet's solicitors.

'I'll ask at the Social tomorrow. See what they say,' Colin mumbled from the couch in the front room. Angel put the letter in her pocket.

'I'm going for a walk,' she said.

'Where are you going?'

'Just for some fresh air.'

'Don't be long.'

Thirty-seven minutes later she was back.

'I've spoken to Daddy,' she said when she came into the front room, her eyes shining. 'He said he'll get in touch with Mr Mullett – he's going to offer to buy him out. Isn't that great? That way we can stay here and be homeowners.'

Colin had brought one of the stick insects' jars downstairs and was holding Greeny in his hand. 'You went out to the phone box? I thought you said you were going for a walk.'

'I was walking around when I came to the phone box and decided to give Daddy a ring. Since ours has been cut off I feel as if *I'm* cut off from everyone.'

'Well, I don't feel cut off. I've got you. We've got each other. Can't you see? He's trying to buy us. He thinks he *can* buy us. I'm sorry, but I'm not for sale.'

Angel fixed her gaze on Greeny. 'I don't think he's trying to buy us. The house will be a wedding present. All parents give their children wedding presents.'

'Yeah, sure. A *house* for a wedding present. A wedding present is usually a toaster, or an iron. Like I said before, a set of tea towels or a kettle like my mum got us. Not a fucking house.'

Angel sat down on the old bust armchair with its stuffing hanging out that Hilly had bought from a jumble sale.

'I suppose you're right.' She sniffed. 'Please don't be angry. All I want is for us to be happy.'

'I *know* I'm right,' Colin said, 'I'm going upstairs to put Greeny back.'

Colin had moved the stick insects into a fish tank he'd found dumped at the side of the lane. With them all in together he hoped to breed, although it was tricky to tell the sex of a stick insect. He'd added extra leaves and some conker shells. He took Greeny out and balanced him on his palm. Of course he didn't know if Greeny was a male but he'd always thought of him as a boy. He heard Angel coming upstairs.

'Look, Col,' she said, standing in the doorway. 'I know you don't like my parents, but I think we should invite them over to talk about the house, and as a way of saying thank you. It would give you a chance to get to know them better.'

Colin let Greeny stride on his stalky legs from one hand to another. Angel blew her nose, kissed Colin on the cheek, and went downstairs. Colin stood motionless in the middle of the room. He could hear her opening and closing cupboard doors in the kitchen. He heard her bang something on the table. A lump of pastry, probably. It sounded as if she was pummelling it with a rolling pin. The kitchen door slammed – the noise reverberated throughout the house causing one of the stick insects to slip down from the side of the tank and land on a blade of grass. He looked out of the window. Angel was crouched beneath the apple tree with her head in her hands. Colin sat looking at the stick insects until he heard her come inside again.

'You know the cake I made for Evie's fortieth? Apparently she said it was so good everyone thought I should sell my cakes. So I told her I *do* sell them – to the post office. And suddenly I came up with this amazing idea. A café. We could run a café, Col. Don't you think that's a brilliant idea? Think about it. It could be amazing.'

'Angel you're mad. Completely off the planet,' Colin said, as he rolled a tiny joint with the small amount of dope he had left. 'You're an airhead. Angel Airhead.'

'No. I'm serious. Think about it. I mean I miss my job and let's face it, apart from the Stringers, we hardly see anyone.'

"Aren't *I* enough for you?"

'Yes of course you are,' she said, sitting on the floor by his feet, running her hand up his shin. 'It doesn't mean I don't love you, just because I've got plans for us to *do* something with our lives.'

'But you see other people when you take the cakes into the village. Surely that's enough.'

'I see Mr and Mrs Robinson. That's *two* people.'

Colin lit the joint, only just managing not to set fire to his fringe. 'Okay,' he said, inhaling deep into his lungs. 'So where's this café going to be?'

'We're sitting in it!'

Colin coughed as he exhaled a splutter of smoke. 'Sitting in it? Angel, you're definitely mad.'

'Listen. I've got it all worked out. We could get three tables in here at a push. If we do a bit of advertising people might come from miles around. I'm already getting orders for my cakes. Evie reckons they're the best in Somerset. All it takes is for a few people to spread the word.'

'You think people will trek all the way out here to eat a piece of cake?'

'But it won't just be a *piece of cake*. We'll have tea, coffee and other drinks. Food…'

'I think it's a mad idea,' Colin said.

'You won't say that when the money starts pouring in.'

'So, we're going to sell out and become capitalists. Imagine what Fabian would have said about that.'

'Fabian would have said – it's far out. Cool as shit. *Everything depends on how we look at things, not how they are in themselves.* That was one of Fabian's favourites. If we look at it as a ...*co-operative.* That's what it'll be. The money we make will be re-invested in the business. I doubt we'll make a lot of profit at first. Just enough to cover our costs and our household bills. That's not capitalism. Karl Marx would definitely approve.'

'Who? Is this someone you've met in the post office?'

'Don't be silly. Karl Marx? Communist dude? Died centuries ago?'

'Oh, that Karl Marx.' Colin turned away to hide his embarrassment.

Colin's job was to transform Crazy Mike's bedroom into a sitting room. Angel worked on an application for planning permission to turn the downstairs into a teashop. Meanwhile she bought a tin of Sunshine Yellow paint, put a kitchen chair in the garden, stood on it and painted the porch.

With the money from her next cake sale, she bought a piece of wood and a pencil thin paintbrush and stencilled the words Angel's Oven. She persuaded Christian Stringer to hang the sign outside. Angel scrubbed the carpets, she made three lace tablecloths and wrote out menus. At night as they lay in bed, they could hear the sign creaking as it swayed in the wind.

Angel's Oven was to open on the first of May. She stored cakes in Evie Stringer's freezer, bought cups and plates from the Oxfam shop in Shapton, and a cowbell to hang inside the door. She was to serve the customers while Colin's job would be to wash up and make the drinks. By nine in the morning everything was ready. Colin watched Angel as she arranged jam jars of wildflowers at the centre of each table. She'd washed her hair that morning and it shone like a golden mane down her back. She wore a long blue skirt, a gypsy blouse and no shoes. The sight of her made Colin want to cry. She was literally the most beautiful thing he'd ever encountered. She had a wild, busy look about her. Nobody could possibly see her and not fall in love with her.

And she was his.

'Aren't you going to wash your hair, Col?' she said. Her words broke the spell and he went upstairs to wash his hair with Sunsilk and cold water. They sat together at the kitchen table – and waited.

'D'you really think this will work?' Colin asked at half-ten.

'I've advertised in the post office, the local paper *and* put notices up in the bar at the university. It's bound to be slow at first. Anyway, it's still early.'

Just as she finished speaking a car stopped outside and the cowbell jangled. Angel jumped out of her chair.

'This is it,' she squealed. 'Our first customer!'

The man standing in the porch was stout with round National Health glasses, and a leather briefcase tucked under his arm.

'Hi,' Angel said. 'Welcome to Angel's Oven.'

'Oh, thank you. Actually, I'm looking for Mr Colin Monk. Is he in by any chance?'

Colin felt himself blush as the man from the Social Security followed Angel into the kitchen. He looked like Richard Attenborough who played the part of a murderer in a film they'd seen in town.

'I'm here about your Social Security claim, Mr Monk.' The man laid his briefcase on the table as he spoke. 'I believe you're running a business from this address. You do realise that your benefits will be affected if you are conducting a business from home? You can continue to claim for a month, after which time your benefits will be cut and you will be deemed to be employed.'

Angel offered the man a green tea, but he declined. After he'd driven away, they sat down at the kitchen table again.

Angel fiddled with one of the menus. 'We're going to make this work, Col. I know we are,' she said, looking slightly less certain than she had an hour previously.

Colin filled the kettle. 'I know we are too,' he repeated but without Angel's conviction.

'You've got to believe in it, Col.'

'I do. I believe in you, Angel. I think you've done a fantastic job. You're brilliant, wonderful, beautiful.'

Angel beamed at him across the table. 'I love it when you say things like that,' she said, reaching for his hand. 'You make me feel as if I can do anything.'

They sat together for the rest of the morning playing Scrabble.

'At least we won't starve,' Colin pointed out at half-past two. He cut himself a double portion of quiche.

At four o'clock they were still in the kitchen reading when the cowbell jangled again. They both looked up from their books, eyes wide with a mixture of excitement and astonishment.

'Just make sure it's not that bastard from the Social again,' Colin said. Angel went into the front room to have a look out of the window.

'It's Evie Stringer, and Christian *and* Martin, and Nicholas and the other son!'

Colin went into the hall. Angel had opened the door and the entire Stringer family – except for the old granddad – stretched down the path as far as the gate. Angel did a little welcoming skip towards them.

The Stringers seemed to fill the whole room. Martin was wearing muddy boots as if he'd come straight from the field. Angel handed them two menus.

'What's all this? Lapsang soo what? *Ahh so*!!' Nicholas made Chinese eyes and creased up with laughter. 'I'll have builders' tea, me, mate,' Martin said. 'Milk and two sugars.'

Colin watched them with disdain, even though they reminded him of himself on the day, only two years ago when he'd arrived from East Anglia.

Evie sat up straight. 'Hush you boys. Can't take 'em nowhere,' she said, handing Christian the menu. Christian mumbled something about not having his glasses with him, so Evie ordered tea for five with a selection of cakes.

In the kitchen, Angel had everything prepared. She made a pot of tea, carried the tray of cakes into the front room then came back to the kitchen and sat down beside Colin at the table.

'Our first customers!' She took her pen to write out the bill. 'Shame we haven't got a bottle of champagne to crack.'

'We can hardly count the Stringers as customers.'

'Why not? Their money's as good as anybody's.'

'Angel! You can't charge the Stringers for a cup of tea and few cakes. They've always been generous to us. We've had Martin's bike for months and Christian put up your sign.'

'But we'll never make any money if we give stuff away.'

'I can't believe I'm hearing this. Take money from the Stringers! They're probably worse off than we are. Think about the proletariat, Angel.'

Angel bit her lip. 'I suppose.'

Colin picked up the bill, tore it up and dropped the pieces onto the table.

By the end of September most people in Lyde had visited Angel's Oven. Angel made salads and sandwiches for lunch. The weekends were the busiest when people came from town looking for a quiet country spot to have lunch.

Colin now dealt with the orders and bills. He spent most of his time in the kitchen, although occasionally he'd have a peek to see who was in the café. He'd noticed a man who often came on a Sunday lunchtime and always ordered a tuna salad and a glass of elderberry wine. Colin thought he recognised him, although he couldn't think where he'd seen him before.

The man turned up the following Sunday – alone, as usual. He obviously didn't have any family, or he wouldn't be eating on his own every weekend. When the order came through for the usual tuna salad and elderberry wine, Colin told Angel he'd serve this one.

'You look as if you need a rest, Babe. Why don't you sit out in the garden for a bit,' he said, as he carried the man's food out. The man was sitting back on his chair looking very much at home. He was wearing round granny specs and had a copy of the *Sunday Times* on the table. He was about thirty, with black wavy hair that curled over his collar. He had one of those rugged faces, like that actor, Tom Conti, all women seemed to fancy.

That was it. The penny dropped like a dead blue bottle from a high ceiling. Colin remembered who he was. The guy he'd seen coming out of the post office when Angel worked there. Colin placed the tuna salad on his table.

'I'll have a slice of strawberry flan to follow,' the man said, removing his glasses and folding them inside a case.

Colin nodded, went back into the kitchen and pulled the sliding doors to.

The bastard hadn't even said 'please'. He lifted the flan from the fridge. Angel had made it that morning. It was soft and round and perfect, with twenty strawberries circled in lime jelly. He cut a small slice and looked out of the window. Angel was sitting on a deck chair with her eyes closed, relaxing in the autumn sunshine. Colin collected a glob of saliva under his tongue, sucked it until it got bigger, before spitting it into the middle of the slice of flan. He watched as it bubbled and dissolved before hiding it with a squirt of cream. He took the flan into the front room. The man didn't even look up to say thanks, but just carried on reading the newspaper.

'Enjoy your dessert,' Colin said.

In October Angel started wearing shoes. The leaves fell from the apple trees in the garden and swirled around the guttering. Rain lashed against the porch. Colin collected apples, picking the ripe ones from the tree before they had a chance to fall into the Stringer's garden. Angel made apple pies, apple tarts, Eve puddings and apple juice. For Halloween they served baked potatoes and on bonfire night Angel made apple cake which she decorated with sparklers. In December she baked Christmas cakes way into the night and displayed them on a table in the café and sold more to the post office.

In January the wind whipped up again. One of the branches of the apple trees broke in a storm shattering the bottom half of the sash window in the back bedroom which was now their living room.

The tuna salad man hadn't been back for months. Colin laughed to himself. Getting shot of him had been a piece of piss. They could survive without *his* custom. But whenever Colin thought about him, he began to worry that if he wasn't coming to the Oven, maybe he saw Angel somewhere else. Although she was almost always at home, except when Evie Stringer gave her a lift to the supermarket.

The supermarket trips were once a fortnight. Angel never asked Colin if he'd like to come with her or go instead. He'd never wanted to go there himself, not least because the thought of having to make small talk with Evie Stringer all morning made him cringe. But the more he mulled it over, the more agitated he felt about Angel going without him – and maybe meeting up with the tuna salad man.

'When are you next due to go to the supermarket, Babe?' he asked casually as he buttered some toast at breakfast.

'Friday. Why? Do you want me to get something?'

'No, I just thought *I* might go, that's all.'

'There's no need for us both to go.'

'Sure. But I'm part of this business. Remember – we're a co-operative. I'll go this time. Give you more time to catch up on the cooking.'

'I'm not behind with the cooking. Things are quiet anyway.'

'But, Babe I *want* to go. Let's at least take it in turns sometimes.'

'Why this sudden interest in supermarket shopping?'

'It's not sudden. I've often thought we should take turns.'

'Okay, but I know it sounds weird, but I really enjoy going to the supermarket. It makes a change from being here all the time.'

'I don't see what's wrong with being here all the time. Anyway, it's only a shop. You make it sound like it's the highlight of your life.'

Angel laughed. 'Don't be silly. It's a change of scene and I enjoy seeing other people, and chatting to Evie.'

'Seeing other people? What sort of "other people" do you see at a supermarket?'

'Just people. You know what I mean. *The outside world.*'

Colin threw the remains of his half-eaten toast into the bin. 'I know what you really mean,' he said. 'You mean you're fed up with just seeing me all the time.'

'Don't be silly. It's just nice to get out, that's all.'

'Why do you keep calling me silly? Maybe it's not so silly to want to experience the luxury of getting out and seeing 'other people' too.'

'Alright. Alright. You go if it's that important.'

The journey to Shapton with Evie Stringer was torture. What on earth did Angel find to talk to her about? The woman was a dunce. Thankfully they reached the supermarket in about half an hour, but they could have got there quicker if she hadn't driven the whole way at twenty miles per hour. Colin suggested they split up once they got inside. He pushed his trolley round the aisles picking things out from Angel's list. Apart from himself and Evie there were only a few women there shopping. The staff on the tills were women too. He saw one man, a manager who walked past when he was paying. But he was an older guy, bald with glasses and a grey moustache. Hardly someone Angel would be interested in. Colin suffered the same torture on the way home. Evie Stringer was like the women his mum worked with. He never knew what to say to them either.

He thanked Evie for the lift and carried the bags of food inside. The minute he walked into the kitchen he sensed something different about the place. He sniffed the air. The house smelled odd. Someone had been smoking. He'd run out of dope and hadn't smoked anything for weeks. The Oven had been closed all morning, so no customers would have come to the house. He placed a box of tinned fruit on the table. Angel was standing by the sink, washing up.

'Hiya,' she said. 'How was the supermarket?'

Colin took a large tin of strawberries from the box he'd been carrying and let it drop to the floor.

'What have you been up to while I was out?' he whispered.

'Nothing. Why?'

'I *said*, what the fuck's been going on?'

Soapy water dripped from Angel's hands. She looked at him with puzzled eyes. 'Col!' she said, 'what's wrong?'

'Someone's been here,' he spluttered. 'I can smell smoke. Someone's been smoking in here, or maybe you've taken up smoking cigars. You must think I was born yesterday. Who is he? Come on, Angel. It's that professor guy, isn't it?'

Angel's hands shook as she wiped them on a dishcloth.

'What are you talking about? My parents have been here, that's all. I was going to tell you. We only had a cup of coffee. We've been catching up on family stuff. Gossip, that's all.'

Colin sat down to compose himself. Her parents. Shit.

'Gossip?' he said eventually. 'Since when were you interested in gossip? Angel, what's happening to you? You're selling out to the bourgeoisie. There are so many important things going on in the world, and all you want to do is sit around gossiping. What about the miners' strike? Or Vietnam? Why don't you discuss things like that? There are people out there suffering for what they believe in. People with no food or money who refuse to be beaten by this government. Fabian never sat around gossiping. He always discussed important stuff.'

'We weren't *just* gossiping. I was telling them about the business …' Angel looked as if she was about to cry.

'What about the business? Why do your parents always have to poke their noses into every crevice of our lives? This is *our* business, *our* lives. Surely they don't have to know each detail about everything we do. They'll be asking for an account of our sex life next.'

He was sitting at the table. Angel put her arms around his shoulders, resting her chin on the top of his head.

'No they won't. I'm so sorry. Please don't be like this.'

He caught the tang of the cigar smoke in her clothes and around her hair.

'I accept your apology.' He eased her gently onto his lap. 'But I don't like to see you changing.' He slid her hair away from her ear and kissed the side of her neck. 'I love you so much. But I love you the way you are. We're alright, aren't we? We don't need other people sticking their noses in, laying some guilt trip on us – and look, now you *are* behind with the baking. What's the point in me doing the shopping if you don't make use of your time while I'm gone?'

'I'll soon catch up,' Angel said as she got up from his lap and lit the oven.

In February the front room where Angel had served lunches and teas was empty and cold. They couldn't afford to light the fire. Then one dull afternoon the cowbell jangled. A shaft of winter sunshine peeked in through the glass at the top of the door and Angel's parents were standing in the porch. Her mum was dressed in a two-piece suit with a white blouse underneath a mauve jacket, and the old man was wearing a trilby and a yellow cardigan and holding an unlit pipe.

'Hello, Colin dear,' Mrs Grey said.

'Hi there,' Colin replied. 'Er… Angel's upstairs washing her hair.'

'Aren't you going to invite us in?' Mrs Grey said with an anxious smile.

Thankfully Angel appeared at the top of the stairs. Her hair was dripping making a damp patch on her jumper. When she saw her parents, she practically skipped down the stairs.

'Angela, how lovely to see you.' The old man had a particular way of talking to Angel like she was a pet dog.

'Go on up to the sitting room. I'll make coffee,' Angel said pointing the way upstairs.

Colin followed her to the kitchen.

'You never greet me like that, Babe,' he whispered.

'Pass me the milk, Col.'

'What are they doing here? They were only here the other day. You didn't tell me they were coming *again*.'

'I didn't know they were coming again.'

'Didn't you?'

'No honestly, I didn't – but it's nice to see them, isn't it? In case you've forgotten, they've recently bought this house for us. We can't stop them coming to their own house.'

'This is exactly what I said would happen,' Colin hissed.

'Shush, they'll hear you.'

'How can they hear me when they're upstairs, probably busy rooting around in our things.'

'What's the problem? If your mum wanted to visit, I wouldn't mind.'

'My mum's different. She would never try to *buy* us.'

Colin followed Angel upstairs. She carried a tray with coffee and homemade biscuits.

Mrs Grey took the tray from her daughter. 'I was just saying to your father, Angela. I mean…' she said, looking up at the ceiling. 'Black paint, darling. Honestly, whatever next.'

Mr Grey shook his head. 'I take it you're not a great one for DIY, Colin?' he said.

Mrs Grey took over at this point as if they'd rehearsed their speeches in the car. 'I know you're both young – and probably busy running this café – but you should take care of the house.'

'You're not renting now, you know.' Mr Grey wagged a stubby but well-manicured finger at Colin. 'If it falls into disrepair it will decrease in value. The market's very unstable at the moment.'

'That's cool. We know what we're doing,' Colin said.

'Sorry, what was that, son?' Mr Grey said.

Why was he calling him 'son'? He wasn't his fucking son. 'It's cool.' Colin repeated.

'What exactly do you mean by that word – *cool*? In my day 'cool' was to do with temperature.'

'Yes.' Mrs Grey shivered. 'It is rather chilly in here.'

Colin looked at the floor. 'Cool means…what it says. Cool,' he mumbled.

'Daddy, what Colin means is that we don't have time for that sort of thing. We're both busy with the café.'

'So how does this so-called *café* work?' Mr Grey was directing his question at Colin. 'I mean, who does what? How *does* it run? In my day, marriage meant a man providing for his wife.'

'Colin deals with the finances, and sometimes he does the supermarket shop…'

'Ah, the finances,' he said, producing a small tin of tobacco from the pocket of his cardigan. 'I've been meaning to ask you about that. Are you making a decent profit?'

'We're not into profit-making,' Colin said. 'It's a co-operative. Neither of us believes in capitalism.'

'A co-operative?' Mrs Grey said. 'You don't give dividend stamps, do you?'

Both of them laughed and Angel offered the biscuits around.

'Have you heard of Karl Marx, Mr Grey?' Colin said.

'Is he related to Groucho?' They both laughed again. Even Angel failed to repress a smile.

Colin sat down on the floor whilst Angel joined her parents on the sofa under the window, the bottom half of which was still boarded up with plywood.

Colin thought again how satisfying it would be to deck him. Mr Grey was filling his pipe with tobacco. He wasn't huge but he was stocky and bigger than Colin. At any rate he made Colin feel slight and undernourished. Instead, Colin picked up the book he was reading. It was called *The Dice Man* and was about a man who made decisions about his life by throwing a dice. He couldn't remember where he'd got up to but opened it at random and pretended to read. Angel and her parents carried on talking. Apparently Angel's grandfather had been ill.

'Do you have grandparents, Colin?' Mrs Grey asked. He looked up from his book. Behind her head was the fish tank – home to his stick insects. One of the largest sticks was climbing up the glass at the side of her head. It was Twiggy.

'No,' he said, willing Twiggy to keep on going.

'Grandpa was asking about your business. He seemed to think opening a café was a lovely idea. Although he has been a bit confused recently.'

'How many customers exactly have you had?' Mr Grey asked.

Colin returned to his book.

'We were busy in the summer,' Angel was saying, 'but it's trailed off a bit at the moment.'

'So you're not making a profit?' The tosser seemed obsessed with money.

'Yes. We are. Sort of. These things take a while to get established,' Angel said defensively.

Colin looked up again. The parents were exchanging knowing looks.

'You would tell us if you needed anything?' Mrs Grey said. 'You look as if you've lost weight. It's no good making food for other people if you don't eat properly yourself.'

'I am eating. Look.' Angel bit into a biscuit.

Mr Grey stood up and clamped his pipe between his teeth.

'I forgot to tell you, Angela,' Mrs Grey carried on. 'Miranda over the road's been ill – only bronchitis, but I've been doing all her shopping. Audrey's retired and so we all miss her. She had a lovely leaving do – we bought her a sun lounger. And do you remember Annette Withy? She's just graduated in Physics, I think it was – this is one of Angela's friends from our road, a child prodigy,' she added, attempting to draw Colin into the conversation. 'There's talk of her doing a doctorate. Oh, and Grandma sends her love. Oh and…' Mrs Grey opened her handbag and produced a newspaper cutting. 'See this,' she said handing it to Angel. 'It's about Christine – Angela's cousin. See – Colin, this is the sort of thing that might interest you. Angela's cousin has been to Tibet and climbed a mountain.'

'Wow!' Angel stood up and handed the cutting to Colin. 'Look, Col. That's amazing!'

He passed the newspaper cutting back to Angel without reading it. Suddenly Mrs Grey screamed and appeared to be propelled forwards from her seat. Mr Grey held out his arms as if to catch her. Colin had been watching Twiggy. The little bugger had done it. He'd climbed to the top of the tank and executed a free fall right onto Mrs Grey's shoulder and slid down into her cleavage. He couldn't have trained him to perform a more perfect manoeuvre if he'd tried. She screamed again, as she tore the buttons from her blouse. Her stiletto heel cracked into her plate which was on the floor. 'Geoffrey, do something. I'm being attacked.'

Colin stood up and strode over to her. 'It's cool. It's only a stick insect – It's Twiggy. He won't hurt.'

'Twiggy? Huh! Get it out. Quickly – Geoffrey! Help!'

Mr Grey dropped his pipe and shoved his hand down his wife's cleavage. 'I can feel it, Marjorie. Don't panic. I'll have it out in a jiff.'

Mrs Grey's face had gone pale, pretty much the colour of the blouse she was wearing.

'Got the blighter,' Mr Grey said as he yanked Twiggy from the side panel of her bra. Twiggy's legs twitched as he held him up for scrutiny.

'Kill it, Geoffrey! For heaven's sakes just stamp on it!'

Mr Grey was just about to place Twiggy on the floor when Colin grabbed him by the arm.

'Give him here,' he said. 'He's in shock. It's not good for them to be frightened.' Colin gently removed Twiggy from Mr Grey's thumb and forefinger, stroked him and placed him back in the tank.

'Frightened! I'll give you frightened,' Mr Grey said as he wiped his hands down the front of his cardigan. 'Do you have any idea what a stunt like that could do to a person? Angela's mother could have had a heart attack. That thing should be destroyed.'

'I doubt it, Daddy,' Angel said. 'It's only a stick insect. They're harmless.'

'I'll give you harmless. What sort of person keeps things like this in the house?'

'It's Colin's hobby.'

'Hobby? In my day a hobby was playing rugby, or soccer. Chess or even snooker is a hobby. Doing jigsaw puzzles is a hobby, for God's sakes.'

'I don't know how he got out. He's never done that before. I think he likes you, Mrs …'

'*Likes* us! Now I've heard everything. Marjorie, I think we ought to be going.'

Colin wanted to laugh as they followed Angel's parents down the stairs. Watching Twiggy disappear under Mrs Grey's bra had been the funniest thing he'd seen in months. He'd give Twiggy some fresh leaves as a reward. Nevertheless, Mrs Grey seemed to have recovered her composure because she'd obviously decided it was time to insult their home one more time before she left.

'The wall on this staircase– it's still half painted. Isn't it about time you finished it off? I mean, it was like that ages ago when your other hippy boyfriend was here. What was his name?'

Angel laughed. 'Fabian, you mean? Actually it was Hilly who started painting it but she got bored.'

Colin stared at Angel as they gathered in an awkward circle at the bottom of the stairs. He was finding it hard to breathe. The walls pulsated around him, as if they were about to suffocate him. He was oblivious as, clearly forgiving him for the stick insect incident, Mr Grey reached for his hand for a manly handshake, and Mrs Grey kissed his cheek. He said nothing as they left the house and drove off.

Angel started washing up and Colin went out for a walk without even telling her where he was going. The words Angel's mum had spoken clouded his brain and blurred his vision. She'd referred to Fabian as Angel's 'boyfriend'. Her boyfriend! He punched the trunk of one of the horse chestnuts in Blackberry Lane and made his knuckles bleed.

That night a shaft of moonlight lit part of the ceiling above Colin's side of the bed. Shadows on the walls played trippy tricks on his eyes. Fizzing black dots joined up into unsettling images – a galloping horse, an ugly monster with a hooked nose. He sat up and touched Angel's shoulder to wake her.

'What's up?' she asked.

'Nothing. I can't sleep.'

'Try counting sheep.'

Colin sighed. 'Your parents freak me out.'

'Why?'

'All that crap about the business really pisses me off.'

'Ignore them. They don't mean any harm.'

'And… what was that about… *Fabian*?' Colin could hardly bring himself to say the word. 'Your mum said Fabian was your *boyfriend*.' Colin clenched his fists, as he waited for her reply.

'Did she? I don't know why, although I did sleep with him a couple of times when Hilly was away. But I doubt Mummy would have known that. She probably assumed he was. I don't know. I'm tired. Let's go to sleep.'

Colin tightened his jaw. 'You *slept* with Fabian?' he whispered.

'Only a few times. It wasn't a big deal. Hilly was away at her granny's funeral or something.'

Colin tried to regulate his breathing and to rid himself of the image of Fabian and Angel in bed together. In the bed he was in now.

'*Where* did you sleep together?'

'I can't remember. Does it matter?'

'You're right. It doesn't matter. Where did you sleep with the other guy?'

'What other guy?'

'The one from the post office. The guy with the tuna salad. The professor. Where did you sleep with him?'

'Col, you're not making any sense. What guy from the post office?'

'Forget it,' he said, unclenching both fists.

He tried to regulate his breathing again. He lay down, as far away from Angel as he could within the confines of the narrow double bed. Eventually he drifted off into dream-fuelled sleep. He dreamed Fabian was lying between them in bed waving a wad of unpaid bills at him. 'Why don't you pay these? You spent too much in the supermarket,' Fabian was saying. 'Twenty tins of strawberries just because they were on special offer. You should have known Angel only uses fresh. And a box of fifty tins of baked beans. Angel would never have anything as naff as baked beans on the menu. Now you're eating baked beans for supper every night. You were too busy looking around the aisles for the cat who looks like Tom Conti. Ha! You're pathetic,' Fabian laughed as he pushed Colin out of the bed so he could only watch from the floor as Fabian made love to Angel. Colin woke at dawn with fear in his heart.

He got out of bed and went downstairs. In the kitchen he put the kettle on. There were boxes and boxes of tins stacked beside the fridge. He found some chamomile tea in the cupboard. Angel reckoned chamomile tea cured insomnia, although Colin couldn't imagine why she'd need to know that. She slept the moment her head touched the pillow, tresses of blonde hair splayed out on the blanket, eyes pinched shut, breathing softly like a child.

One of the things Colin loved most about Angel was her hair. And yet, in a strange way that even he couldn't understand, he hated it too. It was her hair that made people look at her in the street. Her hair was the reason other men wanted her. Men fell in love with her because of her hair. The man who came into the post office and the café probably first noticed her because of her long straight hair. The professor who'd written to her (he still couldn't be sure if they were one and the same person) probably took any opportunity he could to brush up against her hair.

Fabian would have run his fingers through it, caressed it, smelled its musky smell, tingled with the sensation of it against his bare skin.

Colin opened the kitchen drawer to get a teaspoon. It was the drawer where he'd been hiding all the bills under the cutlery box. There was a letter from the Environmental Health Department, whatever the fuck that was. Electricity bills, bills for the rates, water rates, letters from the building society about not keeping up with the payments on a loan they'd taken out, and five brown envelopes he hadn't dared open. They had no funds left to pay bills, the overdraft was at its limit, and, apart from Angel's cakes, they had nothing they could sell. He took all the bills out and spread them on the kitchen table. Slowly he tore at the unopened ones. They were reminders, reminders of reminders, figures in red, threats to cut off the electricity and the water, threats to take them to court. There was even a court hearing to do with their non-payment of rates that had taken place in their absence. Colin bundled all the pieces of paper together ready to shove them back into the drawer.

But something made him stop.

At the side of the drawer in the cutlery section were the scissors Angel used for cutting greaseproof paper. He put all the letters and brown envelopes on the table and balanced the scissors in the palm of his hand.

He took the first letter and cut it through the middle. It was a demand from Shapton District Council for thirty pounds for rate arrears. He took another and zig-zagged around the edges. An electricity bill informing them that the power was to be disconnected the following week. He chopped up more letters, bills, envelopes, then went upstairs to the bedroom.

Angel hadn't stirred. She was so motionless she could have been dead. Colin stood by the bed above her. Once more the image of Fabian lying with her assaulted him. If Fabian was here now, how would Colin know Angel wouldn't choose Fabian over him? Surely Fabian would be her choice. What woman wouldn't choose Fabian? Or the Tom Conti look-alike. Maybe he was married and that was the only reason Angel hadn't gone off with him. But if he was free, wouldn't Angel jump at the chance of being with him rather than

Colin? Mr Tuna-salad wouldn't be the type who fucked up with the bills and got himself into debt.

So Colin knew of two men who loved Angel. Two men Angel *loved*. And they were probably the tip of the iceberg.

He didn't sit down on the bed in case he woke her but stood completely still, bent over her and stroked his hand gently down the length of her hair. It was always the same length. Sixteen inches from her neck to her waist. She didn't cut it and it didn't grow. It had grown as far as it would, she always said.

Her hair was her emblem, the reason she was unique. Colin took a handful of that hair. It was silky soft. She'd washed it the night before. He lifted it up away from her nightdress. It hung down like a horse's tail from his hand. A beautiful, soft, golden horse's tail. The scissors were open in his other hand. His fingers tightened around the handles. He slid them under Angel's hair and cut. The hair was thicker than he'd imagined, more bulky, so he cut again.

She didn't move, only sighed gently in her sleep. The hair came away in a clump in his hand. He held it in his fist. The room was cold, but sweat made his hair stick to his forehead. He crept downstairs still holding the hair, and laid it in the middle of the table on top of all the shredded bills.

Colin stayed downstairs in the kitchen watching the sun come up and then cloud over with grey and the pattering of early morning rain. More than once he dozed off, still sitting at the table. Six o'clock... outside the sun created a yellow light clouded in mist. The mellow mist of dawn rising across the horizon in wisps of torn cloud hanging low in the now pure blue of the sky. Only the fussy chirping of the birds outside broke the stillness.

He thought about dawn again, the way he used to when he was cycling home from the pea factory. Dawn – the goddess of regeneration. The answer to all life's questions. Questions that became dulled and forgotten as the morning embraced everyday life.

Six-thirty. Angel would be up soon. She wasn't one to laze

around in bed. Something outside caught Colin's attention. A rabbit sitting under an apple tree scampered off into the long grass by the overgrown vegetable patch. He stood up and opened the door to welcome the damp air of a new day on his face.

At seventeen minutes past seven he heard the scream. It was the same scream he'd heard that first day when Angel and Hilly and Fabian were contacting the dead on the Ouija board and he'd let his cup drop on the table. The same scream, but louder and more prolonged.

A few spots of rain splashed onto the kitchen floor. Colin rubbed his eyes. They felt hard like boiled sweets again, as they had on that first night in Crazy Mike's room. The mane of Angel's hair still lay across the kitchen table. The echo of the scream died away and was replaced by silence. A silence more unsettling than the scream. He listened to the water dripping from the windowsill upstairs onto the drain cover outside the kitchen window. He heard footsteps.

Colin kept his head bowed as Angel came into the kitchen.

'Colin,' Angel's voice wobbled. She held the sides of her head as if she needed to stop it falling off, clutching the ragged ends of her hair. She was wearing her old Victorian night dress and had bare feet. She walked to the table, gasped and glared at the hair as intently as if she expected it to start moving.

'Col-in,' she said as if she could hardly get his name out between sobs. 'Colin. Say something. My hair. Something's happened to my hair. Someone's cut my hair off. That's it there on the table! Colin, did you do this? What's going on?'

'I know, Babe,' he whispered.

'You're frightening me. I thought you'd gone. I feel so ugly. Don't even look at me. Please. Have you...have *you* cut off my hair? I can't believe you'd do something so horrible.'

'Don't be angry. It wasn't my fault.'

'What do you mean?' Angel screamed at him. 'Whose fault was it? Who else is here?'

Colin bit his fingernail.

'I...I can't stop...shaking. I'm so cold. I'm cold without my hair. What on earth has happened to you? Colin – say something.'

Colin stood up to close the back door. He looked down at the table, so his fringe covered his eyes and tugged at a fingernail, drawing blood.

'Why did you do this? I can't believe you did this. *Was* it you? I thought you liked my hair.'

'Stop it. I know I shouldn't have done it but…'

Angel sat down and folded her arms on the table. 'I feel so, so… *ugly*,' she said.

Rain continued to drip down the pipe outside, splashing onto the windowsill.

'You're not ugly. You're beautiful. It suits you. It's cool,' he added limply.

Angel looked up in disbelief. 'How could you say that?' She pulled the ragged wispy ends of her hair. 'How could you say it's *cool*?'

'I love you, Babe. That's all.' Colin began to cry too. Fuck. He hadn't cried about anything since he got his A level results and that was a totally different kind of crying.

'You love me? Like this? You can't mean it.'

He stumbled into the garden. He walked around to the front of the house. Christian Stringer was in the field over the road with his dog. Colin turned away so he wouldn't have to speak to him. He didn't want to talk to Angel either. What could he say to her that would make things better? Whatever he said or did now could never make things right. She'd go off with another man. Colin didn't even feel like a man. He was a boy – still the little boy whose dad left home when he was ten. A child who came home from school one day to the news that his father was no longer living at home. Colin knew his dad had gone to live with another woman and to make a new family. He felt guilty from that moment onwards. His mum had been deserted and it was his fault. He hadn't been good enough for his dad. He'd been dull and bookish. He hadn't played football or known which team to support. He hadn't joined in when his dad was unkind to his mum.

Now he'd ruined everything – just by being him. He'd violated Angel. The only thing he loved, and he'd damaged her just so he could keep her for himself. To keep her safe from predators, like

Fabian, the guy from the post office, Professor whatshisface. And yet Colin didn't mind if she had long hair or not. He had loved her hair, but he loved *her* more. As long as she stayed with him, that was all that mattered. And yet how could she stay with him? Even *he* wouldn't stay with him. He walked and walked. His T-shirt was soaked. Rain dripped from his forehead onto his nose. He carried on down Blackberry Lane, past the war memorial where an old wilting wreath was propped against the plinth with the list of war dead, on towards the church. He saw the time on the church clock. Almost eight o'clock. He put his hand on the gate and opened it.

Rows of frosty graves appeared to grow from the grass. He went into the churchyard. The second grave on the right had fresh flowers on it. He read the inscription. *Maudie Stringer. Beloved wife, and mother of Christian, Michael and Edmund.* So that must have been Stringer's mother. Poor bastard. At least Colin's mum was still alive. She might not be the most interesting person on the planet, but she was on the planet. And she loved him – apparently.

He walked around the church to the north facing wall where a rubbish bin was overflowing with dead flowers. He stopped and leant against the wall with his hands over his eyes and slid downwards until he was kneeling on the ground. What of Angel's mother – and the dad? Shit. How would they react when they realised what he'd done to their daughter? If Angel stayed, he'd beg her to lie. She could pretend she'd gone to the hairdressers for a change of style.

Colin climbed to his feet only to be encompassed by the most chilling of thoughts. Would Angel leave now? As in, *at this actual minute*, while he was moping about in the graveyard? She might be packing. Throwing her things into a rucksack. Planning her escape. Colin walked quickly away from the church and as soon as he was out of the gate he ran.

From the garden he could see a shadow in the kitchen. Inside Angel was sitting as he'd left her, only her eyes were redder, puffier.

'I'm going to ring Daddy,' was the first thing she said when he came in. 'Ask him to come and get me.'

Colin crouched on the floor and looked up at her. 'The phone's cut off.'

'You're wet,' she said. 'I'll go up the road to the phone box.'

'No.'

'You can't stop me.'

'But your hair...someone might see you.'

Angel fingered what remained of her hair.

'I am sorry, Babe,' Colin broke the silence between them. 'Please don't ring your parents. We're adults. Adults don't go running to Mummy and Daddy every time the slightest thing goes wrong. I promise *nothing* like this will happen again. I can't explain what happened. It was like... like a weird trip. I woke up in the night and I started thinking about all the bills and shit and I had this idea that the only thing we could sell to pay the debts was your hair. It was freaky. I don't think I was fully conscious when I did it. Angel, you know I would never hurt you. Please don't go. Don't ring your old man.'

Angel blew her nose into a piece of toilet paper. 'I am going to ring him,' she said.

'Please don't. If you do, God knows what might happen.'

Angel sniffed again. 'What do you mean? What might happen? Anyway, what are you talking about, bills and debts?' She fingered a piece of paper in front of her on the table. A hacked up piece of an electricity bill. 'I don't understand. I don't know what you mean.'

'The money we owe. Bills and shit.'

'But I didn't know we were in debt. I mean, I knew we weren't rich, but why didn't you tell me? Daddy would have helped us.'

Colin filled the kettle and made some chamomile tea in a brown tea pot. He put Angel's on the table in front of her.

'I wouldn't have asked your old man for money,' he said. 'I wouldn't ask him for anything, and you should stop thinking like that too. I have got *some* pride. I've lived for the last twelve years without a dad – since I drove mine out of my life – I don't need one now.'

'You didn't drive your dad out of your life. He left your mum surely, not you.'

'Same thing.'

'You mustn't think like that. Your dad was a shit by the sounds of things, but you can't take responsibility for what he did when you were little.'

'But I'm scared,' Colin admitted. 'All the time I'm scared that… you'll leave too and, I … just want you to stay and I'd do anything to keep you here. Where you belong…'

'But I'm the same,' Angel interrupted him. She gazed at Colin with wide, bloodshot eyes. 'All the time I'm afraid *you're* going to leave. Even now I'm afraid that you won't want me anymore because of the way I look. I feel ugly, and I know how much you liked my hair, and I don't understand anything anymore…'

The kitchen was quiet. Colin looked at the hair on the table and then at Angel. Her hacked off hair looked kind of horrible. 'You're not ugly,' he said reaching across the table for her hand. 'You could never be ugly.'

Outside the rain had stopped. Only the drip-dripping of the pipe seemed to count away the seconds. A dull glow of early morning sunlight shone on Angel's hair on the table, picking out the gold and darker shades of blonde. A fairer colour at the tip and darker where the growth had been more recent.

Eventually she spoke. 'Do you know,' she said quietly, 'I feel flattered in a funny sort of a way. I mean you tried to protect me from all the money problems and the bills and all that stuff, and the more I think about it, the more I think it shows… how much you love me. And the fact that you thought so much of my hair. It's beautiful that you should value me like this. I actually feel proud.'

Colin closed his eyes with relief as if he'd just reached the end of a very long race.

'And you could grow it again,' he said.

'Yeah, or just keep it like this,' she said. 'Hilly had short hair, and didn't she always look amazing? Everyone fancied Hilly.'

Colin frowned, but Angel carried on with gathering momentum. 'And Hilly always dyed her hair with henna and she wore those long dangly earrings. I'll be able to experiment more now. And it'll be easier to wash. More hygienic when I'm cooking…'

'Yeah.'

'You're right,' she went on. 'It was a fag washing my hair every other day. And I was in a rut. D'you realise I've had the same hairstyle since I was six?'

'Time to move on.'

'And short hair *can* be attractive. Fabian used to say that Hilly was the most beautiful girl he'd ever seen.'

'Yeah?' Colin said, frowning some more.

Colin and Angel walked to the main road into the village just past the war memorial carrying a suitcase each and with rucksacks slung from their shoulders. Angel wore a floppy hat with a wide brim and a silk scarf tied around it. A full moon lit their journey down Blackberry Lane.

'Look at the moon. Do you think there really is a man in the moon?'

Colin looked up. The moon definitely did have a man's face hidden amongst its shadows. 'There might be. He must be some cool dude if there is.'

'Yeah.' Angel laughed. Colin took her hand and stuck his thumb out as soon as the first beam of headlights flooded up behind them on the main road. A van stopped. The driver wound down the window. He was a youngish guy who said he was on his way to Salisbury. He leant across the front seat and opened the passenger door. 'I can drop you at Laverstock, if that's any help.'

Angel jumped in first.

'Nice hat!' the guy said to her with a wink as Colin bundled their bags onto the floor.

'Thanks!' she said.

Colin clocked the way this guy was gazing at Angel. He climbed in and sat next to her, took a deep breath and squeezed her left hand so tightly in his own that her wedding ring dug deep into his palm.

DOBBS

March 1975

B ERNARD DOBBS drove past the war memorial, swung the Jag to the right and coasted down Blackberry Lane.

'Strewth,' he murmured under his moustache. It was years since he'd been down this way. Last time must have been when he'd been invited to tea one afternoon with one of the Stringer boys. Now which one was it? He remembered there'd been a few of them and no mother. Michael, he thought. Michael Stringer had been in his class.

For tea they'd been given a bit of bread and some blackberry jam by a woman who lived over the road and sometimes looked after Michael. Dobbs recalled how pretty she was, with fair hair in kiss curls around her face. Michael said she used to be a famous actress and Dobbs had believed him. Loretta Young, Michael said was her name. Dobbs laughed at how naive he'd been. He'd told his mum about Loretta Young making the tea at Michael Stringer's house, and she'd told him not to be so stupid.

It was March and daffodils doffed their caps on the banks either side of the lane at the big man in his camel coat as he cruised along in his flashy motor. He indicated right and pulled up outside Number Two Blackberry Lane.

Dobbs glanced at the headed notepaper he had on the passenger seat next to his trilby. The instructions concerned the non-payment of rates by the previous occupants. Dobbs ran his eyes down the letter, folded it and slotted it in his breast pocket. He let the engine turn over, waiting a few moments before switching it off. He liked the sound of its soft purr and the warm blow of air it generated. He'd saved for years for this car. Not many people around here had Jags. Admittedly it was an old model, but it was still a Jag.

Once, in the school playground, he'd heard some of the other children laugh when his dad had come in to talk about road safety. Someone had referred to him as 'Mr Plod'. Bernard couldn't put this out of his mind. Plod, plod. Bernard wasn't a plodder. He wanted more than a plodding life. He craved *things*. Nice things that brought status.

He'd started with the car. It had to be something that stood out. His red XJ6 fitted the bill perfectly. But the wheels weren't enough. Bernard craved the clothes to reinforce the image. Like the Italian leather brogues and the cashmere overcoat he was wearing today.

He turned off the engine, opened the car door, grabbed his trilby and stepped straight into a puddle. Strewth. His brogues had mud squelching around the toes and his turn-ups were wet. He wiped his shoes against a tuft of grass and locked the car. He took the piece of paper out of his pocket again and looked up at the house. It was a small place, one half of a semi. Now, which one was his? Number One looked as run down as Number Two. But it was definitely Number Two on the sheet of paper and yet there was a name plate, rather than a number, hanging from the front of the porch. Angel's Oven. What sort of name was that for a house? It sounded more like a witch's house… Or was that a coven? Dobbs had never been that clever when it came to words.

He shoved the gate, causing it to stick in an overgrowth of weeds. As he pushed harder one of the springs broke so he had to prop the gate against the wall. The path was only a few steps from the front porch. Daffodils were hidden by dandelions and spears of grass, and the first tightly budded tulips were showing amongst the weeds.

Dobbs banged his fist on the porch window. He always made a point of checking a property was empty before attempting to gain entry. There were plenty of rules when it came to this sort of thing, and a derelict place could be home to the odd squatter or tramp. The porch door rattled, and flakes of yellow paint splintered onto his sleeve. He peeked through the front bay window. The glass was dusty, so Dobbs took out his handkerchief, spat on it and rubbed a circle on the dirt.

He saw a small room with four tables each with a white

tablecloth. It looked like an extremely small café. He frowned, scratched his forehead and walked around the side of the house. A rusty bike was propped against the wall with bindweed growing through its spokes. He kicked the bike, and its bell gave a half-hearted tring.

The garden was separated from its neighbour by a fence. Three apple trees fought for space and a neglected vegetable patch looked as if it might have seen better days. A punctured football caught his attention and when he went over to pick it up the sole of his shoe squelched into a wizened brown apple, and he nearly slipped.

'Bloody Hell,' he muttered to himself.

At the back of the house was a door. He pushed the handle and humped his shoulder against the door, but it didn't budge. Through the kitchen window he saw a stack of baking trays on the draining board. He looked up. Ah hah! That was better. An upstairs window was boarded up. All he needed was a ladder, and he could see one propped up against the next door's wall.

Dobbs walked round to the front of the house, up the path, out of the gate and through the gate of the house next door. A woman answered his knocking. She had grey, wavy hair clipped back from her face.

'Hello, can I help you?' She was probably in her late forties, although maybe younger than she looked and wore a dress that was too short revealing a pair of knees which were a tad too plump to put on display. All the same, Bernard Dobbs liked to see a bit of leg on a woman, even if she was getting on a bit.

Bernard thought he recognised her. Wasn't she Christian Stringer's wife? Michael's older brother. He certainly remembered Christian. The one who got left behind. He'd heard that Michael and Edmund had done alright for themselves. Both of them had good jobs in London. He'd felt a pang of envy when he'd heard Christian bragging about them in the Ring 'O Bells.

'Excuse me, Madam. Mrs Stringer, isn't it? Bernard Dobbs, bailiff.' Dobbs removed his hat and offered her his card. 'I have a letter here from the Council instructing me to gain entry to Number Two Blackberry Lane. I don't suppose you have a key.'

'No I'm afraid I don't,' she said.

'Then, might I ask if you have any means of contacting the owners?'

Evie Stringer pushed a strand of hair behind her ear. 'No, not me. They done a runner months ago. Moonlight flit. I don't even know who owns the place now.'

'Perhaps you'd be willing to help me. If I don't get in now, I'll have to go back to the office. It would save me a lot of time and petrol,' he said glancing behind him at the Jag. 'If you could just give me a loan of that ladder in your garden, I'd be most grateful.'

She looked worried. 'I ought to ask my husband before I let you take that ladder, and he's way over in the field.'

'Surely not,' Dobbs said, reaching into his trouser pocket for a pound note. 'I won't damage it and I'll not be long. I promise you it'll be leaning against your wall again by the time your husband gets home. Here, take this,' he said, handing her the note. 'As a non-returnable deposit. You could buy yourself something nice.'

Evie studied the pound note. 'Go on then,' she said, taking it. 'And be careful – the third rung from the bottom is broken. And make sure you put it back where you found it.'

Dobbs dragged the ladder around to the garden of Number Two and propped it up under the window. He had a few tools in the boot of the Jag. A hacksaw should do the trick.

He removed the hardboard easily from the window but climbing in was not so easy. He went down the ladder, making sure he missed the broken rung, took off his coat, folded it and laid it on the passenger's seat of the car. Without the coat he was smaller. He climbed up again, knocked out a few slivers of glass and eased himself in, left leg first.

He fell against a sofa and bent his leg awkwardly. Immediately he felt something heavy land on his shoulder. A square fish tank bounced onto the floor shattering and scattering shards of glass, brittle leaves and what looked like brown sticks. On closer inspection he realised these were insects. He'd seen them before – stick insects. Dead stick insects. Bernard Dobbs winced, although, if he was honest, this wasn't the worst thing he'd come across since he'd been in this line of business.

He composed himself, stood up to his full height and brushed the dust from his trousers. He looked around and found himself in a tiny room with a black ceiling and a torn poster pinned to the door. As he walked across the room, his shoe crunched against a piece of glass and a dead stick insect. He went into the bathroom with the stick insect still stuck to his shoe. The bathroom was cold and bigger than the room he'd just come from. Dobbs stood by the sink on the stained linoleum. He turned on the tap to wash his hands and looked around for a towel. There was none. He went on to the bedroom at the front of the house and wiped his hands on the curtains.

Dobbs stood at the top of the stairs and looked down. The stairs were steep and dark. He found a light switch, flicked it, but no light came on. Disconnected – of course. The dark paint on the walls didn't help. Someone had painted the staircase purple but half- way down the purple paint stopped and reverted to orange swirly wallpaper.

In the downstairs hallway the orange wallpaper continued, although some parts were peeling and others were covered with posters. 'Today is the first day of the rest of your life' and 'Make love not war'. Bernard tugged at a piece of wallpaper that was beginning to peel. He pulled it until it came off in his hand in a long thin triangle. He felt a certain amount of satisfaction seeing how much paper he could pull off before it came away from the wall. He enjoyed vandalising other people's properties. Especially ones that had bugger all of any worth inside them.

The room at the front was the one he'd seen through the window with the tables in it. There was hardly enough space for him to get in. Four tables in a room this size, each with a jam jar of dead flowers in the middle. Dobbs emptied one of the pots onto the carpet and screwed the powdery petals into the carpet with the heel of his shoe – just for the hell of it.

A pair of plastic sliding doors separated the front room from the kitchen. He unhooked the handle and went in. The smell hit him immediately. It was like fish that had gone off and then returned with some dead friends. '*Good God*,' he said covering his nose with his handkerchief. The kitchen had white Formica units with red plastic handles. Dobbs opened the fridge. From the smell that came out he might as well have been opening a coffin. The shelves were full of flans and pies all covered in green mould, cake corpses that had decomposed probably months ago. He pulled out a jug of cream which had a surface like dusty, bubbling green moon rock. If he took the fridge, it would need fumigating before anyone would buy it. He'd noticed an old television upstairs and a record-player but this was hardly the crown jewels. He sighed and sat down at the table.

On top of the table were piles of bills, most of which had been shredded, final demands written in red ink. That was hardly surprising. Whoever lived here had been in a financial shambles. But it was something else that made Bernard Dobbs stop in his tracks. He'd entered many houses, most with a sad tale to tell, but he'd never in his entire career seen what was now before him. A tress of long, shining, blonde hair, more than a foot long. He sat down and touched it gingerly as if it might come to life and bite him. It was certainly human hair. Smooth as ribbon. Strewth. He'd come across some strange sights in this job, but this took the biscuit. Maybe the people who lived here had been so desperate they'd decided to sell their own hair. Dobbs had seen it all now.

He stood up to leave, resigned to the fact that he was onto a losing wicket. But he had to touch the hair again. The colour and texture reminded him of Patricia's hair. She'd had a long blonde ponytail when she was little. This hair was so like Patricia's it could almost have been hers. Of course, she'd had hers cut when she was a teenager. She wore it short now and had a child of her own. How quickly time went. He could remember when Lois first told him she was expecting and the journey to the hospital to visit her the day after Patricia had been born. He remembered a sports day at school when Patricia had fallen over inside a sack and twisted her ankle. Her face when he'd told her to wipe off the tarty pink lipstick she'd tried on for the first time. The arguments about Mark Waters when they'd wanted to get engaged. The walk down the aisle when he gave her away. But those were just a few events that stood out in his memory. What about all the in-between things? The ordinary days, the months, the years. Where had all that time gone? In the blink of an eye it was gone. The turn of a key. The flick of a switch. The snip of a pair of scissors. Gone.

Dobbs dabbed at his eyes with a clean bit in the corner of his handkerchief. What had brought him here? A grown man sitting in somebody else's kitchen scouring around for bits and pieces to sell for absurdly small amounts of money. He wound a few strands of the hair around his finger, tighter and tighter until it hurt. The tip of his finger bulged and turned purple. He pulled it off and took the whole ponytail, holding it between his two hands. He tied it loosely in a knot and laid it back on the table. Apart from the television and the record player, there was nothing here of any value. But if he was honest, he couldn't wait to get out of the place. He re-nailed the board on the window, returned the ladder and unlocked the Jag.

He'd never before felt so comforted by his car. He turned on the engine, executed an awkward five-point turn and put his foot down on the accelerator.

CHLOE

June 2004

I'm languishing in the hammock under the apple tree on one of those first balmy June days that make you wonder how you survived the winter. The air is buzzing with warmth and alive with insects. Wisteria petals have floated onto the roof of the orangery, gathering like speckles of snow. I can smell the merest hint of honeysuckle as it scrambles in a tangle of white and pink on the drystone wall. I doze off but have only slept a matter of seconds when I'm awoken by the sound of a car. The noise makes me jump and my book slips onto the grass – my Louise Gluck collection. A ladybird with three spots lands on the spine. Isn't a ladybird with three spots meant to be lucky?

I'm wide awake now. The sound of a car around here is so rare it reminds me there is a world out there beyond Blackberry Lane. Not the chug of a tractor, the roar of a plane, the mooing of a cow. Not the hoot of an owl or the warble of a nightingale or the raised voices of the Stringers in the farmhouse over the road.

My senses are on full alert. The hammock wobbles as I sit up to get a better view. I can see a saloon car, but I don't recognise it or the shadowy people inside. The driver turns the engine off. I have to think fast. My phone is indoors. Everyone is away. Dad emailed me from the South of France yesterday, so I know he and Mum won't be home until the end of August. And Hannah is away – full stop, since she married Sam. I secretly call Sam the garden gnome. I couldn't believe Hannah would marry someone as unattractive as Mr Samuel Garden Gnome. They say opposites attract. But I mean, Hannah! She's gorgeous. She takes after our mother with those long black shiny curls. Shiny bubbly curls like the ripe blackberries that gather and tumble in luscious clumps over the fence every September.

My hair is mousy blonde and straight as the corn in Stringer's field.

The sun dips behind a layer of cloud and I shiver. The trowel and fork I used to dig up the carrots yesterday are discarded on the side of the vegetable patch. With one in each hand, like Billy the Kid with a pair of guns, I creep around the side of the house to the front.

Hannah always says I'm mad to stay here on my own and I'm beginning to think she might be right. She insists I'm a sitting target for burglars, escaped lunatics – that sort of thing. I could run inside and lock the door, but the French windows in the orangery are open, and one of the front bay windows is unlocked. To stop anyone getting in I'd have to fly round the house searching for keys, by which time these guys could have made their way in and hacked me to bits. That's another thing Hannah's always on about – my imagination. But aren't poets supposed to have active imaginations?

Still, Hannah knows what I'm like, probably better than anyone. And she knows about me and this house. It would probably take a lunatic or a murderer to get me out.

I see now that the car parked by the gate is a green Volvo. Two men are inside. Two men – and I'm armed with a set of miniature gardening tools. Great. If I'm about to be slaughtered, so be it. If my time has come, it has come. And I do believe that our lives are mapped out from day one. This day was always going to be, this hour, this minute, me, the trowel and fork, the green Volvo, those two men…

One of them is opening the door on the driver's side. He's parked so near to the wall he has to twist his body to get out. He pushes a pair of blue sunglasses, the type people wear for skiing, onto the top of his head. He's suntanned and wearing a T-shirt and cut-off jeans. He has a smattering of gingery bumfluff on his chin.

'Excuse me! I wonder if you could help?'

He's older than me. Probably over thirty, fair hair, honey tan. The T-shirt has a logo on the front saying University of Sydney. He sounds like an actor from one of those Australian soaps Hannah watches. Or used to watch, before she deserted me to become Mrs

Gnome. On first impressions he looks alright. I guess it's possible he hasn't come here to commit armed robbery. He's not wielding an axe or a machete, and he doesn't look the type to have a hand grenade down his pants.

I pull my cardigan around my shoulders. Maybe he's looking for the tea shop that was once part of Number Two. I know news travels slowly in these parts, but surely he couldn't be a customer arriving three decades too late in search of Darjeeling and scones, or a sightseer taking photos of where it all began.

Or he could be one of Hannah's old friends. Or even one of Dad's *fans*. Maybe he's made a pilgrimage to the house in the hope of a glimpse of the great Ian Barton. That did happen once. A couple from Derbyshire drove all the way to Somerset, found the house and stayed for hours chatting to Dad about his books. Sometimes I get tired of hearing the words *Jolly* and *Dolly* in the same sentence. Of course, I shouldn't think like that. Success has been amazing for Dad, but there's only so much you can say about a series of books about a doll made out of a hot water bottle cover.

Sydney Uni Guy is standing at the gate looking more like he's en route for Bondi Beach than a house at the end of a country lane. The only thing missing is his surfboard. He's scrutinising a piece of paper. I'm on the path still armed with the fork and spade, watching him. The sun comes out and shines on his hair, illuminating him in a bubble of light.

Then a strange thing happens.

For a second, time becomes suspended. I look at him in more detail and feel the fork slip from my grip and clatter onto the path, closely followed by the trowel. I wipe my hands down the sides of my jeans and shake myself out of the weird kind of trance I'm in. But there's something about him. Maybe this is what Hannah calls 'fancying' someone. 'You must fancy *someone*, Chloe!' she's always saying. I close my eyes for a fraction of a second and pray. *Please don't let him be looking for Hannah or Dad.* Please.

Because already I'm prepared to believe that he's looking for me.

Bondi beach boy clears his throat in a theatrical way.

'I'm looking for Stringers Farm? The sat nav's brought us here.

It's there, over the road, right?' He's pointing at the farmhouse. With its dark miniature windows, once painted glossy black and now decaying squares of crumbling wooden frames, Stringers Farmhouse is set back from the lane, a rambling stone-built house almost as big as the whole block of flats we lived in in London, closed off from the world with a four-bar gate and entrenched in mud as black as molasses and thick enough to engulf the sturdiest Wellington boots. Cows gather in the paddock, their necks rubbing against the fence, rows of heads flicking their eyelashes against the invasion of bluebottles, straining to get a glimpse of this unfamiliar intrusion into their world.

'It's just that there's no sign of anyone around and I wondered if you might know when they'll be home?' He ends each sentence as if he's asking a question and I want to answer him but for some reason I can't. I catch my breath, cough and swallow. I haven't done this for years. Not been able to speak, I mean.

We're studying each other like animals in the night. Like two foxes who weren't expecting to meet. I shake myself again – metaphorically – as if that will help me return to reality, albeit a new reality. One where I have to stop myself running at the gate, flinging it open and piling myself into this stranger's arms. Me. Chloe Barton. The girl who's never hugged a man in her life – except Dad, of course.

I still haven't spoken. And although I detest and despise that word, *mute*, that is what I am now. Mute.

'Look...' he says, scratching his head with the piece of paper still in his hand. 'I'm really sorry to have bothered you. I'll err... hang on here for a bit? See ya then.' He turns towards the car.

'No,' I say, relieved to get at least one word out. 'No.' My voice sounds strangled. 'You can wait here. It's market day. The Stringers will be out all day. You're welcome to wait here.' I gesture with my thumb behind me at our house.

He looks at his car. 'Cheers,' he says. 'That's really kind. I'll check my uncle's alright first, although he's been asleep since we left the M4 which means he'll be out for the count for the next hour or so. And if he wakes up, he'll just carry on with the book he's been reading, so, no sweat.'

In the kitchen I open the fridge. Hannah would never believe me – Chloe entertaining a *Neighbours* extra in the kitchen. How cool is this? He's told me his name. It's Saul and he's actually from Queensland. Saul from Queensland is sitting at our kitchen table, golden hairy legs astride the bench.

'Cheers,' he says taking a glass of my homemade lemonade. 'Nice place. Do you live here alone?' he asks between sips.

'I live here with my parents,' I tell him, wondering whether I ought to pretend they are upstairs. After all, he still hasn't proved he's not a homicidal blood relation of Ned Kelly.

'Yeah?' he says. 'So, what do you guys find to do around here all day?'

'I write poetry.'

'Yeah?' he says rubbing the bum fluff on his cheek with his knuckles.

'Yeah. As a matter of fact. Yes. I do. I'm a poet. '

Saul from Queensland smiles. His smile is unexpected and reassuring. His teeth are perfect, like teeth belonging to someone in a toothpaste ad.

'I believe you,' he says holding his hands up in mock surrender. 'Are you famous? I mean, should I have heard of you?'

'No, I'm not famous. But give me time.'

'So, how long have you lived here?'

'We moved here from London when I was five.'

'Five – wow. And that's how many years ago?'

'Fifteen.' He's tricked me into saying how old I am. Saul smiles again and hooks one suntanned knee over another. 'What made your parents want to move here from *London*?' He says this like it's another word for Paradise.

'They wanted to bring us up in the countryside.'

'Jeez, it's hard to imagine anyone wanting to leave London. I mean it's like the hub of the universe.'

'Maybe. But my family never wanted to move back. And Dad always says I was the one who decided we should move here in the first place. Apparently at the age of four I coerced our family away from Streatham and here to the remotest depths of Somerset.'

Saul puts his drink down and frowns. 'Some four-year-old!' he says.

'Yes, I know. I was quite persuasive.'

'I'm fascinated. In what way persuasive?'

'It's rather a long story… It started with a house auction. Do you have house auctions in Australia?'

Saul laughs easily. 'We do, as a matter of fact. We have pretty much most things that you have. Admittedly I'm not massively into real estate, but I do know what a house auction is.'

'Actually, this is a very long story. Would you like to come into the orangery? It's more comfortable in there.'

I throw open the orangery doors. The air's hot and fuggy with a rosy smell from Mum's pot plants – some of which are wilting. I'll need to water them just as soon as Saul from Queensland leaves.

'So your folks bought this house at an auction,' he says settling himself into a cushion of deep blue chintz with his knees directed straight at me, daring me not to focus on them.

'That's how the story goes. Apparently as soon as I saw the photo of this house I shouted "Chloe's house, Chloe's house."'

This reminiscence, when shared with someone who isn't in our family, makes me feel oddly uncomfortable. But I wonder whether it is my reminiscence. I've heard my parents telling other people the story of how we bought the house in Blackberry Lane so often that I don't know whether I remember what happened, or just the telling of it.

'So you're Chloe? Nice to meet you, Chloe.' He stands up and crosses the room, holding out his hand for me to shake. I take his hand and feel his fingers folding around my own. I think his thumb strokes my palm, but I might have imagined that bit. He nestles into the chair again. 'You're Chloe and your family moved here because of you. I'm intrigued.'

'There was a bit more to it than that. For a start, we already knew the Stringers …'

Saul looks blank. 'You know. The Stringers? People over the road – the ones you were looking for just now. Michael Stringer's wife, Amanda, was my psychologist.'

'Oh, *those* Stringers. Yes. My uncle said they were farmers. No mention of psychologists though.'

'So Michael Stringer – he's the middle brother – Michael moved to London in the eighties and married Amanda. Amanda was my psychologist when I was four.'

'You had a psychologist when you were four?'

'I had a few problems.'

Saul lets his eyes slide in the direction of the door. 'Maybe I should make my escape while I'm still in one piece?'

'I'm alright now.' My smile accompanying this statement is ridiculously coy.

I refill Saul's glass with more lemon but decide to offer him a glass of Dad's Chablis too.

'That'd be great,' he says. 'I hope I'm not encroaching on your time.' I'm already liking the way he curls his 'o's around the roof of his mouth when he says the word 'hope' so it's almost 'hape'. He sips the wine.

'So…' He inspects his fingernails and frowns. He seems to do that a lot. He waits a while before speaking. 'So… would it be incredibly rude to ask what exactly was wrong with you that meant you qualified for a psychologist?'

'How long have you got?'

Saul folds his arms. 'I'm on vacation. I've got all the time in the world.'

'Until your uncle wakes up,' I remind him.

'Yup. You're right. I'd better go check on him.'

We smile at each other as he leaves the orangery to go out to the car. And for some reason, although this seems one of the most crazy thoughts that's ever taken root in my head, I want be close to this person, this boy, man, Saul, more than anything I've ever wanted before.

'I was born in a Victorian hospital in South London,' I begin once Saul has returned. 'The midwife who delivered me was called Tulip and she had a smile white and wide enough to light up the whole of Streatham. She cut the cord, and as she handed me to Francesca she narrowed her eyes.

"Hmm, 'dis little one has been here before, hasn't you, petal?" she said. I'd heard Francesca tell this story so many times, always with the same, slightly iffy Jamaican patois. Sometimes her friends would roar with laughter, sometimes the story was met with wide-eyed gasps and silent wonder. The nurse with the beautiful wide smile and dark, luminous eyes must have known what she was talking about. Somehow her words, no doubt innocently expressed, probably even something she said about every other baby she'd delivered, explained a lot of things.

Francesca maintains to this day that I was the one who bought the house in Blackberry Lane. You know, because of the "Chloe's house," thing. But I was only just five when we moved here. What she really means is that if it hadn't been for me, we'd never have met. Amanda Stringer, and if we hadn't met Amanda and Michael we wouldn't have heard about the house in Blackberry Lane, and if we hadn't heard about the house we might still be living in Streatham.

I, on the other hand, believe that somehow, something or someone would have brought me to this house eventually – in fact, there's no way I *couldn't* have ended up here.

Amanda Stringer treated me from the age of three until the time we left London. On Thursday afternoons Francesca sat with me while Amanda asked me questions or gave me puzzles to work out. I preferred the puzzles to the questions. My favourite was a set of cards with heads bodies and legs of different animals that I had to fit together. The questions ranged from *can you draw your mummy?* To, *what do you call her when you think about her in your head?*

Francesca took time off work for these sessions, so they must have been important to her. Even so, I'd heard her mention the inconvenience. But there'd have been no point in Dad taking me. He already did most things a mother normally does. By the nature of my problem, this was Francesca's territory.

"Selective mutism" was the label Amanda applied to my condition. Apparently not an uncommon diagnosis in the world of child psychology, but Amanda Stringer allotted us an extra fifteen minutes per session as she found my case so fascinating. She kept a tape recorder on her desk between a telephone and a photograph of her husband and their daughter. She'd press the button on the tape recorder as soon as we sat down and flip it up precisely one hour and a quarter later. Dad said she was probably writing a book about us or selling articles to *The Lancet* with our names changed to protect the innocent. But was I innocent? I don't believe Francesca thought so. Not that I'd made a conscious decision not to talk to Francesca. It was simply the way things were.

During one session Francesca started crying and Amanda slid a box of Kleenex in her direction saying, "Your mummy's crying, Chloe. Would you like to tell her how that makes you feel?"

I studied the silk scarf Amanda had draped around her shoulders and tried to count the number of dots in the pattern. Amanda wore a different scarf every week. Sometimes she wore pearls too, but that day it was just the scarf with a brooch in the shape of a snake clipping the two ends together. She had a flat face with freckles on her forehead, brown wavy hair and wore orange lipstick. She seemed to be on Francesca's side, like they were friends chatting together in a language I didn't understand.

"I'm beginning to think my daughter's some kind of medical freak," Francesca whispered as she blew her nose.

Amanda leaned towards me again. "Chloe, your mummy's upset. Aren't you going to give her a cuddle?"

I stopped counting the dots on Amanda's scarf. 'She's not my *real* mummy," I said.

'What Amanda Stringer failed to understand was that, not only did I not feel the need to speak to Francesca, but I actually had no choice. I'd been labelled "selective mute", but the reason Amanda's eyes shone above her spectacles with such enthusiastic diagnostic energy was that, although most children who suffer with selective mutism usually choose not to speak to a teacher, their classmates, or at worst, a distant relative, the *only* person I had selected not to speak to was my mother. I'd speak to my father, my sister and my toy bear, Peppo – just not Francesca.

I once heard Amanda Stringer say that never in all her years of sitting in that cramped, file-filled room, across the table from scores of parents flanked by disaffected children, never had she encountered so young a child who spoke confidently to the rest of the world but refused to utter even the simplest word to the woman who'd given her life.

Amanda asked Francesca about her job. She was an absent mother, not in fact married to our dad, but more married to a firm of accountants in Westminster. Francesca dismissed this as irrelevant to our problem. Dad was a budding author and therefore it made sense that he should be the stay-at-home parent. Someone had to go out to work and pay the bills. Surely it made no odds whether it was the mother or the father. *Anyway, it isn't as if it's an illness.* How many times had I heard Francesca say that? Being an elective mute was a "phase" I would grow out of. And if I didn't? She'd always say that she'd never heard of an adult mute. It was like thumb sucking. Lots of mums she knew worried themselves sick about thumb sucking, but who'd ever seen a doctor, or a policeman, a politician or a news reader sucking his or her thumb? Were shops full of assistants twirling cosy blankets around their noses? Or did footballers suck their toes?

Francesca despised all those mothers who fretted. The ones who played tapes of multiplication tables to their babies in the womb in the hope that their offspring would emerge fluent in the nine times table. She had no time for these fussers who spent hours cramming their offspring and carting them around from one extra-curricular activity to another. I was her second child. She already had one perfectly normal daughter. One out of two wasn't bad.

It was at Amanda and Michael Stringer's twenty-fifth wedding anniversary party that my father first heard about the house in the country, half of which was owned by his brother, and was up for sale. He promised to send photos.

A week later, over breakfast, Dad opened the envelope with the central London postmark. Inside were four photographs of the house in Blackberry Lane, two taken from the front, one from the garden, and another from the east side. My father held the pictures up to the light and put on his glasses.

"That's not what I was expecting, Chloe." He sounded disappointed, as he scrutinised the details. "I'd imagined something rather stunning, whereas this place looks run-down like it's been empty for years. Nothing like the chocolate box cottage I'd envisaged from Michael Stringer's description."

He put the pictures down on the breakfast bar. As I bent over to sip my orange juice through a straw without lifting the glass, I was able to peruse the photographs. The house was built of red brick and divided into two identical semis, except only one had a porch. The side with the porch had a broken gate and both gardens were overgrown.

Dad tidied up the photos and slipped them into their envelope with a "we don't want to get sticky hands on these" and opened another letter which was from his agent with news that an illustrator had been found for the children's book he'd been writing.

My father always ate muesli for breakfast. It took a long time to chew. After he'd read the letter from his agent, he still had a good twenty spoonfuls to get through. He took the photographs of the house out of the envelope again. This time he sighed.

"I suppose this property is potentially appealing in a funny sort of way." Dad always used words like "property", "potentially" and "appealing". "Although both houses do look fundamentally sad, as if they're hanging on to each other for dear life. *In need of some modernisation.* Huh. Typical estate agents' jargon."

Dad looked at me and wiped the butter moustache from my upper lip.

"What do you think of it, Chloe?" He held up the photograph for a second time.

"Chloe's house! Chloe's house!" I squealed and slipped from my stool onto the floor.

The bedtime story was Amanda Stringer's idea. Francesca had to leave work early, which meant she hit the rush hour crowds and had to stand all the way from Waterloo. I remember her crouched on the side of my bed. She was still in her suit and her work heels. She had *The Magic Porridge Pot* balanced on her knee and complained that her shoes were tight. She obviously wanted to take them off, but she'd reached the part in the story where all the streets in all the towns were covered in porridge and I'd heard Dad telling her that was my favourite bit, so clearly she didn't want to break the flow. She swallowed a yawn and tried to cover her mouth. Dad never yawned and he put on special voices for each character.

"And so the little girl said, *Stop, little pot, stop!*"

Dad's voice for the little girl always sent me into fits of giggles, but Francesca just gabbled her way through. I snuggled up to Peppo.

At last, the little pot did stop cooking the porridge... And they all lived happily ever after.

I couldn't believe my ears. She'd skipped the last page. I tugged at the corner of my duvet. She always sat on the edge so I couldn't get it up to my chin.

"That was a good story, wasn't it, Chloe?"

I answered her with blank-eyed silence and wrapped the end of my pillow around my head.

"Don't do that! You'll suffocate!" Francesca tugged at the pillow. "What shall we read tomorrow?" She was talking in the voice she used on the phone when she was arranging meetings. She picked up the pile of books by my bed. "*Thumbelina? The Billy Goats Gruff? Fantastic Mr Fox?*" She lingered on *Fantastic Mr Fox*. "Hannah always loved this. It's about three men called Boggis, Bunce, and Bean and a family of foxes..."

I wanted to tell her Dad had read *Fantastic Mr Fox* to me a thousand times and I knew exactly the names of the characters, but I kept my face locked into a frown, which was hard since I too adored the resourceful Mr Fox and his family. I closed my eyes and turned onto my side waiting for the tickle of her hair against my cheek as she leant down to kiss me goodnight.

"You still smell of Mrs Meacher's," she said. "Didn't Daddy give you a bath?" This was more of a thought than a question. She wasn't expecting an answer.

I listened as she went into the living room and heard her flop down on the sofa with a sigh. I knew the envelope with the pictures of the house was on the coffee table and I could tell she was opening it.

"Is this the house Michael was on about?"

"Yeah. Looks a bit of a dump to me. Chloe likes it though," I heard Dad say.

"What do you mean?"

"As soon as she saw it, she became really animated. Kept pointing at the photograph saying *Chloe's house, Chloe's house.*"

Francesca sighed again. "She's in a minority of one then. It looks horribly neglected. Amanda reckons it's going to auction next week."

'A week later I was in Mrs Meacher's front room watching *Postman Pat*, absentmindedly guiding a spoonful of chocolate ice cream into my mouth, when Dad arrived to collect me.

"How's she been today, Mrs M?"

"She's been chattering away happy as ninepence. And she's done some lovely paintings. Look, a lovely picture of a house! Maybe she's going to be an artist when she grows up." Mrs Meacher held up a piece of paper covered in blobs of black and green paint with a red square in the middle.

"Very good, Chloe! Let's take this home to show Mummy."

I grabbed at the paper, tearing one of the corners. "Chloe's house," I stated with a pout.

Ian wheeled me, with Peppo on my lap, back along the same pavement we'd hurried along that morning. At the age of four I was really too heavy for my old buggy, which was slung so low in the canvas seat that my toes scuffed the pavement. We passed the council houses in Mrs Meacher's road, round the corner into the main road where white Georgian mansions lined the street, and across the road by the traffic lights. I bobbed up and down as Dad steered the buggy along the uneven pavements and tipped it over high kerbs. The roll of paper with my painting on it sat in my lap on top of Peppo, wider than the buggy and snagging on the walls of the houses we passed.

"Careful with your picture," Dad reminded me, as we turned the last corner before our flats. As we waited at the traffic lights cars and vans raced through, and a motorbike scraped the curb. This was one of Dad's *reasons to leave London* – the exhaust fumes polluting our lungs. Dad had compiled a list of two columns; one for, and one against moving to the country.

On his list of reasons to stay in London the real one was left out. Dad adored London. Coming from the suburbs he drank in the noise and constant movement. In London something was always going on. You could buy a pint of milk at midnight and still bump into a couple of people on the way home. He loved the anonymity too. No neighbours twitching their curtains to see what he was doing, because nobody cared.

"But *do* you really love London?" I heard Francesca ask during one of their *shall we / shan't we* debates. "I mean, ten years ago when we still went to pubs and clubs, spent days wandering around art galleries or afternoons in pokey cinemas watching obscure foreign films."

"I admit since I went into the estate agents to get the flat valued, I've been thinking more and more about leaving Streatham. Saint Reatham the agent called it. I can't stand that ridiculous trendy way of talking. Streatham is the same place it's always been. Dirty, dusty, banked up with cars and petrol fumes. I can't see the point in trying to romanticise it."

Next morning Francesca opened the front door with her elbow, balancing a piece of toast in her mouth and a briefcase under her arm.

"The phone's ringing. Get that will you, love. I've got to dash."

Mrs Meacher was phoning to say she had an appointment at the hospital with her knees that she'd completely forgotten about until that morning. She wanted to know if Dad could manage without her.

"I'm a bit snowed under today. I have to get the first draft of my book to the agent by Tuesday. Oh hell. No sorry, Mrs Meacher, I don't suppose there any other childminders who might be able to have her. No, I suppose not. Everyone's full. I see. Oh! Do you think he'd mind? That would be great, if you're sure. Is he? What time has he got to be there? Right I'll bring her round at ten. Thanks Mrs Meacher. You're a lifesaver."

"Chloe, come along," Dad said. "You're going on an expedition with Uncle Ken."

I spat pink toothpaste into the sink, jumped down from my block and grabbed Peppo. The thought of spending a day with Ken Meacher was worth hurrying for. He was beanpole tall with grey eyes that matched his hair and he smelled of sweet tobacco. An ex-sailor, who now worked as a builder, he would swing me into the air and loop me under his legs until I landed with a bump behind him. Then he'd hold his hand up to his forehead saying *man overboard!* and pretend to look for me.

When we got to Mrs Meacher's Ken was already in his car.

"This is kind of you, Ken," Dad said as he strapped me into the seat.

"Not at all. She's my little shipmate, this one. She's no bother."

"Give me a ring if you need me. I'll be working at home all day."

"We'll be fine. The gaffer's asked me to go to an auction. He's looking for building land. Wants to get into property development. We'll have a grand time, won't we, my precious?"

'Ken held my hand as we walked into the room where the auction was to be held in a pub called the Coach and Horses in Hounslow. The building was as big as a barn but we had to go through another room with a bar, in order to get to the main hall. Ken stopped to talk to one of the barmen and lifted me onto the bar. I was sitting on a blue and yellow towel.

"What's your poison little 'un?" the barman asked me. He had a dishcloth slung over his shoulder the way Dad did when he was cooking tea.

"She's a funny sausage," Ken answered for me. "Get her a Coke. Probably only allowed organic gooseberry juice at home." They both laughed and the barman squirted some Coke from a silver hose into a glass.

'The hall buzzed with the hum of people. I held tight onto Ken's jacket as he looked for some seats. Lots of the people crowded around boards pasted with photographs of houses, barns, empty fields, and office blocks.

A big man with orange hair and a checked coat pushed past us without even saying sorry. The room was hot and the Coke fizzing in my stomach made me feel queasy. "Uncle Ken," I said. "I feel sick."

"Hold on, Chloe love, I'll find us a seat. You'll feel better once you're sitting down."

Ken had collected a stack of papers from a man in a black suit and put them with a biro on the table in front of the chairs he'd found for us.

"There, sweetheart, you can do some drawing. You like drawing, don't you?"

I looked at the pieces of paper which had photos of all the different houses. A photograph of the house in Blackberry Lane was in one of the papers in the middle.

"Chloe's house! Chloe's house!" I squealed, tugging at Ken's sleeve.

"What's that, my treasure? Your house? No, that's not your house, little'un!"

The man in the black suit stood on a stage and spoke into a microphone.

"Does anyone have any questions before we begin the auction?" His voice boomed like a villain in a play.

"Can I go home and see my daddy now?" I held Peppo close to my chest. A woman on the next table looked concerned.

"What, sweetheart?"

"I want Daddy. I feel sick."

"You hang on, loveheart. I can't leave yet, chicken – that would be more than my job's worth. You do look a bit pale though."

"I feel sick, Uncle Ken."

Ken looked around the room and told me to sit tight while he popped outside to phone Dad to see if he could come and pick me up.

'I soon started to feel better, and I hardly noticed Ken's return so mesmerised was I by the man on the stage. His cheeks were red and his hair so black and shiny it looked wet. The first houses were sold with a flick of a brochure, a nod or a wink. The plots of land came next. Ken took notes of the amounts they went for and who had bought them, but these were just boring pictures of grass, so I sat with my head cushioned between my arms on the table.

"Lot number ten. Numbers One and Two Blackberry Lane, Lyde, near Shapton, Somerset." When I heard those words, my head jerked up. The man in the black suit carried on talking. "We're acting under instructions from Mrs Marjorie Grey and Mr Christian Stringer and we thank them for their very kind instructions. The property consists of two red brick semi-detached cottages built in the 1940s."

I gripped the sides of the seat of my chair and stared, straining forwards, unblinking as the man carried on. "In need of some improvement, set in a garden of approximately one eighth of an acre. Each house comprises an entrance hallway, sitting room, and kitchen. Number Two has two bedrooms, one of which has a concealed cupboard built into the wall and an upstairs bathroom and Number One has three bedrooms and a downstairs bathroom, Number Two has the additional feature of a glass porch. Planning permission may be sought to convert to one dwelling. The usual services are provided, electricity, mains water, with drainage to a cesspit situated to the rear of the grounds. The properties benefit from south facing gardens, one of which has three fruit trees believed to be apple. There is ample parking space to the side of each property and the possibility of planning permission to add a garage.

"I'll call the bidding three times," the man said. "Do I see twenty thousand? Twenty-one thousand? Do I see twenty-two thousand, five hundred?

Dad arrived and scanned the room looking for us. As soon as he caught my eye, he raised his hand.

"Twenty-three thousand, seven hundred," the auctioneer called, registering Dad's wave.

The auctioneer looked at a man near the front. "Twenty-three thousand, nine hundred?" He looked at Dad again as he made his way through the crowds. He arrived at our table and settled me onto his lap. A man to our right had just bid twenty-four thousand, eight hundred and fifty pounds.

"Chloe's house," I whispered to Dad, pointing at the picture on the table. The orange-haired man with the checked jacket tilted a piece of paper at the auctioneer.

Dad was still holding the details of the house in his hand when I pushed his elbow upwards. His arm rose and the piece of paper flapped in the direction of the auctioneer.

"Twenty-four thousand, nine hundred is it, sir?" The auctioneer looked at the orange man and he shook his head.

"Twenty-four thousand, nine hundred. Calling the bidding three times. Are you sure of your bid, sir?" Dad's head appeared to be nodding up and down. "Sold to the gentleman with the little girl on his lap…"

"'So this is the house Daddy somehow *managed* to buy by accident at an auction that he'd somehow *managed* to go to with Ken Meacher!"

I was sucking my thumb, staring out the car window at our new houses. A cow had its head poking over a blackberry bush on the other side of the lane. I spat my thumb out of my mouth and wanted so badly to shout at Mum that she'd only just missed squishing the cow's ears, but, of course, I couldn't and so quietly I stuck my thumb back in and spun round in my seat to make sure the cow was alright.

"It's just as Amanda and Michael described it. Do you like it, darling? It's hardly an oil painting but at least it was cheap and we should be able to knock it into some kind of shape."

I studied the fabric of my skirt. It was my favourite one with an elasticated waist made of cotton with pictures of Big Ben in yellow and grey against a white background.

"You could show a bit of enthusiasm, Chloe. After all, you were the one who liked this house."

I felt all kinds of excitement in my tummy that I didn't want to share with Francesca. A mixture of the fear I experienced every time Dad dropped me off at school, and the happiness whenever he came to collect me. I peeped out of the corner of my eye, past my mother's head and saw the house properly for the first time – and yet it felt like coming home.

Christian Stringer was waiting for us with the keys. A man in his fifties who walked awkwardly with the aid of sticks, he wore black boots, a brown overcoat and had a dog at his heel.

Francesca, tall and self-confident in a navy linen trouser suit shook his hand and introduced herself.

"This here's Number Two," Christian said. He kept his head bowed, seeming reluctant to make eye contact.

"I've just realised," Francesca offered uncertainly, "you must be Michael's brother. I know his wife, Amanda?" Francesca continued, unfazed by his lack of interest. "I've known her for some time." We were standing in the hall looking out at a dilapidated porch. The house was chilly inside and echoed with emptiness.

"We're changing everything. I expect you know," Francesca carried on, taking my hand as we followed Christian around.

"You'll need planning," he said eventually, as if that was the least likely thing anyone might achieve.

We went into a room which smelled of damp. "We've looked into that. This would make a large living space, taking into account the area next door. We'll be knocking through, of course." Francesca tapped the dividing wall. "There's a lot to be done. We're installing a new kitchen with an Aga, and an en suite in each bedroom. Quite a project but we're up for it. I understand we might be able to get a grant."

"I wouldn't know about that sort of thing."

We climbed the stairs leaving him at the bottom.

"Phew!" Francesca puffed. "They certainly made stairs narrow and steep in the old days! When was the house built?"

"1940s – just after the war," he called up the stairs.

"Strange choice of paint," Francesca observed. "A mixture of vivid purple paint and orange wallpaper. What style would you call that? Experimental?" Francesca laughed.

"Hippies," Christian said, by way of an explanation.

We explored the upstairs. I needed the toilet and knew instinctively where the bathroom was. Francesca was in the front bedroom when I'd finished, looking out of the window. Pink roses climbing up the front of the house had budded and died around the windowsills. Across the road the cow was still mooching against the hedgerow.

From the other bedroom at the back of the house, we peered through a broken window at an overgrown vegetable patch and some apple trees with gnarled branches. Then something caught Francesca's eye. A rabbit was shivering in the long grass under the tree.

"Oh, my goodness. Look! A real grey rabbit. I've never seen one before! There, under the tree. How extraordinary!"

I stood on tiptoes but was too short to see anything except sky. Francesca was still enthusing about the rabbit as we continued our exploration of the house. "Oh, my goodness! There's another one. Two rabbits! How wonderful!"

I could see Christian Stringer looking at us from the corner of his eye, as if he thought we were both basket cases, this woman who was thrilled at the sight of a common rabbit, and her silent daughter.

'When we arrived home, this was the first thing she told Hannah and Dad.

"We saw two grey rabbits sitting in the grass. I mean real wild ones. That's what made me sure we've done the right thing. Two real grey rabbits. Two rabbits, and two houses."

"Wow!" Hannah said. "Can we keep the rabbits as pets?"

"I don't see why not."

"Excellent," Hannah said. "I can catch them with my fishing net."

"I know I wasn't convinced about the auction and the house and everything, but now that I've seen it, I think I'm beginning to fall in love with it," Francesca said as she filled the kettle.

"And it sounds like it might be the best place for Chloe," Dad chipped in.

Everyone looked at me.

"Why just for Chloe?" Hannah whined.

"Daddy means for us all. And Chloe liked the houses and the rabbits too, I expect. Didn't you Chloe?"

I turned away and pretended to be looking at the top of a bus that was passing the window. The water in the kettle was beginning to bubble up and boil and although Francesca was in the kitchen, I hid the wide grin that had crept across my face.

'We followed the removal van from Streatham and I slept on the motorway and didn't wake up until the war memorial at the turning into Blackberry Lane. The van heaved along, swallowing up the lane, its roof cracking the horse chestnut branches, leaving them caught on the wing mirrors and scattered in bits behind us.

We began working on the two houses straight away. Francesca was between jobs, and it was school holidays, so we were all there.

Firstly, we had to strip the wallpaper. Apart from Francesca, we each had a scraper, a bucket of water and some washing up liquid. I slopped the wall with water and scraped.

"Chloe's scratching the plaster again, Mum!" Hannah grumbled.

Francesca glanced up from the book she was reading which was called, *Superwoman*. "Let her just do the water." I clung to my scraper. No one was going to stop me scraping. The laps of paper unfurled from the wall and when they stopped unfurling I tugged.

"Not like that, Chloe. Mum, look at her. She's doing it all wrong."

I slapped more water on. Some of the plaster under the paper was crumbly and the smell was like mouldy sand.

"Leave her, Hannah. That bit of wall's coming down anyway."

'We lived in Number Two while the builders worked next door. We all slept together in the upstairs front room while the kitchens were being converted, but the big topic of conversation was the removal of the main dividing wall. An RSJ was installed and we all moved into the box room.

"This is what it must be like for people living in bed and breakfast," Francesca said from the z bed she was squashed into with my father. We lay in our sleeping bags on the floor, and I wondered what she meant. How could someone *live* in bed and breakfast? I visualised my little cot bed in our old flat with a bowl of Weetabix on the pillow.

We ran outside to stare at the builders' van. *Andrew Jessop and Sons* arrived in a white pick-up with CLEAN ME written on the side in the dirt. Gary Jessop carried a pickaxe into the front room, and we bundled into the hall to watch him crack the first blow causing the plasterboard to spill open and the wallpaper on the top half of the wall, where I hadn't been able to reach, come away in chunks. Dust coated Gary's boots and snowed onto his checked shirt. The thick brown hair he'd had when he arrived instantly turned white as if he'd aged twenty years in a few seconds.

"You kids better keep well away," Gary warned as he lunged again, crashing into the crumbling brickwork as we both squealed when the first glint of light appeared through the dividing wall.

Gary leant over to pick up a brick. In a gap where a cupboard had been I could see something silver. He parked his pickaxe by the fireplace and wiped the dust from his eyes. Gary's fingers were like sausages. He reached over and picked up a thin silver cigarette case.

"Hey!" Gary looked around and then stopped himself, at which point Dad walked into the room with a cup of tea.

Dad pointed at the cigarette case. "Where did you find that?"

"Here, where that cupboard was." Gary wiped it down his vest and opened the lid.

"It's real silver. There's a hallmark inside. And it's engraved. *T.L.M.* I wonder who that belonged to." Dad peered into the cupboard as if there might be more cigarette cases in there.

"Hmm. *T.L.M.* Must've belonged to someone who lived here before us."

"I could ask my mum. She's lived in Lyde all her days. She'd know everyone who's ever lived here. Owner could be dead, though. No point in trying to return it now, I'd say."

"No." My father held out his hand for the cigarette case.

'Francesca wanted a housewarming. Dad said housewarming parties were very *London* and therefore not appropriate, and in any case who would come since the only people we'd met were the Stringer family over the road?

After the builders left everything about the house was twice the size it had been. The living room now spanned the whole of the front of the two houses, and we had a kitchen table the size of a canoe.

"I could invite Amanda and Michael," Francesca said. Dad looked sceptical and went upstairs. He spent a lot of time upstairs. The box room where we'd slept squashed together the previous year was now his study.

He displayed the cigarette case we'd found on the mantelpiece over the mock Tudor fireplace that sat at the far side of the front room. He said we should take care of it and not use it as a mirror for our Barbies, which is what Hannah had been doing. It might be worth a few quid. If the Jolly Dolly books flopped, we could always sell the cigarette case, he said.

Francesca got her own way. We had the party and, although Michael and Amanda didn't travel up from London, Christian and Evie Stringer made the expedition from one side of the lane to the other and arrived as the grandmother clock in the hall struck seven. Christian struggled in with the aid of his sticks, and Evie carried a cake on a plate covered with a dishcloth.

"Why are they bringing us food?" Hannah whispered as Francesca cut the cake in the kitchen. "Do they think we can't afford to buy our own?"

"It's neighbourly. The sort of thing country people do," Francesca said. "I think it's nice."

"I think they're weird. Have you seen what she's wearing? An orange dress with some gross purple swirly pattern. And her hair. She looks like a scarecrow. Seriously weird."

"Things are slower here. Fashions take a while to catch on," Francesca said.

"About a thousand years, by the looks of it."

"Don't be unkind, Hannah. They seem nice and they are our only neighbours."

"He's got spooky eyes. And why does he need those walking sticks. He's not that old."

"I think he had an accident. Got trampled by one of his cows," Francesca whispered back.

Hannah shrieked. "Trampled by one of his cows? That's horrible!"

"Exactly, so be quiet. It's not funny – so don't mention it."

"I'm going to make the most of this," Hannah said. "I'm going to ask them all about our house and who lived here before and then we can find out who TLM was."

The Stringers must have felt strange walking into our house since half of it had been once their home. I say *walking* but Christian hobbled, very slowly, and they seemed to need coaxing from the hallway into the living room like shy early arrivals at a children's party.

Christian spent the evening drinking cans of beer that Dad fetched from the fridge. I'd seen them both quite a few times since we'd moved in and yet they both appeared different from normal. Not that they usually dressed like our parents, but they'd obviously put on special outfits for the party. Francesca wore soft flowing skirts that stopped an inch above her ankles. Evie's dress, as Hannah had pointed out, was a pattern of orange and purple swirls but was so short it slid way above her knees, showing the tips of her suspender belt when she sat down. Christian wore a shirt and tie, but the tie was wide and purple with a big knot that he kept trying to pull loose. They were a lot older than my parents and they both spoke like Wurzel Gummidge.

At half-eight I was ordered upstairs to bed, but I crouched at the top of the landing in my dressing gown. They were chatting about how much the houses had changed since we'd bought them and made them into one. Christian and Evie Stringer acted like they were in a temple that had to be worshipped. They couldn't get over the size of the living room. Evie said it was so fashionable she'd like to get their living room in the faermhouse looking the same. The conversation was boring. And after they'd discussed the new fireplace for about an hour Dad pointed out the cigarette case displayed on the mantelpiece. By this time, I was halfway down the stairs. I watched Dad hand the cigarette case to Christian.

"We found this when we had the wall knocked down. Perhaps you know who TLM was?"

I squashed my ear against the banister. I didn't think this was a good idea. We were supposed to be keeping the cigarette case to sell if the Jolly Dolly books didn't take off. The Stringers might pretend it was theirs and we would never see it again.

Christian examined it before passing it on to Evie.

"TLM," she said. "The last people who lived here had plenty of comings and goings – could have belonged to any of them. There was Fabian and Hilly and all their friends, and Angel and Colin."

"'Nah. They were them hippy types," Christian said. "Not the types to have a cigarette case. They never had a penny to their name. Not in them days anyway. I'd say that's from longer ago. Must be someone who lived here before them hippies."

"How many people have lived here?" Dad asked.

"The first were Arthur Blake and his missus. But that was a good while ago. I was a lad when they come. Arthur came to work on the farm just after the war. But neither of them had the initials TLM. Although they did have a little boy by the name of Tommy."

"Then there was the McDonald brothers…" Evie looked down at her glass.

"And … *the one we don't talk about…*" Christian said. Evie took a tissue from her handbag and blew her nose. "And then Mullet and his wife."

"The Mullets," Evie said. "She was a nice woman, Maureen. Not so sure about him, Charlie he was called, but that Maureen was a lovely person."

"Then the hippies, and that's about it. It was empty for years after they left, until you come, of course."

"*To lovely Maureen.*" Everyone stared at Hannah.

"Sorry?" Francesca said.

"To lovely Maureen."

"What do you mean, Hannah?"

"TLM – To Lovely Maureen. That might be what the inscription on the cigarette case meant. Perhaps this Charlie gave it to Maureen as a present."

"But is a cigarette case the sort of thing a man would give a woman as a present?" Francesca said. "That would be like Dad giving me …a pipe."

Everybody laughed.

"Anyway I don't think she smoked," Evie said.

"Yes, she did. She smoked Consulate," Christian said.

Evie glared at her husband. "How comes you're so sure of that?"

"I remember seeing her smoking them, that's all."

"The woman we bought Number Two from was called Grey," Dad said.

"No, there's never been no Greys,' Evie said with a frown. 'Last people in Number Two were Angel and Colin, and their surname was Monk. And I'll tell you something very interesting about them…"

"So who was Geoffrey Grey?" Dad interrupted her. "His name is on the deeds."

Evie examined her plate. "Now, come to think of it," she said slowly, addressing her sausage roll, "the last person to own that side of the house before you was Angel's father. I remember now. Angel told me he bought them the house as a wedding present. Now I reckon he could of been your Mr Grey."

Hannah looked up and laughed. "Weird wedding present."

I watched, listened and rubbed my tired eyes from my position on the stairs. They all seemed faintly absurd, trying to work out who owned a silly cigarette case. I began to drift off to sleep then suddenly felt myself slipping down the staircase. I arrived with a bump at the bottom and clattered into the hallway. Dad rushed towards me. I think I was still half asleep when I picked myself up and stared at the group assembled round me.

"Thomas," I said.

"Who?" Everyone seemed to ask at once.

"Thomas Blake," I said. There was a mumbling of confusion. Dad carried me up to bed and kissed me goodnight with beery breath.'

PIP

IT'S NIGHT-TIME in Blackberry Lane and an inky sky wraps itself around the house. A handful of stars wink at each other and beam their secrets towards the earth. Saul left hours ago and now I can't sleep. I don't want to sleep because if I do, I might not dream about him.

I remember a night like this… many years ago, soon after we'd left London. I couldn't sleep then. All my toys and books were still packed away in crates, and I couldn't reach to get them out.

I got out of bed to go to the bathroom. I stood by the sink washing my hands, cold water trickling from the tap, the room freezing. The radiators were still in the garden waiting to be fitted. Outside the hoot of an owl woke one of the farm dogs and set off a chain of barking.

I shivered and spoke just one word, 'Pip.' The word frightened me, yet at the same time felt like a comfort. As if the name belonged to me. The owl hooted again, followed by the howl of a fox. I heard Dad snoring, the sound of the bathroom door opening.

Francesca switched on the light. She knelt on the floor beside me, so our eyes were level.

'Chloe? Darling, what's wrong? Why are you standing here in the cold?' I flinched as she reached her hand towards me. 'Tell me what's wrong? Have you had a bad dream?'

My lips were as if glued together. If I spoke now, I'd have broken every rule that governed my short life.

She touched my hair, and I took a step away from her.

'Chloe. Please. Just this once. I won't tell anyone, I won't tell Daddy or Amanda or anyone. Please, just speak to me. Just one word.' I wanted to say one word. That same word I'd spoken a few moments ago. I didn't know why or what it meant but the word

Pip repeatedly went through my head. I tried to say it – I opened my mouth and breathed hard, pursed my lips firmly together for the first 'P'. I thought I was saying it, but no sound came out.

Francesca had mostly kept her composure in the face of my silence, but that night, as she kneeled on the bathroom floor, she broke down. The sight of her in tears repelled me. I took another step backwards and banged my ear on the side of the sink. My cry must have woken Dad who arrived dressed in pyjama bottoms.

'What's going on?'

'Daddy, I hurt my ear.'

Francesca visibly shrivelled as I flung myself into his arms.

'Fran, what's wrong?'

'I just want her to talk to me. I'm her mother,' she sobbed. 'Is that too much to ask?'

Dad led me back to my bed and stroked my hair until I fell asleep.

What I'd said to Amanda in her consulting room seemed truer than ever. Francesca might have given birth to me in the echoing hospital with Tulip beside her ready to cut the cord.

But Francesca was not my real mother.

Everything changed one afternoon a week after my sixth birthday. Francesca had a job in Shapton and after work she'd decided – on a whim – to have her hair cut and dyed blonde. She didn't even tell Dad, but just came home looking like someone else. Her hair is grey now, but she used to have a tangle of long, dark ringlets. Hannah said Mum walked into the house that afternoon and it was the strangest thing ever. Everyone was astonished by the transformation of our mother. Dad said he thought he'd get used to it and Hannah decided it was okay, but when she first walked in, it was as if *I* was the only person who recognised her. She stood on the front step with her handbag and some shopping and this new ash blonde hair that she'd had cut to shoulder length and straightened. I went up to her and put my arms around her and whispered, 'Hello Mummy,' into the folds of her coat.

Nobody knew whether to be more shocked by Francesca's change of image, or the change it triggered in me. I had spoken to her directly for the first time in my life, yet to me it seemed the most natural thing. Francesca suddenly looked like my mother after all.

CHLOE

June 2004

DAD BOUGHT the gite in France from the proceeds of the *Jolly Dolly* books, so they spend most of their time there now and it's my job to look after the house in Blackberry Lane. They even pay me. They came at Easter and stayed for two weeks. It was great to see them looking so healthy and happy. Dad's arthritis has improved, and Francesca, well, I think she was always allergic to being at home. She moved around from room to room, but I could tell she couldn't wait to leave.

I write my poetry in the orangery. I decorated the room myself, chose the furniture and the blinds. I've even got a chaise longue, like the one in Keats' house in Hampstead. In the afternoons I write. Lines and lines of verse in my tiny, scrawling hand. I was always in trouble at school about the size of my handwriting. The bookcases that flank the walls are crammed with poetry books. Some of the older ones have gold edges with paper so thin I have to blow it to turn the pages. My *Don Juan* is like that. My other books are in the music room. They surround me whilst I play the piano in the winter evenings. Hannah always says I should have been born in the nineteenth century and been one of those ladies who are *accomplished* and spend all their time improving their musical skills, painting and embroidery. But I've never embroidered anything in my life. Anyway, I don't think of myself as being from that era, but rather from a more recent time.

I've read my poems over and over here, tweaked and turned them about. Printed them off, and sealed them up in envelopes ready to send to faceless names of publishers, with romantic-sounding addresses in London. I sold my first volume last year. *Rain Woman.*

Admittedly Dad helped me, but now I feel absolved. I can spend my time doing the things I love. Daydreaming, looking after the house, taking care of the garden, and writing.

Dad worries about me, living here on my own and keeps asking me what I'm planning for my twenty-first birthday. As if I should throw some huge party. But I would hate this house to be full of people. And anyway, who would I invite? Most of my friends from school went off to uni. I've lost touch with the others.

Saul and I sat together in the orangery for hours on that first day whilst his uncle slept in the car. Days later we met on the village green on the other side of the football pitch where we perched on the bench under the oak tree beside the rubbish bin crammed with bottles and empty crisp packets. We spent the entire afternoon there, until dusk crept in. The tops of my arms were pink by the time he walked me home and he laughed at me, saying I should get out more and that he didn't believe anyone could get sunburnt in England.

We stood at the gate as close as we could without touching.

'When are you going home?' I knew I had no right to ask, but suddenly my life seemed to depend on his answer.

'I haven't decided yet. It's up to my uncle. You're not trying to get rid of me already, are you?'

He came inside the house again. 'It's my twenty-first birthday soon,' I said handing him a beer.

'What're you doing to celebrate?'

'Don't know. I haven't thought much about it.'

'You'll have to do something.'

'Why?'

'Because birthdays are important. You shouldn't let them drift by. Maybe I could help you celebrate?'

I thought for a while. 'You could come to the house and spend the day with me.'

Saul laughed. 'You really are the original hermit, aren't you? Look. I'll check with my uncle, but that should be okay. When is it?'

'The twenty-seventh of June.'

'So that makes you a Gemini.'

'You're into horoscopes?'

'Not especially, but the twenty-seventh of June is an important date in our family.'

'Why is that?'

'It's probably the one time in the year that my parents go to the church? You see, my mum had a baby on that date. The baby died just after it was born. This was years ago but my parents always remember baby Pip on that day.'

'Pip?'

'Yes,' Saul says, studying my face. 'I remember what you said before. That you said the name 'Pip' when you were little and stood in the bathroom. You made it sound spooky. Is it a common name around here?'

'No. I've never met anyone called Pip,' I said.

Saul and his uncle have booked into the Ring O' Bells while his uncle's getting over the 'flu. We're meeting here tonight, and I stand at the bar by a murky half-light of a summer evening praying he won't be late. I order a spritzer and sit down at one of the tables furthest away from the bar, nervously twirling the ends of my hair around my finger. On the bar is a tall, three-pronged candelabra like a prop you'd see in a horror movie. Each candle has molten wax dribbled down its sides.

The door opens. 'Sorry I'm late,' Saul says. 'Terrible time-keeping. I know. It's my only flaw. Have you been here long?' His apology is accompanied by a massive smile.

After he's been up to the bar he sits beside me, close up. He looks clean, like he's just showered, and smells of aftershave. We sip our drinks, and … I wait, wondering if he'll take my hand or nudge me with his shoulder, rub against me with his arm, but at the same time I'm trying to work out what's gone wrong.

Shouldn't he have touched me by now? Why have we talked for so long but with no physical contact? So many words, but little else. I need to ask Hannah about this. Did she make the first move on the gnome? Or did he stroke her cheek with his stumpy fingers? Second thoughts – maybe not.

A waitress arrives with a notepad and pencil. I recognise her from the year below me at school and she gives me an uncertain smile. I think she's called Sarah. I'm pretty sure she used to work in the fish and chip shop. She's one of the ones who got left behind – like me. She asks what we'd like. Saul orders the swordfish and I plump for the cannelloni with goat's cheese.

'When are your folks back?' he asks after we've started eating. A lump of cannelloni goes down the wrong way, forcing me to cough and splutter. Is he planning to spend the night with me before we've even held hands? This is all so confusing.

'Not for a while. In fact, I'm not sure you'll get to meet them at all. If you're planning to go home soon…' I look down at the table, afraid of his response.

He gulps his beer. 'My uncle's still not better but when he's up and about he said he'd like to stay on for a bit and explore the countryside and a place called Minehead? Where he was brought up? Then I'll drive him home. In fact, I'd like to bring him out to meet you, if that's alright?'

'Sure, any time,' I say. 'And he still hasn't been to see the Stringers?'

'The Stringers?'

'The people he was looking for. You know, the farmers. Don't you think your uncle will want to talk over old times with them? I mean he wouldn't have known Martin and Hazel but Christian and Evie still live there.'

'How old are they?'

'Eighty. A hundred-and-eighty. I'm not sure. Ultra old though…'

'Actually, I don't think it was the Stringers he was looking for. The sat nav brought us there, but he says his house was across the road.'

'Across the road? But that's our house.'

The waitress hovers around and asks if we have everything we need. Saul assures her we do.

'I guess. Although he described it as two semis. But of course, you've already told me, your folks did the conversion, so it must be yours.' As he says this Saul strokes my chin with his finger. 'There's no others around, as far as I can see.'

I'm immersed in pleasure. He touched me. Saul just stroked my chin. My insides are in bits but I fold my napkin in half and place it neatly on the table

Saul shuffles on the seat. He's closer to me now and his arm reaches around my shoulder. The feel of him, the smell. 'You're so sweet,' he whispers into my hair… and we kiss. I realise now why I've waited so long for this. This is perfect – no fumbling or doubts. The way he kisses is bliss. It's like he's kissed a thousand girls before me, but at the same time I'm the first. His taste is delicious – despite the swordfish – and eventually, reluctantly we pull apart. A couple of elderly men at the bar are looking at us and chuckling into their beers. Saul takes my hand as if he's about to propose or something. I panic because I think I'm going to cough again.

'Hey, are you okay?' he asks, patting me on the back. He passes me my drink, and when I've calmed down, takes my hand again. My hand feels hot and my mind's a jumble of doubts, fears and an insatiable longing somewhere deep inside me.

I try to nibble more cannelloni before laying my knife and fork on my plate. 'So, to go back to what you were saying…' we both laugh here. 'You're telling me your uncle lived in one of the semis? When was this?'

'He lived here in the fifties with my dad. My uncle owned the house then he sold it to Dad. Mum and Dad lived here before they emigrated.'

'And your mum lost a baby when she lived there?'

'Yeah.'

'Oh my God. How awful. What happened?'

'I don't know much about it, except for the name and the fact that she thought she'd never be able to have any more children. Then lo and behold I popped along out of the blue years later when she'd resigned herself to the fact that she'd never be a mum.'

'Wow. And did you say the baby that died – Pip – did you say the baby was stillborn on June the twenty-seventh?'

'Yes. Why?' An uncomfortable silence hovers between us. Saul calls the waitress over to order more drinks. I peek outside through the narrow pub window. The sun has faded as grey and white clouds amble dreamily by. I wonder how many other couples have sat here cementing their relationships or deciding to part. But we are not a couple, this young man from the other side of the world and I. Half an hour ago we might have been on our way to becoming close but now I'm not so sure.

I suddenly feel hot and quite sick. 'Oh. No reason.' My abandoned cannelloni now looks as appetising as a plate of elastic bands. Saul is still talking but his voice seems to be coming at me through a tunnel.

'What's the matter? You're not angry with me, are you? Chloe, you're not saying anything. Have I done something wrong?'

Goosebumps break out all the way up my arm. 'No. It's alright.' I disentangle my fingers from his. 'I'm not upset. I think I'd better be getting home, though.'

From the village it's not too far to walk, especially with so many thoughts racing through my head, taking my mind off the long stretch with no proper pavement from the outskirts of the village to the war memorial. Meeting Saul has churned up so many memories, forgotten sensations. I hadn't thought about that night in the bathroom for years. And yet I *had* stood there when I was five and said the name 'Pip' out loud for no apparent reason. I run most of the way down Blackberry Lane, arriving breathless at home.

My phone pings as soon as I get in.

Hi. You ok? S x

I tuck my phone under my pillow and lie in bed. I haven't closed the curtains, it's not even completely dark yet. I doze off only to be awoken by another text from him.

Hi. Let me know you got back ok?x

Another text.

Please??x

I put some music on. At two in the morning, I'm woken by Beyonce singing Crazy in Love. I sit up in bed and turn off the music, fumble for my phone and press reply to Saul's messages.

Hiya. Yes I'm fine. Thanks. This might seem an odd question, but do you have a photo of your mum ?x

At eight he rings me.

'Saul?'

'Chloe? You alright?'

'Yeah.'

'Look, I'm sorry if I came onto you too strong last night. I know you're probably not ready yet. But I couldn't help myself. You know, I really like you and ...'

'Err... listen, Saul, did you get my message – about a photo? Do you have one of your mum that I could see? It's really important...'

'Yep I did see it. But my mum? Why?'

'It's important and I thought you might have one with you.'

'I do as it happens. In my wallet. I could come to your house today and let you see it?'

I'm shaking as Saul hands me the photo. His mother in the photo is probably in her seventies. She's wearing a pink blouse and pearls. Her hair is a soft shade of white, styled away from her face. Her eyes are blue, gentle with laughter lines around the edges. She's resting one hand on the side of her cheek. I can see Saul in her face, the lips and the nose. She feels familiar.

'Your mum. She looks lovely. And, I was just wondering, you don't happen to have a photo of her when she was young, do you? When she lived here. I suppose that's not likely. Forget I even asked.'

'No I don't, sorry. What's this fascination with my mum?'

'I know. Tell me if I'm being a pain. But there's something about her face that I recognise.'

'Sorry, Chloe. Much as I love her, I don't lug piles of photos of my mum around the world. Look, can we talk about something else? My uncle's still keen to visit your house. We could come over this arvo if you're free?'

'Ok.'

'You don't sound too keen?'

'Sorry, no it's fine. I was just thinking about something, that's all. But I'd like to meet your uncle.'

'Actually I think he's a bit nervous. I mean, it was his idea to come. The whole trip was his idea, and he seems to have some fond memories of the place, but I get the feeling not all the memories are good.'

The green Volvo pulls up outside the house again. I'm anxious. I'm not great at meeting new people, although this is nothing like the fear I experienced two weeks ago when the same car first rolled up – and rolled over my life. Saul smiles in my direction, walks around the car to open the passenger door. An elderly man gets out.

'Good afternoon. I do hope we're not intruding,' the man says.

Saul's uncle has kind, dark brown eyes that look as if the years have tiptoed in a detour around them. 'This is my uncle,' he says. 'Uncle John, this is Chloe.'

'Chloe, at last we meet.' Saul's Uncle John shakes my hand and holds me with his gaze. 'You live here? How interesting. I've been looking forward to seeing the old house again.'

I take his arm and steady him as he accompanies me down the path.

'So you used to live here!' I begin.

He laughs – a gentle laugh punctuated with a sigh. 'A long while ago, my dear. I hardly recognise the place now. I moved here with my brother in 1955. That's Saul's father, you know. I bought it with a small win I had on the football pools. That was like the lottery is nowadays,' he adds, as if confiding a secret.

We sit in the orangery sipping tea. 'I see the football pitch is still here. After all these years. Some things don't change. Your father used to play football there, Saul. Oh, and the war memorial. And Stringers place is exactly as I remember it. Although I'd never have recognised our house. It looks so different – quite splendid, in fact.'

After we've drunk our tea I show John around the house and garden until we've gone full circle to the orangery.

'Your family have worked wonders. It's changed so. But the feeling is still the same. Do you know what I mean when I say the *feeling*? I knew this was the right house for me as soon as I saw it and it was a hard place to leave.'

'So why did you leave, Uncle?' Saul asks.

'I was offered a better job. Oh, and I was in love too…yes…' he smiles and we both return his smile. 'But I think the main reason was the job. Relocation they called it. Relocation,' he says with a long sigh, 'and love.'

'Who were you in love with, if you don't mind me asking, Uncle? It must have been someone pretty special.'

'She was. Very special.'

'So what happened to her?'

'Oh, we drifted apart.'

'But do you think she's still around? Maybe we could look her up?'

'No, she left the area a long time ago…' As John speaks, Saul's phone rings.

'It's Dad,' he says looking surprised. 'I'll take it outside.'

Saul leaves the room and I watch as he struts around the vegetable patch. He looks in at us a couple of times. I take the opportunity to talk alone to his uncle.

'I don't suppose you have any photos of Saul's mother when she was younger – when you lived here? I'm presuming you knew her then.'

'Ah, my dear. I fear you've guessed my secret. Saul said you were a clever young lady. Yes, I do, as a matter of fact. In fact,' he takes his wallet from the inside pocket of his jacket, 'I have one here. This is Susan when she was in her twenties. It's only a black and white…but it was taken here, in the garden.'

He hands me the photo. It's a bit bigger than a passport photo and crumpled, a picture of a young woman standing by a rose bush. She's wearing a striped A line dress that looks homemade and flat shoes. Her hair is blonde and she has an Alice band pulling it away from her face. Her smile is radiant. 'She is lovely,' I say wistfully. 'And she looks so happy.' I peer closer at her face, but it is hard to make out her features. Even so, I hold the photo flat against my heart.

'I can tell you're taken with her,' John says. 'She was pretty, wasn't she? And charming. And she had the most delightful laugh.'

I examine the photo again. 'Yes, she looks very special.' We sit for a moment in silent reflection. 'So, what was your secret?' I ask him.

John removes the photo firmly from my fingers and slots it back in his wallet. 'I'm wrong to drag up things from the past. Maybe you hadn't guessed after all, and so we'll just leave it be.'

Now I'm even more intrigued. I'll ask Saul as soon as he comes in but when I look into the garden it's empty.

Saul has been gone for the past half hour. He's not answering his phone or my text messages. He seems to have vanished.

'Does your nephew often disappear like this?' I ask with a smile.

'No, I must say it's rather out of character. I wonder where he might have got to. I hope his phone call wasn't bad news.'

'Maybe I should go and look for him.'

'That's a good idea.' Saul's uncle produces a small book from his jacket pocket. '*Pickwick Papers*,' he says. 'I'm re-reading the whole of Dickens. There's always something new to find in Dickens. And books are great companions. Sometimes people can be difficult, but books are always reliable. Books never let you down. But I'm holding you up. You were about to look for Saul, although I'm sure he won't have gone far.'

Outside a blanket of cloud has obscured the sun and a light rain cools my skin. There's no sign of Saul. I check in the car and up the lane. I hear the crack of gunfire from one of the fields. The Stringers' dog starts barking. Then I see him. He's in the field nearest the lane, walking away from the house, still with his phone to his ear. I cross over and shelter under one of the trees as the rain is getting harder, and call him, 'Saul! Come back. You can't walk there. It's private land. Saul!'

He must have heard me, but he takes no notice, keeps walking further and further away from me until he's just a dot in the distance.

I'm tempted to go after him, but judging by the distance he's walked I think it's safe to assume he wants to be alone. I decide to go back to the house to make sure his uncle is alright.

He's still where I left him.

'Any luck?' he says looking up from *Pickwick Papers*.

'I can see him, he's out in Stringers' home field, but I don't think he heard me.'

'Perhaps he's upset. He said the phone call was from David. I hope not bad news. I'm afraid I'll have to wait for him. I'm not able to drive and so will have to impose on your hospitality until he returns. I do apologise.'

'No. No. That's fine. We'll just have to wait.'

Half an hour later Saul reappears. He's only wearing a T-shirt and jeans and is damp and shivering. I jump up to let him in.

'Ah. You're there. We were beginning to get worried about you,' Uncle John says.

Saul looks pale. 'Uncle John; Chloe. I'm afraid something awful's happened. That was Dad on the phone. He's at the hospital – with Mum. She had a fall on her way upstairs to bed last night. She's broken one of her hips, and her arm. He said she's in a …' Saul's voice falters. 'She's in a coma and they're not sure she's going to make it.'

The room goes quiet. It's my turn now to be in need of fresh air and so I take my leave. Outside the dog over the road is still barking. I try to remember its name. It's a golden retriever. Fleur, I think. Or maybe Daisy. Or was Daisy their last dog? I take a few deep breaths before going inside where Saul is on his phone again. His uncle seems to have shrivelled in his chair. After I've found a jumper for him and made him a tea with lots of sugar, Saul sits down beside his uncle.

'Can I get you some water?' I ask John, uncertain as to how I should address him. Saul has only referred to him as Uncle John.

'Yes, my dear.' His voice shakes. 'Thank you. I'm afraid I'm feeling a bit knocked for six. I'll have the water and then, Saul, I think I'd like to go back to the hotel.'

*

SAUL HAS invited me to his room in the hotel because he wants to speak to me. If he's planning to leave the UK and return to Australia, then that is what he must do. The Ring O' Bells is in heart of the village just past the Co-op and before the art and pottery shop. He's waiting for me in the bar and he takes my hand as we climb the dark, winding staircase to the first floor. The windows in his room are framed by maroon damask curtains and a free standing claw-foot Victorian bathtub sits between the bed and a sofa. The lighting is subdued. We are standing awkwardly in front of a plasma screen TV on the wall which is turned on to a cricket match, but with no sound.

'So,' he says. 'I've got a flight booked for tomorrow.'

'Oh.'

'Via Amsterdam.'

'I see.'

'I'm going to miss you, Chloe. I hardly know whether I'm coming or going.'

'I feel confused too,'

His phone is ringing but he checks it and turns it off before leading me to his bed.

Up until this afternoon I could only guess how it would feel to have a man make love to me. I didn't want to even think about it – before I met Saul. His sadness made me tender. Our love making, a mixture of passion and sorrow. I was like a child in his arms, then a woman, then a mother as I cradled his sad head to my chest. He is more beautiful in his sorrow even than he was before.

He gets up to go to the bathroom and in the brief minutes that he's gone I'm suddenly filled with so many different thoughts that when I hear the toilet flush I jump from my side of the bed. I feel a cold, tingling sensation all over.

'Hey,' he says coming round to me and sitting next to me on the counterpane. 'Are you okay? That was your first time? I didn't hurt you, did I?'

For some reason his words, though way off course, make me cry. 'Hey, you, don't cry. I'm not that bad, am I?'

'Saul,' I manage to get out between sobs. 'I'm so sorry, I feel awful about this, but I really don't think we should have done that just now.'

'I guess. I don't want to rush you, but the way things have turned out – I didn't expect to be leaving so soon and …I've never wanted anyone like I've wanted you over these past few weeks. In fact, I was going to ask you if you'd consider coming too. You know – out to Oz? Even if it was just for a short while? I can't let you go now that I've found you.'

'Saul. You have to let me go. We have to let each other go.'

'You don't want us to be together?'

I blow my nose with a tissue. 'No. We can't. It would be wrong.'

'Wrong? How d'you mean *wrong*?' He lies down on his side of the bed. I take several deep breaths before I am able to speak. I twist around so I can see his face.

'You remember what I told you about all my problems when I was little.'

'Yeah, years ago, when you were a kid.'

'It's more complicated than it seems. I always had a sense of not belonging in my family. Of being the odd one out…'

'You mean you thought you were adopted?'

'No, not adopted. I never could put into words the way I felt. I think that's probably why the house in Blackberry Lane meant – still means – so much to me. It became a substitute for something that I lacked within my family.'

Saul is staring at me, frowning. 'Yeah, you said you were a strange kid. Hey, but look at you now!'

'It's not funny, Saul. But there's more to it than that.' I tell him about Francesca and how she changed the way she looked and how I embraced her because she looked different. 'But since your Uncle John showed me an old photo of your mum, of Susan, I can see that Francesca looked very much like Susan once she'd had her hair done, and that's why I ran to embrace her.'

Saul screws up his eyes like he's just come outside from a darkened room. 'But all that's just a coincidence. It's all buried in the past.'

I lean over to get my bag from the floor. 'But supposing it's not a coincidence. Supposing I didn't accept Francesca as my real mother because I'd been born before, here in Lyde, in the house in Blackberry Lane, on the twenty-seventh of June in 1958.'

'Chloe, this is getting weirder by the minute. I've got a lot going on at the moment. I'm just about holding things together as it is, and now you actually expect me to want to discuss this mumbo jumbo about your mother?'

'I'm sorry. I know you're going through a hard time, but you must agree that it would explain a few things. Like why did I coerce my family here? Why did I say the word 'Pip' when I was standing in the house where Pip died?'

'Maybe you felt the baby's presence in some kind of spooky way. Like a ghost or a spirit. But that doesn't mean you *are* that baby. I mean how could you be?'

'I feel that I am that baby. Which changes everything.'

'How so?'

'Because I would be your sister.'

Saul laughs. 'No way. You would so *not* be my sister. I don't have a sister. This has to be the most ridiculous thing I've ever heard. It's certainly a new way to get dumped.'

'I'm not dumping you.'

'No. I see. You're not dumping me, but you're saying you're the reincarnation of a baby that died in 1958 and that baby was my brother or sister. That's crazy, Chloe. That's the most fucking crazy thing I've ever heard. Just because you share the same birthday, doesn't mean you're the same person. Jeez, I share my birthday with Dannii Minogue, but that doesn't make me a famous actress or singer or whatever.'

'I'm not sure you understand. You're missing the point. And anyway, Dannii Minogue didn't die at birth. What I'm trying to say is that I knew I felt close to you the moment I first saw you outside on the front path that day. I knew for years, even when I was really young, that Francesca wasn't my real mother and unconsciously I manipulated events so that my family ended up living in the house where I was *really* born the first time in 1958.'

'You *weren't* born in 1958. That would make you much too old and wrinkly for me. I'd never fancy you.'

Saul leans his head against mine– a simple gesture that could be a lover's – or a brother's.

I shiver. 'No,' I say. 'Please don't.'

'Don't? Don't *what?*'

I hesitate, but fail to find some better way of putting this. 'If you kiss me now it would be like ... kissing my brother.'

Saul slaps his forehead. 'Chloe, this is crap. Are you upset because I'm going away? Or am I too old for you? Is that what it is? I mean, how many boyfriends have you had, stuck out here? There's nothing to be afraid of.'

'I'm not afraid.'

'Yeah? You're scared of getting too close to someone, something to do with the relationship you had with your mother when you were little. Or your father? No one can live up to him, right? But I'm not your father, Chloe. And I'm certainly not your brother. You and me, we've clicked. What happened just now meant something. It meant a hell of a lot, to me at any rate. I like you and I know you like me. There's no way we're related.'

Once more I leave the Ring O'Bells alone, this time in tears. At home I think of phoning Hannah. But would she understand? I've never told anyone about all this. And anyway she'll probably be curled up, fast asleep in bed with the gnome.

This morning I do some writing. My writing is at its best when I'm sad. But 'sad' hardly touches the turmoil inside me today. Saul will have left already and will be on his way to London now. I doubt I'll ever see him again. This thought stops the flow of the poem and sends me into a trance of misery. How often does someone so randomly special come into one's life? And even less likely, appear outside your house? I'm in such a reverie of gloom that I don't realise the door bell is ringing. Of course, it's egg day. Martin should have the sense to just leave them on the step. However, it's not Martin with his eggs who greets me outside, but Saul's uncle. A taxi is doing a six point turn in the lane before rolling to a stop by the gate.

'Hello, my dear. I do hope I'm not intruding.'

I've never been so surprised to see anyone in my life. 'No, not at all. Would you like to come in? I thought you'd gone.'

He takes my arm as we go into the lounge. 'Saul *has* gone. But, as you can see, I am still here.'

'I *can* see that, Uncle John!' I say with a laugh.

I haven't seen him look angry before. 'Heavens above, Chloe, I am not *your* uncle.'

'No, I'm so sorry I didn't mean...'

He leans back on the sofa and clasps his hands together, rolling his thumbs, first one way, then the other. 'Now. I want you to listen. I'm sure you will listen, because Saul's told me a lot about you and you seem the type of young lady who would listen. I've come to talk to you about something very important. Not that I'm adept at solving romantic problems, far from it. But I'm going to have a go. Firstly, I have decided to fly out to Australia. I don't have my passport with me and so I will wait for my housekeeper to post it, and that is why I'm still here. Secondly, the reason I'm going to Australia is not just to keep Saul company.

'Saul told me about your theory.' He looks down at his lap before continuing. 'That you think you are the reincarnation of Susan's baby, Pip. But, Chloe, my dearest girl, perhaps you could be wrong about all this. You are yourself – Chloe, and surely that is enough.'

He stops and we stare at one another. 'And now I'm going to tell the secret that I mentioned before. As I said, when I lived here with Saul's father David, I fell in love. The object of my affection was the young lady in the picture I showed you. Susan. Are you shocked?'

I've been fiddling with a rose petal, squeezing it between my thumb and forefinger. 'Yes. You were in love with your brother's wife? That is shocking.'

'Ah! But she wasn't his wife then,' John leans forward. 'I met her first in Shapton Library where she worked. I was in my twenties then, not much older than you are now, and I was smitten by her. I longed to get to know her. She was a very beautiful woman. I loved her, but I didn't know how to make her love me. I invited her home, here. Quite innocently, for afternoon tea. She came, and just having her in the house seemed like a miracle. Then David arrived. It was a Saturday and he'd been playing football. I invited him in to meet Susan. I practically forced him to join us, little realising that as soon as he walked into the room the course of my life would change for ever. I actually think it was love at first sight for both of them. After that I believed I had no chance with her...'

'So Saul's father stole her from you? Surely he was out of order!'

'All's fair in love and war, or so the saying goes. There seemed little I could do in the circumstances. I capitulated. I kept myself to myself and left them to it, until the pain became too much and I applied to be relocated as far away as I could go.'

'So you moved to Newcastle.'

'Yes. I was very low for a time.' John's voice is shaky. 'Gradually I started to make a new life for myself. I excused myself from their wedding, then David and Susan emigrated and I haven't seen them since. But I never stopped loving her. Not because I wanted to. I didn't. She was my sister-in-law. But there was nothing I could do about it. I never met another woman who came remotely close to Susan in either looks or character, and although I've been happy enough, my life has always been tinged with regret. Regret that I didn't fight for the woman I loved. That I gave in too easily.

'And now, because Saul cannot be here, I am going to fight on his behalf. I want you to consider what you're throwing away, and why. So please come with me. This house might be full of ghosts. But you're not one of them. You're alive. We don't have many chances in life. Think carefully before you lose this one. I'm flying to Australia in two weeks' time. Now, tell me, what does Saul mean to you?'

I rock for a while on my chair, stand up and rub both hands down my cheeks. I actually feel like crying now. Saul's uncle doesn't understand anything – about my connection to the house, about Francesca, about Susan, about Pip.

'I've never met anyone like Saul before. But that doesn't alter what I believe.'

'And what *do* you believe, Chloe?' John sounds weary – with me, with life maybe.

'Okay. I can see it sounds random but I now know deep in my heart that I am the rebirth of Susan's baby daughter, which means I'm related to Saul, to Susan ... and to you, in fact. So the only relationship I can have with Saul is as his sister.'

John ruminates, twiddling his thumbs again. 'Hmm. So, what if I told you that the baby you refer to, Pip, was a boy and therefore you could not be a reincarnation of him?'

'A boy? But how do you know?'

John reddens a little and clears his throat. 'Let's just say I was told.'

I stand up and pace the room. 'Pip was a boy?'

'Well. Yes.' John clears his throat again. 'So I believe.'

'Are you sure?'

'As sure as I am of anything… My dear, we could go to Adelaide together. Look at it this way, I need a companion and I can't think of anyone I'd rather travel with. You could lock up the house. I presume you can write your poetry anywhere. And the house will still be here when you get back. It would do you good to get away from here and all this.' He gestures around the room. 'Living in the past is never a good idea. I know because I spent too much of my life doing just that. And now I will go to the other end of the globe. I will meet with the only woman I've ever loved for maybe one last time and I hope I will see you and Saul reunited.'

I sink onto my knees on the floor. 'No. No. I will never leave this house. Everyone knows that. So what if Pip was a boy? I could still be her. I mean, *him*. I mean, reincarnation has nothing to do with the sex of a person. Has it?'

John stands in preparation to leave. 'So be it, my dear. I'm really not an expert on the subject, but remember, at my age I need a travelling companion. My offer remains open. My taxi is waiting and I said I wouldn't be long. But let an old man offer you some advice. If you really care for Saul, don't let him go. Whatever you do, *don't* let him go.'

He helps me to my feet and, as we embrace, I try to imagine him living here all those years ago, going about his daily routine, but I can't. Maybe I don't want to. Perhaps it's not that important. Because what is important is that Saul has gone and he's taken part of me with him. As John said, this house is full of ghosts, but I am alive.

I'm in Dad's study surrounded by folders, books, photographs, all the trappings of literary success. This room makes me feel close to Dad. I lean back in his creaky, black leather office chair and gaze out onto the garden, the apple trees, and the fields beyond the fences. I'm in the part of the house that was originally Number Two. John said he had the middle bedroom when he lived here. So that would be our bathroom. I get up and move into the bathroom and stand between the shower and the sunken bath. I hold up a grey fluffy towel and sink my face into the warmth and comfort of it. With my eyes closed, I try again to imagine John here, in this room, his bedroom, so many years ago, dreaming about a girl he could never have. What sadness he must have felt here. A sadness that's infused into the walls, the floorboards, the very essence of the building. And for how long have I breathed it all in, letting the spirit of this house saturate my life's blood, needing it as a kind of reassurance and yet brooding on its presence, allowing it to rule what I do. I go into the separate loo, which was part of the original bathroom John's brother, David installed – the room I stood in in the cold that night after we'd moved here, when I said the word 'Pip'. So Pip was probably born here, in the spot where I'm standing now. But that was more than half a century ago, and I'm allowing this to control my life. I bend over and take a deep breath low into my stomach. I straighten up and flip my head backwards, forgetting how near I am to the cistern. Wow, that really hurt. I imagine my head coming out in some huge lump like it did once when I was at Mrs Meacher's house and I slipped on the concrete next to her paddling pool. Except then I had Peppo to comfort me. Peppo the cuddly bear that I carried around with me from the age of God knows what until we moved here. I sit down on the toilet seat lid. Apart from when I told Saul all of this, I haven't thought about Peppo for years. Somehow he got left behind when we moved. Or lost on the way.

Suddenly I'm back in that night and a thought hits me so hard I feel another lump will explode on my head. When I got up that night it was surely Peppo I was looking for, and surely the word I spoke could have been Peppo, not Pip...

*

OUR TAXI stops outside the airport. I look inside my handbag to make sure I've got my passport while the driver humps our cases out of the boot. We join the queue at the Qantas check-in. I drop my boarding pass, I'm in such a flutter of nerves. I bend down to pick it up. I'm leaving the house at Blackberry Lane. Finally. And yet I'm still not sure. I still feel tied. As if I'm being carried out to sea on a current that then pulls me back in the opposite direction with an elemental force. So maybe I imagined all that stuff about Pip. I'm not Pip. The name could have come from Peppo. Is that so far-fetched? All the same, I have to hold onto that thought. Perhaps all my imagined ties to the house are fictitious after all and I will break free.

I'm aware that John looks weary – already – and we are only on the first leg of a very long journey.

'John, are you okay?' I ask him. 'I noticed there's an Angel's Oven upstairs in the departure lounge. Shall we go there for a snack once we've checked in?'

'I'll feel better when we've handed our luggage in,' he says. 'But yes, a cup of tea would be most acceptable. I haven't been in one of those before, although I've noticed a lot of them around, and I've heard they do excellent cakes.'

'They do. And I'll tell you a little story about the people who started the Angel's Oven franchise once we get settled up there with our drinks.'

'I'll look forward to that very much, Chloe,' John says patiently with a smile. 'I've always enjoyed a good story.'

END

Alison Clink is a short story writer and creative writing teacher living in Somerset. She is a graduate of the University of Essex and Bath Spa University's Creative Writing MA.

Her work has been published in mainstream magazines both in the UK and abroad and her stories have been broadcast on BBC Radio 4. She won prizes for her short play, *Ackroyd's Christmas Stocking*, and her memoir, *The Man Who Didn't Go To Newcastle*. *Two Blackberry Lane* is her first novel.

CPSIA information can be obtained
at www.ICGtesting.com
Printed in the USA
BVHW051712130522
636993BV00013B/287